C161056203

THE DESERT MIDWIFE

When outback midwife Ava May meets Zac on a flight to Alice Springs, they tumble into a whirlwind affair. But an exciting adventure leads to a terrible accident with shattering consequences. The couple who had so much going for them now find themselves with everything to lose. Devastated, Ava retreats to her family cattle station to her mother and grandmother, needing their backbone and strength to help salvage what she can of the critical situation. But at home on the drought-ridden farm, her brother is being pushed to his limits, and as his depression intensifies, Ava must step in to prevent another family tragedy. Against the majestic backdrop of Australia's Red Centre, old dreams are shattered, new babies are born, and true love takes flight.

FIONA McARTHUR

———————◆———————

THE DESERT MIDWIFE

Complete and Unabridged

AURORA
Leicester

First published in Australia in 2019 by
Penguin Random House Australia

First Aurora Edition
published 2020
by arrangement with
Penguin Random House Australia

A catalogue record for this book is available
from the British Library.

ISBN 978–1–78782–314–3

Published by
Ulverscroft Limited
Anstey, Leicestershire

Set by Words & Graphics Ltd.
Anstey, Leicestershire
Printed and bound in Great Britain by
T. J. International Ltd., Padstow, Cornwall

This book is printed on acid-free paper

Dedicated to the strong and steadfast families all over Australia who battle the emotional weariness that comes with drought and flood and fire and distance — you are our heroes.

1

Ava

Ava May watched the big guy she'd seen at Sydney Airport fill the empty seat beside her in the aeroplane. She'd been drawn to his strong good looks, like every other woman in the lounge. She'd also been drawn to his hint of sadness. Her mum always called her on being too empathetic, too sensitive to other people's emotions.

She decided her new seat companion seemed to have recovered his good humour, though. As he sat, he glanced at her and gave her the kind of smile that made a girl feel foolishly frisky — even girls who weren't normally the frisky sort.

'I'm Zac,' he said.

'Ava.'

He nodded, then rearranged his seatbelt and snapped the buckle shut. All the while his big shoulders encroached on her space. She inhaled his unique scent — a heady mixture of citrus and something woodsy — and decided it was very sexy. Not that she sniffed blokes' chests often. Without leaning towards him, she tried to catch another whiff and was rewarded. *Niiice.*

He sat back. 'Sorry about crowding you. It's unavoidable for someone my size in these small seats. Do you live in Alice Springs or are you visiting?'

'I live there sometimes,' she responded. 'Midwifery agency work. You?'

'Only for the next month.'

There was no explanation from him on which type of work. His brows drew together and she felt the wall slide into place. It clearly said: *Keep out*.

'It's nice to get away,' he said.

His long fingers waved at the window next to her and she decided he had piano player's hands. She'd always had a thing for men with long, elegant fingers, but maybe that was because she'd dreamed of being a dancer and had needed someone to play the music. Or perhaps most of the men she knew had battered, work-worn hands that could pull a nail from a fence post.

Something in his eyes hinted at that sadness she'd spotted before.

Work and sadness. A combination she understood well.

Midwifery could be the happiest and the saddest of professions, and then there were police, ambulance officers and doctors all out there putting their hearts on the line. She decided he was a policeman because she had trouble reading his face. Probably a detective. She could distract the detective if that was what he needed.

'Prefer not to talk about work?' She smiled at him and his eyes met hers. Maybe actually saw her for the first time.

'You're observant,' he said, making it sound like a compliment.

'It's my job.' She waved her hand dramatically.

'But I won't mention *that* again.'

He laughed and she had the feeling he hadn't laughed in a while. Suddenly, it was important to keep his good humour flowing and she set out to be funny and conversational. Something she normally let others do.

'My family have a cattle station four hours from Alice.' Her gaze brushed over his immaculate shirt and tie. 'You look like a city guy.'

'City born and boarding-school bred.' His tone took on an English accent. 'Political parents who travel a lot.' Then he frowned at himself. 'But that's boring. Does that mean you attended School of the Air?'

'Good guess. The cattle station, which is run by my mother and grandmother, is too far out of town for regular school.'

He shifted, angling towards her. He had a way of focusing his attention on her unlike anybody had before, and she could feel herself responding with an odd recognition of their connection. *Weird.*

'Learning from home instead of school,' he said slowly. She watched the expressions chase across his face, and was gifted a sudden, devilish smile that took ten years off his looks. 'I imagine it would be more relaxing than the dynamics of many children vying for attention from teachers. My schooling had moments that made me happy, but I'm afraid I hated most of it. I much preferred travelling with my parents.'

'Travel, eh?' She had never been outside Australia, but she could imagine it. 'We're not holiday-taking people. Sydney's as far as I've been. It's too far to go anywhere and there's always too much to do on the station. Though we have shed parties after muster and the off-road races my brother loves. And camel and horse races.' She thought about that and was satisfied. 'We have fun at home when the work is done.'

He watched her face as if listening to her was the most amazing, fascinating experience in the world. He was too encouraging, and she could become just a little besotted with this guy if he kept looking at her like she was a rain cloud and he was a thirsty camel.

He touched the corner of his eye. 'You said outback races. Like Birdsville?' he asked, 'I've heard about those outback race meetings.'

She couldn't help the snort. 'Birdsville is in a class of its own. And about two thousand kilometres away. Closer to us, we have the Alice Springs Cup, but it's not quite the same.'

She took in his creaseless trousers, which hugged his thighs in a way that made her think she probably shouldn't notice, and his gleaming leather shoes. 'I can see you at Flemington in a suit. Bet you've been to 'the race that stops the nation'.'

The blankness fell like a dark cloak and hid the thoughts on his face. 'When she was alive, my wife loved the Melbourne Cup. Fashions on the Field.' She saw a frown, then a wince, as if he'd done something wrong.

Okay, then, another closed door. Maybe she should just look out the window. Which she did,

4

and saw they'd left Sydney. At that moment the seatbelt sign pinged off.

He sighed, unsnapped his seatbelt and stood up. 'Excuse me.'

She tried to figure out what it was that made her so determined to understand him when he was proving to be such hard work. She'd felt that tingle of attraction and she wanted more. Lots more. But if he returned the interest, which she was sure he had for a few shared heartbeats, he'd just told himself to stop.

They were strapped and trapped in narrow airline seats on a three-hour flight from Sydney, so it was almost inevitable for them to talk. As the flight attendant came around with miniature bottles of West Australian pinot noir, Ava grabbed a couple. A drink might be what he needed to loosen his oh-so-constrictive reserve, because this could be interesting.

When he came back, he seemed to have recovered from whatever had troubled him and he accepted the wine from Ava.

His beautiful eyes were self-mocking. 'I forget to be sociable.'

She laughed and decided not to ask about his work or his wife. 'So what music do you like and who's your favourite actor?'

He laughed. 'You're a delight.'

He raised his glass, they carefully touched plastic to plastic and, bizarrely, for Ava it felt as if that tiny spark of attraction had flared into a scrub fire. Incendiary attraction, both of them needing comfort, both well over the age of consent. This was going to be a memorable flight.

The conversation barely faltered from there — seriously, the people in front of them must have wanted to knock their heads together to get some peace — and they'd only covered the surface stuff. His political parents and private Sydney boarding school versus her School of the Air and matriarch-run outback station. He was a widower and she single, and yes, he was an emergency doctor, not a policeman, but he didn't want to talk about his loss or his job. Something in his gaze made her want to squeeze his fingers.

They shared their tastes in music — his piano and jazz, hers everything — as well as books — biographies versus a happy ending — and travel — Sydney being Ava's most distant city and his love of Zurich. They made a game out of avoiding his topics of employment and family except for the basics.

They had so much unexpected rapport, such foolish fun exchanging foibles. His discovery of the health benefits of kombucha tea and her love of Bonox around a camp fire at muster. His aversion to heights and her love of off-road driving. So it seemed natural to share a taxi after landing, and then stand grinning at each other as he checked in to his swish apartment — not room — at the hotel where they intended to eat.

Food. Honest.

★   ★   ★

The sunrise tinted a pink swathe across the wall of the room, blushed across the white duvet, and dusted the beginnings of Central Australian heat across Ava's cheek, warming her skin. Hazily, as she shifted her head, she squinted at the unfamiliar rose-coloured room and frowned.

She could see the flecks of floating dust motes crystallise but, unfortunately, that wasn't all that formed as clarity returned. Her cheeks burned as the fractured pieces of last night re-emerged, and she stifled the urge to groan. Good ghastly grief.

She'd had a one-night stand.

You're a grown woman. Her inner voice shut down the embarrassment.

That may be, but oh my. She had to admit, she would hate to have grown much older without experiencing last night. Talk about lust at first sight. It had been complete enchantment, and they'd been soulmates for at least the length of the spell.

She was no blushing virgin — though her virginity could quite possibly have grown back because it had been more than five years since she'd last been with anyone . . . for good reason — but darn, this morning felt uncomfortable. Especially when she was a novice at waking up next to a stranger from the night before, with the heat from his body still warming her hip.

She knew the outback rule: never leave your car if you break down. Were there rules for one-night stands?

Her stomach growled and she lifted her hand carefully to cover her eyes. Did this get any more awkward? Maybe she could slip sideways out of the bed. She wasn't game to turn her head in case he woke up.

'Would you like coffee?' Deep, rumbling masculine tones with just a hint of amusement sounded, and she shifted her head to meet his eyes. Yep, those unfairly chocolate eyes were twinkling and not at all abashed.

She sighed and tried not to breathe her dragon breath on him. Another new skill she needed to learn.

Her hand dropped from her face. *Right. Toughen up, Ava.* 'Weak black tea would be wonderful. Earl Grey, if you have it. Thank you.' She wriggled up the pillows, strategically holding the sheet. 'Then I have to go.'

'Of course. Would you like a shower while I'm making it? There are extra towels in the bathroom and a bathrobe on the back of the door.'

She thought about a shower, feeling refreshed, more relaxed and restored to her normal unshakable composure, or, alternatively, the messy, crumpled walk of shame without one.

'That would be great,' she said. 'Thanks. I won't use the robe, though, I'll just get dressed.' She could do this. Calm and composure were her middle names; nothing fazed her. Everybody in Alice Springs knew that.

'Umm . . . ' More amusement sounded in the dulcet tones of his voice, and she turned her head back his way. 'I think we may have popped a few buttons on both our shirts.'

Her hand came back up and slapped her forehead palm up as the full glory of their lustful exuberance returned.

'A night to remember,' she managed in an even tone.

'I'd like to think so,' he said. 'Your Central Australian charisma fascinates me.' Then with less amusement he said, 'I'll put the kettle on.'

Zac Logan — at least she recalled his name — tossed back the sheet, swung his long, muscled, naked body to the edge of the bed and stood. All six foot plus of solid, sexy, sinfully seductive stud. And he didn't pause to put on any clothes. He just strode to the bench with the kitchen appliances and reached for the switch.

Ava blinked, dragged her eyes from his tantalising backside and scrambled to get to the bathroom before he turned around and gave her a front view.

2

Zac

Half an hour later, Zac watched Ava walk out the door, and to his horror, it felt as if the ground was falling away from his feet, like it had a year ago when the accident irrevocably damaged his wife. *What the heck had just happened?*

Guilt pushed his lips together: this infidelity after Roslyn's death touched so many emotions. He blew out that other shaft of guilt that he had lived with since his wife had become comatose. So many, many emotions and he seemed to have lost the good ones. Like humour, joy. Anticipation. He could barely remember when he'd last experienced those feelings, and yet in one night with Ava he'd felt them all.

Memories of the accident still made him shudder with regrets and he just wanted peace.

Peace from loss.

Peace from survivor's guilt.

Peace from wondering what he could have done differently.

After twelve months of being suspended in a horrible limbo, he'd decided to spend a month as a locum in Alice Springs to lose himself in remote medical care. Last month, on his first posting as a fly-in, fly-out emergency doctor, those four weeks in Weipa Hospital hadn't brought peace.

Quite the opposite, in fact, but that had worked. At times frantic and crazy with emergencies, alongside challenging and stimulating chaos with the remote location and the lack of services, Weipa had at least made him feel alive.

Hopefully the next month at Alice Springs, a post his friend George had suggested as not quite so isolated, would be equally restorative and he'd be able to go back home with a fresh perspective and positive energy.

He hadn't realised his resilience had been so badly eroded by the drawn-out nature of Roslyn's death. And the heart-wrenching strain of sitting opposite his wife's broken-hearted parents for so many hours at her bedside. He hoped to hell he'd never have to watch a child of his wither away and die without waking, and the thought of ever again being responsible for another person's well-being in that way made him shudder.

Which was a good reason not to see Ava May again. *Don't get involved.*

He'd spoken to women on flights before, had laughs even, but never, ever had he connected like he had instantly with the blue-eyed, blonde-haired Ava May. To the point of shock. And never had he invited a strange woman back to his place and rocked the earth like they had done last night. Never had he lost himself so completely in another person. And felt that joy. Ever.

Hence the guilt.

It was as if their stars had collided and their mutual gravitational forces had snapped together, despite what was in their pasts or futures. Melded, for one short night. But that was ridiculous. He'd come here to get away from emotion.

He wanted peace, remember?

To remain isolated and insulated from others.

Just a FIFO locum, using his skills to the max and forgetting about Sydney and all the trauma it held while the house sold. The plan was to shake the exhaustion that was bone-deep from twelve months of grieving.

Then Ava had happened.

Bloody hell. He really had intended just to have a meal together.

If only he hadn't slept with her. He felt more ensnared by strands of the searing memory of last night and the almost desperate pure lust he'd let loose than he could possibly hope to deal with. It wasn't just her strong, sweet face or her innate calmness that had captured him.

He shook his head. It was nothing. Just fascination.

As if he could seriously fall in love with this woman in one night.

That was crazier than him being here in Alice Springs to work instead of back in Sydney. This was all temporary. He and Roslyn had grown up in the same world, but even that hadn't turned out perfectly. What hope did he and an outback midwife have to live happily ever after?

He'd stop this. Ava had gone, and despite there being a crossover of their professions, he was an emergency doctor and she an agency nurse for maternity. There wasn't much chance they'd interact. He wouldn't ring her number, and he had the solid belief she would wait for him to call first.

His hand reached to the back of his head and pulled the hair at the nape of his neck until it hurt. He needed to wake up. Shake it off. A one-night stand in a place thousands of kilometres from where he lived?

It wasn't too bad.

He could handle that.

He decided to go for a run. Wear himself out and then get a couple of hours' sleep before he started work tonight. And. Forget. Ava.

★ ★ ★

Sixteen hours later, just after midnight, Alice Springs Emergency Department looked like the floor of the stock exchange during a financial crash, with arms raised and voices loud. The dozen or so partially curtained cubicles surrounding the central office had reached capacity, the staff had doubled with call-ins, and there were trolleys bearing patients in the walkways around the central computer hub where nobody had time to sit to type or even answer one of the insistently ringing phones. The majority of the patients came from a busload of inebriated young footy players. Most had not been wearing seatbelts and had been thrown violently forward when their vehicle had ploughed into an unfortunate camel herd out of town. The impact had catapulted passengers down the bus corridor and resulted in broken bones, multiple lacerations and some magnificent bruises. They'd arrived in a convoy of ambulances to enliven the night.

Though the injured men were partially anaesthetised by their alcohol consumption, the emergency department rang with groans and muttered expletives and some not-quite-so-muttered outbursts. Zac stood to the left of the ambulance entrance, examining tipsy and torn players who were triaged his way. There weren't enough ED staff to manage the patient flow, but help came from other wards, pulled from less frantic areas in the hospital until the rush could be contained, with an efficiency he could only wish for in his Sydney hospital. Thankfully, the emergency department had been rebuilt recently, so the layout and lighting made for effective flowthrough.

He looked up as an additional two nurses appeared from the staff entrance and he waved to direct them his way. His come-hither head signal froze as he took in the shorter blonde woman gliding towards him and his breath hitched in his chest — Ava! Recognition and a flare of something else ignited. Something he didn't know he had inside him as he glanced around at the alcohol-infused patients that filled the room.

Ava's delicious curves were hidden beneath the purple scrubs she wore, but he didn't need to see them to know. Every delectable inch lay imprinted in his brain. He dragged his eyes to the taller nurse, who reached him first, and kept them on the unknown woman's face.

'I'm Jade and this is Ava, from maternity,' the nurse said. 'The nursing supervisor said you guys need extra hands down here for a while?'

Zac's grip loosened for a second in shattered concentration, and the swollen, tattooed arm he held shifted under his fingers. The man groaned in a cloud of alcoholic fumes, and Zac muttered an apology as he focused back on stabilising the fractured humerus. When he looked up again, he had himself under control.

'Thanks. One of you with Ruth over there.' He nodded his head towards a tall young woman in a white coat bandaging a bloody leg. 'And one with me would be great, thanks.' He knew which one he wanted, but he shook that thought and focused on the task at hand.

'I'll stay here.' Ava spoke crisply, and Jade nodded and moved swiftly towards the other doctor.

'What can I do, Doctor?' Her voice was professionally neutral and she didn't meet his eyes. He would have loved to know what was going on inside her head because he surely didn't know what to think. Just when he'd decided it was best he never see her again . . . That certainly wasn't what he was thinking now. His emotions were cheering and whooping and totally letting him down with the delight of the moment, and he was ridiculously aware of some of the ribald comments from the footballers when Ava passed them. She completely ignored them, but he found himself wanting to growl with an unexpected silent baring of teeth in the direction of the other men.

'Could you check with X-ray to see if they're ready for us?' At least his mouth was working. 'I think this will set with stabilising, without a trip to theatre, so as soon as we have the pictures then we'll head to the plaster room.'

He caught the glance she slanted at him and the tiny smile on her lips.

Had that sounded like a come-on? His voice had dropped. Hurriedly he added, 'To hand this guy over to the physios for some plaster.'

She flashed him a grin and turned for the phone. He watched her go and told himself it had just been a spur-of-the-moment connection. He'd already chosen to close that door. This had no future and the attraction was too strong to save them from hurt.

When she returned, he leaned towards her and said quietly in her ear, 'I know already that this place works like a small town. Probably better not to mention we've already met to avoid unnecessary gossip.'

She raised her brows at him, then inclined her head. 'Who's our next patient?' she asked slowly.

He'd just asked her to lie to everyone here and she'd only looked at him and moved on. He needed to do the same. He searched the room. 'That guy just in on the spine board.'

That was the last time they had a chance to talk about anything other than work. They were too busy dealing with a neck-injury patient who needed a collar and a CAT scan before transfer, not to mention treatment for a slew of nasty glass cuts from his rapid exit through the broken back window of the bus.

'Dr Logan?' Ava called out to him from where she stood by the man brought in after falling from a tree. Zac had just handed the man over to

16

Ava to admit for observation overnight for any further developing injuries. They could do further tests on him when the others had been triaged. 'I think there's a difference in air entry now. On the left side,' she said.

Zac shifted back beside her and listened with his stethoscope. He met her eyes. 'Great pick-up. There's a definite change in breath sounds.' He could hear the difference himself and noted the uneven chest rise as the lung began to collapse. 'X-ray ASAP for pneumothorax.' Zac looked down at the man and touched his shoulder. 'Sorry, mate. We've more to do yet. Feeling breathless?'

The pale, quiet guy gasped a little and nodded, and Zac walked alongside his bed, heading for a phone, as the orderly whisked the patient towards X-ray.

'I'll set up the underwater sealed drain down there.' Ava's voice carried from the other end of the stretcher where she helped the orderly push the patient swiftly away. Zac nodded and picked up the phone to warn X-ray to clear for an urgent patient before he followed.

She was good at diagnosis. He might have missed that deterioration considering his workload if she hadn't asked his opinion. As for the treatment, he had no doubt she'd acquire the necessary equipment and be ready to assist with the decompression drain. The hidden depths of this woman he'd passed in the night continued to amaze him. He'd scored the one-woman assist team he could see the other doctors envied.

Which wasn't helping the attraction he tried to

mask with a set face. There was no denying the fact that he noticed whenever she moved his way, or that his eyes would follow her as she worked. And once, when a high-as-a-kite footballer put his hand out to fondle her backside, Zac was between the two of them in an instant, casually blocking the guy's reach and delivering a hard stare.

'I can manage,' Ava had told him with a smile, 'but thanks.'

A couple of the stroppy men had needed a firm word and a glare before they behaved for their purple-scrubbed nurse, and Zac had delivered both out of sight of their target. If he'd hesitated over something she was there with a suggestion, her knowledge of emergency treatment the adjunct to his.

'Ava,' a man called out. Zac looked up as a blond guy, one who seemed to know her well, put his hand out to grab her arm, but she steered around him deliberately, with an emphatic shake of her head. Something about the smirk on the man's face made Zac want to pin him to the wall by the throat. Interestingly, the other midwife who'd arrived with Ava made a beeline for the man and towed him away before Zac could insert himself between them. Which really was out of character for him — he never lost his cool and concentration at work. He didn't know where this caveman act was coming from.

After nearly two hours of frantic sorting, there were poignant moments in the mayhem. The older gentleman admitted for palliative end-of-life care, with his wife needing a hug from both

18

Ava and Zac, showed such gratitude when the pain relief began to work properly and he could relax. And a three-year-old girl who'd stuck her mother's earring into her ear canal, making Zac produce some pretty fast wheedling for permission from the small child to remove it with success.

At last, most patients had been shipped off to wards or home, the triage area began to clear, and Zac finally was able to lift his head to allow less immediate thoughts to intrude. He could see the nurses had begun the mammoth task of restocking for the next onslaught, which could come in an instant or in many hours. He stood back and watched the ED as it reverted to quiet calm with many empty, freshly made beds. Someone was missing. He scanned the empty open area again, but there was no sign of her.

Ava had gone. She'd left the emergency department without saying goodbye, and he felt jolted. Stupidly bereft. But of course she wouldn't say goodbye. There could be no future between him, with his city practice, and the bush midwife, so why would she waste any more of her time with him? Plus, he'd been the one to mention he didn't want to be the cause of any awkwardness for her. He'd be leaving soon, but she had to work in this community. There was no need to advertise their connection if nothing was to come of it.

'Hey, Ruth. Did you see where Ava went?'

'Back to maternity. She's good, isn't she?' The tall woman smiled. 'She's one of the desert midwives and works here as a casual nurse. She spends most of her time doing outreach midwifery with the stations and remote communities between Uluru and Katherine, and she's pretty passionate about it.'

'I can imagine that.' The words were more to himself than to his colleague.

Ruth hadn't finished. 'I guess she needs to deal if she's the only medical person in an outreach settlement, and it makes for good intuition.' She glanced longingly towards the staffroom. 'I'm going for coffee. Wanna come?'

Zac followed Ruth thoughtfully. He'd been wrong to assume Ava would be here a long while and it would be his job to avoid her. She'd be disappearing to another post soon, possibly hundreds of kilometres away, and when this shift ended in the morning, it might just be his last chance to see her before she vanished into the outback.

3

Ava

By six the following morning, Ava decided the drama of emergency had moved to the birthing suite. She'd hardly had time to catch her breath all night. She'd had to press the emergency response bell for reinforcements fifteen minutes ago, and thankfully there had been ED staff free to respond and things were settling.

As she surveyed the carnage of the birthing room, she could see blood from the mother's post-birth haemorrhage pooled on the bed and dripping on the floor. A few drops had splashed on the TV screen that was suspended from the roof of the unit. *Still*, she thought, as she tried to be as gentle as she could in rubbing the new mother's abdomen, *at least I can rejoice in the now firm uterus below my fingers*. Ava glanced at Zac and nodded with relief. 'There's no further bleeding.'

Ava couldn't help reflecting on the emergency situations she'd spent with Zac in the past eight hours. And here they had another good outcome, despite the gory mess of the room. But that was a minor issue. The room would scrub clean and mum and baby were safe.

She remembered other places where she hadn't been so blessed with instant expert help like Zac. It was so important to have cohesive teamwork come into play when there was an unexpected haemorrhage after a birth.

This time they'd been lucky, and the last quarter-hour had been tense but ultimately rewarding. She watched Kareena, a strong Mutitjulu woman from the community near Ava's family station, snuggle her new son. Ava had known Kareena since they were chubby toddlers, and Kareena's grandmother knew Ava's through their shared *mukata*, or needle-felting, classes, so their history and rapport had helped keep the new mum and her support women calm during the drama. Even the shock in Kareena's mother's eyes had begun to fade into pride and excitement.

While she shifted to take Kareena's pulse, she watched Zac as he talked to another doctor who'd also responded from ED. My, hadn't seeing Zac at work been an eye-opener on her laughing lover of the night before. He had been easygoing but firm with the inebriated footy players, so gentle and kind with an elderly couple, and cleverly relaxed with a frightened toddler. But she couldn't help noting that now, five hours after she'd last seen him in ED, his eyes read absolutely shattered. She felt the lack of sleep herself, but he seemed as if he had no reserves, and she wondered about that. Most people had reserves, and he'd only just arrived.

She had her own problems. The hardest part was pretending she didn't know or care about him. She looked away. It wasn't so easy to stop that subliminal awareness she felt when he was near.

She turned to help Kareena's baby settle at the breast, careful not to interfere, but her mind lingered on Zac. If what had been between them had all ended yesterday, she wasn't going to chase him.

Dammit — she didn't regret learning what her body could do. Though she did feel like she'd been dreadfully uninhibited. Luckily, she supposed, nobody else knew. But they would. They always found things out. Her mother would be horrified. Her sister-in-law would be thrilled to hear of Ava's escapades. And her grandmother ecstatic. The thought of her family's input, which was inevitable because they dragged everything out of her, made her mouth kink upwards. *Oh my.*

And, regrettably, she remained mightily attracted to the man in an *I-could-wake-up-next-to-him-for-the-next-millennium* way. She couldn't help feeling depressed about the waste of what could have been an amazing, if only short-term, relationship. But, if the secrecy he'd asked for was an indication of their lack of future together, that was that.

She peeked quickly back across at him and their eyes met. He smiled at her with a tired little waggle of his determined brows, the relief of another life saved between them. Although the deep chocolate eyes swirled with other emotions that baffled her.

She was used to being able to peg people — her job depended on it — but Zac resisted all efforts to peg him, and she really hated that. And it now seemed unlikely she'd get the chance to know the real man.

'We really have to stop meeting like this,' he mouthed quietly.

She half laughed. That was the most ironic understatement in the world. 'I know.'

Then he looked away, pushed himself upright off the wall and nodded to the room in general. 'Right. Good job, team. You're all amazing. I'll go type some notes and then head back to ED.' And with that he walked out, his shoulders slumped.

Ava narrowed her eyes. When you were the only medically trained person in a remote town — which she often was — you learned to be observant. Her instincts said this guy, this absolute champion of a doctor who'd done as good a job at triage as anyone she'd worked with, one whom she'd incidentally spent most of the last twenty-four hours with, was on the edge of collapse. And she didn't think it was her newly awakened libido that was killing him.

Despite the fact that they'd spent hours wrapped together in the same bed — not that they'd slept a lot — she didn't have any right to nag him about looking unwell. Mostly because of that big 'keep out' sign she kept running into. Nope, she was not going there without an invitation, and he obviously thought the craziness of yesterday had to burn itself out.

Except — judging by the fresh sparks between them overnight at work — the fire still had some fuel in it.

Thankfully, the first of the three shifts in maternity she'd taken at the last minute — silly her — had almost finished. Soon, she could go to the family flat and regroup, and contemplate the final chaste kiss of yesterday morning. Jock and Hana, her brother and sister-in-law, were residing there for a few days this week, so Hana would lend a sympathetic ear if they could shake Jock for long enough to have a sisterly chat.

Ava felt the woolliness of fatigue. They'd certainly had an influx of first-time mums. The mums who'd been sitting from thirty-eight weeks in the lay-in accommodation, eager to test them. She'd bet they were just waiting for Ava and the 'A' team to come on duty before they brought out their strange and wonderful complications to run the staff through their emergency drills — at least it felt that way.

She checked her watch. The morning staff would be here in thirty minutes and she needed to get her own computer work up to scratch, check up on the baby in the Special Care Nursery and get Kareena and her mum to the ward so they could sleep. Then the night staff could all head home to bed.

On their own.

Sigh.

At least she would be going on holidays soon. Once she'd done three more shifts at the Yulara Medical Centre. A change of scenery back at the family cattle station would take her mind off not seeing Zac. At work or play.

4

Stella

Four hundred kilometres away Stella May lifted the dusty top of the miniature homestead mailbox that her mother's love of fusing metals had left mounted at the gate to Setabilly Station. The apex of the replica tin roof lifted on a side hinge, and since gaining an exotic Italian penfriend, Stella liked to collect the mail from inside the little fabricated house herself. Her stomach dipped as she found two bills, which she tucked into her pocket, and then fluttered upwards in delight as she uncovered the textured envelope, postmarked Italy, from Lorenzo, which she clutched to her chest in a crackling hug.

She glanced up the deserted orange dirt road and back towards the homestead. Nope, there was nobody in sight. She hadn't told her mum, Mim, or daughter, Ava, that she and Lorenzo had been corresponding. She'd never thought anything would come of their chance meeting at the races in Alice last year. Not with a man who lived in Italy, even if his backpacking son did jackaroo around outback Australia.

Looking at the letter in her hand, she could feel the excitement again. The thrill of meeting the tall Italian, his obvious admiration for her that no bushman would put out there so candidly, the sensation of fluttering femininity and desirability that he created in her, were all emotions she'd almost forgotten in more than twenty years of widowhood. But lately, Lorenzo's letters had taken a more insistent note. He wanted to come to her. His son was looking for a station somewhere in the Red Centre, so he would be coming and going between Australia and Italy. Perhaps he could see her? If she wanted him to?

His request last year to write to her every four weeks when he returned to Italy had increased to fortnightly, then weekly, and she still hadn't told her family, though they had been corresponding for almost a year.

It had seemed such an old-fashioned idea to write letters to a strange man, and embarrassing to tell the others, especially her mother, who would tease her unmercifully, but she'd relished penning every one, and loved receiving them even more.

She'd taken to describing her month, then her week, enjoying the idea of conversation with her male friend, and their distant rapport had supported her in times when she'd felt she needed it. But he hadn't written last week and she'd missed his endearments, his descriptions of life on his olive farm and his office in town, and his thoughts on her own news and challenges.

Her fingers shook as she carefully unstuck the envelope, pushing it into her pocket and unfolding the crackling paper so she could read. The sun shone so brightly it was hard to decipher the words, so she backed over to the shade of the mulga tree at the gate.

27

My dear Stella,
I desire this finds you well and happy.
Though not too happy without me, I
hope. Thank you for your letter. I am
glad to hear your daughter-in-law is well
with her pregnancy, and that your lovely
Ava will be home with you soon for her
break.

I have been busy, but that is no excuse
to have you wait for my letter, so I write
you a short one to say you are in my
thoughts as always and all is well with me.
Though I miss you and wish, always, that
you would consider coming to visit me in
my home.

She looked unseeingly into the distance. She couldn't fathom the idea of spending money to gallivant around the world and leaving her family here to struggle. They'd be lucky to keep the station from bankruptcy as it was, without the burden of her blowing a bundle on chasing a distant Italian. She'd been tempted but embarrassed when he'd offered to book and pay for her flights, meet her in Milan, and generally spoil her. It was a nice dream, though.

She looked back at the letter.

I see I lacked decision. But more on that
soon. Know I have not forgotten my
Aussie rose, but I am holding you dear to
my heart. Do not forget me.
With much affection, Lorenzo.

She folded the letter carefully and slipped it back into its envelope and away in her jeans pocket. As if she could forget him.

She strode back to check the solar pump that carried water to the cattle troughs in the front paddock. The red rocky ground lay bare, with only the occasional chewed tuft of saltbush. The only happy sight was the shiny surface of the solar panels soaking in the afternoon sun as they should.

New technology. It was so different from her parents' days of clunky windmills, she thought as she dusted the panels, their strange flat faces now clean. They remained undamaged in the red desert. The sun beat down upon her hat and shoulders. Her son, Jock, had pestered for the panels and she admitted he'd been right, despite the cost. There was always more sun than breeze. She'd decided the panels were even oddly, bizarrely, beautiful, like strange square birds on the evocative landscape.

She turned to look behind her, and even in its barren state the land held beauty. It calmed her. The MacDonnell Ranges in the distance made the perfect backdrop to the open space. Stella savoured the perspective the purple-blue crags gave the expanse of desert.

Perspective.

It wasn't just something she admired in her favourite Albert Namatjira painting. She and her daughter needed to appreciate there were other things in life than financially supporting the family's dying station.

Stella squinted at the puffy clouds, which only

very occasionally brought rain, and acknowledged the last few days had been unusual. But
that was home for you. The family liked to do
something unexpected, just like the weather.
There'd been no rain since last January and
none this month, so the soil had started to lift
with the breeze. There might be a dust storm
instead.

Teasing stratocumulus clouds had appeared
on the western horizon and moved east quickly
to cover the sky. It was more the feel you got in
March than April, Stella thought, as she strode
back to the truck. The wind lifted her hair and
the temperature felt cooler against her skin, so
maybe there was a chance they'd be blessed with
a spot of moisture.

Jock normally did the bore run, but he and
Hana had gone into Alice Springs for a few days
for an ultrasound. The next generation for
Setabilly Station. Jock had married Hana in a
rush, and Stella still struggled with their youth,
though Mim had whooped and danced when she
heard because young blood was the future out
here.

I need to be less abrasive, Stella thought with a
sigh, *though Mim thinks I've started to grow a
few clucky feathers with the prospect of a grandchild.* She felt the shiver of anticipation and
unconsciously crossed her fingers that all would
go well. Unlike Ava's loss. Ava was twenty-five
now. She should find someone decent before her
life was gone, like Stella's. But someone from
here, not the city.

Stella disliked this business of looking fifty and

feeling twenty inside. What had her mother said? 'You're drying up like a cow pat.' She'd looked in the hall mirror after that and there had been those crow's-feet at the corners of her eyes and fine lines around her mouth. Cow pat indeed.

'Thanks, Mim,' she said out loud as she slapped the corner fence post, and a puff of red dust rose and blew away as she walked back to her car. She'd been hearing that in her head all day today since her mother had spoken the words. And apparently, acting just a little irrational and emotional to go with it. That was Lorenzo's fault. She couldn't help wondering why he hadn't written until now, and if her refusal to visit had finally worn thin. *He's just a penfriend*, she reminded herself.

The sound of an approaching vehicle from the usually deserted road drew her gaze, and a bottle-green Lexus turned in to their gate and slowed to a stop beside her. Unlike her own heart, which, after pausing in shock, did the opposite and began to increase until it pounded erratically.

Stella stared with disbelief at the tall, dark-haired man who climbed out and her breath came in a gasp as she blinked rapidly. It was the man himself — Lorenzo! Not one of those shimmering mirages that lived on the horizon during the summer. Her gaze roved his bulk from head to toe and focused on the blood-soaked bandage that was wrapped around his wrist.

She fixated on the injury almost with relief. Dealing with that was much easier than dealing with the shock wave of the man who held her thoughts arriving at her door. 'What have you done? Show me.'

Her voice was gruff as she strode towards him, and she took his arm almost roughly as she tried to disguise the shaking that seemed to have overtaken her whole body. Ridiculously, her eyes stung with suppressed tears — How had he come? Why had he come? Now she'd have more of those foolish dreams — and she kept her head down so he wouldn't see. But his big, warm hand on her shoulder stilled her.

'Stella.' The rolling *a* at the end as he said her name made her close her eyes. 'Have you no welcome for me?' She heard the touch of humour in his voice, but nothing was funny to Stella about this hallucination that might disappear in a moment.

She glanced up and his dark eyes were smiling down at her with such warmth that she lost herself in the intensity of his gaze on her. His strong Roman nose, that square chin, with a touch of dark regrowth along his firm jaw. That sexy mouth curved as he watched her. 'What are you doing here?' she asked.

'It is good to see you, too, dear Stella. But I think I have shocked you? You know my son wishes to settle here.' The smile stayed in his voice. Then he gestured dramatically with his good hand, a very Italian trait that she loved about him. 'My son is in love with this place. You knew that.' He shrugged. 'So, I have bought Dreamtime. Your next door, though it is kilometres away. Because the woman I want lives near there. And I have come to lay siege.' He gestured to his bloodied arm. 'But first, she must suture this wound caused by a piece of metal I cut badly, or so my housekeeper says.'

Stella raised the bandage and the immediate swell of blood over the jagged wound made her wince. Thank goodness Mim was out on the other boundary, so she'd have a chance to think. 'Lay siege. What rubbish. Come back to the house and I'll fix that for you.'

'Stella.' His voice held a hint of seriousness that made her look up. 'Is it good I am here?'

She couldn't lie — wouldn't. There had been enough lies in her life. 'Yes.' But oh, what a mess. She wasn't sure what was messier — the situation or the arm. Then he stepped forward, and despite his bloodied arm he gathered her in and kissed her. He was making no bones that he was hungry for her. And she could not deny he tasted wonderful.

Their first kiss. He really was here.

He reluctantly eased her away from him to look at her and she clung a little. His eyes darkened and she couldn't miss the satisfied quirk to his brows. 'The rest we will sort, then,' he said, and gestured to her dust-covered vehicle. 'Drive and I will follow in my car and then I will explain.'

Stella could do nothing else; her brain had turned to mush. She climbed into the truck and checked behind her as if to be sure it wasn't all a trick of the heat. But there he was. A crazy Italian millionaire behind her in his car. Stella's fingers shook on the wheel. She who had the steadiest hand around.

Her romantic mother would be in seventh heaven when she heard that Stella had a beau. But this? This confrontation of a man who had made it clear that he found her attractive and was looking for a future. She didn't know what to think, or whether this was exactly what she'd dreamed about, hoping he would come here. As if she'd been waiting for him.

5

Zac

Zac found himself waiting outside the door to maternity, despite his intention not to. It was funny how he was aware he'd rediscovered the emotion of anticipation, which he'd lost for the last year. He shouldn't be doing this, but Ava the midwife warred with his common sense, even though Alice Springs was nestled 2700 kilometres away from Sydney.

The connection with Ava he'd felt on the flight, and definitely after that, had been incredible, but he knew he should be letting her go. He needed to find the peace he'd come here to find and go home unencumbered. This was not a good place to find his heart open and expect his blonde sprite to follow him home. But last night had made him rethink that strategy.

So here he was, leaning against the wall outside the ward with his inner voice demanding, *You'd better get your backside into gear and see what today brings, because you might just have to work out the rest as you go along.*

He thought about Roslyn, and how when she'd hung suspended in a coma for those last twelve months, his fidelity and focus on her had remained rock solid. These short two months since she'd passed had been the same.

Until the flight.

It was just too soon for a blue-eyed 'desert midwife' to have smiled her way to his core. In one day and one night together, not counting work last night, which had strengthened the bond. A one-night stand with a woman he'd bonded with more closely than the best friend he'd been married to for five years.

Guilt draped thick, disapproving tendrils over him until he almost lifted his hand to wave them away. To make it worse, he'd already been unfair to Ava — asking her to lie to everyone here, to pretend they hadn't spent the previous night together. He had thrown her generosity back in her face. Even as they'd worked together, he'd told himself the previous night had just been a fling.

Yet here he was. Making it a two-day fling. And he suspected he'd want tomorrow as well, because his gut had sunk when he'd heard she'd be gone in a couple of days.

Maybe it wasn't a fling? Maybe it was a tumbling, stumbling, impossibly crazy love-at-first-sight situation with a woman from another world? After the night they'd shared, the rapport he'd found again, the attraction he felt for her despite his guilt, the thought of not having her body next to his when he went back to his hotel this morning had driven him to stand here. Waiting. In full view of everyone.

Where was the voice whispering hints that he was overreacting?

Where was the voice saying stop?

Nowhere.

The door from maternity opened and Ava's

chin lifted at the sight of him. A beam of mischievous promise swirled in those blue eyes as a tingle of recognition and reciprocation zinged along his not-so-tired-now limbs and down into his gut. With a look?

As she came closer, he held up his hand with a hint of apology. 'Can we meet for breakfast? My hotel? Maybe talk?'

Her brows twitched. 'Talk? As in, tell me we're both going to work in the same ward and pretend we don't know each other?' He heard the scepticism, but he didn't miss that her beautiful mouth lifted at the corner. He had to give her that one. It had been a shock. And there was the distinct possibility that talk might not happen at all if they spent time together.

But she hadn't finished. 'And promising me food again?' She smiled.

He warmed under the promise of her curved lips and couldn't help smiling back at her. 'I guarantee I'll supply breakfast this time. We both need the sustenance,' And he needed to talk to her. Get to know her. Hell, he hadn't asked any real questions about her family, her life. He promised himself they would eat before he took her back to his bed. If she'd come.

She'd crinkled her eyes at him in disbelief when he said 'breakfast'. But she did say, 'Sure. Your shout.'

His gut kicked with a different kind of hunger as she slid into place beside him, her hips swinging next to his as they walked a little too quickly towards his hire car. His heart pounded like a young Jock's, not like one belonging to a widower of thirty. Desperately, daringly, his fingers itched to take her hand. But he didn't.

Ava was the opposite to Roslyn: sun-blonde hair, not black; thick, sensible ponytail holding the masses of unruly hair away from her face instead of sculptured helmet style; and blue eyes that soothed the world, which he could lose or find himself in.

So self-sufficient. Self-reliant. Self-everything. He'd never seen anybody so quietly, unobtrusively confident and competent regardless of the disasters being enacted around her. Even those disasters he set in place.

Like now? his inner voice asked. What did he expect? That in a month's time he would forget her? Or that she would come back with him to his brash world of corporate hospitals and city life and just be with him? Or that he would stay here?

He shouldn't be doing this, but darn it felt good to watch her walking beside him. He could feel the smile tug at his lips, easing the emotional exhaustion he'd been dragging around like a two-tonne rock since the accident.

If he was sensible, instead of savouring the joy of the moment like a kid with a lollypop, he'd be thinking how to explain about Roslyn. How to explain that he felt bad about having slept with someone else so soon after his wife's death, and that, because of where they each lived, they had no long-term future.

Some of the joy seeped away and he glanced down at Ava. She looked up at him and smiled, and he forgot all that and tasted sweetness again.

6

Ava

Excitement effervesced along Ava's veins like a dropped can of cola shooting fizzy streams outwards to her fingers and toes. Maybe she had a chance to get to know this man properly. Find out why he hadn't wanted to talk about his life before now. Learn about his loss, hear about his work and family. Most especially, find out why he'd waited outside maternity for her this morning when he had reduced a connection she'd thought special to something gossip-worthy.

She tried not to hold her breath in case he reverted to being distant if they ran into someone from the hospital. Nobody passed before they came to his four-wheel drive.

He opened her door first, and when she was settled she watched him stride around to his side.

Nice manners . . . Nice butt.

What was it about this man that penetrated her barriers? Apart from mind-blowing sex the night before last, that was. There'd been plenty of guys around at work and at the few social occasions on the station since Jai but she hadn't been interested.

Was it a positive sign that he was obviously

doing this against his better judgement, or a bad sign? And all that baffling subtext. Was it a lack of real feelings and he was just a sex maniac who fancied her, or was it something else?

Maybe she should just ask. For her own protection.

He climbed in and shut his door, then glanced across at her as he reached for the key. When he smiled, she felt her resolve soften and the need for answers fade.

'We're mad,' he said.

That took her words away until she managed, 'It's only breakfast.' But they both knew it wasn't. As a reflex she added a little too forcefully, 'Why did you want me to pretend we didn't know each other last night?'

His hands rested on the steering wheel, fingers open. A good sign he planned on telling the truth? 'I told myself I'm leaving in a month.' He said it slowly and very clearly, as if reciting something he'd said over and over. 'It's nobody's business except ours. And I didn't want to kick the rumour mill into gear and fly away unscathed.'

Ava nodded. 'Okay. On the face of it.' But why was he worried? She believed she had enough credit to survive one affair without damage from the gossipmongers. 'I know you lost your wife — you told me on the plane — but is that why I'm getting mixed messages?'

He started the car and it surprised her that he still took off. They were having a big conversation — maybe too big for multitasking after a long night shift.

Ava watched his hands — confident, competent and far too sexy — as he drove out of the hospital car park and onto the road to his hotel. He had beautiful fingers, and her skin shivered with goosebumps as memories of their night together flashed through her mind, and suddenly she wished she hadn't asked about his departed wife. She dreaded the answer, actually.

Then he said, 'My wife died two months ago. Car accident.'

She tried not to suck her breath in too loudly. *Ouch*. She'd never thought he could have been so very recently bereaved. He had to be feeling guilty and chock-full of Regrets'R'Us. Should she ask him to pull over and let her out? Her stomach sank at the notion.

Before she could act on her jumbled thoughts, he went on. 'Roslyn had been in a coma for a year after the accident.' His voice remained level, like he was describing an unknown patient. Too level for the occasion, which hinted to her that emotions ran deep, and he wasn't letting them out. That was fair enough, but his wife being in a coma for a year made his actions more understandable.

'Her EEG showed flat since admission.' He turned the car left. 'She was cared for privately until she succumbed to a respiratory infection twelve months later — two months ago.'

Ava furrowed her brow and tried to think. Once she'd handed over her patients to the next shift, her mental processing after night duty took that little bit longer. While she tried not to get too bogged down with his guilt, or the fact that she was the one he was feeling guilty about, her brain reeled with the inconsistency of what she knew about long-term coma patients. It wasn't a situation she'd had much experience with in Alice Springs, as any such patient would be airlifted out. 'Is long-term care usual with a flat EEG? To be maintained on respiratory support for that long?' Ava had always thought flat brainwaves meant flat brainwaves — forever. Tragedy in a shell of a body. The ultimate donation of life with a harvest of organs.

His hands tightened on the steering wheel and she winced and looked away. How badly did she need to know? She shouldn't have asked. He deserved his privacy. 'Don't answer if you don't want to.' Then she had another thought. 'Or maybe it would help if you haven't talked about this stuff with anyone.' It wasn't exactly her idea of a light pre-breakfast conversation, but if it would help Zac, her new friend, ex-lover — whatever he was or could be — then she would survive.

A minute passed, then two, but it didn't faze Ava; she and patience were old friends. It was a part of her work.

'Yes,' he said finally. 'After the accident, within a day, the hospital suggested organ donation and the removal of ventilatory support. It was Roslyn's parents who insisted she be admitted to a private facility. In case of a miracle.' He shook his head and she knew he didn't agree. 'I didn't feel I had the right to overrule them.'

His hand lifted briefly from the wheel, as if trying to catch the sense of the past. 'But she lay for months, unchanged, except towards the end her chest became worse — a hospital-acquired infection. Her body was racked with fever and she wasted away in front of us, every day thinner, more wraith-like, trapped in our decision to maintain life support despite the fact that everything real, everything that made her Roslyn, was gone.'

'Pull over, Zac. I'd like you tell me, but you don't need to do it while you're driving.'

He looked at her a little startled, but he did what she asked. When he'd stopped and turned off the engine, staring straight ahead with his hands resting lightly on the wheel, she murmured quietly, 'Thank you. Did she die or was life support withdrawn?'

'We turned it off.' The words fell like cold stones between them and she blew out a breath. Tough love.

He shrugged helplessly, with his hands tighter on the wheel. 'It became obvious, even to her parents, that we were increasing her suffering without any hope of a future. They finally agreed to a day.' Although he was talking, she felt it wasn't to her. Maybe to himself, maybe to his wife, maybe to her parents or his friends, who didn't understand.

But she was the one listening. She and listening were old friends, too. 'That must have been heavy on you.'

'Thank you.' His face turned towards her. 'Funny how you pray for someone's suffering to pass, yet when the time approaches you wish for more time.'

She nodded. 'I've had a little to do with palliative care, with babies who come home to die because nothing can be done for them. I've seen that. Felt that tension, that maybe if we waited something would change.'

He nodded. 'I think you do understand.'

She did. Life was precious. But sometimes the cost was too high.

He sighed. 'So the morning came.' His voice dropped and she strained to hear. 'It was a beautiful day. I think that made it harder. Like that song about the seasons in the sun. Her seasons were all gone and Roslyn needed to sleep in peace, and this machine that hissed in and out, dragging the air in and out of her reluctant lungs, had to let her go. We had to let her go.'

'And this was two months ago?' No flipping wonder he'd looked emotionally drained after one night shift. He wasn't just physically empty, he was also spiritually empty. Her heart ached to give comfort. To him. To Roslyn's parents. To Roslyn, even.

He said, 'The machine stopped. I'll never forget the silence in the room as we watched her heart slow, falter and stop. No breaths. No heart rate. Nothing. What was left of her was gone. It was tragic. Horrible. But Roslyn's death was a release for us all.' There was another pause and then he said, 'Especially Roslyn. Twelve months is a long time to be held back from peace.' His eyes briefly met hers. 'But those internal conversations make you guilty, too.'

Ah, guilt. Ava understood feeling guilty even

when everyone else said you were innocent. She'd been there. Guilt explained a lot. Poor guy. He'd made the sort of horrible decision she hoped she'd never have to make. 'It's tough all around,' she said, and impulsively rested her hand on his arm. She squeezed and felt his muscles tense under her fingers.

He lifted his other hand and touched hers briefly in appreciation, then put it back on the wheel. He huffed out a pent-up breath. 'After the funeral, I needed to get out of the city. Thought I'd try remote locum posts. Last month, Weipa . . .'

Ahhh. 'This month, Alice.'

'Correct.' He ran his hands through his hair. Roughed it up very nicely, Ava thought, with a tug of attraction.

'Weipa proved to be a steep learning curve and a good reality check from all the sympathy that hung around my own hospital. I went back to Sydney for a few nights and then I was on a flight out to Alice for a month while my house sale is going through. It was Roslyn's dream home and it's far too big for me on my own. The plan is to return a new man and start a new life. That's it.' He looked at her for a moment and shrugged, then turned on the engine.

Then he'd met her, Ava thought. Of course he was still going back to Sydney in a month. His intention to not form any lasting relationship with her made a little more sense now. She should have the same sense. He had given her more than enough to chew over, and maybe regret she'd come back with him. 'I'm sorry for your loss.'

'Thank you.' He pulled out into traffic and

drove the short distance to the hotel. In no time, he was slowing the car for the hotel entrance.

He parked and switched off the engine, and they gazed at each other. His story sat between them like a heavy mist they were trying to peer through. Funny how sure she was that on the other side of that mist there could be glorious weather.

Well. Ava scooped her handbag off the floor. It was too late to wish she hadn't come, and being out of the car and in fresh air would help. 'Breakfast?'

'Please.'

They left the car and walked together towards the main entrance. After a small silence, strangely not awkward as it should have been, she said, 'I hope one day you'll tell me about Weipa. That's one of the places where I'd like to do a stint, and they say it's an amazing flight into the town.'

He laughed without amusement. 'I hope you'll tell me about your world out here, too.' He gestured behind them, 'But shouldn't you be criticising me for being an uncaring husband? Cheating on my just-buried wife?'

She shook her head. 'That's not my call. Out here we promote the 'don't judge others' habit and I agree.' Then she stopped and he paused too. She held his gaze. 'From the little I know of you, you're not a cold person, Zac. Not someone who's uncaring about your wife's recent death.' She raised her brows. 'You might be conflicted about what we did.' Wicked thoughts swirled in her brain, and no doubt in her eyes, and she

46

flicked him a very brief smile, then started to walk again. 'But you're not cold.'

'Not cold now.' His voice followed her, low and definitely more upbeat. The glance he sent her as he caught up promised as much warmth as she could handle, and her cheeks heated when he said, 'What we had two nights ago warmed me right up.'

With a room full of people inside the hotel, they needed something else to think about. The air between them had shrunk like plastic wrap, and she could feel the warmth of him and the sizzle of her own skin. Her belly swirled with remembered sensation and she dared not meet his eyes in case this new wanton woman inside her, the one she didn't recognise in sensible Ava, took his hand and steered him upstairs instead. That would not be a good idea.

Say something, she urged herself. 'Um. We really should think about food.' Or she wouldn't get to eat.

He said, 'You could sleep here today and we could go to work together tonight.'

Oh my, she thought, but she couldn't stop her smile from forming.

7

Zac

Zac closed his mouth. Well, that had come out in a rush. He glanced at the profile of the woman beside him. Who wanted food?

But he'd promised. Both of them. And he did want to know more about her. Needed to. She was a mystery to him. A being from another world brought up on a far-flung station and extremely comfortable in her own desert skin. Ava was capable, skilled and quietly amused at life without ever mocking it. An outback oracle and a dancer who made him think of another kind of dance. And boy did he want to tango.

'You know when you move, at work, or outside, you move like a dancer. Have you ever danced?'

'I grew up on a cattle station. But funny you should say that. I'll tell you the secret one day.' She smiled at the doorman, who opened the door for her, 'Hello there, Ken. How's your wife? And the baby?'

'Great, thanks, Ava.'

'Say hi. And thanks for the door,' she said over her shoulder as they sailed through. Zac nodded his own thanks and wondered how many people in this town she knew. He guessed it was proportional to the number of babies she'd helped deliver. Ava showed kindness and warmth towards others because it was right, but he couldn't help thinking this was not something Roslyn would have thought of. She wouldn't have seen the doorman. Comparisons. He shook his head at the memories that were guaranteed to bring him down. Not today.

When they were seated and had given their orders, he said, 'Thank you for coming with me this morning. Despite my odd behaviour.'

'Right, then.' She lifted her chin higher and stared straight at him. 'Do you regret what happened between us after the flight?'

'Regret?' He felt cold that she'd think that. 'Lord, no. I don't regret what happened between us. I couldn't have stopped asking you up to my room if my life depended on it.' His gaze rested on her and he recognised that same thrill. 'It was as if we'd been together forever.' Then his scalp crawled at the disloyalty to Roslyn and he ran his hand through his hair. 'But . . . my wife died two months ago. What sort of man does that make me?'

Her bacon and eggs appeared before her. 'I've been thinking about that.' She considered him. 'I've thought about it all the way from the car.'

She played with her fork without taking her eyes off him and he couldn't look away from the gentle expression she regarded him with. There was no judgement there, and as if by osmosis, his tension eased away.

'I think you're a man who's been grieving for twelve months already,' she said, her tone careful. 'You said there was no brain activity from the first day. It isn't only two months since you lost her. You lost Roslyn more than a year ago.'

Why did his own theory sound more plausible coming from her?

'Thank you. That's the argument I've been using, but until now it hasn't helped.'

The waiter came with his food and all of a sudden he had a big appetite.

She put the fork down with a metal chink and nodded at something he suspected had nothing to do with him. 'We do love to make ourselves feel guilty.'

'I feel guilty about making you lie last night.'

She nodded. 'I wasn't going to call you on it. I felt confused too.'

Lord, she was so honest.

Her chin went up. 'Maybe I wanted to come back, even if it was on your terms,' she said, meeting his eyes and laying herself bare.

He could do the same. He hoped. 'I couldn't process it. Pretending I didn't know you kept things distant.' He spread his hands. 'At least I did come to my senses after I left you in maternity this morning. I'm sorry.'

She shrugged, but he knew he had caused her angst. Then she confirmed it. 'I'm not an expert on the morning after with a stranger, but I'll survive.'

'I see that.' He admired her resilience. 'But I don't want to be a stranger to you. I want to get to know you.' These were words he didn't know he'd been going to say, but they felt so right once they were out.

'Why?'

His gaze swept over her face. 'Because I have to?'

He heard her swiftly drawn breath, saw her hand lift to rest over her sternum as if her heart hurt.

She said very slowly and quietly, 'We both need to slow down. We come from different worlds.'

The problem was, she didn't look any more convinced that she could slow down than he was.

'We could eat breakfast slowly before we go back upstairs,' he suggested.

She grinned at him. 'I dare you.'

8

Hana

In a two-storey flat in Alice Springs, Hana May felt her baby's feet drumming against her uterus, and a warm surge of maternal love made her eyes mist. Life felt so darn good it frightened her, and she stared at the ceiling of Jock's mother's townhouse. She missed the serenity of the station, but they were lucky they had this, a place the family used if they had to come the four hundred kilometres into town for the monthly shop or a doctor's appointment. Or in her sister-in-law's case, agency midwifery work.

Hana sent up a little prayer for her wonderful life to stay wonderful. Normally she was not a worrier, but pregnancy had heightened her awareness of risk, and this drought, which was affecting Jock's family station, made her neck prickle with unease. Especially with her normally easygoing husband's unreasonable and escalating guilt that the station's perilous financial position was all his fault. She had her own small online baby-clothes business and was grateful that she could contribute towards their household expenses.

She couldn't dispute that he talked less and less and seemed to have trouble finding anything to smile about. Which was crazy when they were having a baby. And then he'd made that off-the-wall comment that if anything happened to him, she should 'find a good man and be happy'. The chill had well and truly run up her arms at that, but he'd waved her concerns away with an 'accidents happen' and he was just thinking of their baby.

She pushed the thought away as her baby kicked again.

She loved Jock with all her heart. She'd upped the tempo of including him in all of the baby news to try to make him focus on the future and not the present drought.

She remembered the first time she'd seen Jock. An agricultural studies student from Australia. His broad shoulders and slim waist with his subtle, whipcord strength had been so different from the muscular Maori men she knew. Jock's blue, blue eyes had smiled at her under the big Akubra hat that shaded his face. He'd looked at her more than the crops at the exchange-student ag farm she worked at.

'Psst.' She reached for Jock's hand even though he was sleeping and dragged his work-roughened fingers scratchily across her belly so he could feel what was happening. Jock shifted and rolled onto his side, and as he woke properly, his hand pressed a little more firmly to sense the vigorous movements of their child. She watched his mouth curve and felt the echo of her own.

'He's a wild man like his dad,' she whispered as Jock's hand came away from her belly to gently caress her cheek, the roughness of his skin testament to the manual labour he loved.

'Our baby will have dark, wavy hair and

chocolate eyes like those that captured me,' he whispered back and leaned over and kissed her. 'Our daughter will be beautiful like you.' He smiled. 'And a strong Maori woman like you.'

'I'm not the strong one. You are.' Hana tamped down that frisson of fear and sighed into him. Forced herself to relax. She loved this crazy man so much. When he'd rested his blond head back on his pillow, she turned her cheek to look at him. Her big, strong cattleman she'd fallen in love with from across the Tasman Sea and followed home. Home to this desolate expanse of red earth, distant grey-blue mountains, and wonderful, caring people. But a Central Australian cattle station? She still shook her head over that one.

The landscape was so vastly different from the vibrant green hills of New Zealand's North Island, and it was surprising she wasn't more homesick. Though with dear Poddy, her brother, following her over and becoming Jock's right-hand man, the rest of the family's estrangement — and their horror that she'd married outside New Zealand — made it bearable. Her hand slid down her belly and she soothed another jab from the baby within. They were building a new family. 'You sure you don't want to find out the baby's sex today, when we have the ultrasound?' Hana did feel a little guilty she'd suggested they wait.

He shook his head. 'I waited all my life for you, I can wait to know more of our baby.'

She snorted. 'Twenty-four years is not all your life.'

54

'Ah, wife, I've only been alive for a year now.'

Hana laughed. 'Your big sister would not believe how romantic you've become.'

Jock blinked. 'Which reminds me. How come Ava didn't get in until yesterday morning? I thought her flight came in the night before?'

'She had delays,' Hana said serenely. 'She should be home after seven-thirty this morning, and she has two more nights, so don't make a noise while she's sleeping or she'll kick us out.'

Jock's pale brows rose. 'We're going home tomorrow, anyway. But she can't kick us out. It's Mum's house.'

Hana poked his shoulder, 'Sometimes you are so pedantic. And it's almost seven and we have to be at the ultrasound by nine. I'm getting up.'

A big, calloused hand slid caressingly around her wrist and tugged gently. 'Do you have to?' Then he said very softly, as he kissed her, 'Life's too short.'

* * *

Two hours later, Hana's phone light flashed beside her and she reached over and lifted it from her handbag.

Happy ultrasound. Having sleep over again with hunk from plane. Turns out he's a doctor from ED. Not expecting forever, but today is very, very good. See you back on Setabilly. Xx A

As she read the message, Hana's eyebrows crept up and her lips curved. She shot a glance at Jock, who was flicking through a magazine in the hospital waiting room. Her voice remained

55

serene as she shared chosen parts of the message. 'Ava's staying at a friend's today. She wishes us fun at the ultrasound and might not see us before we leave tomorrow. She'll see us next week.'

Jock shifted his eyes to her. 'Which friend?'

Hana studied the message, keeping her eyes fixed there. 'I don't know this one. She has lots of friends.' Hana was saved from further creative sidestepping by the receptionist calling her name.

They both stood, and when she took Jock's hand his fingers shook slightly and she realised he was nervous. She'd discovered that men, especially big, strong ones like her husband and her brother, didn't like hospitals. Even ones that showed them cute 3D pictures of their baby. But she understood that the base hospital was a necessary part of life. Especially when you were pregnant with your first baby in the centre of Australia. There was no use having a birth problem out with the cattle, even if your sister-in-law was a midwife and your mother-in-law a nurse. And then there was Mim, the matriarch of them all who had handled an inconceivable number of isolated incidents in the fifty years she'd lived there.

Nope. Hana would come into Alice Springs when her time was near, they'd stay in town like all remote women did, and wait close to the hospital for their baby to arrive. Then they would celebrate back among the wide-open spaces she was growing to love once her baby was safe in her arms.

Hana felt surrounded not just by her husband's love, but by strong women, and since she'd been pregnant, even her no-nonsense mother-in-law had softened a bit. Luckily, Hana had the ability to not be fazed by the forthright Stella. Jock was her dream man, and she knew that the love of her life would be a dream dad. She couldn't wait.

9

Ava

The last thing Ava had expected when she'd agreed to the three shifts at Alice Springs was to sleep over at Zac's for all three days before work.

But she had. By the third day, her mouth held a secret smile and her cheeks had a glow about them that didn't have much to do with the midwifery job she loved.

The polished floor in the maternity hallway looked like a deep, dark pool as she trod silently up the hall at the start of her last shift. The door had just shut behind the evening staff and the yellow Dolphin torch in her hand shone a path of white light on the shadowed floor as she confirmed that intravenous infusions were working correctly, attended to observations that needed to be done, and checked on sleeping mums and babies. She liked the serenity of night on the ward, be it sensible or dramatic like it had been the first night with Zac.

Zac. She smiled to herself.

A baby's wail drifted towards her and a call bell pinged from one of the mothers on the ward. She moved swiftly down the dim corridor, humming softly. She also loved it when the maternity ward enjoyed a rush of babies.

Every room had a mum and baby tonight

— even the two- and four-bed wards were full — which meant the chances of sitting down would be slim, but the night would fly as new mums soaked in the secrets of the night and were initiated into the realm of snatching sleep between feeds.

She'd met some of these mums earlier when she'd visited them in the Indigenous communities hundreds of miles in all directions from Alice Springs. Outreach midwifery visits meant Ava connected with women on their country, answering their questions, sharing advice. She also carried a heart-rate doppler to listen to the unborn babies, measuring tapes to measure bellies and babies' growth, blood-pressure machines and tools to take pathology specimens to send back to Alice Springs.

For the mums, it meant they could cut down on travel hours to see their doctor or midwife. When they did have to come into town, they would hopefully see the midwife they'd met on their home ground if she was back in her rotation in Alice. Or, if an illness or complication cropped up during the pregnancy, they would come into Alice early and be admitted to wait on the ward or in the accommodation near the hospital, and Ava or one of her colleagues would see them there.

Often, the trip to the hospital a couple of weeks before the birth meant a poignant wave to the woman's family and a lonely outback bus ride that would take hours to reach Alice Springs — so the idea that the women would know their midwife was a reassuring one.

Sharing the births of the outreach patients, and the connection she felt with these strong Indigenous women, represented everything Ava had moved into midwifery for. The births were gentle, often with older wise aunties or grandmothers in attendance. What's more, the deliveries were unhurried and driven by the mother's wishes for how she wanted to birth, despite having to travel to Alice Springs and waiting there for the day to arrive.

Considering the calm, beauty and rhythm of these births, Ava wasn't the only one who wished these babies could be born in the country of each woman and her family. As long as everything went smoothly, of course. Which it didn't always do. Having the backup of medical science came in handy way too often, and Ava couldn't see an alternative to coming into a centre of high acuity for these remote women. Every settlement needed backup for emergencies, which just wasn't possible.

With amusement, she realised that now when she thought of medical backup, she thought of Zac. Her sexy city doc. In a perfect world, she and Zac could run a flying squad for outreach maternity, like the obstetric heroes had in the 1930s for home births in the United Kingdom. Except in Australia, distances meant they really would have to fly in the air and swoop down on isolated settlements. It was a nice dream though. A pipe dream. And as things stood at this time, it simply wasn't going to happen.

Which led to something else that might not happen. Despite the fact that she'd spent the last few days with Zac, today her Alice Springs midwifery shifts ended and she would travel to her last placement before she took holidays. Last night, for the first time since they'd hooked up, Zac had mentioned he could fly to Uluru on the weekend to see her at the Yulara clinic. The question was, would he actually arrive there so she could introduce him to her favourite place in the world? Or would something crop up to prevent it?

Maybe she wasn't the only one who felt they had something momentous happening between them. Was she dreaming that he looked at her with a special light in his eyes whenever their paths crossed at work?

Another call bell rang and she slipped into Kareena's room where her baby had begun to howl with distress. Kareena's pale face looked drawn with weariness, even in the dim light, as she rocked her new son without any reduction in noise. Her mum snored loudly on the corner sofa. Kareena sniffed when she saw Ava, and a tear trickled down her cheek. 'I'm no good at this,' she whispered.

'You're perfect. Just tired. And your baby doesn't know the rules yet.' Ava held out her hands and Kareena passed the baby over with relief. 'You're exhausted. How about I take him for half an hour? I'll rock him while you have a power nap. You'll be surprised how little time you need to feel better.'

'Thanks, Ava. That would be good.'

Ava helped her to the toilet and back, checked Kareena's tummy when she returned to bed to see that her uterus was still firm, and then carried the newborn down to the nursery to change his nappy and discuss reasonable sleep patterns with him.

The nursery, a long, dimly lit room with the unattended radio chatting away in the corner, held two recliner rockers, a baby bath and a bench. In the past, all the babies would spend most of the night down here with the midwives and be taken out at regimented feed times to their sleeping mums. However, in these enlightened times of demand feeding and babies rooming in with mothers, most nights it was only used by the midwives when exhausted mothers needed half an hour of down time for a brief nap and babies needed a one-on-one with their midwife.

'Now listen here, young man, your mummy is tired,' Ava whispered as she swiftly undid his nappy, wiped the meconium from his bottom, and pinned a new nappy in place. 'You need your arms wrapped and a good burp. Then you can close your eyes and go to sleep.' She patted his bottom in a slow, steady rhythm. 'Then I'll tuck you back into your bed beside your mum because you've had a big day, too.'

She began a thorough check of his observations, ensuring nothing was out of the ordinary that could be upsetting him. Once he was wrapped and settled, she carried him back to his mum's room and tucked him into his cot. She stood quietly in the dark and rocked the little wheeled cot back and forth until he was asleep. Kareena's breathing sounded deep and untroubled. Her mum still snored and Ava grinned as she left the room to return to the desk to complete her notes.

The clock hands seemed to spin towards morning, until finally dawn arrived with another pink sunrise and a sense of promise. She hoped. She waved goodbye until next time to the early-morning staff, agreed to look out for a young woman of unknown gestation of pregnancy from up north who had slipped through the midwifery caseload system and was supposedly in Yulara now, and opened the door to greet the promise of Zac waiting for her.

He was there. Zac stood tall and solid against the wall, idly swinging his car keys, looking so much better than he had three days ago, despite another night in emergency.

This time when she greeted him, they were given a few raised eyebrows as night staff from other wards walked past, but Zac just smiled at them and took her hand. He raised her fingers to his lips and kissed them before tucking her arm into his. Ava hugged that to herself and tried not to plaster herself against him in a declaration of 'mine'.

She raised her large bag in her other hand. 'I brought breakfast cereal and toast to celebrate the end of night shift and thought we'd have a picnic somewhere special — oh, I don't know . . . in bed?'

She watched his eyes turn hot, and darken to almost black. Her belly kicked as he smiled that slow, devilish smile. He leaned down and whispered in her ear, 'No restaurant? No waiting for a meal when what I really want to do is kiss

63

you? What a fantastic idea.'

Especially as they only had the morning before she had to leave. *I'm a basket case*, Ava thought. But so was he.

They both quickened their pace and were laughing and practically running by the time they reached the car. She felt like she was sixteen, not twenty-five, and couldn't wait for Zac to get into the car and drive. She liked this extravagance of staying in his apartment at the hotel — no housework, lots of conversation, and a gorgeous man who wanted to meet her needs, while she met his. It was such a shame that it had to end.

★ ★ ★

Just before three, after she'd fallen into a deep sleep beside Zac for almost six hours, Ava slowly opened her eyes. As she lay there, she remembered this room from that first morning — was it only four days ago? This time the room was shrouded in darkness from the pulled curtains, so essential for daytime sleepers.

No chink of light entered today except from the clock, the green numbers telling her she needed to go. She sighed. If she wanted to get to Uluru before dark, she needed to leave now, and if she closed her eyes for a snooze she'd be driving in the dark. So she slipped from the bed and padded across to the bathroom, gathering her things to pack silently behind the closed door.

Which was a good thing because she needed

to prove to herself by saying goodbye to Zac that he was not as necessary to her as breathing. She still didn't know if the craziness between them would falter now that she was leaving Alice. They wouldn't finish work together, meet in emergencies, or sleep in the same bed. But they'd made tentative plans — that he'd visit. Plans that she had no control over. All she could do now was wait to see if those plans would come to fruition. It really was outrageous to think of the depths to which she would miss this man after so short a time.

Ava slipped out the door of the hotel and across the car park to her car, which she'd moved here yesterday in preparation for the trip today. But once inside, after winding down the windows to let out the heat, she sagged against the seat. Instead of starting the car, she phoned her sister-in-law. Hana would be back at her little house on Setabilly, which was just out of sight of the main homestead to give the newlyweds privacy. Ava wished she could transport herself there for an hour, because she desperately needed to talk to Hana about Zac, and Hana could keep a secret. A phone call was the next best thing.

'Hey, Hana.'

'Hey. Sneaky Ava.' She could hear the laugh in Hana's voice. 'Are you still 'sleeping over'?'

'I was. I'm just about to drive down to the medical centre at Yulara township.' Her voice wobbled unexpectedly.

'You okay?' Of course Hana would pick that up. Intuition was her strong point. 'Feeling sad about leaving your new friend?'

'Zac.'

'Is Zac short for something?'

Ava laughed. 'I don't know.'

'And that's okay, too,' Hana was quick to reassure her. 'You have all the time in the world to find out because I knew immediately Jock was for me. Instant attraction.'

'Attraction doesn't cover it,' Ava said. 'We exploded.'

'And lucky you. Things are pretty explosive my way, too.'

'Give my love to my brother, then,' Ava teased. 'How was the ultrasound?' The medical reports arrived on the ward for filing into the mothers' charts but she had resisted the temptation to check the report herself, which was not easy considering she'd never had a niece or nephew before and it was all pretty exciting. She surprised even herself sometimes with her self-control.

'Excellent, apparently. He or she is growing well. Due date of birth still on track.'

'That's wonderful. Is the baby moving well?'

'Playing football.'

They both laughed and Ava could feel her tension ease. Yes, she'd needed to hear Hana's voice. She'd always wanted a sister, and Hana had slipped unerringly into that warm and wonderful spot. 'Awesome. I'm about to head off. It'll be good to see Denise.' Ava's best friend, Denise, always offered a warm welcome.

'She'll be glad to hear you've broken the drought with Zac.'

'That's disgusting,' Ava protested, 'and too Australian for a Kiwi like you.'

Hana chuckled. 'Give my love to Denise. I haven't seen her since she started as Aboriginal liaison down there. Is she still out at the arts centre?'

'Yep.' Ava glanced at the dashboard clock. 'I felt a bit down leaving here and just wanted to touch base with my fave sister-in-law. Thank you. I feel better now.'

'Give it a chance. You be happy, Ava.'

Well, she'd certainly been doing that — giving it a chance. Ava blew out some of her misgivings. 'Thanks, Hana.' It did help. 'The problem is my cautious side keeps whispering about the way I tumbled into love before and the disaster that became of it.'

'Five years ago.' Hana puffed with disgust. 'I wasn't here then, but I've met that Jai and I can easily believe he tricked you. The guy is a sleaze.'

He was actually. Shame she hadn't seen that when she was nineteen. 'I saw him in emergency with a bunch of his drunken mates the other night, but one of my friends dragged him away so I didn't have to deal with him. He's still making a play.' Jai hadn't liked that she'd ignored him.

'Sounds like him.'

Zac was the opposite. 'Zac is a caring, wonderful man,' she told Hana, and she had no doubt about that, and the way he looked at her . . . But everything that had happened five years ago, with Jai, and when Amelia was born and then died, had been a watershed in her life. She

67

did not want to go through such pain again. And tomorrow marked Amelia's birthday and she wanted to be at Uluru for dawn.

'Thanks, Hana. I just needed to hear you. I'd better get going. Get to Yulara before dark.' And towards the end of that five-hour drive, the wildlife might start to step out in front of her if she didn't leave now.

'Any time. And sending hugs for tomorrow for Amelia's birthday. Love you.'

Ava felt the sting of tears and brushed them away. She composed herself to say goodbye, but before she could Hana added, 'Drive safe.'

She always did. She'd seen too much heartache not to.

'Bye, Hana. Love you.'

Speaking of heartache . . . Zac understood heartache. Which was why she wondered if he'd risk following her to Yulara when they'd part anyway. He had to head back to Sydney shortly and she belonged here. Neither of them had discussed that but soon it would be time to do so.

★ ★ ★

Very early the next morning, Ava wasn't thinking about Zac. This was an Ava Zac hadn't met. It was the day of her yearly dawn pilgrimage to Mutitjulu, Uluru's family waterhole, to celebrate the short life of her infant daughter. She chose to celebrate the beauty of Amelia's soul on the date of her birthday rather than with pain on the date that her spirit flew six weeks later.

She'd risen early to allow the pilgrimage before her first shift at the medical centre, which, unlike the maternity ward, began at the reasonable hour of nine. She'd go from here back to the nurse's flat and get dressed for work.

The sun hadn't yet risen above the red sand hills of the horizon as she drove slowly around the silent base of Uluru. In the predawn light, even the parking area near the waterhole looked magic as she switched off her headlights.

It was five years already since she'd been a young single mum birthing a child in the nurturing embrace of her family. The gossamer memories of Amelia's tiny, pale starfish fingers clung like gauzy threads to the edges of her mind. It was too personal, too painfully private to share this date with strangers, or to share her reconnection moment with this place that mystically eased the burden. Hence the reason she'd come very early today.

She switched off the ignition and sat for a moment as the engine ticked down in the empty parking zone. It was early enough that the tourist buses were all parked on the far rise, disgorging the first-time visitors onto the red sand in the middle of the desert well back from here. Rows of awestruck sightseers dragged from their dark beds were ready to capture the iconic moment with their cameras and smart phones as the sunrise finger-painted the desert and, more dramatically, the rising monolith in crimson and gold. Their sleepy eyes would be strained across the sand as dawn light began to hint at the deep-red mounds of Kata Tjuta in the distance as well.

'Happy birthday, Amelia,' she said aloud. For such a short time, mother and daughter had met and fallen in love.

As she climbed from her vehicle, tendrils of desert night clung to the air, and those ghostly fingers brushed cool kisses against the tears on her cheeks. Though she was alone, except for the call of the morning birds that made her peer into the sparse bushes as she walked the red sand of the path, she didn't feel lonely.

To her left, a plump western bowerbird with his curved neck and rounded head hopped on long legs, the thicker feathers near his body dressing him in feathered trousers that made her mouth relax in a smile. To her right, a crimson chat, dark brown with his bright-red crown and feathered back and his black eye mask was scanning the area. He poked among the fallen leaves, scratching for small insects, but no doubt thinking carnivorously of a caterpillar. Overhead a lone wedge-tailed eagle, the magnificent *walawuru* of the desert Anangu people, soared and searched with his keen eyes for something, anything, that moved.

As she absorbed the silence of the winding path that carried her to the creases of Mutitjulu, she felt the sharpness of her burden of loss, which grew heavy on this date each year, gradually ease.

To her right, the smooth, soaring cliffs on the face of the sandstone seemed to disappear like the walls of a cathedral into the pale, eggshell-blue of an early sky. Those towering cliffs always made her pause on the way in, to soak and sit on the polished wood branches of the free-form seating and listen. Absorb. Feel. The anticipation building.

The deep scores of the grained wood of the bench seeped like the stroke of cold fingers into her skin as she sat, the crisp morning air soothing her heart, the silence broken only by the soft rustle of the leaves in the gum above her. The crackle of creatures in the undergrowth calmed her.

She spied the tail of a lizard. Watched the thorny devil as he shifted, patient beside the ant trail, until his tongue flicked out to gobble up another small worker. Denise had told her that the *ngiyari* could drink with his feet, standing like a spiky armoured vehicle in a puddle and shifting the water up capillaries along the grooves to his mouth like a marvel of science.

She was so glad she'd come. She stood and walked slowly towards the end of the gully where the water flowed into the smooth folds of the secret place and the captured pool, absorbing the peace as the gully enfolded her in a mystical embrace in welcome and empathy. It was always healing.

At the end on the fenced wooden platform, she sat and drank in her personal restoration, allowing her senses to open fully to the spirit of the rock. To renew. To breathe. Slowly, the residual agitation beneath her skin seeped away, flowing down to the earth to be absorbed into the red dirt beneath the wood, and her muscles eased. This was the reason she'd been drawn here before. This quiet, spiritual place gave her calm and strength, and re-energised her depleted stores, because this date always held sadness for what might have been. A birthday that never grew in years. This place of families understood.

She always came here at least once as she passed on her way to Alice Springs, or when she could fit it in around the shifts at Yulara — and every time she came away changed. Setabilly Station lay closer to Mount Conner than Uluru, but each time Ava visited she wondered if this was where she'd been born in another life.

The sound of approaching voices — tourists — echoing quietly from the soaring granite walls around her made her stand, murmur her thanks, blow a kiss to the sky and leave before the seclusion was broken. Then she walked back to her car and drove to work.

★   ★   ★

Yulara township was the service centre for Uluru and sat outside the national park. The village was set around a circular roadway, approximately twenty kilometres distant from Uluru and fifty kilometres from Kata Tjuta. A hub of different levels of accommodation, from high-end to backpacker, with a shop and tour office, bus service and restaurants, the centre was self-sufficient on the whole and was surrounded by desert. The airport was a further ten minute's drive away.

The medical centre and ambulance bay were both small, ground-level buildings set amid gardens and pedestrian paths that ran alongside the roadway. The medical centre ran as a weekday-only modern clinic, catering for locals and tourists who suffered minor injuries, mild medical conditions that needed monitoring, dressings and assessments, as well as being a centre for the critical transfer of emergency patients. Although it was well connected to telephone and internet higher-level support from Alice Springs and the RFDS, those too sick to deal with at the centre were airlifted or road-transported out to higher care as soon as possible.

Still, the excellent first-line emergency treatment onsite at the centre saved lives prior to such transfers. Usually it was a slow-paced general practice type of clinic, and Ava hoped this two-day visit would prove to be typical. However, when she pulled up outside the clinic, her best friend, Denise, a statuesque, ebony-skinned Anangu woman, was already waiting outside the door for her to arrive.

She'd known Denise since they were children. Ava knew most of the families from the local Anangu community, many as artists, and neighbours who hunted on lands adjacent to her family property — but she and Denise had struck a close bond from the outset. Denise, who was an artist and traditional healer, had a wicked sense of humour, and she and Ava had become known over the years as the laughing pair. Between Denise's strong-boned face and gorgeous black plaits, and Ava's blonde hair and blue eyes, they were a striking pair, and the fact that they laughed a lot together drew even more attention.

The two women hugged in greeting. Ava

unlocked the door to the clinic and Denise followed her in. The nurse hadn't arrived yet and Ava switched on the air conditioner to cool the room before any patients arrived.

'You been out at Mutitjulu? I can feel your peace.'

Ava smiled. Denise just knew things sometimes. 'Yes. Amelia's day today.'

Denise hugged her again. 'Thought it was.' An unusually harried look crossed Denise's face and Ava frowned. Her friend said, 'I need you to visit the local community to see someone today. Maybe at morning tea time?'

Ah. Ava suspected the reason for the concern on Denise's face. Perhaps it was the woman the maternity ward had mentioned? 'Is this Big Jim's partner? The young woman that's come down from up north? About eighteen and pregnant? None of the midwives have managed to catch her at any of their outreach visits. They asked me in Alice if I could look out for her.'

Denise nodded and some of the tension left her. 'That's her. Jessamine. So pleased you've heard of her. Nobody knows when she's due to go to the hostel in Alice. I'm thinking very soon, so I'm glad you're here. I spoke to her the other day and I think she's terrified of labour or something. She needs to talk to you.' Denise shrugged and smiled. They'd had a few discussions about Denise's two past births. 'I also think she could be due pretty soon.'

Ava hadn't heard this. 'What makes you say that?'

'One of the other girls told me she wants to have her baby born on country for Jim.'

74

They both knew that most of the mums and aunties agreed with the health authorities that it was safer if their babies were born in Alice Springs. 'Has she got anyone on her side?' The elders added their weight to the health directives and did well to encourage the women that it was better to go home with a baby afterwards than have a problem at home and need help that took too long to arrive.

Ava understood it wasn't easy for a displaced young woman to leave her new family or the father of her child and wait alone in a big town like Alice. And if she was new to the area, it would be unlikely she'd know any of the other women. Without her own midwife champion, the hospital could be unaware of other fears she had.

Ava knew that Hana wished she didn't have to wait in town either, but Jock would go with her, so she'd have someone to support her and she wouldn't be alone. But the men from the communities usually didn't go with the women because it wasn't their way. More often a mum or aunty would be there for the birth if they could be.

'Anyway,' Denise said quietly, 'she dreamed the baby is a boy. So now Big Jim says maybe he should be born on ancestral land in the old women's camp like his dad. Get some of the old aunties to help. Then the baby could be smoked here. So when he grows up he can say he was born on country.' Denise shrugged, but Ava could tell she was worried. 'I think it also has to do with Jessamine being new. She wants her baby to belong.'

Ava sighed. That made sense, and one of the most difficult parts for the Indigenous parents was not to have their babies born on country. Ava had been told many times that in Aboriginal culture the land was everything.

The problem was it was so darn far to get out here if things went wrong that the risk factors stacked up against any expectant mums. They had the emergency clinic, but if a mum needed help during birth, there were really only the nursing staff and one non-obstetric doctor for nearly five hundred kilometres. Ava had no desire to deal with a post-birth haemorrhage like the one she'd had with Zac in Alice Springs — Big Jim's brother's baby, in fact — without backup.

Ava rubbed her suddenly itchy hands. She had an odd feeling about this. 'I remember my mother telling me Jim was born prematurely here. It's probably coming from there. Lucky Jim was a tough little baby before they flew him out to the NICU.'

She checked her watch. Amelia had been ten weeks early, but Ava didn't want to think of sadness any more today. 'Perhaps if we go and speak to Jim and his mother, they can persuade Jessamine to feel okay about coming into town if we explain there are other girls there she can talk to.'

Denise screwed up her nose. 'Don't like your chances.'

'Thanks for the heads-up. I'll come, and hopefully together we can convince Jessamine to wait for her baby nearer to medical help.' *Much*

76

nearer. And much sooner.

'Before we catch a baby here.' Denise laughed. It wasn't funny, Ava thought, but the nurse arrived and smiled at Denise's infectious mirth, and Ava found herself relaxing again.

★ ★ ★

Two hours later, after dressing an ulcerated leg, inserting three stitches in a cut finger, and washing out a sand-filled eye, Ava drove out with Denise to the desert community on the outskirts of town. Her first sight of Jessamine made her brow furrow.

To Ava, the young woman seemed big around the middle, even in the baggy dress which was a few sizes too large for her, her pregnant belly hanging ominously low for someone not supposedly near term. Had Jessamine put on body weight under that dress, or was the billowing fabric concealing a big baby?

Hiding her concern, she smiled. 'Hello, Jessamine. I'm Denise's friend, Ava, the midwife who lives on Setabilly Station. Nice to meet you.'

Jessamine didn't answer and the silence stretched. Ava waited, still smiling; she had no urge to rush it. 'I heard there was another baby due sometime over here, so I thought I'd drop by and see if you're going okay.'

Jessamine kicked some dirt at her feet and didn't look up. 'I'm good.'

Ava knew the fine line between nosy and nice and had perfected the art of not being pushy. Everyone had reasons to choose their own time for things. 'I see by your belly that baby's growing well.' *Quite a lot, actually.* Ava acknowledged another niggle of disquiet. Sometimes, if a mum developed diabetes, the baby put on a lot of weight because of the mother's sugar-rich blood. 'Have you had a scan?' she asked.

'Machine broke down when they booked it. I don't need one. My baby's good.'

Ava smiled. 'Baby's moving well, then. Lots of kicks?'

'He's good. Dreamed he was a very fast hunter. Got a way to go yet, though.' The girl looked away as if many interesting things were happening anywhere but where Ava stood.

Ava doubted the 'long way to go', so she tried again. 'He's a good size like his dad?'

'Yep.' Jessamine stood awkwardly.

It seemed Ava had worn out her welcome, if there'd been one to begin with. Something was troubling Jessamine, and Ava wished she knew how she could help the young woman feel more comfortable. 'I'll let the group-practice midwife know you're here. She'd like to come out and check you and your baby on Monday. Though I could check today if you wanted?'

The girl gazed off into the distance. 'Maybe.'

Ava felt a tiny surge of hope. 'I'd love to see you and I have my baby doppler. You'd be able to hear your baby's heartbeat.' She put her hand to her ear as if listening. 'The heartbeat sounds like a horse, you know. A fast *clop, clop, clop.*'

Denise smiled at that, and finally, like a promise, Jessamine did too. Her smile lit up her whole face and Ava had to smile back. This was

78

why she loved doing what she did for women like Jessamine, who needed understanding.

Encouraged, Ava added, 'It's all in my car. I could check your sugar levels and blood pressure now. Let those midwives know everything is fine.' *And feel your tummy to find out what's going on,* Ava added silently with a tinge of urgency.

There was another flicker of interest. 'Gotta go somewhere now, but maybe later today,' Jessamine said. 'Or tomorrow.'

Ava nodded. 'After lunch today would be good at the clinic. You wouldn't have to wait then.'

The girl turned away and something made Ava say with the utmost sincerity, 'You can come to the clinic anytime if you have a question. I'm at the clinic here till Friday at five. Let us know if you want to go to Alice Springs before that and I could help Denise arrange a ride.' It was such a shame Ava wouldn't be in Alice next week to see her there.

Jessamine paused and she looked back over her shoulder, then nodded once. 'Thanks.'

'Good to meet you, Jessamine.'

Denise's nod said she'd go with Jessamine, and Ava didn't doubt her friend would try to bring the young woman in later that day. Or they'd make a plan for tomorrow. If she didn't turn up for a check, at least Ava could say she'd seen the young woman and that she looked well in herself.

10

Zac

On Saturday afternoon, Zac heard the satisfying clunk of the undercarriage not long after the aircraft's wheels rose from the Alice Springs tarmac. As the plane's acceleration pushed him back into the seat, his mood lifted with the cabin. He'd missed Ava like a limb, even though she'd only been gone for three days.

Since Ava had left Alice Springs for Uluru, a journey that would take him fifty-five minutes to fly instead of hours by car, he'd had plenty of time to think. And act. And, after she finished work today, they'd have two nights and a day together. He had plans. Not just fly-down-and-see-her plans, but outrageous plans. Him-staying-here-forever plans.

Zac had bought something he hadn't intended when he'd gone to buy Ava flowers this morning. Strangely, the impulsive purchase had eased an odd, disquieting feeling of impending doom that he'd finished night shift with today.

It was nothing to do with the business of the emergency department, so maybe it had just been that he wanted to be with Ava now and not have to wait until this afternoon. Either way, he'd bought something so special, he couldn't believe his desire to put himself right out there at

80

the end of a very long tree limb and declare how he felt.

Hopefully, his idea would hold its weight. He could have been fuzzy from lack of sleep on his shopping trip, because while Ava had been gone, his work had been hectic and he'd had trouble sleeping in his silent bed. The apartment had sighed with an emptiness he couldn't fill.

The four days prior with Ava — well, they'd used up a lot of hours not just making love. They'd laughed at the television together, swum in the hotel pool, and spent hours telling their life stories on the comfy lounge as they'd sat by the window looking over the scrubby distance. They'd fit some wild and woolly night shifts in there, too, saving the world together. It had been perfect, as if he'd found his soulmate. Did the culmination of all that explain the bizarreness of his purchase? Like how the item had shouted to him through a shop window in diamond speak that nobody else could understand, like the snake in Harry Potter? Drawing him to the glass to peer at it and marvel.

Yep, something like that. A ring all by itself on a stand with a backdrop of a pink Central Australian sunrise.

The perfect engagement ring for Ava.

It was a big decision, and a big pink diamond, but he consoled himself that if he looked like a fool, at least he'd dared to dream. He'd certainly made the jeweller happy, and the weight of the velvet box in his pocket made his heart rate settle and his vague worry recede a little. He'd stopped drumming his fingers. They would have a long

81

engagement, he decided. There was no need to rush her into a wedding. There were so many things to discuss, people to see — parents, family — and decisions to make. But just knowing he'd found the right symbol of how he felt was enough.

The aircraft bumped through some turbulence and brought him back to the present. He glanced down to where he'd slipped the box into his bag. It was safe, and he resisted the urge to look at it again to confirm the tightness of the design. It was simple. Bold. Beautiful. Like Ava.

And he'd made the right choice with colour. It was the exact shade of the sunrise that had shone on their bed that first morning as he'd watched her wake up, and the colour of her cheeks as she'd met his gaze so bravely that first day. The diamond glowed with a blushing, rosy pink, the colour he wanted to see on her hand and cheeks as he woke with Ava beside him every single morning for the rest of his life.

He had no doubts about that. He'd realised it this morning, when he'd simply nodded his head and bought the ring. Not because she would lust after a big diamond — he'd learned possessions wouldn't sway Ava — but because the strength of the stone's pull reminded him of her. Irresistible. One-off. And he was taking a giant leap of faith.

Because he loved her.

Zac felt the ramifications of that statement race along his veins. He'd loved Roslyn, his childhood friend, his society wife, and mourned her loss. He would always hold her memories dear, but this was a different love.

He'd never wanted anyone more than he wanted Ava. Did that make him a bad person? It wasn't just lust — though bucketloads of that clouded everything. It was the unexpected pleasure in her company, the need to be a better man for her, the desire to make her smile and see her happy. And since she'd been gone, he'd seen that where and how they were together truly wasn't important. They could figure out the details later.

But so soon? So fast?

Yep.

This was assuming biblical proportions, and strangely, he wasn't feeling the need to run. The outrageously unexpected purchase of the ring in his pocket attested to that. He wanted to take away all her worries and sit her in front of that big red rock she loved so much and hear her passion for her work and laugh and tease her. He wanted to meet her friends and family, and reassure them that he was worthy.

He'd listened to Ava's love of the majesty and mysticism of Uluru. As he stared out the window, searching into the distance for the resplendent structure, he thought, *It's the perfect place to propose.* He was having some pivotal moments in aeroplanes lately.

Zac heard the engine note change as Ayers Rock Airport swung into view, and the window tilted as the aircraft swung in over the low scrub of the iridescent rust-coloured desert to land.

Now he could see Uluru in the shimmering distance, impassive, mystic, rising from the desert like a long, low pyramid. Even from this distance, it impressed with its magnitude, and he couldn't wait to see it up close. Actually, he couldn't wait for Ava to show him up close.

Because this timeless, enduring monolith would become a symbol of their future.

11

Ava

Zac was coming! He was due to arrive after lunch, and Ava glanced around the clinic and decided it wasn't too untidy to show off. The patient load was calming down now that the half a dozen seats in the waiting room had nearly emptied. She methodically completed her assessment of a child with asthma and was relieved to see the wheeze Zoe had shown yesterday had lessened, as they'd thought it would. 'You did well with your puffers, and your chest sounds much better,' she told Zoe with a smile, then turned to the mother. 'Keep following the asthma plan and ring the helpline if you get worried.'

'Thanks, Ava. Will do. Come on, Zoe.'

Ava washed her hands and moved on to the elderly diabetic gentleman from the community whose ulcer was also improving, and then dealt with an elderly lady with a scraped knee and a twisted ankle.

'I've wanted to come here to Uluru for years,' the lady was saying, 'and I fall over and twist my foot on the first day.'

'It's a shame but all is not lost,' Ava reassured her as she bandaged her leg. 'If you put your feet up today, you should be feeling even better tomorrow. You can take the bandage off for your shower in the morning, but put it back on for walking, as support.'

'Yes, Nurse.' The woman looked doubtfully down at her foot. 'You sure it will be fine?'

'You can take your weight on it now, but it will only get better if you rest it. Watch the sunset from your room and pop your feet up on the outdoor table. It's a beautiful afternoon.'

Yes it was, she thought as she helped the woman to the door. And Zac would be here soon. She gazed through the window at the dark sapphire of the sky. The colours seemed deeper, the bird-song louder, everything brighter and crisper, despite the warning that they might be in for a dust storm later. But not before Zac touched down.

By two pm, she knew Zac's plane would have landed. She pictured his big frame on the bus from the airport to Yulara, but she kept her head down as she carefully cleaned the gravel from another scraped leg.

By the time it was done, her stomach jittered with tiny twitches of excitement and her mouth kept smiling at the clock as if she had a new friend in the ticking hands. For the last three days in her staff accommodation, in the back of her mind, she'd been planning Zac's introduction to Uluru, the park, the base walk, the cultural centre, Denise and her husband. All the places to watch the sun rise and set. And other things . . .

She needed to calm down. Anyone would think she'd fallen in love with a guy she'd known for a week. Had she been that foolish?

Her mind skittered back to Zac. He'd jumped on her suggestion to book a rock-view room at the Yulara resort, so they could step out onto their own verandah in dawn's light and know exactly where they were. It was impossible to miss what stood on the horizon from that vantage point, and she wanted him to see it too.

Surely he'd drop in here as soon as he'd unpacked. They only had tonight and tomorrow and then he'd go back to work and she'd go on to her family's station.

The clinic door opened and suddenly he was there, watching her, hand still on the doorhandle as if frozen by the sight of her, checking her out with a warmth in his eyes that made her skin heat and her delight bounce in her chest.

'Hello,' he said, his voice deep and familiar like a much-loved song. The door closed behind him and the room felt as though it had shrunk to the size of a telephone box.

They grinned at each other like loons and she crossed to him and held out her hands because, really, she wanted to launch herself into his arms, and it just wasn't professional to do so at work. He took both of her hands in his and searched her face as if he wanted to memorise every feature, and yep, her belly flipped and flopped. She was alone in the clinic as the other nurse had dashed to the supermarket to pick up milk for tomorrow.

'Perfect timing. We're just closing.'

'Beautiful,' he said. And if she heard that right, so much more was being whispered underneath. Whether he meant her or the circumstances, she didn't care. Both boded well for the night and the coming days.

That was until the hubbub of noise erupted outside and the screen door scraped open in a hurry. Denise ushered Jessamine into the room and the mood flew away like a startled lorikeet. Zac stood back to allow the women to push past into the clinic area and Ava knew they'd just taken a raincheck on their reunion.

'Jessamine's waters have broken,' Denise blurted out.

Jessamine's face screwed up in pain. 'Baby's coming.' Judging by the grunt that followed, she was spot-on.

Well, then. Ava's eyes met Zac's, and she thought, *Just like in Alice! Did drama always follow this guy, or was it her?*

She snapped out of that thought as Jessamine took a step back when she noticed Zac. Ava kept her voice low and tranquil, as if it was a lovely coincidence that the women had visited. 'Jessamine. This is Dr Zac. He's an emergency doctor from Alice Springs. I worked with him when Kareena had her baby and he was a big help. Do you know Kareena?'

Jessamine nodded reluctantly.

'It's so lucky, really.' Ava drew her in further. 'If your baby's coming, he'll be here to help us. It's good to have a doctor around. I'll look after you and he'll look after baby.' Ava glanced at her friend. 'Denise will stay too, of course.' Denise's relief at finding the clinic still open was evident and Ava smiled at her. 'Good job.'

Denise shook her head. 'I found her walking in

from the community. I'm happy to see you still here.'

Jessamine's fingers were white on the internal clinic doorframe. Then another contraction began to build and her breathing sped up. Her eyes darted around the room as if there was somewhere she could hide from the pain in her belly.

Ava saw the edge of panic and rested her hand very lightly on the young woman's shoulder, sharing her calmness through touch as older, wiser midwives had shown Ava in the past. In response, Jessamine dug her fingers into Ava's hand and squeezed as she bore down. 'Don't you let go,' she ground out and Ava smiled.

'You're safe, just breathe slowly and let the tightness roll over you like a wave.'

The outside door opened again. 'And now we have Nurse Jill — ' the short, grey-haired nurse raised her brows at Ava in question — 'who is back from the shop, so there are plenty of hands to look after you.'

By the time they'd helped Jessamine into the treatment room, another contraction had pushed a small rivulet of pink fluid to drip onto the floor, confirming Denise's warning about broken waters. At least the colour of the liquid was reassuring, Ava thought, as she began to run through what she needed to do for an imminent delivery. The nurse grabbed a towel and dropped it on the puddle before someone slipped.

'I can't lie down.' Jessamine leaned forward over the day bed the clinic used for critical patients, and with a nod from Ava, Denise moved around the other side to gently take the young woman's hands in hers for comfort. Denise began to murmur soothing Pitjantjatjara words that dipped and hung quietly around her.

Relaxed a little by Denise's crooning, Jessamine rocked and swayed, almost in a dance. Jessamine's dusty footprints began to form a circle like a painting around the towel on the cream vinyl of the floor where she stood. She rocked and stepped through the escalating contraction, and Ava imagined the young mother was creating her own circle of safety. She liked the idea. They'd take all the help they could because she doubted any RFDS plane would make it in time for this baby.

Ava didn't want to interrupt that instinctive response to her body that Jessamine had found to direct her labour. They wouldn't have to wait long for another change that would indicate the labour had reached the point where Ava would have to look.

Jessamine made a strangled noise and Ava exchanged a glance with Zac that said, *Right now.*

'Can we lift your dress, Jessamine, and see if the baby's coming?' Ava asked.

'You'd better,' Jessamine said with a groan as she shimmied out of her wet underwear, which plopped onto the floor. ''Cause somethin's happenin'.'

When they lifted the damp skirt up to her back, a much thinner back than Ava expected, they could see the roundness of a tiny baby's buttock.

'Breech,' Ava breathed as she caught Zac's eye, and Zac frowned worriedly at her. *Be calm,* she told him with her eyes. 'All the spontaneous ones I've seen had no complications, so let's keep it like that,' she said softly. Zac's eyes still held concern, though, so she said quietly in an aside, 'Good thing I did a refresher in Sydney. *Allow the presence of trust,*' she said, repeating the mantra they'd pushed at the course and smiling at him. To Jill she said, 'We'll let mum and baby do the work, but get ready for a baby, Jill.'

Nurse Jill's fingers shook, but she handed Ava and Zac a pair of gloves each from the pack beside the day bed. 'I'll phone for the RFDS.'

'No.' Jessamine shook her head as tears rolled down her cheeks. The young woman turned her head to look at Ava. 'I shoulda come yesterday.' Ava had been to see Jessamine again yesterday, but hadn't been able to cajole her into allowing an examination.

'We talked,' Ava soothed her. 'You and Denise did well coming here today. And Jill will call the RFDS to pick you up so they can make sure you and baby stay okay.'

Jessamine shook her head and glanced at the door as if she was going to run away. 'You can ring 'em. But we're not goin' on that plane.'

Ava guessed something had happened to Jessamine or one of her family to cause this fear of hospitals or aircraft, but they didn't have time to find out now. They needed to be calm for the next stage. 'I hear you. We won't worry about that yet.' Ava met Jessamine's eyes and said quietly, 'Nurse Jill has to ring so they know we might need help. I understand you don't want to leave country. We'll talk later when you're not so busy.'

Zac peered around the now crowded room. 'How did you get here, Jessamine?'

'I walked. That's how I saw Denise.'

'It's a good thing to walk,' Ava said gently. 'Most breech babies curl themselves into a ball and sort themselves out. Movement helps that.' She turned to Denise. 'What about her man's mum? She not here with you?'

This time Jessamine narrowed her eyes. 'I didn't tell anyone. She'll be mad I didn't come in after you left yesterday. We don't get on too good.'

Better she's not here, then, Ava thought philosophically. Emotional friction didn't go with birth. She repeated, 'Walking through labour is good. Really good because your baby is almost here.'

Jessamine nodded and swallowed. 'I can't stand. I wanna kneel down on the floor.' With that the girl pushed off the couch and awkwardly knelt down until she'd buried her head between her elbows and then into a pillow Denise hurriedly dragged off the nearest bed. Nurse Jill was like a sprite dragging towels from cupboards, helping Ava put protection under Jessamine's knees and body to shield against discomfort and cold, then tossing a thin blanket over her back.

Even Zac, who hadn't done a lot of obstetrics, didn't look surprised that a strongly labouring woman wanted to throw herself into the best position. Ava knew Jessamine had listened to her body telling her the most useful way to use gravity.

Ava saw that Zac had found a stethoscope for the baby and was making a space on a nearby bed to examine or resuscitate the infant if he needed a work surface, a task Ava was glad wouldn't fall to her.

As Jessamine knelt down, Zac used his foot to slide a little footstool for Ava to sit on so she could hover close by and help if needed. In the background, she picked up the quiet rumble of the tumble drier. Jill must have switched it on to warm towels and a blanket for the baby on her way to the phone. This wasn't the first time a child had been born in the clinic, but it was certainly unusual. Everything had better work out well because there was no backup aside from those present.

A few minutes later, Jill returned with the emergency birthing kit and an injection drawn up to give after the birth. Ava flashed her an appreciative smile. They certainly didn't want a post-partum haemorrhage.

'It's coming,' Jessamine gasped as the baby's body gradually appeared with the help of gravity and the mother's pushing.

In slow slides, centimetre by centimetre, the baby's hip descended. Denise's eyes grew huge and even Jill looked incredulous. It became apparent that Jessamine's dream about a new male in the family was right as a tiny scrotum swung into view. Her man would be pleased.

'Let the legs come themselves,' Ava murmured to Zac, even as she privately thought, *It's so hard not to flick those legs out!* She was mindful of the words of her recent instructors and explained quietly to Zac, 'While the legs are folded inside the mother, they're stretching everything for the head. If the legs are flicked out too early, the birth canal misses out on the extra stretching that helps the rapid descent of the head.'

He nodded. 'Sensible.'

As Zac hovered, and Jill scurried away and came back with a warmed towel to wrap around the baby, first one and then the other of the baby's legs dropped down, all by themselves, so that the curve of the baby's belly and a stretched part of the umbilical cord appeared.

She spoke to Jessamine, but she was really talking to Zac. 'Same for the cord. People used to ease that loop of cord out to save strain on it, but now we're taught to leave it in case we cause a spasm in it.'

'Got it,' he said and they smiled at each other, both aware of how amazing the natural birth occurring in front of them was.

They watched a section of the slippery rope tumble out of the birth canal. Ava chanted to herself, *Wait. Wait.* All she needed to do was wait.

In fact, it all made beautiful sense to let the baby drive the birth. With progress this smooth, it would go well as long as she didn't interfere and startle the baby into lifting his chin and interrupting the curve of his spine.

Ava continued speaking softly to Zac. 'See that dip between the baby's nipples on the chest wall? See the space it makes for the cord to sit protected? Isn't that wonderful.' The little pale chest and legs hung between the mother's buttocks, and slowly the tiny calves and thighs began to jiggle, as if the tiny human inside his mother had decided to slowly ride an invisible unicycle.

'Will you look at that.' Denise's awed voice floated across in a whisper.

Jessamine moaned.

'He's moving his legs to help him come down,' Ava murmured to Jessamine. 'That's what you can feel. Soon he'll be sitting on the ground under you, so let me know if you want to move.'

'I ain't goin' nowhere,' Jessamine ground out.

With the baby doing his circus act, first one arm and shoulder appeared and then the other. Now there was only the head to come. The baby was sitting almost cross-legged under his mother, until suddenly his chin dipped forward and Ava had to lean over quickly to catch him before he fell face first onto the towel. 'Spontaneous breech birth,' she announced, wanting to laugh with the exhilaration of it all. Instead she asked, 'Born at?'

Zac made a noise. 'Good catch,' he said with an exultant note in his voice. He took the warmed towel from Jill and rubbed the baby firmly until the little boy screwed up his face and roared with disapproval.

'Born three thirty-one,' Jill intoned as if they were in a normal birthing suite, and they all sighed out at the same time. 'Will I give the injection?'

'Wait.' Something wasn't quite right, though Ava wasn't sure exactly what it was. She hadn't had a chance to feel Jessamine's uterus and she knew the young mum hadn't had a lot of obstetric care. This baby seemed too small for the size of his mother's belly. While she thought about it, she allowed a minute for the extra blood from the placenta to flow into the baby. Anaemia could be a problem for some outback and especially Indigenous babies if the mother was anaemic, and the extra blood could mean a much healthier start to life. After a moment's pause, she clamped and cut the cord to allow Zac to lift the baby away and around to the front of the mother.

But Jessamine was busy again. Another gush of water, not blood, flowed from her, and another tiny buttock slid into view.

'Second baby,' Ava breathed.

'Exciting times,' Zac murmured.

'I did wonder,' Ava said, glancing quickly at Jessamine. 'Jill, can you put a cannula in for Jessamine? I want Zac free for the babies. Then give that injection, IV. With twins, our PPH risk just went up.'

The second baby was also a frank breech, and again two little buttocks presented and another little scrotum. Ava couldn't help a tiny laugh as once more the procedure was accomplished easily. This baby's trunk delivered quickly and Ava allowed the infant to rotate slightly to the left as the natural curves of the mother's pelvis facilitated delivery of first one shoulder and arm and then pivoted the other way so that the other arm came free. Then there was a *plop* as the baby's head eased out and he fell forward into Ava's hands. Another baby who knew what to do.

Ava waited again for an extra minute before

she clamped and cut this cord, too. There was a small gush of bright blood and the cord lengthened suddenly as the placenta began to come.

'Needle now,' said Zac. Ava had no doubt he'd be thinking about the last post-partum haemorrhage they'd had in Alice Springs.

Ava nodded. 'Jessamine, I'm worried that you'll bleed. So we have a needle here to give you. Is that okay?'

Jessamine eyed the needle in Jill's hand with trepidation. 'Better be quick before I change my mind.'

Ava marvelled at Jessamine's fear of the needle when she'd just pushed out twin boys. She said soothingly, 'Needles make people nervous, but Jill's really good at it.' At Jessamine's nod, Ava said to the nurse with a smile, 'Now would be good, Jill.'

Jill tightened the tourniquet and inserted the cannula. Denise helped her strap it, and then Jill slowly inserted the uterotonic injection, then assembled an IV line. The look on Zac's face was priceless — it was so full of amazement.

'We've worked together before, you know,' Denise told Zac. The whole procedure was completed quickly, before Jessamine could change her mind.

Very soon after the injection Ava delivered the enormous placenta, and after a quick check down below, she encouraged Jessamine to roll over so she could massage the mother's stomach. The idea was to reduce the placental site on her uterus and squeeze off any haemorrhage vessels.

97

To Ava's immense relief, everything settled with remarkably little fuss and they all breathed more easily for the moment.

Zac made light work of helping Jessamine up to the day bed to lie down. Ava and Zac put the babies back against their mum's skin, while Jill put a warmed blanket across the trio. Done.

Ava laughed and stood back, stripping off her gloves. 'Oh my. Now that's an exciting event. Alice Springs maternity will be horrified, and jealous, that we had such a fabulous outcome here. Brilliant birthing, Jessamine.' She couldn't help thinking, *That's one way to keep off the labour-ward bed: a few kilometres of walking.* 'But don't go starting a trend.'

Both babies looked less than three kilograms, and to Ava's surprise Jessamine didn't seem perturbed that there were two. 'Jim will be real pleased,' she said quietly. 'They're both good, eh?' she asked Zac. 'They can stay on country?'

Ava knew she couldn't promise that. Everything might be fine, but they were too isolated. 'I don't think so. But we'll wait for the team. You've done amazingly well, Jessamine. But twins! Your poor uterus is stretched and tired. I'm sorry. They'll want you to go to hospital for at least a day or two so they can watch you don't bleed, and these boys need to be putting on weight.'

Jessamine's face dropped. 'I don't want to go.'

'We know.' Zac crouched down. 'But these little boys need their mum, and having two babies at once makes your uterus risky. If something happened to you, their life would be sad. It's best to go to the hospital and then you can come back in a day or two when everything is settled. You were amazing.'

She sighed and there was a long pause. Ava held her breath. Finally Jessamine said, 'At least they're born here.'

Zac nodded. 'A big story they will hear from you when they grow up.' Zac lifted his stethoscope. 'Can I have a listen to them while you have a cuddle?'

Good job, Zac, Ava wanted to say, but she glanced at the clock. Jessamine had been there for less than an hour and so much had happened. They were having a very big week.

12

Zac

Zac sat outside the clinic on the tiny verandah and waited for Ava to finish handing over Jessamine and her babies to the flight staff from the RFDS. Jessamine had wanted to breastfeed and he'd left them to it. Denise had collected a bottle of red soil for Jessamine to take with the boys as a symbol of country.

Above him the sun had drawn closer to the horizon. Thinking of celestial movement made him feel remarkably blessed to have been present for Jessamine's babies' smooth arrival. The young mum had held it together so well, helped by Ava's calm action and management, which kept him shaking his head. His girl had been like the conductor of nature's incredible symphony of birth. How had he been so lucky to have been there to see it all?

In Sydney he'd seen twins born by caesarean section but had never witnessed a natural twin birth. Although those times were special, the absolute amazement of seeing a first-time mother achieving what could have been a very complicated birth without any unnecessary hands interfering had truly blown him away. And made him rethink his medical-school risk-management ideas. His new motto was going to be: go natural birth until proven otherwise. The only vaginal breech birth he'd seen had been fraught with drama and declarations of what could go wrong, and he wondered now if that had been so dramatic because everyone had been hands-on when they should have been hands-off.

It was a pivotal moment in his life, showing him that things could turn out well if he gave them a chance. He could see luck played a part. Ava had been here, obviously, and he had been backup in case the twins were compromised. But maybe you made your own luck.

For some reason, the arrival of the twins au naturel reminded him that he should trust the arrival of Ava in his life. His Ava, who continued to astound and astonish him with her clarity of purpose, her intuitive skill and warmth when dealing with crises, and her unconditional generosity to allow him to enter her private world, dealing with his crisis, too.

He could hear the dull murmur of voices from inside the little clinic, and he stood up and walked down the steps to the native gardens laid out like small green artworks of nature's design all around the resort complex.

Soon he would have Ava to himself. Someone in Alice Springs had suggested they attend the Sounds of Silence dinner between Kata Tjuta and Uluru, and he'd booked that for tomorrow night. Apparently, one of the local Aboriginal elders shared Dreamtime stories from the night sky while the attendees looked through tele-scopes. It would be marvellous to just sit out under the starlight with Ava and soak it all in with the stories. He decided he liked the sound of the traditional names more than 'The Olgas' and 'Ayers Rock', which had been given by the Europeans.

But not tonight. Tonight he wanted Ava. Just Ava. Considering his plans for tonight, it was strange that tomorrow would be their first real date. He was just grateful for all they'd had up until now.

The gratitude word had become his biggest lesson since meeting Ava May. To learn to be grateful for the blessings instead of bitter about the pills in life. It wasn't new or groundbreaking, but he'd missed that basic truth in the rush and drama of his world away from here. Life before Ava.

She'd gently suggested he shift towards being grateful for the good times, the friendship and early excitement with Roslyn, and that he'd had the time to say an extended goodbye, despite his ambivalence about her parents' decision to continue life support. He certainly needed to be grateful that he'd been able to share the exhilaration of today.

But now he'd like to have time with Ava to resolve their future, to put his feelings out there and be sure she felt the way he did, because if she didn't then he needed to move on from here before he was so far in love with her he'd never recover.

They needed to talk about whether they could both fit into each other's lives, and that conversation required privacy for him to present his ring and ask to marry the woman he knew he was falling more and more in love with every day. He'd shifted the ring to the zipper compartment on the back of his wallet. He had no loose change and it couldn't fall out, and he hadn't wanted the bulky box to give away the surprise. He'd been hoping for a few hours before sunset, but they were running out of time.

'You do draw drama.' Ava's voice came from behind him and he turned to look at her in the afternoon light. Her face was haloed by the sun, and every line and shadow seemed precious to him, making his chest ache with emotion.

'Look at you in this light.' It was an effort to keep his voice level. 'I want to carry you away and learn your magic' He was very glad he'd made arrangements before he'd come to see her. 'I don't suppose I could invite you over to my hotel room for some contemplation of . . . ' he pretended to search for inspiration ' . . . the afternoon view from our verandah?'

She laughed. 'It would be nice to have some alone time with you that didn't include babies or medical emergencies.'

He reached for her hand, and once they were joined he felt ridiculously complete to have her fingers in his. Hip brushing hip, they walked up the curved footpath towards the hotel. The sun cast long, thin shadows away from them and he waved his other hand back at the health centre. 'All good on transfer?'

'Amazing. Jessamine's breastfed the boys twin fashion. She's calm about the flight now. The pilot told her how many thousands of safe landings he's had.'

103

She squeezed his hand, her mind obviously on other things, but that was fine by him. He loved the way her mind roamed. In fact, he loved everything about her.

'It's five years away,' she said musingly, 'but when these babies go to school, I'll talk to Jessamine about looking at a scholarship in health. She'd be an incredible nurse. Maybe even a midwife if it isn't too far for her to travel for study.'

Five years. She expected to be here? Of course she did. That was food for thought but not unexpected. Given his feelings, there was a big chance he'd be here too. For the moment, he only said, 'You're a midwife. From here. Nothing stopped you.'

'No, it didn't. But everyone is different. I do think she'd be such a great resource. We don't have enough Indigenous midwives, and her inner strength shines. That's where the change will come from. When Indigenous midwives can support Indigenous women in communities, we'll see more outreach births. More babies born on country.'

There was a long road to travel and a lot of red tape to cut through before that would be a reality, but if anyone could encourage it to happen, Ava and the friends she had here could. 'No matter how good your set-up became, you'd not get twins booked to be born on country,' he commented with a small laugh.

'Yes. Except for today.' They both smiled again at the thought. 'Jessamine was brilliant with those babies coming out so well. Probably the long walk did it.'

He'd thought about that. 'She's lucky she didn't have them on the way.'

Ava pretended to punch his arm. 'Stop. I don't want to think about it. Having you here helped a lot, too. If you hadn't been here, I'd have been terrified the babies would need more than I could give them.'

He laughed at that. Ava terrified? He seriously doubted that could happen. But at least he'd been useful. 'Thank you.'

Ava was still chewing over the problem. 'I don't know. I think she'd get a lot of help from Denise in finding support and assistance to study, too. She has a long-term goal for helping remote pregnant women, not just Jessamine. I've read about the Inuit women, where a system of local maternity support showed better outcomes for births at home, so I'm sure it could work here too.'

He leaned in and kissed her. 'Absolutely.' Then he kissed her again and stepped back to re-tuck her hand into his arm.

'I'm ranting again,' she said with a sheepish smile.

'You do it beautifully. If enough people feel the way you do, things will change. But I'm more selfish and wonder if I can entice the desert midwife to hurry a little faster across to my hotel room.'

He felt the tension ease out of her and she touched his cheek. When their eyes met, her expression grew teasing.

Tonight. I'll tell her tonight, he thought. The declarations were threatening to burst from him.

13

Ava

What an afternoon she'd had. And now this. She was mad. Intoxicated. The man just had to waggle his finger and she was there, ready to follow him to his bed and kiss him all over. She'd planned to drive him out to the viewing places to see the first sunset, but they'd never get out of his bed once they got to his room.

As they turned left through the greenery and gravel paths between the buildings, she couldn't wait to be wrapped securely in his arms. To know without a doubt that they were together again.

He gestured for her to precede him up the stairs to the second floor. They would have the best views up here. *My extravagant hero,* she thought just a little smugly. Her heart pounded with the need to get him alone. Her heart also pounded because he'd walked her faster than her legs normally walked and she cast a sideways glance at his determined face. He was a man on a mission, apparently. Her mouth struggled to stay straight.

He paused at the door with his key in his hand and turned to stare down at her with such an intense look. This was another face of Zac's she had trouble reading. But she'd learn all of his expressions if she had the chance. Their gazes locked. Time seemed to stand still. Distantly, she heard a bird call out, and someone rumbled a suitcase over the path below. She could pick up the subtle scent of his aftershave, and the even more subtle scent that was Zac. Everything seemed more noticeable when she was with him.

With his gaze still on hers, he bent down and kissed her gently on the lips, his breath warm on her cheek as he turned his mouth to her ear and she closed her eyes. Very quietly he said, 'I love you, Ava.'

Her eyes flew open. Men didn't say that. Especially ones she'd only known for a week. 'What?'

His lips tilted at her shock. 'I love you.' The words came out again, each word defined as if he savoured it.

In that instant, time felt like a slow train that ran over her ghostly self as she stood outside his door. Two carriages. *Bump. Bump.* He'd said it twice.

'I'll explain inside.' He slid the key into the lock and opened the door for her. As he steered her through to the verandah, her eyes automatically crossed the glorious red and olive of the desert and lingered on the majesty of Uluru in the distance. Indented soaring cliffs were burnished orange and gold with the late-afternoon sun. She loved this view at sunset. If he'd planned the moment, he'd executed it perfectly.

Then she saw the rest. The table set with flowers, glorious desert blooms in an ochre bowl, crystal glasses and a beaded bottle of what she suspected was champagne in a bucket with ice. She shot him a glance and saw his lips twitch.

'And still in time for the setting sun.'

'This looks very special.' But her mind reeled from his words at the door, her heart tentatively testing the echo again. Did she dare hope? She remembered how her day had been coloured by the promise of his arrival, by her first sight of him this afternoon. She'd felt like throwing herself into his arms and had had to hold her hands out instead for control. What if he really felt this craziness too?

He watched her, then shook his head with a smile. 'Ava. I probably deserve this incredulity, but it's no game I've played before. What I feel for you is not a lukewarm feeling. It's hot. Urgent. Terrifying,' He gave her a searing glance that could quite possibly have singed off all her clothes if she stood any closer to him. On the verandah, in full view of the road.

'But my feelings aren't just about the sexy you. You're generous. Fearless. Limitless. I'm stupendously lucky for what we've already had and I'm gambling on the fact that you care for me as well. I missed you too much when you left. And I want you to know this is not a fling.'

And if it isn't, what then? she wanted to ask. Instead, she said, 'You do know we come from different worlds?'

'I know, but they're worlds that I'm very willing to negotiate.'

She stared up at him and said softly, 'What does that mean in practical terms, Zac? I'm not a city girl . . . I doubt I could leave the outback for good.'

'I know. I'm willing to do what it takes to

make our relationship work. Share the dislocation of moving between city and centre. Move to Alice or somewhere like it.' He paused, looking down in thought and then back into her eyes. 'Finding something like we have deserves whatever it takes to work.'

She drew in a breath, wondering if he was quite ready to be so far from his old life, or she from hers. Were they both willing to live for six months of the year for the other, to make their relationship work? This needed sorting, but she didn't know how.

Then he said, 'Will you kiss me?' That she could do. Had in fact been waiting all afternoon to do. She slid her arms around him and he lifted her up so her feet left the ground, hugging her to him. She sought his mouth and infused it with all the love she'd been holding back, all the frustration of him being away from her. She felt like she'd been starved of this — that she'd waited weeks, not just days, to be back in his arms.

'This was why I came to Yulara, to talk about this, to make plans that suit us both, and to share my epiphany from our very short, very intense time in Alice.' He lowered her gently and released her. 'It's crazy, but . . . I. Love. You.'

Ava still felt the shock of each word.

'I was going to get to this more slowly.' He ran his fingers through his hair and she realised she'd missed that gesture. Missed the need to brush it back into tidiness again. Missed everything about him, and now that he was here, her world had righted again.

Zac smiled at her. 'But we had Jessamine's babies to deliver and the sunset is getting away. The sunset on Uluru is part of my plan.' Their eyes met and his were soft with understanding for her confusion. 'You'll see. I've had time to get used to the idea and you haven't.'

More ideas?

He stopped and then pulled her hand so that she leaned into him. He gathered her securely in his arms. 'I love you, Ava. And after a reasonable, I-promise-I-won't-rush-you engagement, I want to marry you.' His voice reverberated low and deep through her skin and the wonder lifted the rays from the rock straight into her heart until it felt like it glowed as well. 'But I'm offering commitment now. I want the engagement. A proposal of the old-fashioned kind. It feels right.'

Engagement?! But he wasn't letting her think.

'I've learned the hard way that life can be cut short,' he went on in a rush. 'When you left Alice it hit me. I'm not losing the opportunity to love you through faint-heartedness. And you're not losing me. The distances between us in the next month mean we will be apart, so I want you to know I'm telling the planet. Here I am. Putting us out there. If you feel the same.'

Crazy man! She gestured to the desert as if the answer lay there. But he still hadn't actually asked. Was she mistaken about what he meant?

He was watching her as she stared at the monolith in the distance. Listening for an answer. 'Would it be easier for you if we drove there now? We have time before sunset. I wanted to ask you there.'

Her gaze jumped back to him, incredulous. How had he sensed that?

'We could stand together and I'll ask you properly.' He raised his brows, gesturing at the champagne and flowers. 'Then we'll come back and celebrate. I want this to be the moment you dreamed of.'

'And if I say no?' she asked, more of a tease than a possibility, because suddenly she believed him. They could make it work.

'I'll leave as fast as I can to try to forget you,' he said, only half teasing back. 'And if you say yes, we will have a longer engagement than courtship, I promise. And I will never leave you,' he vowed with a smile. 'Would you like me to propose properly at Uluru?'

She was saving this moment to hug forever. Her romantic Zac. 'Yes, please.'

★ ★ ★

Ava had never been this happy. Zac's hand lay on her thigh as she drove, maintaining the connection between them. They were almost there, excitement building, Uluru growing larger in the windscreen as they curved towards the final approach, the rays deepening into glittering gold on the rock. It was so beautiful. So . . .

Something flashed ahead — a vehicle, a white campervan careering sideways around the last bend towards them on two wheels. Ava didn't have time to understand as it grew larger and larger, approaching with ridiculous speed. She swerved, but there was nowhere to go.

111

The oncoming vehicle hit Ava's car with an explosive *whoomp* of force, and spun them over the guardrail. Ava screamed as everything seemed to slow to one-second increments. Their bodies moved up in the seats, then sideways as the vehicle tilted and hung for a moment, before someone pressed the fast-forward button on disaster and the car crashed down onto its roof and then spun away in a furious blur of speed as it rolled over and over across the desert.

Ava's forehead hit the steering wheel and white light burst in an explosion of pain. Everything went black and her last thought was a fervent prayer to see Zac's face.

*   *   *

When Ava's eyes opened, the smell of diesel saturated the air, and through the cracked front windscreen the last of the late afternoon sun shone serenely down on the wreckage to ironically paint the scene in beautiful Central Australian gold and yellow. Steam rose in escaping tendrils from the mashed bonnet, and the steering wheel in front of her was slimy and dripping with congealing blood. Hers.

She sat strapped upright, the car on its wheels, but as she slowly turned her head, her neck and face and shoulders sent spikes of pain along her nerve endings. Then she saw him and her own discomforts became nothing.

Zac.

Her heart thumped as she saw the way his head lolled.

112

'Zac?' His name was a croak from the depths of her throat. He didn't move. Blood lay everywhere. His arm, his chest, his head.

She strained to see his chest rise or fall, but there was nothing. Slow tears began to drip and mix with her own blood. 'You said you'd never leave me,' she whispered, and she closed her eyes because it was too heartbreaking to look.

Then Ava heard him moan.

Her eyes flew open. Urgency pushed away the lethargy of shock and she fumbled for her seatbelt.

★   ★   ★

Four hours later, Ava stared out the clinic window and tried to ignore the pounding in her head. Outside the dust storm hid the night sky. So much for the help from Alice Springs she'd begged for, because Zac still hadn't woken up.

Jill had dressed Ava's head wound and made her shower, then she'd put a pillow and a blanket on the easychair in the corner of Zac's curtained area because she'd refused to leave.

Ava looked back towards the bed and Zac. Unconscious Zac. The man who'd introduced her to the hidden depths of her own body, who'd caught her eye and grinned wickedly as their occasionally macabre humour clicked silently at work. The man who had been going to propose.

The dust storm had rolled in not long after the ambulance had moved them to the clinic. It had shrouded the township and grounded the RFDS aircraft before it could come back from taking

Jessamine and her babies to Alice Springs with extra medical help.

Now, hours later, she knew that in the dark the great Uluru would be dusted with eddies of sand, and red dirt would coat all the trees and the grasses in the desert as far as the eye could see when the sun rose. They'd blow away soon.

She wished she could go outside and scream away the fear and pain and mental exhaustion, but it would hurt her head. And she wouldn't leave Zac. Wouldn't leave him in the understaffed centre that was meant for daytime clinics only. They'd recruited a doctor from the other private medical clinic. After checking Ava and Zac, he and Jill had taken over the care of the occupants of the other car, who were in need of emergency resuscitation and Ava had said she'd watch Zac and call out if he deteriorated. And she had, mostly alone, until Denise had heard and arrived as support, though she was away briefly now to find Ava a drink.

Ava stared at the small window showing the empty road. Denise had been amazing, and Ava allowed herself to be soothed again by the bush medicine leaf pattern on the curtain material, copied from one of Denise's Dreamtime paintings. Her friend would be glad she was drawing strength from the flowing motion and undulating rhythm of the vivid lilac and white strokes. The brushstrokes seemed to ripple across the material with their significance to local traditional Aboriginal culture and healing. Healing that she needed desperately for the man she loved.

For the last two hours, as she'd twisted her hands in fear and Zac's pulse had grown more erratic, she'd tried to keep him stable until the flying doctor could airlift him out. He'd been too agitated, restless, and Ava had been beside herself trying to calm him. Visibility was down to mere feet on the road to Alice, so there was nothing they could do until a plane could land.

She feared she'd lose her big, beautiful man, with the extent of his head injury unknown and the torn wound on his arm, which she'd bound in the car as he'd threatened to bleed out. It was the simple things that could kill you. She stared at his pale face and beautiful eyes, which were shut to the world, his long, dark lashes lying still now against his ashen cheeks.

She'd leapt on Denise's idea of traditional healing for his soul at least — anything to keep him calm before more help could arrive — because she'd almost admitted defeat. Denise had studied Zac, seeing to the spirit within, and murmured about a build-up of negative energy which had placed a stone of bad magic inside him. She'd said that the stone was preventing his return to consciousness and she'd danced and smoked the accumulation out with a solemnity that had brought tears to Ava's eyes.

So was it coincidence that from the moment after the cleansing smoke and chanting from the traditional healer had finished, Zac's restless movements had settled and his galloping, thready pulse had begun to even out? She didn't know. But she had hugged her friend in gratitude.

Since then she'd been able to sit and watch, and she was trying to keep him calm with her voice. She was so immensely, wearily thankful that she could.

She watched her man's large, capable hands and those long, strong, brown legs lying too still. And that broad expanse of tanned chest and ripped upper abdomen, which had been slick with agitated sweat, but now lay cool and dry.

Tiredness swamped her, and she opened and shut her gritty eyes. She swept back the curtains to the early-morning darkness and allowed her gaze to drift over the roadway outside. There were few cars at this hour, and the ones that did crawl past left an unfamiliar muffled noise of dusty bitumen and tyres. Not your usual Yulara sound. The silence of the night calmed her and sent a shallow burst of new energy through her.

When would he wake up? Had he been damaged? Would he wake up? The questions bombarded her as memories of Zac on the gurney from their one ambulance skittered through her mind like that staccato gecko making his way down the wall of the room. *Stop. Start. Freeze.*

His unfocused eyes.

The blast of concern at his continuing unconscious state.

The panic she'd stamped down because of her helplessness at not being able to get him to a higher level of care and knowing he could only become worse — at least that had passed for the moment.

Now all she could do was wait.

14

Zac

When Ava's car had hit the guardrail on Zac's side, it had been so fast he didn't have time to shift away. Something in the deafening maelstrom of their crazy spin ripped his shoulder open and smacked the back of his head, and his vision blurred until they stopped spinning and landed with a *thwump* back on the vehicle's wheels, but he'd stayed awake.

Blinking with difficulty, Zac opened his eyes. Red dust swirled around them, and for a full minute he couldn't see. Then his breath caught at the horror of red streaming down Ava's face from a gaping wound in the middle of her forehead.

A wound he'd seen once before. Exactly like one he'd seen before. This was his fault. Again.

His brain screamed *No!* so loudly it escaped in a moan through his lips. Ava was dead. Or worse. Comatose.

Panic surged like a swirling black tornado in his brain, ripping his consciousness with the horror of his worst nightmare and swallowing him. His mind churned and the edges of the world grew dim. Everything went blessedly black.

★ ★ ★

When Zac began to take in his surroundings, it was the familiar routine sounds of a hospital he noted. Which hospital, he had no idea. In fact, the events of how he'd arrived here remained strangely elusive. His head pounded and he raised his hand to touch the spot. A thick bandage met his fingers at the back of his skull. Head injury? And his arm hurt.

Below the fog in his mind, a panicked urgency fluttered to get out and his heart pounded with the need to remember. He'd almost woken several times, pushing through the gentle weight of unconsciousness, and sometimes a whisper of an elusive feminine voice clamoured for his attention. Always it said the same thing. 'Zac?' There was something about the voice that calmed him, until eventually, the nightmare receded as he clawed his way up through the mists of confusion.

He remembered saying, 'Roslyn?' And then the patient in the next room cried out and some instinct made him swing his legs off the side of the bed to render the fellow assistance, but before his feet could touch the floor a nurse hurried towards him.

'Back in your bed, Dr Logan, please. Dr Fithers will be here soon. You stay resting till the doctor comes.'

When she saw that Zac was in no more danger of falling, she hurried out the door and he heard her soothe the other man's distress.

To Zac's relief, someone he knew, George Fithers from med school, appeared at his side, and after a moment's hesitation he perched

118

awkwardly on Zac's bed.

'It's good to see you alive, Zac.'

'Hello, George. Was I that close to death?'

'You've had a big couple of months.'

What month would that be? he thought but he didn't ask. It would come back. 'Where am I?'

'Alice Springs.' George studied him. 'A bit hazy on that, are you?'

'A bit,' Zac admitted cautiously.

'Not surprising.' George steepled his fingers and considered him. 'You came to work for me here a week ago. A locum appointment, though.' He gave Zac a mock glare. 'You're off sick now.'

'Sorry about that.' Zac was never sick. But that wasn't what he needed to know. 'What happened with this?' He slid his hand around the back of his neck again and winced when the pressure stung.

'Car accident. Impact and roll over, and a branch came through the side door and knocked you out. You're lucky it didn't take your head off.'

Zac winced. 'Harder to get over that one.'

'Beyond my help,' George agreed. 'But you'll be fine. It happened on the road out to Uluru. You were hit by a speeding campervan.' He sat back. 'You had to wait for a storm to pass before the RFDS flew you in here.'

George seemed to be watching his face intently, but none of this rang any bells.

'What can you remember?' George's question seemed careful, and Zac had the impression the doctor was trying not to upset him.

Why would it upset him? Zac closed his eyes and tried to remember the events of the last few

119

days. 'Today is Sunday?' he asked, and George nodded. He even looked slightly relieved, so that was good.

'I'm not cheering yet. You had a one-in-seven chance of that being right. Try the date,' George urged gently.

Zac could remember asking patients these questions. He stared down at the white hospital sheet for a moment. 'I can remember Valentine's Day. Roslyn's funeral. I got home from Weipa last week. So mid-March? I had lunch with my parents and signed the papers for the house sale. So maybe the twentieth of March?'

George didn't meet Zac's eyes, but he nodded as if he'd confirmed something he'd suspected. 'Today is the fourth of April.'

Zac forced down another of those sudden panic surges and had to concentrate to keep his voice even, which hurt. 'How long did you say I've been here?'

'Twelve hours.' George sat back and stared at him. Zac wanted to know what he was thinking.

April? He shook his head and winced. He'd lost a couple of weeks. 'It feels like March.'

'There's no doubt you sustained a major blow to the head, but you were lucky. The X-rays we took show no fractures to the skull and the CT looks clear of any clot or haemorrhage formation. Apart from your memory glitch, the injury shouldn't cause you any further trouble, but of course, I'd prefer you avoid small aircraft flying for a few weeks.'

Memory glitch? Zac's knuckles whitened on the bed as the panic attacked his throat again.

120

He needed to remember something, but it was completely out of his reach. 'Was anyone with me in the accident?'

George hesitated. 'There was a nurse, an agency midwife, Ava May, from one of the cattle stations out of town.' George's voice stayed carefully expressionless. 'She works here a fair bit. You two met last week. She'll be in to see you in the morning.'

Still no bells. 'Was she injured?'

George touched the middle of his forehead. 'She'll heal. She was knocked out briefly as well, but you were both very lucky to be strapped in, apparently. We're keeping her overnight, but she should be allowed to go home in the morning sometime with her family. They're here with her.'

At least not like Roslyn. But another car accident. Another woman injured. 'Who was driving?' He fervently hoped it hadn't been him.

'She was.' George stood.

Relief flooded through him at that. He slid his hand back to where he felt the bandages at the back of his head and the pressure made his head throb. The name Ava May struck no chord of recognition, and no matter how hard he tried he couldn't remember the accident. At least the amnesia was focal and he remembered who he was. It was the when that eluded him. All things considered, it could be worse.

'Focal amnesia.' George echoed his thoughts. 'Tricky and possibly permanent. Usually, it's the result of trying to block out a particular incident or fear. Not surprising really. It's been a tough few months with Roslyn, then this accident that nearly took you out.'

Zac shook his head. It was all too much and none of it made sense. 'How did I get to Uluru if I was working here?'

'You went down for the weekend. Many locums do.'

He couldn't remember any of that. He'd just have to wait for his memory to come back.

George glanced at his watch.

'How long do I have to stay?' Zac asked.

'We'll do another scan in the morning and talk about it after that. The crazy part was, although it's a small wound, you could have bled out if Ava hadn't put pressure on your arm. You nicked a vein and we had to give you a transfusion, so your loss of blood made you more critical than you should have been. She watched you at the Yulara clinic despite her own head injury. The staff had their hands full with the occupants of the other car. This was tough on her, but she's known for her toughness. Anyway, must go.' George looked anxious to get away.

'You pressed for time and manpower?'

'Yes,' he said sardonically. 'One of my locums nearly killed himself with a head injury.'

'Thoughtless fellow,' Zac quipped.

'Indeed.' George smiled, but it didn't reach his eyes. 'I'm glad you're okay.'

When George left, Zac tried to sleep. Until the panic came in the form of dreams and fractured scenes in the middle of that sleep and he tried to stay awake. But the vat of emotional bleakness stayed with him, cold and unforgiving and ominous.

Maybe he'd be more settled when he met the woman who had driven the car tomorrow.

* * *

Except he forgot she was coming.

He was dozing the next morning when a quiet knock at his door made him turn his head. A blue-eyed, blonde woman stood in the doorway. She had a plaster across the centre of her forehead and a huge purple bruise on her cheek. He winced in sympathy. That must hurt.

Despite the professional face she wore, he noticed that her hands jittered with a slight tremor, even though she held them tight by her sides. For some absurd reason he wanted to comfort her.

'Can I help you?' His voice croaked with dryness and he reached for the glass of water.

When she didn't answer he wondered if he should ring for the nurse, but he was just too tired. He leaned back against the pillows. 'Have you come to the wrong room?'

'No. This is the right room.' She drew in a distressed, shaky breath.

A suspicion formed in his mind that perhaps the last person who had been in this bed had died and she hadn't known.

'I'm sorry, but do I know you?' Although he felt inadequate, she wasn't his problem. He had enough problems. He looked away.

The woman lifted her chin as if annoyed with herself, then drew herself to her full height. 'I'm sorry, Zac.'

His eyes flew back to her. She knew him.

'I'm Ava. I should have started with an introduction. I was in the accident too. We've known each other for a week.' Her voice had evened to become low, melodic and caring.

Ah, the nurse George had mentioned. He should have remembered. She had a good voice for a nurse.

She closed her eyes for a second and he wondered if she had a headache as well. Of course she would, with that bruising. She opened them again, then added, 'Are you okay?'

'Ava. Yes. Thank you. You stopped the bleeding, apparently?' To his surprise, tears began to trickle down her cheeks until she dashed them away impatiently.

He sat up, held out his hand and pretended he didn't feel as weak as a kitten. Her body looked lithe and well balanced and it allowed her to move almost silently. Like a dancer. She crossed the room and let her small hand rest in his palm. The physical touch of her warmed him in a place that had been cold for too long. This was becoming stranger by the minute.

'You should rest, Zac' The way she said his name rustled like a breeze against his memory, but before he could pin down the thought she gently pushed him back against the pillows. 'I'm so happy to see you.' She bit her lip and swallowed, and he realised she was quite emotional about their meeting. 'But I can see this isn't the time,' she said calmly. 'You don't remember me.' It wasn't a question.

'Sorry.' He wanted to comfort her yet didn't

124

know how. 'Everything's pretty fuzzy about the last couple of weeks.'

'Dr Fithers warned us.' There was a strange expression in her eyes. 'I'm sure it will come back if you don't push it.'

'Of course . . . Us?'

'My family. They've come into town to be with me. You haven't met them.'

He touched his bandage uncomfortably. 'Well, sorry I don't remember you, but thanks for checking on me.'

She reached out a hand to smooth the sheet. Zac thought she might be going to cry again, but then she pulled herself together. Thankfully. That would have been awkward.

A week. He didn't know her well, then. That made him feel a little better that he'd forgotten her. She watched him warily. Waiting for him to say something, the colour a little high on her cheeks. He couldn't help noticing her freckles. He liked the softened angles of her face and the lush mouth that hinted at a sensuality he hadn't thought about for years.

The silence stretched and Zac found himself filling it. 'So, we were driving out to Uluru at sunset?'

'Yes. We were hit and the car rolled.'

And they'd survived. That was good news. 'I'm sorry I can't remember you, but I'm glad you're okay.'

'I'm glad you are too.' She looked at him again and then she blinked and straightened. 'I'll come and see you before I leave.' She gestured behind her to the empty doorway. 'Do you have plans for when you leave the hospital? If you wanted, when the hospital releases you you could come home with us — we live on a property not far from here — until you got better. My mother's a nurse, too — so was my grandmother — so you'd be well cared for.'

Maybe they ran some outback convalescent home? He wasn't sure how that could be a viable business, but who was he to doubt? 'Thank you. I'm sure I'll be fine and will be back at work soon.'

She looked as if she was going to say something, but then seemed to change her mind. 'It's up to you.'

'Thanks for the offer.' He hesitated. 'I'm sure it's very nice there.'

She smiled as some memory lit her face, and he was struck by the thought that he could watch her forever. He felt his own lips curve in response. Perhaps it could be worthwhile to follow her up as a possible means of prodding his subconscious, if his memory didn't come back by the time he left here.

'Think about it,' she said. 'I'll be in town for another day or two. I need to organise new transport. If you'd like to, we'll arrange for you to stay with us later. It might help you remember. Anyway, get well.' Then she left, with her back straight and her head high.

Zac stared at the empty doorway and his heart pounded, but he didn't know why. Although he couldn't remember her face, there was something about her voice that stirred those deep memories he was only allowed glimpses of.

She was beautiful, and he wondered if he'd been tempted to make a pass at her while working with her. That would be out of character for him, and unlikely given his recent loss, but it would be dreadfully bad manners not to remember if he had.

Zac sighed and a wave of tiredness engulfed him. This was becoming more complicated than he'd bargained for. The anxiety came creeping back, building, rising in his throat and tingling his arms and legs with stress. He couldn't pinpoint the source.

His head began to throb, so he manoeuvred himself awkwardly down in the bed and closed his eyes.

15

Ava

Ava walked slowly back to the hospital room that they'd made her sleep in overnight under observation. The blank look in Zac's eyes when he'd regarded her hung cold around her like a damp fog that was worse than any lingering effects from the accident. His memories of her were lost. What did you do when the love of your life forgot who you were?

It had to be transient. Temporary. Surely. He was awake and functioning, so that was the most important thing. That was what really mattered when it could have been so much worse. The dread she'd felt when she'd watched over him at Yulara chilled her skin again. Thank God he was awake.

But he didn't remember her. Didn't remember *them*.

Had it all been a glorious dream to be grabbed back like a child's longed-for Christmas toy? That incredible instant connection to the man she'd given her heart to after only a few days. The love she'd never believed would find her after Jai's betrayal.

They'd been pushed off a bank by a stupid campervan and now he didn't know her. At all. Their last week together had evaporated from his heart like rain in the desert. Without a trace.

Her head pounded. What was she supposed to do? She could tell him the truth, say he'd proposed, force him to look at her and describe what they had. 'Daunting' didn't begin to describe what that would be like. And what if he didn't believe her? A proposal after a week, to a woman he didn't recognise, in a place he was passing through? Ludicrous. If their positions were reversed she wouldn't believe it.

Should she patiently wait here, hover around like a lost soul, until his mental recovery took pity on her? Pass time until he did remember? *If* he remembered. She didn't even have an excuse to stay. She was on leave.

What if he *never* remembered her?

Stop it, she told herself. *Bemoaning the fact won't help you or Zac.*

Ava blew out a long, pent-up, anguished sigh and let it go. She drew in a steadying breath and tried for the unshakably composed Ava. *Okay.* As soon as this bloody headache left her she'd make a plan. She had to. Because she was not losing the man she loved to a bloody white campervan.

Granny Mim and her mother were waiting when she returned. They took one look at her face and closed in for a group hug.

After several seconds of intense hugging, Stella was the first to step back. 'Well? How is your friend?'

Ava hadn't had the chance to say more than that Zac had flown down to see Uluru for the weekend. Her mother knew Ava had only known him for a week, so it wasn't strange he'd be labelled 'friend'. But it hurt. She couldn't explain now, and Stella wouldn't want to believe her, either. She'd always had a thing that city people were different, which was a double standard considering she'd married one who'd been the love of her life. Ava settled for 'He'll recover.'

Her mother examined her face with some scepticism. 'Good. Does he remember you?'

And there was the hell of it. 'No.' She looked for reassurance. 'Most people get their memory back, don't they, Mum?' She needed to refresh her understanding of amnesia prognosis. There wasn't a lot of call for amnesia knowledge in obstetrics.

Stella nodded decisively. 'Yes.' Good old Mum. 'Often a mirror incident or aural trigger can help. Is he having flashbacks?'

Ava thought back to their awkward conversation. 'I don't know. I told him we worked together, but that's gone too. Dr Fithers said he's lost a chunk of time since March, which would be just before he came here.'

There was a gasp from Mim, and Ava realised she must have given some indication of her hopes because Mim looked horrified at this stumbling block. Incurably romantic Mim.

'He doesn't think he's still married?' Mim asked.

'I didn't ask him.' Ava lifted her hand to her forehead, which had begun to ache with renewed enthusiasm.

'Mother.' Stella's voice commanded Mim's

attention. 'Ava needs pain relief and rest.' Then she turned to Ava. 'We'll go now and come back later and pick you up after lunch, not before. I'll tell them at the desk. I'm not sure you want to drive yourself to Setabilly on Tuesday, either.'

Ava would drive herself, but there was no use asking her mother not to talk to the nurses. She already had them terrified. And her head did hurt. If she was honest with herself, it was nice not to have to worry about anything when her mother had it all in hand. As long as Stella didn't have Zac in hand. She couldn't deal with that at the moment.

'On one condition,' Ava said quickly before they left the room.

Her mother stopped and turned back. 'Condition?'

'Promise you won't go see Zac without me.'

Granny Mim and Stella exchanged glances. If she wasn't mistaken, they both looked disappointed. That was a lucky escape.

'As you wish.' Stella gave a firm nod. 'Now rest. They'll be in soon with something for that headache.'

Ava took off the wrap she'd put on to visit Zac and laid it across the blanket, then raised the head of the bed with the remote control. She'd been spoiled with a single room, she thought as she climbed up onto the mattress. Thankfully. She couldn't imagine dealing with this behind the curtain of a shared room within earshot of other patients. A staff bonus. She should be grateful, and she really was trying to be.

Her thoughts turned to Zac once again. She

131

tried to imagine what he must be feeling to wake in a strange place and with a time gap of two weeks. Not knowing how he'd arrived or the people he worked with except a colleague from the past. She guessed she had some luck that it wasn't common knowledge she'd been sleeping with Zac, now that he'd forgotten her. Something else to be grateful for. She closed her eyes.

★   ★   ★

After lunch, Ava woke with her headache dulled enough to allow her to make decisions. She would be proactive and fight. Fight for what Zac had believed in enough to fly to her to do. He'd believed so much that he'd proposed they spend their lives together. They needed to recapture the connection that had been so strong from the first moment they met.

Although she could smack Zac upside the head for holding onto telling her he loved her until Yulara, when he could have shared his feelings earlier. Right now, the brief episode of him skirting around asking her to marry him felt like something she'd dreamed up before all this horror started.

Ava slipped on her robe and padded up the hall to peer into his room. He was alone and awake, and sat in a chair, staring out the window. She took a deep breath and knocked. She watched the frown as he tried to place her, then recognition that she was someone he'd met once before. She could be grateful for that, at least. 'Hello there, Zac.'

'Ava.' He even remembered her name. 'Come in.' He stood, his face inquiring more than welcoming, and she had to stamp down the feeling of hopelessness as he gestured to the other chair.

One day since the accident, she told herself. *It has only been one day. Everything will be fine.*

'Thanks.' She pulled the chair closer to his and sat. Glancing at her hands in her lap, she gathered her thoughts to convince this stranger he needed to spend time with her. 'I'm going home this afternoon.' She lifted her chin to hold his gaze. 'I've come to ask you again to consider convalescing with us on Setabilly Station when you're discharged.'

He studied her, as if trying to see through to her reasoning. He was an intelligent guy so he must be wondering. At least he didn't say no straight off. 'Setabilly Station?'

She answered the easy part first. 'Down near Mount Conner, towards Uluru. A cattle station. We're setting up a sideline as a farmstay, like an ecotourist retreat. It's early days, but we're geared for guests.' She shook herself. 'I just wondered if you'd like to try our hospitality while you're still isolated by loss of memory. I understand you can't go back to work for two weeks. And you shouldn't fly either.'

The way he searched her face gave her a tingle of hope. Then his measured 'Thank you' dashed it. 'I'll probably just stay in the apartment George says I have at the hotel.'

Ava forced a laugh and pushed a little more. 'Or you could come with me and be an ecotourist and at least I could keep my eye on you for a few days.' There. She'd said the words.

He raised one dark brow. 'To your family station? A stranger?'

Ava lifted her shoulders. *To hell with it.* 'Not a complete stranger. We did have a six-day relationship that you don't remember,' she said quietly. 'And my family know we're friends, so they understand why I want you to come.'

She waited for him to dispute the information, but he didn't. His eyes met hers and his brows went up. 'A relationship? Did we? I wondered.' Although she listened for it, she didn't detect disbelief.

Still not sure what he was thinking, she said firmly, 'Yes. We did. I haven't forgotten.'

'And I have.' Their gazes met and held. Finally, after the slowest two seconds in the world, he said, 'That would explain my somewhat out-of-character fascination with your womanly wiles.' Then he gave her that beautiful smile she'd fallen in love with and she thought her heart would break.

Oh, Zac.

After a brief struggle with the lump in her throat, she whispered huskily, 'Nice to know something still rings a bell.' She gestured vaguely. 'The thing is, I'll worry about you if I leave you here. I was driving that damn car, and if you came as a guest I'd be able to check on you. At least till the ten-day mark.'

Still he watched her face intently. 'Make sure I don't have a secondary cerebral bleed or something?'

'Something like that. Such disastrous complications are strictly forbidden.' She gestured to the window this time. 'We have cottages, pre-fab corrugated-iron mini homesteads that my grandmother designed. They're air-conditioned, self-contained and have desert views. So it's not like you'd be living in the main house.' Though her mother or grandmother might still veto that. Old nurses didn't trust in nature as much as midwives did, and she'd be overruled. In this particular case, her mother and grandmother were the only people in the world she'd allow to overrule her. But that was a worry for later.

He didn't look convinced and she could feel him slipping away. *Make it happen,* she told herself, *or lose him.* 'As the one responsible for your loss of memory, I would prefer you to spend the next week or so this way.' *Please,* she silently added. 'And I can't hang around here because I help at muster this time of year. I'm not back in Alice for a month. But it's up to you.'

'It's good of you to offer, but please don't feel responsible as the driver.' His face twisted a little as if he understood the price of that, and she thought of his past trauma. Yes, he definitely understood. He probably didn't connect that she knew about his wife, either.

Had she put too much pressure on him? Was recuperating with a strange woman the last thing he wanted to do and he didn't know how to say no? For a moment she cringed, feeling pushy and desperate. Then she pulled herself together. She was fighting for their love. For them. For a future Zac had seen as wonderful, if what he'd said in Yulara was true. This guy was a high-flying city emergency doctor. He knew how to say no if he wanted to. He had amnesia, not a personality transplant.

Tensely, she waited for his answer, watching him warily. Trying not to let him see how awkward this was for her.

'I'll think about it,' he said.

She could almost read his thoughts. Could read them a little better than when she'd first met him, anyway. She'd bet he was thinking, *What sort of relationship have we had? It can't have become too much in a week, surely?* She hoped she didn't look like a woman who needed him to escape her life, or needed to grasp at men who didn't remember her.

She added, 'If you like, I could drop in here before I leave this afternoon and introduce you to my mother and grandmother. They can add their invitation to mine. They'll be going back today ahead of me and you could see if you feel comfortable with them. I don't want to pressure you.'

Yes, she did, but she'd try not to. Honestly. Now, however, it was time to go.

She stood. 'I pick up my replacement car this afternoon and will be heading to the station tomorrow before lunch. We'll talk again tomorrow but then I'll be gone.' She tried to look calm about his indecision, to look like the patient woman she was known as. Funny how she couldn't find much calm resignation at this moment. Soon she'd be leaving for a month.

She hoped he'd make the right decision.

16

Stella

In her flat on the outskirts of Alice Springs, Stella gripped the verandah rail and stared down at her work-roughened fingers and tried to bend steel. It wasn't working.

Her fingers were white and ugly. She did not possess a sophisticated woman's hand — like Lorenzo would be used to — with all her cracked, short nails torn in places from hard work. She eased the pressure and looked away from her offensive digits through the buildings across the street to the glimpse of desert beyond. She could just see the sand-crusted hill with saltbush and drew in a deep breath as if the freedom out there could settle her agitation.

'Are you all right, Stella?'

She turned to see her mother poking her head out of the bedroom door onto the verandah, as if unsure whether it was safe to venture further. Considering Mim didn't know the meaning of fear, her expression made Stella smile, if a little reluctantly.

'My brain feels like an overfilled chaff bag ready to explode.'

'I can tell that, dear.'

Oops. If her mother was calling her 'dear', she'd been difficult to live with.

137

'Sorry, Mim.' Stella gestured to the two chairs on the tiny balcony and Mim came out and sat down. Stella watched as Mim donned her listening pose with her hands settled demurely in her lap, and her smile grew a little. So many times her mother had settled herself in that pose.

Stella could remember her sitting like that with her father on the verandah at Setabilly while some weighty matter had needed to be discussed. After he'd died, Mim's attention had focused on Stella and her children, and they were truly blessed. Mim the listener. And the sage, with her sometimes wickedly insightful comments that could make you blush or cry.

Stella made herself sit and blow out a breath. 'Lorenzo's arrival has thrown me.' She threw up her hands with the agitation that rose just hearing herself say that. 'I'm confused like a fifteen-year-old would be, not a woman of fifty. How could I make such an impression on a man in one afternoon a whole year ago?'

Mim raised her brows. 'Men remember attractive women. And despite hiding it in those farm clothes, you've worn well.'

'You said I looked like a cow pat.'

'Got you with that one. I was trying to wake you up.' Mim's eyes danced with mischief.

Mim had been aware all along and never said a word? Maybe Mim did understand her fears. Stella lowered her voice. 'I'm scared he's going to ask me to marry him.' And thought but didn't say, *I did so badly as a wife last time.*

Mim surveyed her from head to foot and then her gaze softened. 'What if he does ask you? It'd do you good to be looked after for a change. To have a strong man's arms around you.'

Stella sighed. It was all very well to dream. 'I can't waltz off into the sunset with a European Casanova and leave you all.'

'Why not?' Mim's question was placid, a gentle puff of amusement on the warm air. As if she had no idea what Stella was het-up about.

Stella rolled her eyes. 'We're all stressed to the max about the station. You know — the drought! Especially Jock, who is turning my hair grey with the way his spirits are sinking, and with Hana expecting the baby, and the bank's grumbling about the improvements he's overdrawn on. I need to be here to help and support them.'

Stella blew out another breath and looked at her mother. Then there was Mim's advancing age, which she didn't mention. 'I have a mother and a daughter who need me as well,' she said instead and shuddered at the memory of searching for her mother for almost a full day after she'd come off that horse. Someone needed to make sure Mim didn't do anything else so stupidly dangerous.

Mim made a rude noise. 'Don't you put me in there as your responsibility. Young Hana has already invited me, very prettily, to live with them.' She thought about that. 'I'd enjoy having a baby about again.'

Stella blinked. 'Are you all talking about the possibility of me leaving?' Why was she the last to know anything?

'Not all of us. Ava doesn't know.'

Ava was one of the reasons her head was going

139

to explode. Imagine if she'd left with Lorenzo. 'And now Ava has almost been killed by an idiot in a campervan. Imagine if I had been in Italy when that happened.'

'She's fine. She's tough like us. And you would fly home.' Mim smiled beatifically. 'I think Ava's in love.'

Stella felt like the little balcony had just cracked off the side of the building, fallen to the ground twenty feet below them, and carried her with it. 'Not with the city doctor? The one with amnesia?'

'Just a suspicion,' Mim said serenely.

Stella wanted to twist her hands together and cry. Or break something. Neither of which she ever did, but lately the feelings were bubbling inside and tearing to get out, and fifty was a stupid age to lose control.

This was all her fault. She waited a little until she could speak more calmly. 'It's a penance for the lies. I should have told them the truth. That love isn't enough if that person is from another world . . . '

'Stella May.' Her mother's voice broke in. 'Stop it. Your father and I were from different worlds and that worked out very well, thank you. Hana and Jock are from different worlds.'

Stella said softly, 'What about Noah? What about me? I deserted their father when he needed me and then he died.'

'You got homesick. Tell your children now, be done with it. You were pregnant and lonely. He did something stupid and then he died. It's time to let go of that volcano of bitterness you've carried for twenty years. It's done enough damage. Don't let it damage others.'

This was Mim at her most determined. But how could Stella confess she'd lied to the very children she'd promoted truth to after saying she'd been happy in Sydney, and very much in love?

Stella stood up as if to take a turn around the room, but the verandah was so small. So she sat down again and thought reluctantly of the painful past. Well, they had been happy for a while. But Ava in love with a man from the city? Her darling Ava, who'd been hit by that camper-van and almost killed along with her companion, the amnesic companion her daughter wanted to bring back to Setabilly to convalesce? It all began to make horrible sense and her dread grew.

★   ★   ★

Three hours later, Mim and Stella had packed the car in preparation for returning to Setabilly and had driven back to the hospital for Ava.

Stella walked into Zac's room to meet him, as requested by her daughter. The instant she saw the way her daughter looked at him, she knew. It took all of two seconds to confirm her mother's suspicions were correct. Two seconds.

Oh, she was polite and said the right things, but inside her heart pounded with regret, and she had to force herself not to hope he never got his memory back, because she could also see that he wasn't returning the affection. He really had forgotten Ava, and despite her misgivings, she could see it was causing her daughter pain.

Karma had come back to slap her for her dishonesty, because now her daughter had fallen in love with a man from the city like she had and the same struggles would be hers, and Stella hadn't warned her. If Zac did get over this temporary memory loss, he'd remember he loved Ava, too, and then he'd want to take her back there with him and Ava would be miserable like Stella had been, and history would repeat itself.

Maybe she deserved it. Ava, however, did not. Stella could only hope this city stranger would decide not to come back to Setabilly.

17

Ava

That afternoon in Alice Springs, Ava watched the side of the road flash past as her mother drove her from the hospital to the family flat. It wasn't far, and despite their protests that she should travel back to the station with them, they were dropping her off against their better judgement, and heading back to Setabilly before dark.

Ava said again, 'I'm fine. If he agrees to come, I want to bring Zac back myself.' More importantly, she wanted the alone time in the car with Zac to see if they could find the rapport from their previous closeness. It wasn't much of a plan, though, and it relied on both Zac agreeing to convalesce at her home, and also the privacy while they became acquainted before then.

There was silence from her mother and a nod from Mim. Her mother would have to deal with whatever reason she had for her tepid response to Zac.

'So you met him on the plane back from Sydney?' Stella finally spoke from the front.

'Yes, and then we worked together in Alice.' It was the second time she'd asked, and Ava thought again that her mother was behaving oddly.

'Hmmm,' said her mother. 'And he's going back to Sydney in a month?'

Mim interrupted. 'I think the idea of bringing him back to the station is a good one, Ava. You'll be able to look after him and show him around. I think that would help take his mind off the horrible feeling of losing a slice of his life. Don't you, Stella?'

Ava smiled her thanks at the back of her grandmother's head. Every few minutes, Granny Mim would turn and give her a little smile. She needed to have her family's understanding, but when her grandmother's sympathy came her way, she felt reassured that her heart would not break. That things would turn out well.

She deliberately breathed in slowly and then out. In and out. She needed to let everything go, and just concentrate on healing herself from the shock of the accident and her own small injuries. She also needed to believe that Zac's memory would return.

She'd visit him again tomorrow, convince him to come, and start again. She needed him to come with her. To let whatever their future together would be to grow naturally, because loving someone couldn't be forced.

Or forgotten.

Or lost.

Could it?

She slowed her breathing again as a wave of sadness rolled over her, and she brushed away a lone, stupid tear as it threatened to run down her cheek. It could have been much worse. She had to keep telling herself that. He'd be physically fine. Dr Fithers had said he was happy with the scans. It was the amnesia and the loss of the last weeks that felt like a chasm between then when they'd only just found happiness.

Mim turned her head again as if she knew what Ava was thinking. 'He'll be fine, darling.' She smiled encouragingly at Ava. 'He seems very strong . . . ' She paused and her eyes twinkled. 'He seems like a particularly virile man, and I imagine his recuperative powers are impressive.'

Was there innuendo in that statement? Surely Mim couldn't know that they'd slept together. Ava felt her cheeks warm and the sudden lift of her spirits was something she'd not have believed possible even a minute ago, but such was the magic of Mim.

Darling Mim. Nobody could love their family more, nor mischievously direct from the sidelines in the loving way Mim did.

* * *

The next morning, Ava drove back to the hospital, her fingers tense on the steering wheel. She went early, deciding she'd come back to the flat to pack after she knew Zac's decision. She had things to do in town before she left.

Mostly she was thinking about if he said no. Which was the opposite to what she should be doing — affirmations and all that. Hopefully that wouldn't happen because she'd convince him. But what if he did? Then she'd have to try to forget him and also the fact that she'd found the man she instinctively knew could have given her

145

a happily ever after.

Once at the hospital, she climbed softly so her feet wouldn't echo in the deserted stairwell. It wasn't visiting hours and she hoped she wouldn't meet any staff on the way, more for the fact that she didn't feel like conversation than any worry they'd tell her she had to leave. Coming out on the second floor, she crossed to Zac's doorway and found him standing at the window looking out over the hospital grounds. His broad shoulders were silhouetted against the light and there was tension in the stiff set of his neck. She wanted to come up behind him and put her arms around him in comfort. Instead, she knocked quietly on the doorframe and waited, and when he turned, his face lay in the shadow with the light behind him.

'Ah, Ava. Good morning.'

'Morning, Zac' She could hear too much cheery brightness in her voice and pulled it back. She only just managed to stop herself from asking, *Are you coming?* Taking a calm breath, she said, 'How are you?'

'Feeling remarkably well,' he replied, then he paused and gestured for her to come in. 'And you?'

'Fine, thanks.' She could feel her heart thumping and this precipice of the future was killing her. She needed to end this indecision before it did her head in. 'Have you thought more about where you will convalesce?' she asked as coolly as she could muster.

He nodded. 'I have. George has been to see me already and I can leave today. He thinks going with you is a better idea than staying on my own at the hotel, and he'd prefer I didn't fly back to Sydney yet because my parents are in Greece for a couple of weeks.'

She felt her heart lift. He was coming.

'But I still think it's an imposition on you.' She could hear the hesitancy in his voice.

'It's no imposition if you'd like to come.' She kept her voice light, though the idea that his parents knew at least her name now made her feel anxious. She'd been driving when their son had almost been killed.

'Though I'd better tell you now in case you change your mind — Mum wants you sleeping in the homestead so she can watch you.'

His mouth opened and shut.

She grimaced. 'That conversation went as expected. I suggested you'd want a cabin and your privacy but was howled down because you 'need watching'.' She shrugged. 'You could stay a couple of days in the house and then move out. I gave up trying to reason with her.'

To her surprise, he didn't seem fazed. 'She seems a strong-willed woman.' She could hear the smile in his voice, which reassured her.

She couldn't stand this any more. 'I'm leaving at twelve, so yes or no?' She had a pretty good poker face for work and she hoped it was doing its job now because her stomach was twisted in knots.

'If you're sure it's no imposition, then yes, please. I'll be ready at twelve. George picked up my things and checked me out of my hotel.'

Ava tried not to sag with relief. 'Thank you.'

Now she really wanted to throw her arms around him. She'd better get out of here before she made him think she'd be offering inappropriate gestures of affection if he went with her.

'You've made me happy. I'll be back in a couple of hours then, at twelve.' She smiled blindly in his direction and bolted to the stairwell, where, after trotting down to a landing, she leaned against the wall and closed her eyes. Who knew that would have been so hard and so fraught? She just hoped she was doing the right thing for both of them, because if this didn't work it was going to be hell for her. She really hoped these obstacles they'd encountered were not fate trying to warn her.

★　★　★

At twelve exactly, Ava pulled up at the entrance to the hospital. Zac appeared at the front steps looking pale but with the tilted smile she remembered from the plane, and she reassured herself that she wasn't doing anything that was going to hurt her more than she already had been.

She jumped out and hurriedly opened the passenger door for him. 'You look like death warmed up,' she teased, although she was questioning whether he was actually well enough to travel four hours in a car. Especially after the last time she'd been driving.

'I'm fine.' Zac eased his long legs into the front of the vehicle. He glanced wryly at her as he settled, and the nurse who had followed him out handed Ava his bag.

'Packing and getting himself sorted took a bit. You sure you'll be right with him? What if he faints on you?' The nurse, Jodie, was an agency nurse Ava had done a few shifts with.

'I guess he's better with me than alone in a hotel room here. If he deteriorates I'll phone RFDS for advice.' This was her one extravagance — she always carried a satellite phone.

Jodie nodded and stepped back. 'He's a nice guy — it's a shame he's sick. Say hello to the mums and bubs at the community.' She looked a bit wistful. 'Enjoy.'

'Thanks, Jodie.' The nurse waved as she turned away.

Enjoy, Ava thought with a pang, as she buckled her seatbelt and glanced at her passenger. He stared straight ahead, his profile strongly defined as if he were clenching his teeth. Which made her ask, 'Are you in pain?'

He didn't turn. 'Only from hoisting myself on you.'

She laughed softly and turned back to the road as if the bitumen held a world of fascinating sights. Without looking at him she said, 'You can change your mind now. Otherwise, you'll be stuck on an isolated cattle station surrounded by red earth, mountain ranges and bossy women.'

She tried not to hold her breath in case he did just that — underlining the fact that he must be wondering if he was doing the right thing in trusting her. A woman he didn't remember. She grimaced at that. The one positive was that it had been recommended by his doctor.

What was it about this man that had made her put herself at risk like this? The feelings inside her were too big for the occasion now that it was all one-sided. She knew he didn't feel the same urge she had to reach across and touch his cheekbone to reassure herself he was fine.

She had to believe everything would work out. If it didn't it wouldn't be for want of her trying.

She pointed to the floor. 'There are two rehydration drinks and some muesli bars in the cool bag beside your feet.'

He raised his brows with a slightly mocking smile. 'Thanks. You've packed my playlunch?'

That sounded more like her Zac and she smiled at him. 'Cheeky blighter. I'm keeping you hydrated and your glucose levels up. This way there'll be less chance I'll have to phone a friend to save you.'

He gave her his heart-melting smile at that and she was lost as her cheeks heated. 'Ready?'

Zac shifted in his seat to look at her properly. 'Yes. Though I'm still not sure why you agreed to let me lump myself on you in this state. Doesn't seem fair for your holidays.'

'I know.' She threw up her hands, pretending horror, before she started the vehicle. 'Crazy. But your sparkling company grew on me in just a week and I'm hoping to find that again,' she said lightly. She was still a little surprised he'd agreed to come. 'I'm sure you'd do the same for me if our roles were reversed.' She wasn't, but it was a standard answer she used when people tried to thank her for an act of kindness.

'True.' And he gave her another singularly

sweet smile that reminded her she'd liked this guy on first sight. Loved him by day two. And maybe that smile was why she'd been drawn to Zac. That, and seeing Zac's genuine caring and compassion for the young, the old and the staff, despite the maelstrom of a busy ED and maternity department. But he didn't remember any of that.

He said, 'I looked up your family station on my phone and I'd like to at least pay the tariff for accommodation on the web page. Lack of finances isn't a hardship I suffer from.'

She opened her mouth to refuse and then stopped herself. She guessed she'd want to do the same. Charity sucked. And her family could use the money. 'I invited, so you don't have to. But if you'd prefer to pay, then no problem. You can do it online later.'

It was funny how hard that had been to say, which was probably why she was a midwife and not a businesswoman.

The awkwardness passed as she pulled into traffic. 'We're all looking forward to you coming.'

'It was good of your family to drop in yesterday.'

'My mother is tough. As is my grandmother.'

'And yet they both look so sweet. I'll look forward to knowing them better. And you.'

You do know me, she ached to say. She stared at the road, but in her peripheral vision she could still see his broad shoulders resting back against her passenger seat. Could detect the tang of his aftershave, a mix of wood and citrus, and feel the heat from his big, rangy body a foot away

151

from hers. He was her man, a man whose bone structure, musculature and skin she knew intimately.

Taking him with her had better work.

'Is Uluru near your station?' he asked, and Ava thought, *Thank you. A welcome interruption.*

'About seventy kilometres. Mount Conner is closer and also impressive.'

'I feel ripped off that I've been to the centre and I don't remember any of it.'

Now there was a nice, safe topic, and Ava grabbed the opportunity. 'We can drive out when you're feeling up to it. I do the base walk around Uluru as often as I can. I start after sunrise and it takes me about three hours, but I love the different facets. The folds and the angles in morning light, and the up close and personal is less populated with tourists at that time.' She thought about the moments just leaning against the smooth granite, feeling the vibration in her aura. He'd think she was a crackpot.

He leaned back in his seat and said quietly, 'I must do that one day. How long is the base walk?'

'Nearly ten kilometres around.' She glanced quickly at him. 'Maybe give yourself a couple of weeks before you do. I hike the base most times I work down there. It's good for my soul.' She shrugged a little self-consciously. 'I see something different every time. And it's good exercise. Bit different to a gym, I imagine.'

'I like the gym.' He half laughed. 'But I'll have to go back to see what you see before I return to Sydney.'

Her confidence took a hit. Of course he was going back. He remembered nothing about his promise to do what was necessary for their relationship to work.

After a few minutes of silence, awkward for him and tense for her, she said, 'Before the accident, you told me you went to Weipa last month. That's one of the places I'd like to do a stint. They say it's an amazing flight into the town.'

He blew out a breath as if to loosen the sudden tension between them.

'Weipa . . . ' He paused. 'I remember that. It was nothing like I expected. Nothing I'd done before in Sydney. Which was what I wanted after my wife died.' He turned to look at her and she briefly met his eyes. 'I'm guessing I told you about that?'

She nodded and eased the grip she had on the steering wheel. And his honesty, again, eased the ache in her heart for what she might lose. He too was trying.

'Flying into Weipa is spectacular.' He stared straight ahead with the slightest smile on his face, and she could tell he had shifted his thoughts to that flight.

She was glad. Of course the loss of his wife made him hurt and clam up, and also feel guilty that he'd had some sort of relationship with her so soon after his Roslyn had died. And getting him to talk was for her benefit, too — she loved the sound of his voice. Unfortunately, she loved a lot of things about him.

18

Zac

Zac glanced at the profile of the woman beside him. He didn't know her, but he had to admit he was attracted. Hopefully he hadn't slept with her. Surely he wouldn't have — it was too soon after Roslyn's passing.

It seemed they'd developed a friendship. A strong rapport, he could feel that. Ava looked capable — according to the other nurses, she was supposedly super skilled at emergency midwifery and nursing — and from her point of view, it must be awkward that she had a man in her car who had completely forgotten her. From his point of view, it was a little hard to believe he'd actually got close enough that she felt responsible for him. Maybe even moved on her a little. He ran his finger around his collar at the thought.

Speaking of moving . . . 'Have you ever been a dancer?' he asked, more to distract himself than her.

'You've said that before.' She smiled at the road ahead as if he'd said something amusing. *Good, then*. His tense shoulders relaxed a little in relief.

'I did actually promise to tell you about that. So, when I was five, I fell in love with ballet. I dreamed of it, I thought ballet dancers were princesses and I wanted to be one sooo badly my mother sent away for DVDs of ballet tuition because I wanted to learn. To expect to find a ballet teacher would be impractical on a cattle station four hours from Alice Springs. Anyway, I used to spend hours practising in front of the TV and would follow the steps. My grandfather fixed a ballet barre to the wall in the house. I haven't danced for ages but I loved it for years.'

Wow, a torrent of words. He sat there watching the expressions cross her face like clouds across the sky on a windy day. Then blinked at his own poetic thoughts. *Good grief.*

She looked across at him for the briefest moment and he saw her shrug away a tinge of embarrassment. 'You seem to think it shows.'

'A dancer in the middle of Australia is taking me to her home.' He sat up straighter. 'Life is very strange.'

He heard her breathe in and hold it for a moment. As if she was going to say something and wasn't sure. Then she said, 'I'm taking you home because I hope that spending time together will bring back your memory. But I won't harass you. If it doesn't work out I can accept that, too. Until we get to that point, well, we can look after you properly and show you the outback.'

He was impressed with her level tone, and his mouth kinked upwards. 'Thank you. I know where I stand with you. Nothing airy-fairy about Ava.'

'Except the dancing,' she said, and he could

see the dimple — the cute dimple — at the side of her smile. The tension between them had lessened again, and he was glad.

'So you're a legendary midwife, I'm told. Do you always work in Alice?'

'Not that legendary. I work for the Alice and Elsewhere Nursing Agency. Most times I travel between Alice Springs and Katherine communities as a midwife, but I work as a nurse as well.'

'I think the staff on the ward had a vested interest in me remembering you. They all had a tale about you and some medical drama in the outback.'

Her cheeks turned pink and he smiled. She said, 'They exaggerated.'

She wasn't used to compliments. He didn't know why he found that endearing, but he did. 'I don't think people out here are into exaggeration. There's some major respect held for you.'

She lifted her chin at that. 'That's very kind of you to say.'

He studied the way she kept her eyes on the road. Avoiding his? 'So, where and how did you gather all that respect and experience at such a young age?'

'Right.' She made a rude sound. Obviously, she was not taking his sincere compliments seriously. 'You sound like an old man. How old do you think I am?'

He studied her dusting of freckles. Such smooth, unlined skin. The vibrancy that was inherent in her seemed to shine. 'Twenty-five?'

'Spot-on. So, five years since graduation, you get experience.'

'True, but you don't always get respect and deference. The staff at Alice love you. Jade came to see me and we talked about that crazy first night in the ER. She thinks the sun shines out of you.'

'Bull.' She tossed her head, still not taking her eyes off the road. He liked the way she drove. Just under the speed limit, both hands on the wheel, scanning ahead and watching for animals and potholes, yet she was relaxed.

'They're a good crew,' she commented. 'But that's not love. They like me because I do the night duty they don't want to do. And I know where everything is and how it works. That's always good for making friends. I know how to troubleshoot the machinery and monitors and follow procedure and guidelines. I offer to help out when I can. It's just common sense when you don't work there all the time, and I read the communication book so I know what's going on. It's not hard.'

It's the extra stuff, he thought. Communication would be important to her, and collaboration. Getting the best out of other people. Anyone who worked on their own or worked remotely in communities had to know how to communicate and collaborate and demonstrate respect for others. He couldn't look away. He should turn his head, look out the window, but he couldn't. Was he remembering or was he just thinking there had to be risks in her job with the isolation between outposts? Car trouble, weather issues, tiredness, travelling as a single woman. He wondered how long she thought she could do it for. The concept left him unsettled with wisps of a dormant, protective instinct he didn't know he had.

She said, 'I know they liked your work in ED and maternity as well, even if you don't remember it.'

There was something about her that touched him. On a different level to anyone he knew. But he didn't understand how he could have been so thoughtless, to expect her not to be hurt when he left Central Australia. A relationship between them would never work. What had he been thinking, trying to get involved with her?

Now, by forgetting her — even though he couldn't help the amnesia — he'd hurt her, and that wasn't his intention either. He was hopeless at not hurting women, wasn't he? He'd hurt Roslyn in the worst possible way.

'I'm sure my memory will come back,' he said, but he wasn't really. He shook off his intensity in the guise of resettling himself in the seat, then he turned slightly towards her so he was primed to amuse her. She deserved that. 'I was going to talk about Weipa.'

'Yes. Tell me about it.'

'I always wanted to be a storyteller, with people sitting around listening to my tales.' His wife had rolled her eyes and gone off to repair her make-up whenever he'd started one of his stories, but he'd drawn kids and older people to laugh with him. He hoped Ava laughed.

'Good,' she said, 'Tell me a story about Weipa. For some reason, the idea of flying into the Top End like that captures my imagination.'

He marshalled the memory of that morning

when he'd flown to the top of Australia for his first outreach locum. He closed his eyes and let himself sink into the memory. It wasn't as hard as he'd thought it would be. And it was nice to have some memories. Or maybe that was the audience.

'So, imagine you are flying into Weipa with me. It's bumpy through the humidity and the clouds, and then you soar in over a ridge that opens up onto a river delta with a forever amount of red dirt and grey-green shrubs and trees.' He paused. 'Got it?'

'Got it.'

'Okay. There's a gleam off the water. Apparently it often looks like a deep steel grey, like the day I landed, and there are islands in the delta and outcrops of rocks catching shade. And the borders from the mining demarcations look stark and harsh against the curves of the land-scape, despite the areas where they're attempting the regeneration of the land.'

'The water glitters over Albatross Bay with the angle of the sun when you fly over the railway bridge above the river, and the plane completes the figure-of-eight shimmy it needs to do to approach the strip. Then you see the Mapoon community on the tip, a dot on the peninsula surrounded by ocean, then closer to the ground you see the height of the termite mounds near the airfield, the green of pandanus palms, and the shine of beach hibiscus trees.' He opened his eyes and looked at her. 'We've landed. Are you okay?'

'It was a bit bumpy,' she murmured as she drove.

'Always bumpy, stumbling into a roll along the strip because the air pockets are tricky and the plane always wobbles, or so I'm told.'

'Don't stop,' she said.

He grinned to himself. 'We can see the airport building coming up now — actually it's more of a shed — and there's a wire fence at the side, and Indigenous kids behind the wire are jumping and waving at the plane. A dozen people are waiting out the front. Waving. Excited to greet passengers coming home.

'Finally, we stop adjacent to them with a little jerk.'

'Are we the last off?'

'We are. We're the last off, and the heat hits us like that oven door has just opened and the blast of it almost singes our eyebrows. You don't notice the humidity for a while. Just the heat of it.'

'Worse than here?'

'I haven't felt it like that here.'

'Don't let me stop you. Go on.'

'Through the fence the kids are screaming with enthusiasm and families gather and hug and laugh, but we don't know anyone, so we follow the tide through the shed and out the other side to the lawn behind it to wait for the luggage. It takes a good fifteen minutes. There's one big frangipani tree that offers the only shade and we all move like cows in the heat to find a position under the branches.'

'You might have moved like a cow, but I moved like a dancer.'

He laughed. He loved that answer, he

reassured himself. But suddenly he was unsure, jolted out of the game. He would be leaving, there was no doubt about that, so why was he was flirting with this woman?

'Your turn,' he told her. *Please.* What was it about her that drew him? Had drawn him in the time he couldn't remember. 'Where is your favourite place to work?'

'Yulara.' She glanced at him very briefly. 'Except when dust storms hit and accident victims with head injuries remain unconscious and threaten to die on me.' The answer came promptly, ironically, and he had to smile.

'Yes. I imagine that would have been stressful. Just keeping you on your toes.'

'I'll say.' She shook her head. 'Attention seeker. I'll sleep for a week when I get home.'

Leaning his head back against the seat, he continued watching her expressions. He needed to stop beating himself up about the lack of future between them because she must understand. And she intrigued him. 'What is it about Yulara that you love?'

'The proximity to Uluru,' she said in another prompt reply. There was no hesitation, only a warm, rich feeling in her voice. 'It's a magical place. Something people don't believe until they've been there.' There was no holding back with her. No artifice. 'The Anangu people are great. I have wonderful friends there. My best friend is an artist and traditional healer, and her husband is a dancer and teaches didgeridoo.' She laughed. 'He was born in Melbourne — Uluru is not didgeridoo country.

'I love all the communities, but I feel connected to the Anangu people for some reason. The artwork, the bush medicine, the desert, the sky at night. Very good friends like Denise, who works at the cultural centre.' She gestured with one arm to the desert they skimmed along the edge of. 'This is Albert Namatjira's country.' This time she glanced at him and her cheeks were dusted with pink. 'Sorry. I get passionate about the centre.'

He wished he could feel so enthused about something, but that too would pass, he was sure. It had to, because everything changes eventually. Early on in their marriage, Roslyn used to say she loved his enthusiasm. But that changed. He pulled his thoughts away from that dark hole. 'There's nothing wrong with passion. It's clear in your voice.' It had been years since he'd had that kind of passion and it was nice to know it still existed. He felt himself being more drawn towards her, and thought, *To hell with it, I'm not going to fight it any longer.*

Feeling a sort of release, he relaxed even more into his seat. 'Tell me more about the Anangu people — more about them that you admire.'

She wrinkled her brow. 'Aren't you sick of listening to me?'

'No.' He wondered if he ever could be, and the thought brought a puzzling mix of fear and hope and guilt: standalone emotions he didn't need to feel all at once. But that was what he suspected summed up Ava May. Feeling. All or nothing. He'd lost faith that he had the kind of fearlessness she seemed to have.

She shrugged and went on, her eyes scanning ahead, their speed along the strip of tar steady and eating up the distance towards their destination. 'The Anangu have been the custodians of this desert around Uluru and down south for a very long time. I guess it's their resilience and ability to change that I admire so much. They believe the responsibility for keeping the land safe lies with them. I do too.'

She slowed to steer carefully around a lump on the hot tar in front of them. When he glanced back, he saw it was an echidna, uncurling to keep crossing the road. She grinned at him. 'They call him the Tjilkamata in Pitjantjatjara.'

'Tjilkamata.' He stumbled a little over the pronunciation, unlike her. 'Great word,' he said. 'Though I like that in the English language baby echidnas are called puggles.'

She laughed. 'I did not know that.'

'So tell me more about the Anangu.'

'Well, as custodians, they guide and welcome those who visit the national park, wishing them safety and helping them with Indigenous teachings to appreciate the sacredness of their world. Uluru and its surrounds are a lot like non-Indigenous people expect a cathedral or mosque to be — sacred.'

'That's reasonable.' *But not always true*, he thought.

'The Anangu believe in the creation of the region by ancestral beings, and that they are direct descendants of those beings. They care for the land using their *Tjukurpa* — Anangu laws.'

He could see from her profile that she was

reliving memories and concepts she'd spent time considering.

He considered it too. 'I still think they must find it pretty hard to get that across in today's society.'

'Yes, it's ongoing, but their people are finding ways to gain support from the government now. Fewer tourists are climbing Uluru — it will be closed completely to climbing soon — and more are hearing the stories and walking the base track.'

He remembered something she'd said earlier and asked, 'Is that why you walk the base? To respect the local communities?'

'I have no need to climb Uluru, the same as I wouldn't want to climb Westminster Abbey. If an elder offers to show me the beauty of a hidden spot, though, I am respectfully thrilled. The Anangu have immense and detailed knowledge of everything in the history of the park. The flora, fauna, habitats, seasonal changes and landscapes. Even today, a lot of this knowledge remains unrecorded. That's why conserving oral history and tradition is vital to the wellbeing of Anangu culture, and to the ongoing management of the park.' She waved her hand. 'I warned you. I get emotive.'

'You know a lot about it.'

She scoffed. 'That's only the tip of the iceberg. Or out here, the tip of Uluru. The biggest part is underground and can't be seen.'

He turned to look ahead at the red earth and scrub that never seemed to end. It felt like the two of them were on a deserted planet of ochre sand and blue sky. Leaning his head back, he mused, 'What was it like growing up in the centre?'

'Hot in the day and cold at night. Wonderful. An adventure.' She gestured with her arm. 'Being blessed by good fortune despite the constant threat of drought. Great people. Diverse people: on the stations, in the communities, and the travellers passing through.' She shrugged.

The answer was a good one. Open and giving, like her. Right then, he fell a little more under her spell. 'So how did Setabilly Station start?' he asked.

She gave him another one of her smiles. 'My great-grandfather's family settled there. Then my grandparents met in Alice, when Granny Mim was nursing. Pops had been thrown from a camel, in a race. She said it was love at first sight. We think he saw an indomitable woman to found his dynasty with and pounced on her. He was second generation on Setabilly.'

He watched her face soften as she talked about her grandparents.

'My grandmother, Granny Mim, is up to my chin, but she's the toughest woman I know.' She laughed. 'At seventy-eight, she's tougher even than my mother, who's a force to be reckoned with. I followed both their footsteps to become a nurse and my own to become a midwife.'

And matched their toughness, he thought, *that's clear.* He enjoyed watching her. She made him smile inside, and the more time he spent with her, the clearer his attraction to her became. It was so easy, so natural to spend time with her.

'What happened when they fell in love?'

She laughed as if it was a much-repeated story. 'My grandfather took Granny Mim back to Setabilly when it was nothing but a stone croft and a windmill from the bore. Just a lot of barren-looking land that could hold a mob of cattle and keep them alive as long as it rained. She thrived, and anything he could do, she mastered as well.

'She loves a challenge and says she always will. It's diverse country. Borderline. Has extreme heat in the summer, a brief wet season like the Top End, and a high mountain range that runs with waterfalls when it rains — though that's rare. I love the glory of it. With a passion.'

She swept her arm out to the side, where the distance stretched endlessly away from the road into the never-never. 'Unfortunately, we've had a run of poor rainfall years and need a major injection of cash. Mum and I use our wages to help, but that's still only providing the bare essentials. Plus, there's a limit my family will let me give.'

They were quiet for a few minutes as he allowed that to sink in. The scope of the past, the trials of the future, the meaning of family supporting family. Someone was missing, however. 'What about your father? You haven't mentioned him.'

'My dad died not long after my brother was born. He was a policeman in Sydney and Mum moved us to Granny Mim and Pop's after he died, so we grew up on the station. Then, ten years ago, my grandfather was killed in a gyrocopter accident, mustering cattle.' Her voice softened with the remembered distress.

'I'm sorry. That must have been devastating.'

She sighed. 'It changed everything. My brother was only fourteen, I was fifteen. Suddenly, Granny Mim and my mother had to run the station. We would have gone under without the support of the Aboriginal families who worked with us, and the families from the other stations.

'Granny Mim's heart hasn't really recovered, but she certainly stepped up to running the show. And she was doing really well until the big drought eight years ago. We had an extra two thousand head, and winter coming on with no feed. Granny Mim took a crew and my brother, and they went droving for six months. She home-schooled him along the way, but it was hard for her without my grandfather. He was larger than life and as tough as old leather — you had to be, in the times they lived. But they made it through with the cattle, and the money from the sales saved our home.'

He had no concept of that sort of physical determination, and now he'd met a whole family capable of it. 'It's a tale of amazing people, and you're a part of it. You have a proud family history stretching behind you.' Which was even more reason for him not to pursue her. She'd never leave here. 'Have you ever wanted to live anywhere else?'

'No, but sometimes I hanker to join the RFDS and see more of the north. Like Arnhem Land.' She grinned at him. 'Like Weipa. But I need to be closer and not away too much as Granny Mim gets older.'

He thought about her in that role. 'You'd be good as a flight nurse. An asset.' He'd looked at RFDS too before he'd started the locum gig. But it would have meant commitment, and for the moment he needed to be free to run when he felt it necessary.

Except for some reason, Ava might have made him want to stay.

Just then Ava pushed the indicator and began to pull over. She parked under one of the rare trees at the side of the long-deserted road.

'We've been driving for an hour and a half. Let's walk for a minute. I make myself do it. It only takes sixty seconds to sharpen your senses again.'

19

Ava

The ground crunched underfoot as she walked away from the car, and she savoured the stretch to her legs.

A burnt-orange lizard scuttled under a leaf beside her and she heard a bird shift leaves to watch with hungry eyes. Then she saw the cross she'd forgotten about. The white roadside crucifix with dusty, faded silk flowers at the side of the tree.

Zac was slower out of the car, but as soon as he saw the marker he stopped, closed his eyes and turned away.

Damn. Of course that would hurt. She felt like stomping her foot. *Damn, damn.* She'd reminded him of his wife when he was already fragile. 'Sorry, Zac. I'd forgotten about that.' She said it softly, not really to him, aware she could only make it worse by pointing out she'd noticed his distress.

He heard her. 'No. They're everywhere and I know why. I agree they should be if it will slow some other silly bugger down and save a life.'

They had their own example of this just four days ago. But there was no use talking about that now since he couldn't remember. 'Was someone speeding when you were in the accident with

169

your wife?' She hoped it hadn't been him. For his sake. If he wanted to talk, she'd listen.

'Yes.' And as though he'd heard her question, he added, 'Not me. But we were all travelling motorway speed.'

'Let's walk for another two minutes.' Out of the car or house was better for emotion, her grandmother always said. 'Where did you meet her?' She didn't know why she asked — probably because she wanted to change the subject from the accident — but she regretted it now that the words hung between them like a dark little cloud. If she'd thought before she opened her mouth, she probably didn't want to know more about his wonderful dead wife.

He fell into step beside her along the deserted road. 'I knew my wife since we were children. She was beautiful even as a child, vivacious and my friend, and we were destined to marry. It was a steady progression. Roslyn's parents were distant business associates of my father's and it all began to cement into permanence with ridiculous ease.

'Before we knew it, we were post-wedding, and sadly we drifted apart far too quickly. I dived into work, and she disappeared back into the social whirl she'd come from. We smiled at each other at breakfast or dinner, whichever one of those events we occasionally met at, until one day I realised I'd let her down. We'd lost each other in the rush of life.'

Ava glanced at him and then away. You couldn't lose people if you lived on a remote station together. They were all you had. She didn't understand his dilemma but had seen it happen in Alice. 'And then you had the accident?'

'A romantic trip to the Blue Mountains to try to salvage the warmth of our marriage. That ended in the middle of a six-car pile-up with Roslyn comatose. If she hadn't married me, she'd still be alive. I'm sure her parents think so, too.'

'That's crap and you know it.' There was a trace of impatience in her voice and she reined it in. 'I don't subscribe to that theory.' *You can't explain it, you can't change it, you just have to learn from it.* These were her grandmother's words, and Ava agreed with them. 'I think we make our own luck. Or what happens to us teaches us a skill we need for later.'

He kicked a rock and it skidded across the road and disappeared into the bush. 'Well, I was lucky and she wasn't,' he said. 'She never woke up. I respected her parents' wishes for prolonged life support, but I hated it.'

'She's at rest now.'

He nodded and glanced back at the tree and its marker. 'And I share a story of loss with those little crosses all over Australia. I'm not special for being there.'

'Were you hurt?'

'Barely. But Roslyn's head injury was obvious. Frontal lobe.' He blinked rapidly and she put her hand out to steady him as he swayed. His face drained of colour until it was as white as the cross at the roadside.

'Enough walking,' she said and steered him

171

until he leaned against the car.

'I'm sorry. I'll never lose that picture. Everything went dark for a minute there.'

'We walked too far.' Or grief could do odd things. She opened the door and nudged him to sit. 'Do me a favour and have a drink. You're an interesting shade of pale.'

'Sorry,' he said again as she closed his door.

Shock from his recent accident combined with grief, Ava thought as she climbed in and started the engine. She'd been there. She thought of the flawlessness of her infant daughter, Amelia, as she lay in her tiny white coffin. Pale-pink lace around her alabaster face of unmoving perfection. Cold porcelain fingers that lay still and straight against her own trembling palm.

That picture would never leave her, either. She'd never shared it. Yet now seemed a good time, 'Five years ago, I lost my daughter, Amelia. She was ten weeks premature, and by the time I was flown to Alice we couldn't stop the labour. She died from necrotising enterocolitis. The lining of her bowel was just too injured when we started the feeding and she passed away at six weeks.'

'I'm sorry,' he said. She didn't look to see his expression, but she heard understanding in his voice. 'You've known loss.'

Well, he would understand, wouldn't he? 'She was perfect,' she said softly. 'My family were amazing. It took me six months before I could go back to work and twelve before I could go back to midwifery. But I've found peace. And I wouldn't change it to avoid having gone through

172

the pain if it meant not meeting her — even for that brief time.'

There was silence for a minute, then he said, 'And the baby's father?'

'He wasn't the man I thought he was.' She shrugged. 'He was head stockman here after my grandfather died. I thought we were both in love, but the month we found out I was pregnant, he left. Took off to work as a contract musterer. I suspect he'd also discovered that Setabilly wasn't going to make him a rich man and that my family had debts from previous years. I'd never gone into the finances and it wasn't a pleasant surprise for him.'

'Not someone you'd want to spend your life with.'

'Absolutely. But he did make me wary of allowing my heart to rule my head.' *Lot of good that's done me in the last week*, she thought.

'So your mother and grandmother were supportive?'

'Every step of the way. Like lionesses, lined up beside me, unmoving, warrior women guarding me during labour and early motherhood, and while surgeons tried to operate on my baby. The first two they were successful with. Nobody could help me with the third.' She remembered the morning she'd met Zac. 'Before I met you on the plane, I'd been thinking of her at the airport. It was probably why I was vulnerable to your scintillating conversation on the flight.' She wondered if he'd been thinking about Roslyn.

He said, 'Any age is tough for loss, and twenty and single is tough for any birth, let alone one

173

that ends in a baby dying.' He thought about that. 'No wonder you're composed in your work.'

'I've been blessed. My mother and grandmother were rock-solid supporters through everything. They showed me they were proud of me, and reminded me to be proud of myself. I remember every minute of being a parent and regret none of it.' She glanced at him. 'But you're right. Guilt is out there ready to pounce. Forgiving yourself is underpromoted. I was a mother for a very short time and she changed me. Having known Amelia helps me every day in my work, especially the midwifery.'

'I can see how she would. Thank you for telling me.'

The car sped down the highway towards their destination, and despite the emotion and scars from the past, despite the solemnity of the little white crucifix at the side of the road and the shared grief from different tragedies, empathy had cracked the walls between them and they both stared ahead with mutual understanding.

20

Zac

An hour and a half later, the sun appeared and disappeared as clouds skittered past in a grey-blue sky. Zac's legs ached for a stretch, despite it being less than ninety minutes since they had last stopped.

As Ava slowed to pull off the road again, he glanced at her profile. Their rapport took no effort, yet it still surprised him. However, there was still no hint of a past memory of them in his mind, no matter how hard he tried. She touched the corner of her eye every now and then and he wondered if that was a mannerism he used to know.

They pulled in at a red cairn piled under a wizened palm tree and the engine ticked down as she unclipped her belt. 'We'll only do a minute here.' She opened her door and he followed suit.

He pushed his door and stepped into a flapping twist of red dust that wrapped around him like a coat then blew past, leaving him disorientated with grit in his eyes. He blinked and picked at the corner of his eyelids. Through the blur he saw her hand cover her smile. Her other had lifted to check he wasn't going to fall. No, he wasn't. He felt stronger every hour and the drinks she'd given him were doing their part. His private nurse?

Ava grinned at him. 'You were hit by a willy-willy. Funny stuff. My friend Denise says it's good luck to be brushed by the wind.'

'Lucky? Guess I've had my fair share of it in the last week.' He patted himself down and glanced after the tiny wind spout as it twisted and danced up the road on its merry way.

She smiled, then turned away and stretched her arms up. He kept his gaze on the horizon, even though she wasn't looking at him. 'We'll just stay a few minutes. I think another dust storm is brewing and I want to get home in case it does something crazy like cut visibility again.'

'Do you want to go now?'

'No. I like to stop, and we'll turn off the highway soon. I make myself do it where there's a chance of traffic. Just in case my vehicle doesn't start again.'

'Does it do that?'

'Not yet.' She was so sensible, unlike him; he often drove from A to B with only the thought of getting there as quickly as he could.

They fell into step to pace the road for her required stretching time, and once again he thought how odd the ease between them was. 'Can I ask what you were doing before you met me on the plane in Sydney?'

'It seems so long ago,' she said and shook her head at the series of events neither had expected. 'I'd been to a conference on obstetric emergencies and breech births. Which was lucky for us, but that's another story. I'd been trying to get there for a while because I'd won a scholarship for it.'

He was distracted from the 'lucky for us' by imagining her there at a conference. A sponge soaking up knowledge and ideas and analysing where she could use them to improve her practice. Standing quietly on the edge of the noisy ones.

He said, 'I used to teach paediatric life-support courses a couple of times a year but stopped after the accident.'

'You'd be good at it. Paediatrics are a specialist game. You have to have the knack to calm fear.' She stared into the distance. 'Kids get sick so fast, but at least when they turn the corner they heal swiftly, too. In clinics, I might put up a quick drip, and once they're rehydrated they don't look back. Let's walk for another minute then we'll go.'

He slanted a glance at her. 'It's not so easy to put up a quick drip in a dehydrated child.'

She smiled. 'Everything is doable if it has to be done. Kids are like mothers. They know when people want to help them, so getting rid of the fear is the main thing.'

'You're amazing. How has nobody asked you to marry them all this time?'

She looked at him soberly. 'I've been asked. But I don't want to talk about it.' She turned away from him and headed briskly back to the car. 'Come on. Let's go. We'll be there in an hour.'

21

Ava

The swirls of dust had blown from Ava's windscreen as they turned into the stone entrance of Setabilly Station. There were only a few kilometres of driveway to go.

The conversation had flowed easily, except when she'd passed the SOLD sign on Dreamtime, the neighbouring station down the road from their gate. That had kept her quiet for a few minutes.

Granny Mim had said the Wilsons had gone, and Ava spared a thought for the family who had been there since the fifties. Like the Masons and the Mays, the Wilsons had been part of the struggle and the triumphs of the last poor years. Part of the serious discussions about rainfall, the good-natured teasing about comparative cattle weight, and the rollicking shed parties that raised money for the RFDS. All the community-minded stuff that station life encouraged to celebrate good times and the end of muster.

She wondered who'd bought the holding.

Almost immediately she thought, *Does it matter?* And then, terrifyingly, *Will Setabilly be the next to change hands?*

'Is that a dam away there to the right?' Zac's voice interrupted her less than cheerful musings and her gaze fixed on his big arm as he pointed. Those arms. Good grief. She'd never had an arm fetish before, but then she'd sat beside Zac for nearly four hours. Every time she'd glanced sideways, his arms were right there. Big, sleekly solid, tanned and taut. And close to her. With him pointing, she couldn't help following the sculpted musculature all the way to his long fingers.

She sighed for the loss. His fingers had been one of the things that had attracted her back on the flight from Sydney. So expressive and long, and capable of such gentle caresses. She really liked his hands. And his arms. And his chest and shoulders. And his eyes.

Seriously. Every barrier she'd erected to protect herself if this didn't work out had fallen on the way home. His loss and guilt had made her want to hug him, and his Weipa story had slid under her guard. It had made him so human and had joined them on a flight of fancy that had made her want to sob for what they'd lost.

'The dams?' he repeated with a friendly poke at her shoulder.

Right. 'Yes. My grandfather put the dams in and that makes us a little more durable when the drought hits. The last drought hurt badly though: we were handfeeding, carting water, battling to get the cattle shipped out before they died. That's when Mum decided to try the ecotourism. She modelled the concept on a station in Queensland that includes experiences and not just bed and breakfast. Mum enjoys the cooking and Granny Mim will enjoy showing people what we do.' She shook her head. 'I'm a bit sceptical that people would want to see how to cut and dress a carcass, but Mim is impressive when she gets into it. Maybe it's feasible.'

'It must be expensive to build cottages?'

'Mim decided she could design the small cottages for minimal cost if she did them herself and had Jock, my brother, and Poddy — that's Hana's brother who came out from New Zealand after her — put them together.'

'Hasn't it started yet?'

'They're still setting up. You'll be the guinea pig. Once you're well.'

'I've never been called that before.'

She shook her head. 'It'll do you good. You're too sure of yourself.'

He smiled at that but only said, 'You mentioned your brother before.'

Ava thought of Jock. Tall, a little too serious, big-hearted, too aware that he was the only man around the place but not allowed to be the boss. 'My brother has delusions of being the father figure for the family. Nobody listens to him except his beautiful wife. So he tries to be discreet as he does what he believes is best for the family. We're lucky we have him.' She slowed the car for a cattle grid and they rattled over it. 'Jock's twenty-four and has a level head, though he did a few dumb things when he was younger and Mum won't give him as much slack as he needs to run the station completely.' She glanced at him. 'I think she's wrong. But that's between her and Jock.'

'Does your mother work as a nurse?'

'Yep. Two out of three of us do. Mim hasn't nursed for years, but she handles emergencies fine. But Mum is the calm head. As well as nursing agency work, she does part-time clinics. She takes relief work for the communities to the west and south, and the elders will come, or send people to her for emergency first aid when the normal clinic is shut. The workers and family at Dreamtime Station used to come as well if they needed her because we're the closest medical help.'

'How far away is the nearest Aboriginal community?'

'About eight kilometres. Then there's the community at Yulara. I have a group of antenatal ladies and new babies over there, who I catch up with. I knew them growing up. The caseload midwives are their midwifery contact, and all mums transfer to Alice for birth, but I like to know where everyone is at when I come home, and admire any new additions. The ladies make me welcome, and sometimes I can help when important things don't get passed on to the other midwives. Granny Mim is a favourite over there.'

'So it's a big community?'

'It varies, depending on the season, and some of the stockmen who work for us and their families still live here on Setabilly in the cottages some of the time.' She gestured to the land on every side of them. 'It gets busy. Mum and I both roster ourselves off the agency nursing during May and September for the mustering seasons when it's all hands on deck.' She tried not to sigh. 'And this muster had better be good

181

or the bank won't listen again.'

'Money problems?'

And the rest. 'The drought by itself we can handle. It's a way of life and good times roll around eventually.' But the timing of outside influences had hit them hard. Her brother was feeling the weight of the world, and Hana was worried enough to pass her concerns on to Ava.

'Sounds like other worries?' Zac could be perceptive.

'Just stuff.'

'Sure, but I'm a doctor. You can tell me.'

She laughed, tempted to confide in him.

He pushed. 'Think of me as someone to listen and not repeat. If it helps.'

'I know. And thank you.' She really wished she could share her worry with someone not related to her. And quite probably, Zac would be a good option. He'd be gone soon. Or he'd forget. No, she admonished. *That is unfair.* 'Don't tell Jock I told you.'

He made a show of crossing his heart.

This is a dumb idea, but here goes. 'This drought is longer, harder, and we'd spent extra on infra-structure. I'm worried Jock will take it too hard if we do go broke. Blame himself for innovations we needed to have but he thinks now we could have waited for. I'm worried about him coping with the unfounded guilt that goes with responsi-bility. I know he's seen the livestock perilously decline in condition as well, and that knocks you down.' She thought of the baby. 'Then there's the usual stress any first-time dad has when his baby is coming soon and he's the breadwinner.'

'You're worried he's heading for depression?'

She didn't know whether to nod, which felt disloyal to Jock, or shake her head and pretend she didn't agree. 'He's not smiling as much as he used to. Hana tells me he's even stopped working on my grandfather's old gyrocopter, which I know he's been rebuilding in secret. Granny Mim doesn't know about that — she'd be horrified. It's one of Jock's dreams to be able to fly over the property and it always excited him. In the past, if he ever had any spare cash, he'd buy parts and spend a few hours tinkering and it always made him feel better. One day he wants to get his helicopter licence. Take an aerial view. But he's stopped now, and won't go near it. And Hana is worried.'

Zac drummed his fingers on the dashboard as he thought. 'His wife shared her worries with you?'

'Yes. So now I'm worried too. But maybe having you here, another man to talk to, will help as well. He's outnumbered by all the women, although it's much better since Poddy came to live here.' She blew out a lungful. 'But I've got it off my chest, so thank you. Enough is enough. Let's talk about how a city boy like you won't die of boredom while you're here, instead.'

'With all this going on? And Granny Mim slaughtering a beast?' He gestured the way she had earlier. 'Not going to happen. Besides, that would defeat the purpose.'

She frowned. 'Meaning?'

'I'm here to see and experience the outback. And find my memories.'

'I'm all for you experiencing the outback. You are also here for the drive. Seeing as I knew you were good company on a flight.' *And you thought I was good company, too.*

He turned and she could feel the intensity of his gaze. 'I wish I could remember that.'

'I wish you could too.' But they'd get there, one way or another. 'But it's not going to dominate the next few days.' They both smiled at that and Ava realised their relationship had shifted again. And it felt good. Right.

This was the Zac she'd found hard to forget. And he'd given her the opportunity to share something that had been worrying her. Something she hadn't been able to share with anyone else. If they had a future, sharing stuff would be a part of it.

'Thank you for listening about Jock.'

He didn't pretend not to understand. 'I will cling to him like a limpet.'

Ava laughed. He was quick. 'His wife might have something to say about that, but that's very sweet of you. Thank you.'

'Either way, I won't be bored. I'll have you and hopefully I'll be here for the musters?' Zac's voice held a spark of definite interest. 'I'm keen for that. It's fascinating stuff for a city boy to see. I could notch up an experience and trial it from the tourist's point of view?' Then,' he lowered his voice, 'I could give you all a review on RateYourTrip.' He nodded sagely and held up his hands to imply he'd only give his honest opinion.

'Excellent. Ten out of ten. Mum will like that.

But not for another few days. You're here to recuperate under my watchful eye.'

He raised his dark brows with a hint of challenge. 'Am I to sit on the verandah and rock while everyone else works?'

'Just a little. A day or two will do it. If you get too bored you could run some community clinics,' she teased. 'It's hard for all the mums and kids to be there when the clinics run.'

He showed his palms. 'My boss has told me I can't be a doctor for a fortnight.' They exchanged smiles. 'Tell me about the station.'

'The station? Wow. Where to start?' They'd be at the homestead soon. She tapped the steering wheel. 'Setabilly has been in our family for a hundred and ten years. Compared to Aboriginal history, which sits something past forty to sixty thousand years, of course that's nothing, but for us we have loved it for a long time. The holding sits at over a million acres and technically could carry up to eight thousand head, but we don't have the people power for that at the moment. It's around two thousand now, plus calves, which is about a thousand too many breeders for the drought in Granny Mim's opinion, but my brother disagrees.'

She turned to look at him. He watched her thoughtfully. His brows had climbed at the numbers she'd been listing. 'What's that acreage in hectares?' he asked.

'Four hundred and sixty-two thousand, eight hundred.'

He smiled. 'Is that roughly?' The teasing Zac was back. 'It's hard to comprehend one holding of that size. It sounds so enormous.'

She shrugged. 'Anna Creek Station in South Australia is Australia's largest station, and it's six times our size. So much of the land is dry and the foliage is sparse, so you need the size to carry the cattle.'

'So what do you do for water in the centre of the Australian desert?'

'It's not all desert. We have eighty kilometres of frontage to the Finke River, though most of that runs water thirty feet below the surface, so dams are the mainstay. It helps that we have a few permanent surface waterholes, but that still leaves a lot of distance between water for the cattle. That's where the dams and bores come in.'

'I can't quite get my head around that amount of land. So how do you muster the cattle?'

She laughed. 'Watch a lot of cattle shows, do you?'

'Not a lot, but I did see the Paul Hogan crocodile movies when I was a kid. Do you use horses and dogs like on the TV?'

'Not us. That's a different part of Australia. Though we have a yard dog. In the centre of Australia, the lack of surface water pretty well takes working dogs out, though there are a few. Too much distance between water for them — they get too hot, exhausted and die if they get too single-minded chasing cattle. There are plenty of wild dogs, but I'm not sure how they survive. We mostly use quads or bikes, and aerial mustering, which we rent. And now with Jock's bores we do bore management and the stock automatically move closer.'

'And other water sources?'

'We use a solar pump to feed tanks on the hills and run pipes down to troughs for the different paddocks. Part of the workload is to check the fences and gates, and especially troughs to make sure they're full and the solar pumps are working. We check every three days or so, or maybe less often when it rains and there's surface water.'

'So that will be all part of your registered tourist business.'

'Yes. Jock's drawn up a list of all the duties and it's an ongoing discussion. That's my mother's baby. She's an excellent cook and manager, and she's devised a program of 'experiences' that we're trialling from this muster.'

'Like me?'

'Mum suggested including you, yes,' she told him, 'as long as you're healthy enough. We'll have safety briefings. Granny Mim's pretty good at keeping people under control.'

'I'm terrified of her already.' His voice dropped to a dramatic whisper.

'Be very afraid.' Her voice dropped too.

'So tell me about a muster. What does a muster mean for you?'

'For me?' She thought about that. 'Holidays from work. And hard work. Muster involves more than rounding up cattle that have spread far and wide. It can take days or weeks, but usually around six days for us. That's working from dawn till dark. You don't want the cattle upset, so it's slow and steady, walk them in and sort them into

187

those to go onto the trucks and those that will return to the paddocks.'

'Do you hire the trucks, too?'

'Yep. The vet comes in to check them and give any treatments, we do branding and then loading, and cattle-drive the rest out again.'

He was watching her and she smiled at him as she slowed for another cattle grid. He looked genuinely interested and that was a plus. She drove slowly over the noisy grid.

'It's easy when you know how,' she told him, before she sped up again. 'Do you ride a quad bike?'

She caught his smile before she turned back to the road. 'I did have a motorbike in my misspent youth,' he said. 'Though not for long once I started medicine and the attraction of skidding along asphalt using my skin as a brake was lost for me. There were too many skin-graft examples in the emergency department.'

Ava nodded. She'd seen that. 'I know what you mean. Though that's riding in the city for you. Here we get speed accidents and just pick up the pieces and bury them.' A small silence followed that heavy statement. 'Sorry. That was morbid.'

'A bit.' She could see he got that, because he had also seen too much. 'The nature of our professions,' he said. 'There are many temporary Australians out there living on the edge of good sense.'

They both stared thoughtfully into the distance. Then she went on. 'You asked about horses. We don't keep horses, though some stations do. There aren't so many of the Indigenous stockmen who ride horses now. The ones I know like the motorbikes and quads. Granny Mim would like to ride, but she had a nasty fall from her ancient horse, Red, and it took us a little time to find her. She takes the truck now because my mother insists on it.'

'It's all fascinating. A whole different world to my life in the city. You said you don't have your own helicopter?'

'Not since my pop's gyro. 'We hire the helicopters for the aerial part of the muster. Since my grandfather's death, Mim has been strongly against Jock getting his helicopter licence. I'm not game to stick up for him.'

'Not game? I wouldn't have thought you were afraid of anything.'

'I'm afraid of doing the wrong thing by omission. It's a cop-out, I know, but I'm not sure what else I can do. He's his own man. And his wife's,' she added. 'Hana is amazing. You'll like her.'

'You're a good sister.' He smiled at her and her insides turned to mush.

So she made fun of it. 'And a good daughter. And a good granddaughter.'

He looked at her as if trying to read in her face what had been between them. 'And a good nurse and midwife. But what about when you were with me?' he asked. 'Were we good together?'

She slowed the car again and she turned to face him, so their eyes met. 'Yes, Zac, we were very good together. You made me feel like someone I didn't know I was.'

22

Zac

Someone she didn't know she was? Was that a good thing? How far into this relationship had they been? Zac felt the ramifications of Ava's statement lodge in his brain. Had they reached the point of sleeping together, then? So soon after Roslyn? The thought stunned him.

They drove along the dusty red track in silence for a few minutes. Past another square red hole in the earth with a solar pump, the dam quarter-filled with red water, but all around the land stretched dry, covered by saltbush and scarce tufts of olive-green bush.

On a small rise, Zac saw the long verandahs of the homestead resting among the scrubby trees and a cluster of smaller buildings that were scattered like petite mushrooms around the mother.

'Here we are, then, Setabilly Station,' he said.
'Yes.'

And she drove this most weeks to come home? In Sydney, he used to complain about the half-hour travel to work, through traffic.

The craggy mountain range behind the house was distant yet close enough to see the fissures and valleys in the purple-coloured haze. The house seemed set into the small hill, not just simply standing on it. Probably because it was made of what looked like mortar-joined, hand-picked red stone. As they drew closer, he could see that the brown trunks of timber verandah posts held up a never-ending story of corrugated-iron roof like the one in *The House That Jack Built* — it had new rooms and extensions added haphazardly until it sprawled like a gnarled hand with a few stubby fingers poking out. The patch of sparse greener grass under the surrounding trees and a roundel of roses sat it in an oasis among the saltbush like a rustic prize.

As they drove closer, red-earth tracks disappeared left and right towards other scattered buildings and stands of low trees. Another line of trees veered off at a tangent and Zac realised the homestead looked down on a watercourse. He wondered if it was the Finke River, but he didn't ask. He'd detected a shift in Ava's mood, a crease between her eyes, a quieter, almost absent tone, and he wondered what sobering subject held her thoughts.

He'd pestered her with questions for most of the way because she intrigued him, and every answer opened another line of thought for him. His mind kept bouncing back to that game of 'imagine' about Weipa, which had been a hoot. He hadn't been so engaged with conversation on a drive for years, and he still wasn't sure what made them get on so well.

Perhaps it was her matter-of-fact answers, or the dry humour, or the understated tenacity of her family in times of hardship. Or, on a less noble level, the visceral sexual awareness between them that shimmered so much he felt like he was smoking hot and ready to ignite. Her strength, determination and sheer will were certainly unique in his world.

That wasn't a reason to push him into a relationship with a woman so far disconnected from his world, but it wasn't something he could ignore either.

They passed another of the natty FARM STAY signs he'd seen at the main gate, the shiny, metal, scaled-down, three-dimensional home-stead board mounted on a post, about a metre across and complete with miniature working windmills and an arrow pointing the way to the house. The metal house models made his mouth twitch because they were clever, and he remembered them from the website he'd visited. He wondered where they'd purchased them, or whether they'd made them. Knowing what he did about Ava's family, the latter wouldn't surprise him.

A thin, mature, black dog ran up to the car, barking, tail wagging, the intelligent doggy face alive with curiosity to see who was in the car with Ava. Zac loved dogs, and one day he planned on adopting one. He might need an object of affection for when he looked back at these times with the increasingly fascinating Ava May, the desert midwife. He stared at the excited canine and he laughed out loud in response. He might need a dog quite badly, in fact.

They pulled up at the main entrance, though it seemed every room in the house facing them had its own door outside to the verandah. He recognised the main door by the welcome mat and the row of boots standing to attention outside.

The door stood open and he saw Ava's grandmother — Mirium, she'd told him at the hospital — though Ava referred to her as Mim. The small, well-tanned, white-haired woman called, 'Reggie.' The dog obeyed immediately and came to sit, very still, beside her at the door. She bent and rubbed his ears and the black tail slapped the floor of the verandah in ecstasy.

Then Ava's mother, slightly taller, equally well-tanned, with Ava's blue eyes and snub nose, stepped past her and smiled in Ava's direction as she climbed out of the car.

He couldn't help comparing the welcoming delight on the faces of the two women to the gracious acknowledgement his wife had showed when he'd arrived home each day. *Poor little rich boy*, he mocked himself, and opened his door.

Ava's mother smiled at him, nodded and gestured them towards the door. 'Come in, come in. Come and have a cold drink. And late lunch. You must be starving.'

23

Ava

Ava turned her head to survey the familiar surroundings and felt the peace wrap around her like her grandmother's arms. If anywhere could heal Zac, then her home could. She believed that with all her heart and quashed the doubts that tried to surface again about his memory.

When she entered the homestead, she could hear the clatter of a pot going onto the stove and guessed her mum was heating soup already. She turned back and saw Zac coming in after Granny Mim, his bag in his hand, a little diffidently, as if unsure if this really had been a good idea. She drew a deep breath and plastered a smile on her face.

'This way, Zac, I'll show you to your room. You might like to freshen up — you have your own bathroom — and then meet us back in the kitchen.' She gestured to where the noise was coming from. 'Mum's onto lunch already.'

His face cleared. 'Thanks.'

Granny Mim followed them and Zac moved closer behind Ava as if afraid of getting lost.

The main hallway walls showed the red-stone mortar work of the original homestead, and the different seams of colour through the rock made her want to run her hands along the familiar cool stone for comfort. Immediately to her right, a door led to the long room with the day bed and a blood-pressure machine. She saw Zac glance in. On the other side, a doorway led into the lounge area.

Zac said, 'It's cool in the centre of the house with the stone walls.'

'Yes. It helps a lot in the summer. We don't turn the aircon on usually, but we had it installed when we built all the cottages because it seemed silly not to have it here too when they had it.'

She gestured with her arm. 'This is yours. All the rooms have a door to the verandah. Nobody is next door to your room, then it's me, then Granny Mim, then Mum. So you can find us if you need us.'

He tilted his head. 'Would I need you?' The why was unspoken but still there.

Why indeed. 'You might feel unwell,' Ava reasoned, then paused and met his eyes. 'Or remember something.'

She saw understanding that she was hoping he would very soon. 'None of us mind being woken up.' The last word almost wobbled so she turned away. 'Anyway, see you in the kitchen when you're ready. Mum doesn't like to wait.' She stopped again and waited for her grandmother to follow her. 'Come on, Mim.'

'Good to see you here.'

There was a wealth of something in her grandmother's voice — Ava hesitated to label it 'satisfaction', but that was what it had sounded like. Incurably romantic Mim. Ava just hoped her grandmother was right. Zac would be experiencing the many strong personalities in this house, but that was okay. Ava had warned him.

'We won't have any of that nonsense of you staying in a cabin until you're stronger,' Mim said. 'We'll feed you up and give you a few days under three pairs of nurses' eyes.' She looked him up and down as if he were a large schoolboy. 'We may let you escape after that.'

'Thanks, Mrs May.'

'And call me Mim, like everyone else does, Zac.' Ava saw Zac only just manage to contain his smile.

'When you've washed up — ' Ava bobbed her head towards the end of the hallway — 'through that white wooden archway is the kitchen. We'll be waiting for you.'

She sent him a smile and they left him, standing in his allocated room.

'Oh my, oh my.' Ava could hear Mim rubbing her hands and muttering as she followed her to the kitchen. She hoped he couldn't hear Granny Mim extolling his virtues as a big, strong man, but he probably could. *Oh well.* He would get used to Mim's forthrightness, she was sure.

Ava put her empty water bottle next to the sink and then turned and leaned back against the bench, looking warily at her grandmother. No wonder she didn't tell her family everything that happened to her. 'Did you want something, Mim?'

'Just wondering how the trip went.' Mim winked and Ava couldn't be cross because she knew Mim missed having her around to tease. 'A few hours in the car with that man would be no hardship.'

'Grandmother. Behave.' Ava raised her brows. 'Or should I tell him you fancy him?'

'If he were fifty years older, maybe. But — ' she shrugged magnanimously — 'I'm happy if you fancy him.'

She certainly did. 'He has to remember me first.'

Mim waved that away. 'You could make him fall in love with you all over again, I'm sure.'

Ava wished she was that positive.

Mim cackled quietly. 'Don't suppose he has a grandfather or handsome older uncle he could recommend for me? Seeing as how you're all finding fellas. Good genes, and good what's in the jeans.' Mim snorted.

'Mother!' Stella frowned in their direction as she stirred soup in a pot on the stove. Then she switched off the heat. 'Stop chuckling like a madwoman. Have you seen Jock?'

'Not since this morning.'

'He knows I want him to check in or he's to let us know he's back safe. Or his wife could.'

'He'll be fine. You should go ring Hana to check. Or go for a walk and get rid of that glint in your eye. I've something I want to ask your daughter.'

'Be civilised. We have a guest,' Stella admonished and disappeared from view.

'Well?'

'Well what?' Ava crossed her arms.

'I'm not blind.' Mim huffed in exasperation. 'He looks like a lovely man.' She lowered her voice. 'I'm not a complete goose. I think you two have done it.'

Ava blushed and Mim, noting it, rubbed her hands. 'I thought so,' she said, nodding vigorously. 'How was he?'

'Mum,' Ava called out. 'Can you help me, please!'

Mim frowned and glanced warily at the empty doorway. 'She's gone. You didn't have to do that. I'm just teasing.'

'Mum has ears like a bat and you know it.'

Mim screwed up her face. 'Well, I've been hinting you should get a life apart from commitment to work, and he seems perfect for the job. He can't take his eyes off you.'

'He's trying to remember who I am.' Ava rolled her eyes and pushed off the sink. 'And anyway, we've been here all of two minutes — you can't tell that. You said I should take up travelling, buy clothes, remember? Are you changing your mind?'

'Yes. I'd much prefer you found a man.' Mim peered through the screen door to check Stella wasn't in earshot. 'You are your own woman, but you need to take a break from being careful all the time.'

'Really? Do you think so?' Ava rubbed her palms together softly as if they were cold. She'd lost her daughter and now she'd almost lost Zac — she might still lose Zac.

Ava saw Mim's face crumple as she looked at the calendar. 'Oh, sweetness, I missed Amelia's birthday.' She crossed the room and hugged her granddaughter and Ava hugged her back. *Dear*

Mim. Ava's throat scratched as she hugged harder.

Ava whispered, 'She'd have been five. Starting school.' Then she lifted a resolute face, despite the pain behind the eyes. 'Does it get any easier? Pop's been gone ten years now.'

Mim nodded, understanding in her faded blue eyes. 'Not easier, but kinder. Though I have memories of Max while you have unfulfilled dreams for your Amelia. But,' she stepped back and searched her granddaughter's face, 'you know neither of us would have missed the pain to keep the joy.'

'True.' Ava hugged her fiercely. And she felt that way about Zac, too. The thought gave her strength. 'Love you, Mim.' She stepped away and picked up the framed photograph of Amelia they kept on the kitchen dresser. The one beside Max. 'I went to the waterhole. It was beautiful as always.' She put down the photo. 'But I'm a little tired after the drive, so don't tease me about Zac.'

'Okay, sweetie. You do look bushed.'

'He just needs TLC for a few days. You're good at that.'

'Tender loving care. I can do that. Stella can fatten him up with her food.'

'And no stories of me as a little girl.' Ava winced. Mim loved those when visitors came. 'Or embarrassing teenage ones, either.'

'Of course not,' Mim said innocently.

Ava sighed. It was probably too much to ask. Hopefully, she'd be out of earshot when they happened. Zac in her family home without amnesia would have been a whole different experience. 'He's a fascinating man.' She winced at the satisfaction that statement caused Mim, her mouth making a delighted 'O', and hurried on before Mim could form any more embarrassing questions.

'But that's enough. Give me a little space, Mim. It's been a pretty torrid week.'

'Of course, darling,' Mim said, all sweetness and light, which worried Ava more. Mim was making plans, she knew it in her very bones. But she could no more stop a dust storm than stop Mim, so she let it go. Reluctantly.

'It's good to be home.' But she needed a moment, and needed a long debrief with her sister-in-law. 'How's Hana?' *Where's Hana?* Instead of sitting down, she moved across the room to look out the door in the direction in which her brother's house lay.

'She's keeping your brother close to her, though I think it's more for him than her.'

'Then she'd have a good reason to. I'll go have a wash. Be back soon.' As Ava left the room, she could hear her grandmother muttering to herself, 'A wedding. Excellent.'

Ava sighed. She'd known Mim would be on to her like an eagle to roadkill about Zac's prospects as a husband. Since she'd finished her training and started her midwifery agency work, she'd been doing ten-hour shifts with four days on and four days off, then driving back to the station most weeks. With two months of the year dedicated for muster and spending time with her family, Ava's life had felt very full. Who needed men when the work was there?

Her goals had been to gain the confidence and respect that Zac had seen from her peers, and even harder to achieve, the confidence and acceptance of the women in the many communities she visited as a midwife. Though their homes were simple and their amenities few, the women inspired her with their ingrained sense of family and ability to rise from challenges with such strength.

She believed her being there helped their experience when they came in for birth and recognised the midwife. And she loved the babies. The brown-eyed, round-cheeked, happy babies she saw everywhere she visited. She loved her life.

Mim had scolded her often for being single-minded, telling her that work wasn't a penance she deserved as a young single mum whose daughter had died. Ava had come to accept, if not rail against, the fact that it had been Amelia's destiny to visit fleetingly, and there was no one to blame for what had happened, herself included. She also knew her mother and grandmother worried about her lack of male company, but she had plenty of male acquaintances. Just none, until now, who turned her on.

Zac Logan's face insinuated itself into her mind and she couldn't help the forlorn smile that tilted up her mouth. Well, she'd certainly been 'socialising' lately, and she had to admit the colours in her world had turned brighter before they'd been photoshopped viciously into the monochrome of amnesia.

But, she reminded herself, the last part of the drive had been good. This afternoon had shone with the connection she'd felt with Zac in the car. However, today became more precious for the tragic possibility that it too could be fleeting. She accepted that if his memory didn't come back, he'd return to Sydney soon. She knew the promise he'd seen between them before the accident had gone, and if it wasn't restored she'd have to survive.

Ava opened the screen door and stepped out to pat Reggie for a few minutes as she gazed over the paddocks. She leaned against the rail and stared out over the dry landscape.

The cost of possibly falling even more deeply in love with Zac would be the price she'd pay. She ruffled Reggie's neck. Probably. But she needed to be brave for both of them if she wanted to fight for something her gut said was a future people dreamed of.

24

Zac

Zac stood at the door to a large kitchen with a big, scrubbed wooden table set for lunch. He'd passed an airy sitting room with cane furnishings, plants and bright-yellow cushions. It looked welcoming. This room vibrated; it was the heart of the house, full of family photos, polished pots and pans hanging from the ceiling, letters, books and knitting needles. A big, yellow, old-fashioned stove took one wall and the largest refrigerator he'd ever seen stood in the corner.

Across the room, the screen door to the outside showed the sky as blue as a kid's paint pot. He had no idea what had happened to the storm that had spat dust at them less than an hour ago: the heavens hung cloudless above endless rock-strewn ground.

He spied Ava out on the verandah to the left and started forward before he saw she was coming in. She approached with that light step of hers and he felt his heart lift. Which was crazy. Too crazy to feel this earth-shifting awareness just looking at her after fifteen minutes apart. There was certainly something going on.

She looked him up and down critically. 'Do you feel better? It was a long drive.'

'I'm perfectly well.'

She shrugged and smiled. 'You look like you'll shake off the lingering effects of concussion if you take it easy enough.' He heard the unspoken *please take it easy* in her tone, which was reflected in her eyes.

He touched her shoulder lightly, in comfort, suddenly shatteringly aware that he hadn't thought enough about the psychological cost that had been paid by this woman he barely knew. The drain on her emotions looking after him as they both lay in the wrecked vehicle. And afterwards as she waited for his retrieval. Oh, he'd seen that she was physically tired, but she'd been hurt herself, and according to George, she'd thought he'd die and there was a cost to that concern — he knew. And his prognosis had looked grim there for a while — he'd seen his medical records.

He lifted his hands to cup her upper arms and stared into her eyes, those pools of blue, like that sky without any clouds, blue that could lift a dark day. Abruptly, it felt as though the room held only them. He and the woman who'd put her own injuries aside to keep him alive. 'You're an amazing woman, you know. And I haven't really said thank you for saving my life. I'm sorry you had to carry that.'

'I'm glad you pulled through.' Her voice sounded a little strained and he realised someone else was in the room.

Over her shoulder, Mim's face came into focus, faded eyes so like her granddaughter's surveying them both, a delighted grin beaming his way, her hands gesticulating for him to keep going. He couldn't help the embarrassed laugh. Already, as he dropped his hands, he could see that Granny Mim was a menace. 'You have an incredible granddaughter, Mim.'

'I know.' The older lady smiled even wider at him and stood to move across the room to the refrigerator. Ava's mother came in from the hall. He guessed he should be thankful he hadn't had another spectator to what had just passed between Ava and him.

Though maybe, from the look Stella was sending, she'd decided he was a pesky city boy playing in the outback. But she shouldn't have worried, because they couldn't have long-term plans. He knew Sydney was where he belonged, and the more he saw of Ava he knew where she belonged — here. What had he been playing at, becoming involved with her? These were dark thoughts for a bright afternoon and he felt his spirits sink.

'Look.' Ava touched his shoulder and pointed to the verandah she'd just come in from. And he did. The tall trees shaded what was apparently a shallow watercourse set well below the house. It would be cooler down there. That must be where Ava had said permanent waterholes lay under some overhanging trees, but mostly all he could see of the watercourse showed dry red gravel curving away into the distance. Even dry, it looked extremely inviting, and he'd definitely like to see it with Ava.

'There's a chair out there,' she murmured so the others couldn't hear, 'on the verandah, for when you need time away from the family — '

she glanced across the room — 'or Mim. It's my favourite spot. You can watch the birds and the wildlife come down to drink and let the world go by.' Then she smiled and directed him to a chair. 'There's no time for interesting views when lunch is on, though.' She nudged him.

He looked down at her, her head near his shoulder, her compassionate eyes slightly concerned.

'You're looking a little peaky again,' she told him.

'Pale and interesting?'

She pointed to one of the kitchen chairs. 'Pale,' she said.

'Come on, you two. Sit,' Stella called as she began to ladle an aromatic orange soup into bowls on the table. Fresh, home-baked bread and a small bowl of butter sat in the middle.

Ava gave him another nudge, as if to say, *See*, and he pulled out a chair. Then, to draw attention away from him, she spoke to her mother as she sat beside him. 'After the accident the dust storm closed Yulara. Did you have it here?'

Mim snorted. 'Not like you had out at the rock.'

'You were lucky it lifted,' Ava's mother said, then sent a piercing inspection Zac's way. 'I can see we'll have to get some colour into your cheeks, Zac. Eat up.'

25

Ava

Ava tried not to stare at the man at the table. Tried to stamp down the excitement of having him here. He'd been so earnest just then as he'd held her shoulders, as if he'd woken from a sleep. It could just be his brain catching up with the last twenty-four hours, or it could be a breakthrough with his memory. The thought bounced in her head like a bower bird hopping across the paddock.

He looked damn fine, despite the occasional bruise. Gorgeous, in fact. How was she to deal with this overwhelming pull she had for him, now, in front of her family? She was thrown by the way his damp hair curled over his ears. He must have washed his face and wet the edges of his hair, probably to stay awake. She had to physically restrain herself from asking him about it, though why on earth that tiny fact was incredibly interesting she didn't want to consider.

She felt herself relax as he smiled at her. As if he was glad she was within arm's length. She had the strangest feeling he wanted to reach out and touch her hand, which was a crazy idea at the lunch table of people he didn't know.

'It's beautiful here. Thank you for allowing me

to come.' He spread his hands and gestured to the windows, to the room in general. When her mother put a bowl in front of him, he asked, 'Is that pumpkin soup? My favourite.' He sniffed it appreciatively and took another admiring glance around the room.

Ava wondered fleetingly what he saw. Their kitchen was open plan, like the rest of the house, except for the original hallway and the formal sitting room. The walls were white, the rooms airy with lots of cane, magazines scattered across the side tables, and a couple of resilient plants spreading quietly in pots in the corner.

He was returning her regard when she turned back, and she felt her cheeks warm at the appreciation he directed not at the room but more personally at her. She tried not to blush and give Mim something else to crow about.

Mim wouldn't have missed any of it. She was busy perusing the full breadth of him sitting at their table, his broad shoulders taking up the whole of the carver chair back, and she even patted his hand. Ava stifled a laugh as she saw the funny side of her grandmother's approval.

Mim smiled at him, her mobile face easily drawing a return smile from Zac, and waved her hand as if she'd known him for years. 'It's lovely to have you here, Zac. A new face to brighten us up.'

He looked smitten. Ava remembered the story he had told on the way in and changed the subject. 'Zac worked in Weipa for a couple of weeks.'

Stella paused and her brows drew together.

'Really? I know a nurse who worked up there. I'd love to hear about that while you're here.'

So over the lunch table, the three of them sat and listened to Zac's description of the gulf communities, crocodiles and other exotic wild-life, and medical emergencies managed with the barest of essentials. Ava felt a stirring of almost envy at his words. Maybe Weipa could be a bolthole if she needed it. It was a little more distant from home, wilder, and full of unusual characters. Zac had mentioned the most extraordinary patients escaping the world — or hiding — in the Top End. It sounded so fascinating and like a true challenge. She would definitely enjoy the experience.

'I've always been captivated by remote medicine. And Weipa sounds a little different to what I do now,' Ava said.

He shook his head. 'It's primitive, stinking hot and the mosquitoes try to kill you all the time.'

She returned his stare calmly. 'You seem to like it well enough. Are you attempting to scare me off being attracted to Arnhem Land?' Ava teased him and surprisingly he bit back.

'Are you interested enough that I have to worry?'

She tipped her chin up. *Whoa there.* 'It's really none of your business what I do, so you don't have to worry.' Where had this come from? Now they were eyeing each other thoughtfully.

Mim cleared her throat noisily as each tried to stare the other down, and Stella jumped when the phone rang.

'I'll get it,' she said, and the curiosity in her

voice was patently clear. She glanced at Ava as she went to answer it in the sitting room. 'It's Jock,' she said when she returned. 'He's not coming for lunch but will bring Hana for tea.'

Ava said to Zac, 'Hana's thirty weeks pregnant. She has an online baby-clothes business she runs from their cottage.'

'She has the most beautiful sewing skills,' Mim added. 'It'd be good to add some of that into the bloodline. None of us are much good. Though my knitting sells well at the Beanie Festival.'

Zac looked bemused. 'You have a Beanie Festival?'

'It's a big event in Alice Springs.' Ava made sweeping gestures with her hands. 'Huge.' She pointed to her grandmother, pride in her voice. 'Mim's on the committee.' Well, it was pretty cool that Mim could go from metalwork to crochet. 'Granny Mim has diverse skills.'

'I'm not satisfied.' Zac spread his hands. 'What's a Beanie Festival?'

Mim waved her on so Ava answered. 'It started with beanies crocheted by Aboriginal women in remote communities. Sharing the knowledge before it was lost. Now it's become a huge fun event where Aboriginal and non-Aboriginal artists share their culture and exhibit together. There's an incredible amount of community participation because it aims to develop Aboriginal women's textiles, promote women's culture and promote handmade textile arts. It runs at the end of June. It started with traditional spinning and basketry and now everyone showcases their beanies. Granny Mim enters every year.'

Stella came to the table and joined them. 'And usually brings home a prize. They have themes.'

Ava said, 'Last year was *Weaving the Magic*, so think Dreamtime or fairytales. What was the year before, Mim?'

'*Spirit of the Land*,' Mim said, and Ava could see her granny enjoying the attention. She cackled and Ava had to smile.

'So, Mim's the crochet and knitting queen, but Hana is much better at needlework and using a sewing machine.' Ava gestured to the other two women. 'Granny and Mum are also good cooks.'

'Your mother is. You take after me, or worse.' Mim peered at Zac. 'Did she tell you she can't cook?'

He smiled at Ava. 'I'm sure she can. She has a few good recipes for saving lives.'

'More important,' Mim agreed with a look of approval at Zac.

Ava raised her eyebrows at him. 'Don't tell me.' She sighed. 'You're a fantastic cook?'

'Not bad.'

Spare me, she wanted to protest aloud. She didn't need further reason to be even more attracted to him. 'Excellent,' she told him. 'When it's my turn to cook you can take over.'

'Gladly. I wash dishes as well.' He said that smugly.

She had to laugh. *Better and better*. 'Be still my beating heart. That's what I usually offer to do instead of the cooking.'

Everyone was smiling, even Stella. 'You want to take me on in a cooking competition? Should

I dare you to show us?' Her mother arched a brow at Zac with a gleam in her eye.

'I could,' he said, not backing down.

'Zac's going to give you a run for your money,' Mim crowed.

Stella sniffed. 'I'd like to see that. But for now you should rest,' and she stood up and waited for Zac to stand. He raised his brows but did as she indicated, and then proceeded to follow her out of the kitchen. He cast a glance back at Ava and shrugged.

Ava hid her smile and she suspected Zac held one in, too. It was lovely being here with her family, having a meal together. And Zac being a part of it all. She'd done the right thing bringing him here.

26

Stella

Stella saw Zac to his room after lunch, checked he had his window open to let in the fresh air, and shut his door. She had the feeling that their family lunch had been unlike any he'd ever been present at. Ava had said he was an only child. There'd been too many flashes of surprised delight in his eyes as they'd all bantered, with Mim the stirrer and Ava giving as good as she got. When he'd met Ava's eyes there was some connection there because they smiled at the same things together often.

She shook her head. She didn't want to like him, but it was hard not to. He seemed like a lovely man, and yes, she might be jumping ahead, but she knew the risks and Ava didn't. She didn't want her daughter to suffer the same heart-wrenching challenges Stella had as a lonely partner in an unfriendly and distant place far from home.

To her surprise, Zac had looked a hundred per cent better than when she'd seen him yesterday, despite the continued amnesia, which made the nurse in her think it was more psychological than physical, and he'd held his own at the table with a quiet, incisive humour. Stella sighed. There was no doubt that Ava was on the way to quietly loving him. It wouldn't do. Talk about a foolish, headlong rush.

Instead of going back to the kitchen, Stella continued on to her own room. She needed a moment, and couldn't be sure she wouldn't say the wrong thing to Ava if she went back just yet. She seized on the basket of unfolded clothes as if they were old friends waiting for her. She'd brought them in from the long wire line this morning and put the basket in here to tidy when they'd run out of time as Ava and Zac arrived.

As the familiar task of sorting and folding soothed her agitated hands, her mind cast back, trying to remember if she'd even thought about the future when she'd first seen Noah. Probably not. She'd been too busy kissing him.

Oh my.

It had been a nurse's party, Svelte Stephanie's birthday, and the cowboy Stella had gone with hadn't been the fun she'd thought he'd be and they'd drifted apart. She'd looked around for new faces. There'd been a police conference on in town and she remembered how Stephanie had always known how to gather fresh men to her parties.

Stella remembered that rush of attraction when she'd caught sight of Noah, taller than the others, his head above the crowd, his smiling eyes meeting hers across the room. She'd asked Stephanie, catching her arm as she'd gone past, 'Is he single?' The next thing she knew, he'd been beside her with his gray eyes smiling at her, and at her zip-up full-length denim jumpsuit, though even then it had been ten years out of date. Her mouth curved at the memory. He'd made her feel incredibly beautiful with that one long look and they'd shifted closer to each other. There was something wonderful about a really tall man and your nose in his chest.

Stella sighed again as the memories poured in now that she was allowing herself to think.

They'd moved out of the noise of the crowded room, the lounge room of a ground-floor flat not that far from the one she had now, a little on the edge of town and near the often dry Todd River, and they'd leaned against the courtyard fence and stared at the myriad stars. And talked. And finally, he'd put those big arms around her and pulled her closer and kissed her, and she could still remember her incredulous delight.

Nobody had ever kissed her like that, as if she'd been waiting for just the right man. Noah's mouth and lips had had the perfect pressure, his tongue the perfect erotic feather. It was her first enjoyable kiss after a small net of fish-mouthed fumblers that had left her unimpressed and unawakened. And in that moment, she'd thought she'd found her home with Noah.

She threw down an orphan sock in disgust and one lone tear plopped into the centre of the empty plastic base of the washing basket. *Poor Noah.* And no, she hadn't thought about the future, where he lived, where she'd live. She had just fallen helplessly, heedlessly in love and agreed to follow him. And hadn't that been a disaster.

Jock is like his father rang through her mind and she wiped her eyes. Funny, she hadn't thought about that for a long time. Noah was a strong man with a soft heart, like Jock. And she herself was doing it again. There were aspects of Lorenzo that reminded her of the qualities she'd admired in Noah. The sudden, definite attraction, the outspoken honesty of feelings, the protectiveness that big men couldn't help projecting, the sexy eyes and mouth. Her lips quirked. And Lorenzo could kiss too. And he wanted to take her away and nurture her. Which would be a change from her previous marriage. But again, he was unsuitable, because she wasn't moving to Italy. She would see how long he lasted out here on his son's property.

Ava's Zac was another big man, with admiring eyes for her daughter, though she could see his puzzlement as he tried to remember. Was there anything she could do to stop it happening all over again? Probably not.

Except share her own truth with her daughter. Finally. Not that it would make a difference.

It was intriguing to see Zac acting protective when Ava mentioned her interest in some far-flung outpost because he'd raved about it. Her daughter could do what she wanted. She'd managed to look after herself for the last five years without Zac helping her to avoid risks. The girl was always off in her four-wheel drive, travelling to some remote outpost, often the only white woman, connecting with her smiles and her respect for others. It seemed perfectly normal to Stella that Ava would want to work at a remote outpost with dedicated clinicians because that's what she did. So for Zac to have

216

reacted, she wondered just how intense their relationship had been that it could seep through a wall of amnesia. Had there already been long-term thoughts of Ava moving to Sydney?

Stella would dig, do a few internet searches on this Zac, and check him out.

When she returned to the kitchen Ava still sat at the table, though her shoulders were drooped and her head was resting in one cupped hand. Stella's heart ached for the stubbornness her daughter had probably inherited from both her mother and grandmother. Ava had been determined to do the drive herself — to have the time with Zac — she understood that. But the girl was pale and needed a rest. She wasn't glad her daughter had met Zac, but there was no doubt that Ava's pain was real. And she deserved none of it. Unlike Stella herself, who still hadn't told her children she'd left Noah and that their father had taken rash and reckless risks until it had killed him the week she'd left.

She'd lied to her children. Lied to everyone, though her mother had always known. Would Lorenzo still think she was an angel when she told him? Would she tell him or continue the lie forever?

No, she decided right then and there. When all this settled down, she would tell them all. Clear her conscience at least of subterfuge. Then she would see what Lorenzo said.

27

Ava

When Stella walked back into the kitchen, she pulled Ava into her arms, one hand reaching up to pull Ava's head down onto her shoulder.

It felt so good. Ava let herself relax, could smell the soap her mum used, always jasmine, and the slight aroma of cooking that hung around her. She breathed in the scent of the calm her mother was known for but had struggled to find lately. When her mum spoke, the words brushed over Ava's skin like a caress. 'I imagine it was very tense. You must have been under enormous pressure. And then there was Amelia's birthday. You need to walk along the riverbed and heal a bit. Recharge. No work for you today, either.'

Ava let her mum's arms hold her for a moment longer and let the strain go. She felt the tension draining like water into sand. Stella had her own medicine. It was called love, and on the rare occasions when she brought it out, they were all blinded by the strength of it. 'Thanks, Mum.'

Stella stepped back but held onto Ava's upper arms. She gave her a little shake as she searched her face. 'You need to look after *you* as well. You're too precious to burn out doing too much.'

Ava nodded. 'I will.'

'That Zac might help her,' Mim said slyly.

Stella glared at her mother. 'Don't go putting ideas in his head. Or hers.'

'Ha! I'm thinking the ideas are already there in her head. And he sounded protective to me.' She hummed the wedding march as she left the room, much to Stella's disgust.

'That woman drives me mad,' Stella huffed.

Ava laughed. 'You'd be lost without her.'

They looked at each other and the smiles died. 'Yes, I would. So much so that I don't want to talk about it.' She tried a joke. 'Or about weddings.' They both knew that comment fell flat.

Ava stepped back to try to explain. 'We connected last week, Mum. Big time. I know there's a chance Zac won't ever remember and I'll have lost something very special. So thank you for having him here.' She drew in the air to calm herself. 'He makes me feel so incredible, so . . . different.' Her belly kicked as she thought of them tangled together and she glanced away as the heat rose in her cheeks. He made her feel sexy as hell. Like a desirable woman. Resolutely she went on. 'I know that it's probable, especially now, that he'll go back to his high life, which I could never fit into. Even last week in Sydney at the course, the busyness of the place drove me mad.'

'I think so, too.' Stella nodded, and Ava couldn't miss the relief that flashed across her mother's face. And something that looked strangely like guilt. Why would her mother feel guilty about that?

'Don't celebrate too soon, because I have to believe Zac will remember me and then it will be our business. Then all you have to do is bless us. But at least my trust bone has healed after Jai. And maybe if there has to be a time 'after Zac', I will be more open to the idea of trusting someone else. Get married, have children.' Her thoughts spiralled to a little white coffin. 'Though that would be scary,' The idea of losing another child made the sweat break out on her body. She couldn't go through that again.

Stella nodded again. 'I understand. It's your life. I just don't want you to set yourself up for disappointment like I did,'

'What disappointment? You always said you loved Dad?'

'I loved Noah, all right. Very much. But — ' her mother stepped back and lifted her chin — 'I haven't done everything right in my life.'

Ava didn't understand where this was coming from. 'You didn't have much choice with Dad dying while you were in Sydney.'

Stella sighed. 'Except I wasn't in Sydney when your father died.' Her eyes met Ava's and there was a plea for understanding in them. 'I'd already left him. The week before.'

Ava's breath hitched. 'Mum?'

Her mother went on, staring at nothing over Ava's shoulder. 'I'd run home to my mother, with you, from the homesickness. Missing my family.' She shook her head. 'It was his long, long hours at work, with my time in a horrible brick house and no friends. Not many people talk to their neighbours in the city, and when I tried they'd just look at me as if I was trying to steal their washing.'

'You were lonely,' Ava said very quietly.

'Very. He was devastated, of course. I found out, a fair while after the funeral, that he went a little crazy and took stupid risks and continued to until that got him killed. I blame myself. I've always blamed myself for Noah's death.'

Ava's head was spinning. 'But we were always told you came home after he died.'

'I lied.' The statement clattered in the kitchen like a dropped knife and her mother's eyes filled. Ava's throat closed in sympathy. She couldn't remember the last time she'd seen her mother cry, and she slipped her hand into Stella's and squeezed.

Her mum didn't seem to notice as she hung suspended in another world and time. 'I left him and he died. And the lie I told you has eaten me for all this time.'

Ava didn't know if the tears were for her father or for the fact that her mother had carried the burden for such a long time.

'Oh, Mum.' Ava stepped up closer and returned the love her mother had given her. 'You were young, alone, maybe even post-natally depressed, without your mother nearby. And pregnant again. What did Mim say when you came home?'

She half laughed and it was not a happy sound. 'She said go back. Talk to him. That there was a place between the two worlds where we could find a solution and we needed to work on it together.'

That sounded like Mim.

Stella sighed. 'But before I could go back, it was too late.'

'Oh, Mum,' she said again. 'You poor thing. And you've carried that and worried about what we'd think all these years? That's why you were worried I'd end up like you if I went with Zac? Why you looked worried when he arrived, with our obvious rapport?'

She nodded.

Ava reeled, but her mum needed this sorted. She could rearrange her own brain later. 'Firstly, I love you. Jock loves you. Neither of us is going to judge you for something you thought was right twenty-four years ago. Dad should have seen it coming too.' She squeezed her mum's hand again.

'Secondly, you couldn't know he'd be killed. You didn't know you'd never see him again. That's a tragedy. Horrible. But that's life. It's capricious and doesn't do what you expect, and we have to grow with it. We have to learn from it because that's our journey.'

'Like Amelia,' her mum said sadly.

'Yes, like Amelia. And like me taking risks with Zac if we want to go that far. But we'll see what happens.'

Her mother reached up and dropped a kiss on her cheek. 'How did you get so wise?'

Ava hugged her. 'I picked it up from my mother and grandmother.'

'Really?' Her mother's voice was uncertain and buried in the hug.

Ava gave her an extra squeeze. 'Yes, really. Let

it go, because your daughter thinks you're amazing, and that you deserve happiness, and I hope you find it.' They stepped back and eyed each other mistily.

Her mother looked at her for a moment and opened her mouth to say something, but Mim walked in chuckling. Ava watched her mother's mouth shut with a snap. *Now what?* she wondered. *Was there another secret her mother had been holding on to?*

To fill the sudden gap in conversation, Ava said, 'Just so you know, I intend to remain my own woman and I always will be.'

'I can see that,' her mum said.

Ava couldn't suppress the smile. 'And I have to acknowledge that no matter how things could pan out with Zac in the long run, having him here is wonderful. But we have a week at least, maybe two if we don't drive him away, to see if there's a chance we can find what we lost.'

She studied her mother, blonde and upright, a determined frown on her face as she tried *not* to tell her daughter what to do. She'd inherited a lot of her mother's need to control and she understood what she was going through.

'It's okay, Mum. I know what I'm doing.'

Her mother smiled at that, very dryly. 'Excellent' was all she said.

Granny Mim, observer of these last statements, looked at them both and cackled like a madwoman. The two younger women shook their heads at her.

28

Zac

Zac stepped out at three o'clock and quietly closed the door of his room. He'd slept, as instructed by Stella in no uncertain terms, which he had to smile at, but he'd had enough rest today. She epitomised the bossy nurse, so unlike her daughter's gentle, midwife-like suggestions to listen to his own body. If he stayed more than a few days, he could see a time when moving to one of the tiny chalet-style cottages overlooking the desert could be more relaxing than following Stella's orders. Then he could invite Ava to come visit. Now that was a fantastic idea.

Before he'd drifted off to sleep, he had admitted to himself that he wanted to know more of Ava May's background and what made her tick. Well, this was his chance. They would be living in close quarters for a week at least. Even under such intense chaperonage as at lunch, he'd felt the pull of attraction, which he guessed was what had happened when they had met initially. However, there wasn't much chance of acting on any of it without being observed, Mim and Stella had watched them like desert hawks which he supposed was a good thing to keep things moving safely.

Zac walked down the hallway, taking in Ava's

world in a more leisurely manner than during his arrival. Once again, he admired the way the stone hallway kept the centre of the house cool. It was such a clever design by the pioneers of this family, who spent their lives in the highs and lows of the Central Australian winter and summer.

Now that he thought about it, he realised that he'd lived in an air-conditioned atmosphere almost all his life, both at home and at work. And since arriving in the outback, he found he really was enjoying the purity of the more natural atmosphere, even though at times it was terribly hot. If he was honest, he doubted he was actually cut out for this life. The stories of drought, the people who lived here and the battles won — this was a whole new world Ava was inviting him into, and the opportunity to experience it was great. He just had to remember that this wasn't his world, and make sure that the risk of causing Ava pain in the long run didn't outweigh the benefits for him. He needed to remember his track record for not keeping the people he cared about safe.

If he'd been sensible, he wouldn't have come here with Ava and risked her heartache, but he'd seen how much she wanted that to happen, to give him a chance to remember, and he hadn't been able to say no.

All he knew, in the present moment, was that he ached with the need for exercise and to clear his head with space, and this place had more space than he'd seen before.

He stepped out onto the back verandah and

spied Ava's Granny Mim as she dragged a long metal rod from an organised stack of metal sheets and rods towards a long, low building he hadn't noticed before. When he strode across to offer help, she flashed him one of those twinkling smiles he already recognised as a trademark of hers.

'Now are you officially an invalid or not? Should I let you?'

'Not an invalid. I'm a doctor, I can make that call.'

'Then a big, handsome man like you wants to help? Absolutely. You go right ahead and drag that into my shed.'

She cracked him up. He took up the rod and tried to keep his face expressionless. It was surprisingly heavy. And yet she'd been dragging it, at her age! He decided not to lift it onto his good shoulder and began dragging it too. 'This your shed?' he asked, and she nodded. 'And what mischief do you get up to over here, Mim?'

Inside the naturally lit shed, with sunlight streaming in the windows illuminating Mim's work, he saw the almost completed miniature homestead, just like the ones he'd seen on the way in. 'So these are your creations.'

She reached out with one veiny hand and stroked the sloping tin roof. 'They are. They're models of the chalet cabins, scale versions of those we've made to use for the tourists.' She looked at it with pride. 'It has all the things I like in a cubbyhouse.' She chuckled. 'Full-sized, though, the metal gets a bit heavy for me.'

Indeed! She was so tiny beside him. 'You're a

marvel,' he told her, truly meaning it.

'My late husband taught me to weld and I enjoy it. It's one of my artistic bents.' She pointed to the windowsill and there lined up like the Dubbo Zoo were tiny native animals in all sizes made from metal.

Zac studied them. 'I like the emu.'

'He's my favourite, too. Cheeky.'

'The tourists will love them. You're onto a winner there.' He thought of the woman who'd driven him here — physically and figuratively. 'Which one is Ava's favourite?'

Mim inclined her head at the sill. 'The lizard — the thorny devil. *Ngiyari.*'

This was not what he expected. 'He's fierce.'

Mim chuckled. 'He is if you're a black ant. He can eat up to a thousand a day.'

'Ah. He's high maintenance. Like me.' Zac listened to himself with some shock. Was Ava changing him already? He was employing self-mockery, something he hadn't thought he'd mastered, and he liked how amusing it felt and the way it lightened the load of drama his life had held lately.

Mim cackled. 'I heard that about you.' Unfortunately, she didn't expand and he wondered what Ava had told her. 'I think this little fella reminds her of Uluru. She reckons she sees one every time she goes there. Her friend, Denise, says it's her desert friend. Once that granddaughter of mine saw a nest of tiny baby devils just hatched and fell in love. Strange girl.' She looked at him from beneath her white brows. 'She's tough, but she's softer than her mother.'

Mim waited after this statement, so he weighed up the thought and didn't fill the sudden silence to interrupt her. He was rewarded when Mim said, 'Did Ava tell you about Amelia?'

He felt the weight of Mim's sadness as it drifted towards him, and he remembered Roslyn's parents saying, *The young should never go first.* 'Yes. She did.'

The older lady seemed to sag with relief. 'I'm glad. She would have been an amazing mother — was a wonderful one for the short time she had — and now she's a good midwife. But I'd like to see her be a mother again.'

Mim wasn't pulling any punches. And strangely, he wasn't alarmed. 'They told me at the hospital she's an amazing midwife. And I can see she's a wonderful woman. She'd be very easy to grow fond of.' As soon as he said 'fond' he felt stupid.

Apparently, Mim thought so too because she laughed and waved him away in disgust. '*Fond's* nothing to write home about. Doesn't do it for me. Let me know if you warm up to scorching.' Mim glanced out the window. 'Volcanic. That's as warm as you need to go before you bother.' She snorted distastefully then muttered 'Fond' under her breath and he grinned again. This woman. If Ava turned out like her grandmother, then the man who won her heart would've won the greatest lottery in the world.

He had a sudden urge to buy as many tickets as he could.

Mim interrupted his thoughts. 'There she goes.'

Ava had stepped out of another small building

across the yard. She saw him and their eyes met, and when she smiled, he felt his spirits lift. *That must mean something.* She changed course towards him and he savoured her approach. Felt anticipation lift like a wave in his chest. *And what did that mean?*

Her pale jeans hugged her hips and the long-sleeved top sat loosely enough to keep her cool, but her clothes were fitted enough to let him know there was a very desirable woman underneath. Her blonde hair had been tied back with a checked ribbon, the ponytail off her neck to keep her cool in the heat, but it left the lovely curve of her throat so softly vulnerable, he had the sudden urge to run his finger down its line.

It was going to be an interesting few days to see how long he could keep her safe from the bigger danger: himself.

He met her on the dirt path outside. 'Are you going for a walk?'

She pointed. 'Down to the river — I want to check the level in the waterhole.'

'Okay if I come? I need to stretch my legs.' He could hear the warmth in his question and he suspected she did too, because she nodded, her mouth kicked up and she gestured to the path ahead.

'This way.'

'I hope I'm not intruding on your walk.'

She turned her head to look up at him. 'You're not intruding. I enjoy your company, which was why I asked you to come here to convalesce.'

To Zac it suddenly seemed natural when he lifted her hand to take it in his as they began to walk. Her fingers sat cool, despite the heat, and strong beneath his. He wrapped his hand around her palm and she fitted perfectly.

She didn't pull free when he thought she might, especially with Mim watching. 'You're a confusing man, Zac Logan,' she muttered, and she shook their clasped hands to illustrate her point.

He looked down at their entwined fingers. 'This is just to stop me from falling over.' He squeezed gently and contentment surged like a fluid wave of warmth, unexpectedly sweet and calming.

'At least you'll have some control over the danger if I start to wobble,' he said.

'What? We both fall together, is that your idea?'

'That would be the best scenario,' he quipped.

She stopped in her tracks, shaking her head at him. 'So what are we up to now?'

He thought of Mim. 'We're getting warmer. How does that sound to you?'

She tossed her head. 'Boring. Let me know when it gets hot.'

'You sound like your grandmother.'

'Oh dear,' she said and laughed.

29

Ava

Her flippant comment notwithstanding, Ava thought that 'getting warmer' sounded promising. There was that hint of amusement in his deep voice and Ava savoured the spread of euphoria that reminded her of how she'd felt with him on the plane and after that. This wasn't a shared memory, but it was perhaps a shared connection rebuilding.

'Do you remember anything when you hold my hand?' she asked.

'It feels good,' he admitted, 'but no. It feels like the first time.'

Ava swallowed the disappointment. She should just be happy that he was here with her and try not to wish for the stars. They were walking down the side of the bank that led to the bottom of the river, arms swinging, fingers clasped. The day shone blue and clear, with no sign of a new dust storm or rain. The demon of drought aside, the magic of the moment swelled inside her with the scent of crumbling red earth under her feet, the leaves of the tall gum they were passing under, and home. She loved the smell of home. Unexpectedly, joy opened like a desert flower inside her.

Zac swung her hand. 'You have slim fingers,

fingernails not too long, a little rough at the edges from constant washing, like all health workers, but the whole hand fits nicely in mine.'

The air seemed to vibrate between them, in spite of his clinical assessment. What the heck was that?

He lifted her fingers to his face and kissed her palm, then repositioned her arm back by his side and they continued walking. 'It's a particularly nice hand.'

She sucked in a breath, shocked by the impact of his warm lips as they brushed her skin and the slow burn he'd started with his words, which burst into a wicked little camp fire.

Her inner voice cautioned, *Calm down. It's just a walk.* 'Thank you, kind sir, for the potted description of my hand,' she said, hiding in humour, but she felt a little breathless and struggled to keep the conversation light. He'd held more than that on their hot nights, but there was something sweet and unhurried about a man wanting to hold her hand and saying he enjoyed it. Something romantic. It wasn't a trait she was known for, but what girl didn't smile at a hint of romance? Maybe this new relationship she hoped to build with Zac could start with romance instead of sex.

Ava went along with the attraction, and the frivolous conversation hid the depth of tension slowly building into a fog of lust between them. The residual heat from the day warmed her legs, Zac warmed her middle, and a slight breeze drifted towards her every now and then, trying to cool her down. It wasn't succeeding. 'You're confusing me.'

The almost silent tread of his footsteps made her aware of his powerful frame. He suddenly laughed and she closed her eyes briefly at the warmth in that sound. He didn't do it enough.

'I'm not surprised I confuse you,' he murmured. 'I confuse myself.'

'That's no good.' Ava exhaled noisily. 'Someone needs to know what's going on.' She shook their hands. 'I'm not sure what happens next with you and I find that hard to cope with.'

'That's another thing I'm finding I like so much about you — your honesty.' He sighed. 'I hope I can be the same.'

His comment made her feel uncomfortable because there was so much he didn't know about her, such as her dreams and the reasons she had brought him here, which actually warred with her fears and insecurities. Her need to stay connected to the land. His eventual commitment to spend long passages of time in her setting if this all did work out. She didn't understand this man or his world, and it terrified her the way he could rouse her emotions with a word or two and a quick squeeze of her fingers and then dash her down with a facade that said he didn't know her.

What would he do when they went back to the house? Pretend there was nothing between them, like he had once before? Mim knew there was more between them. Her mother had sensed it, too. Was he aware of what he did to her or was it just she that was supersensitive?

It was all too hard to think about and she'd come down here to relax, so she needed to change the subject. They'd made it down to the dry riverbed, her hand still in his. 'When the rains come properly, once a year if we're lucky, or every few years, this whole creek bed is flooded. The water rushes through here like a red torrent and anything caught in it gets washed away too. Even men like you.' Big. Strong. Mortal. The thought of Zac in a flash flood made her shudder and she acknowledged her lack of faith in his ability to survive in a remote landscape.

She wasn't a small woman, but he looked down on her from his height and she wanted to hug him. Keep him safe. It was probably the tiredness that had crept up on her since she'd arrived home. She was possibly allowing it to swamp her because she now had some support mechanisms in place.

He must have seen her sizing him up because his voice lowered teasingly. 'Does it bother you? I seem to tower over all your family like a big lummox. I hope your brother is big.'

She laughed. 'Big is beautiful. Your size was handy in the emergency department with our stroppy football players.'

'I'm glad to hear it. Was that all?'

She cocked an eyebrow at him. Did he expect her to be all coy and embarrassed because they'd enjoyed each other's bodies? 'You are big,' she teased him. 'Of course height is fine lying down, but it could be awkward at this angle. You up there, me down here.' She dared him with her eyes, then said, 'You could kiss me and I'll tell you.' The comment came out of her mouth before she could stop it, and hung in the hot air between them loud and clear.

He paused and surveyed her in a way that made her think it might be time to head back to the house before she said anything else that would make it awkward to spend the next week together.

'Forget I said that.' She turned her back on him. 'Come on. It's just a walk.'

Unexpectedly, he took her fingers in his big hand again and squeezed them for comfort. A sudden rush of empathy welled inside her and ran through her entire body like a cooling draught. He was so lost without his memories and she was pressuring him. She squeezed his hand back. She needed to console him more than he needed to console her.

She stopped and he stopped with her. There had to be more than this, and she could almost see in his eyes the shadows of the past crowding like cloaked figures around him, and sadly, his inability to pinpoint any of the faces.

'I'll have to get used to not having those memories, I guess,' he said in an echo of her thoughts. He tightened his grip. 'Is there something big between us that I should remember?'

Her lips parted, but she couldn't say anything. The words were stuck in her throat because of the lack of recognition in his face. She tried not to let her heart shine out of her eyes. He stared at her mouth and she tried not to dwell on his.

'Maybe you're right. What if my memory needs jogging,' he said, his voice gravelly, 'in another way?'

Below the wave of dark hair on his forehead, she saw his eyes darken. It would be so easy to reach up and try that connection. To risk the awkwardness that had to follow if he didn't remember her when they kissed. She could feel the undercurrent between them, the heat rising even though they only touched hands. How could two people create such intensity without him remembering?

She took a calming breath, then another. Not yet. If nothing jogged his memory when he did kiss her, then that disappointment would sting and kick her and frustrate the hell out of him as well. Make him wonder why he'd come to the back of beyond to their station when nothing was ringing any bells.

She saw the moment his eyes changed, the decision made to not go there. He probably saw her struggle because she was pretty darn sure that was sympathy crossing his face.

'Cooee.' The call came from towards the house. Ava pulled away unsteadily. Her chest rose and fell as she tried to slow her breathing, and when he put his hand out to catch her fingers to steady her, she found him holding her hand again.

She licked her dry lips. 'My brother.'

Zac seemed to be watching her mouth. 'Your brother.'

'Jock,' she said.

'Jock,' he repeated.

Maybe he had been feeling what she had, after all.

'Echo,' she quipped.

He blinked and focused on their surroundings. 'Right, then. What were we looking for down here before we go back?'

'Just the level of the waterhole.'

They walked around a small dark-red pool about the size of a child's trampoline and climbed back up the hill, and this time she took his hand and clasped his fingers because she didn't want to let go, and she decided then and there that they would walk like this for the whole world to see if he let her. Their tenuous relationship had subtly changed.

She'd changed him. And to her amusement, her brother's stance was something else that changed as they walked towards him.

Jock's brows lowered, his chin went up and he gave Zac the once-over that said, *You'd better be careful with my sister.* She glanced at the man beside her but he didn't seem to mind. He just smiled at her brother's protectiveness.

'Zac,' Ava said, pretending she was oblivious to the glare shooting past her, 'this is my brother, Jock. Jock, Zac. We worked together in Alice.' She let go of his hand and Zac reached out and took Jock's grudging one aimed his way. They shook firmly. Maybe a little too firmly. Ava hid a smile.

'Zac or Jock. I need someone with height. Have you got a minute?' Mim called out, and Ava caught Zac's questioning look that said he didn't mind the diversion.

'Coming!' he called to Mim with a wave. 'It'll give Ava and you some space to talk. Good to meet you, Jock. I hope I get a chance to sit down with you and hear more about the running of the station when you get time.'

She saw the flick of Jock's brows as he nodded. 'Sure thing.'

'Better go then,' Zac said.

30

Stella

Stella watched her daughter and son from the window in the sitting room as they talked outside. Something was going on. She'd seen Zac and Ava arrive from the river holding hands and she suppressed a sigh.

She watched as Hana refitted the bobbin in Granny Mim's sewing machine. Hana hadn't run away. Hana hadn't dragged Jock back to New Zealand. And she and Jock seemed happy. But this was only their first child. Would they remain happy as their family grew larger?

'Phew.' Hana stood awkwardly and shifted her belly around a small table. 'Got it. I think that's fixed it. She had a ball of old cotton catching on it.'

'Thank you.' Stella put her hand out to stop her. 'How are you and how's that grandchild of mine? Moving well?'

Hana glanced at her in surprise. 'We're great. Everything is going well and the midwives are happy with me.'

'Are you happy? You and Jock?' The words were out before she could stop them.

Hana froze and straightened, and Stella flushed. She'd been abrupt. She deserved it if her daughter-in-law snapped at her.

239

Hana's face softened and she touched Stella's hand gently. 'We are very happy,' she enunciated slowly and with definite emphasis. 'I'm fine. Jock's fine. The baby's fine. Poddy and I both love being here. It will be even better when the baby arrives.' She peered at her. 'Okay?'

The girl was perceptive, she'd give her that. Stella's spirits lifted. 'I have to admit, the idea of a child in the house is very exciting.' Actually it gave her joy, something in short supply lately with her disordered emotions. 'I can't wait.'

Hana nodded and moved towards the door. 'Good.'

'And Hana?' The girl turned, causing Stella to flush again. 'Thank you.'

Hana nodded, her head high like the strong woman she was. 'You're very welcome, Stella.'

She waited a moment until the stupid swell of relief passed before she followed Hana down to the kitchen. Except Hana had moved out to the yard and Zac was eating an Anzac biscuit by himself at the table. He started to stand when she came in and she shooed him back down again with her hand.

'All alone?' She glanced around. 'Where's Mim?'

'She said she had something to do.'

'Up to mischief, then.' She shrugged. Her mother would return in her own good time. She studied the first man her daughter had brought home in five years. He looked pale, but not as pale as he had on arrival. There was no use asking how he was feeling because he'd just say 'fine'. Maybe she could pump him for more background information. Make him see the disaster of he and Ava together in the city because again she could feel that vague hostility of foreboding when she thought of Ava with him in her future.

'I'm sorry to hear about your wife.'

'Thank you, Stella. I'm sorry to hear about your husband.'

Well, that served her right. But she didn't give up easily. 'Were you married long?'

He smiled at her. 'Five years. You?'

Smart alec. 'Five. Was she from Sydney?'

Now his eyes positively twinkled. 'Yes. We grew up together. You two?' Ping-pong. But she didn't bite this time because she'd found her opportunity.

'My husband and I were from two totally different worlds. Though lust blinded us. I nearly went mad when I went back to Sydney with him.' There, she'd said it.

He studied her face for a minute and then said kindly, 'I'm sorry to hear that.' He looked towards the door as Ava laughed from somewhere outside. His face lit up and Stella had the crushing realisation that she'd just wasted her time.

'Tea, anyone?' she called, half exasperated and half amused. As if anyone would have been able to change her or Noah's mind all those years ago. It really was a shame that it had ended so badly. 'Sorry for the inquisition. You'll get used to us.'

'I'm enjoying myself,' he said and grinned at Stella, who simply shook her head.

Reckless, foolish young people. Yes, it was

Ava's right to choose, and the big man with his beautiful, tired eyes was a lovely-looking specimen. Perhaps her daughter would risk withering in the city's soulless world of money and mayhem for him. Maybe she'd be fine. But she'd have to work in the fast lane of transient patients in a busy Sydney hospital or be stuck home alone with kids while he did his thing.

Stella thought back to those days. To being surrounded by neighbours who never talked to you and rushing traffic that never stopped. Would Ava shrivel into herself like she had until she cracked?

Stella sighed again as she glanced out and saw her son's unsmiling face. Jock. There'd been a lot of grim looks lately. There were so many things to worry about when she really wanted peace.

31

Ava

'Never seen you hold a bloke's hand before, Ava.' Jock scowled at the house.

Ava narrowed her eyes. *What's eating him?* 'I never found one sexy enough.'

Jock nearly choked. 'Hope there's more to him than that?'

She was tempted to say 'Is there more?' to get a rise out of her suddenly protective younger brother. But Jock looked bowed down with some emotion and she glanced back at the house to see if Hana was there. She couldn't see her. Hana kept him on an even keel.

'Hana tells me the baby is growing well.'

A rare smile crossed her brother's face. 'It kicks like there's no tomorrow.' His face appeared sad for a moment before he seemed to drag a smile from the bottom of his boots. 'We still don't know the sex, but we don't care either way, so the surprise is nice for Hana.'

She tilted her head at him. 'The surprise will be nice for you, too.'

'Of course.' He brushed that away and faced the house again. 'We've got a couple of weeks before we have to go back to Alice Springs. There's the muster to get through first.'

'We'll manage. We always do.' She lowered her voice. 'You okay?'

Jock combed his hair back from his face with his fingers. 'The stock look terrible. There were even a few that we've had to shoot. They're starving. Mim says the rain will turn up, but I'm thinking I might have blown it.'

'You're not responsible for the drought. And the improvements you made were needed,' Ava said. 'Do you want to go for a drive together? See how the back looks?' She wouldn't let him go alone again if he came back from the paddocks looking like this. 'I guess we could bring Zac?'

Jock looked thoughtful. 'Mum says he's sick.'

'He's recovering.' *Boy, was he recovering.* 'But I've seen him in action, and if you needed a hand with a steer he could help.'

He laughed, but it was bitter and angry and she frowned in concern. 'I blew the budget and it's going to wipe us out.'

'This isn't like you, Jock, all doom and gloom. Stop it. You can't take the blame for the weather.'

Jock positively vibrated with self-loathing. 'I should have waited another year for the solar pumps.' She'd never seen him like this. He'd obviously been stewing on it for some time. He dragged his hand through his hair again and she could see it was shaking. He was worse than she'd thought.

'Overcapitalising happened to the Wilsons. And the Johnsons before that. Mum should have stopped me.'

His voice had risen and now Hana appeared at

244

the back door. She glided across the grass to put her hand on Jock's arm. 'Hey, cowboy. Getting loud there.'

Jock's stiff expression softened. 'I know. Sorry, honey. I was telling Ava about the cattle. She said she'd come with me to count.'

Ava didn't remember saying quite that, but she would. She'd bring Zac if he was up to it. And she hoped they wouldn't find too many ill cattle. Jock didn't look like he could take it. But then he'd been here day in, day out watching the feed disappear while she'd been in Alice in another world. Maybe he needed to get away for more than an ultrasound in town. She sighed. But they couldn't afford that, either.

'Tomorrow morning, then, rather than today?' She was thinking that Zac would have had another night's sleep and he'd managed the walk to the creek bed with ease earlier. Managed to hold her hand with no ill effects. She'd ask him if he thought he'd be up to sharing Jock's run later.

Hana sighed and rested her hand on Jock's arm. 'Mim's just told your brother he's not to go looking for bad news.'

Jock brushed that aside. 'We can say we're showing Zac around. Take some food, call it a picnic.' His voice was bitter and harsh. He must have heard it himself because he ended with his voice calmer and softer. 'Mim will be happy with that.'

She and Hana exchanged looks. Ava wasn't so sure Jock was looking at this rationally, and judging by Hana's expression she didn't think so either, but they could both see Jock was taking it hard. Ava couldn't blame her brother. Everyone was struggling.

'What does Mum say?'

'She's focused on the ecotourism.' Jock waved his hand in disgust. 'Believes it will save the day.'

'It might.'

'Tea, anyone?' Stella's voice floated out to them and Jock set his jaw.

He glanced at the house. 'Better go in if we want to do this thing tomorrow.'

'You go ahead.' Hana's voice was quiet but determined, and Jock nodded. 'I want to talk to Ava for a minute.'

Ava watched as Zac stepped out onto the verandah to wave them in. 'I'll go out with you tomorrow, Jock, and see if I can help. After 'we' — ' she used her fingers for inverted commas — 'show Zac the station.'

Hana's relief couldn't be mistaken as her husband walked away. 'I'm glad you're going with Jock. I'm in no state to go bouncing around in the Polaris looking for him.'

'He's lucky he has you.' They turned towards the house and started to follow more slowly. 'How's your pregnancy going this week? I know you said the baby is good, but are you keeping well?'

'I feel great. And Jock makes a fuss of me.'

Ava smiled. 'He should.'

Hana shrugged. 'And I think your mother is getting just a little bit clucky.'

They both laughed. 'She's got a lot on her plate with the tourism stuff.' Not to mention the bombshell she'd dropped on Ava today. 'She's glad of your help. One day Jock will take over the station, and Mum and Mim will go to Alice to live. You'll miss us all then.'

'I wish Jock had your conviction. This drought has really knocked his confidence, and I think that responsibility at this moment could be the last straw. I'm worried about him.'

Reggie rushed up to Ava and she reached down for a pat of his soft neck as he sat against her legs, a warm quivering weight. 'Me too.' Then she said to the dog, 'You're a sook, Reg.' Then lowering her voice she said, 'This visit I'm thinking Mim is looking frail, too. What do you think?'

Hana nodded. 'She works very hard and she's worried about Jock as well. So is your mum. Mim won't slow down on the station, even though Jock says he can do half the stuff she does. He tries to lighten her load, but she's stubborn. And her hip hurts.'

They started walking again. 'I know. I'll have a talk to her. Maybe suggest Jock needs to feel like he's pulling more weight. I'll see what I can do.'

'Thanks, Ava.'

'Thank you. We're so lucky Jock found you. Just take care of yourself and the next generation of Mays. Don't work too hard.' Hana was as bad as Mim on that front.

'I'll try.'

They pushed through the screen into the kitchen and her mum was there holding up the teapot as a question.

'Yes, please.' Ava sat herself next to Zac and smiled back at him. 'So, you've been closeted with my grandmother and now my mother on your own. Still surviving?'

'I'm enjoying myself,' he said, and for some reason her mother laughed.

32

Zac

Zac woke the next morning before light with only some stiffness and a few aches, and he felt better than he had for a week. Possibly better than he had for a whole year, except for the confusion of losing two weeks of his life. He didn't know if it was the place or the people making him feel this way, though he suspected the latter. Especially the company of one particular person. He couldn't remember when he'd slept so deeply once his head hit the pillow. The only discomfort was the itching around the suture lines at the back of his head and his arm. This morning, the silence seemed to beckon with cool desert whispers enticing him to slip outside and watch the sunrise. *Come on. Come on. It's nice out here.*

He sat up and swung his feet to the cool floor, but before he could stand his door opened just as quietly and Ava poked her head around. When she saw he was awake she slipped into the room.

All his Christmases came at once. 'Good morning, Nurse.'

She put her fingers to her lips, but he noted with satisfaction the quirk of her smile behind them. 'I'm more of a midwife. Would you like to see the sunrise? We've still got time if you're up for it.'

'Oh, I'm up for it,' he said, and decided he'd said that cheekily, which wasn't like him, but something about her just made him smile. Rather than think why, he obediently reached to pull his shirt over his bare chest.

'You're wearing boxers.' Their eyes met and he saw amusement from her that he didn't understand. There'd been a few of those moments between them and he was learning to let them slide.

He nodded. 'There might be a fire and Granny Mim would be shocked.'

Stella stifled a laugh. 'Granny Mim would be delighted. Though my mother might be shocked.'

He wasn't sure he agreed there. Stella was an interesting woman. Any lady who had raised the woman in front of him had to be interesting. 'Your mother might surprise you. I'm looking forward to knowing her better. I think she has hidden depths that will help me understand you.'

'Really?' Ava smiled. 'We can ask her later. Now you need to pull on your jeans and a jumper because it's freezing out there. I've brought you one of Granny Mim's beanies.'

She waited until he was dressed before she pulled it out from behind her back, and he tried very hard to laugh quietly. It came out more as a snuffle than a laugh.

Ava held it out. 'I said last year's theme was *Weaving the Magic*.' The beanie resembled an intricately knitted magician's hat reminiscent of that worn by Gandalf in *The Lord of the Rings*.

She handed it to him and he pulled it on. It held an incredible fuzzy warmth, but the conical point dipped over his left eye. 'You're kidding me.'

From where he stood, he could see that words had deserted his nurse. Her cheeks were sucked in and her eyes were almost shut as she tried to keep her face straight. He could see the enormous effort she put into not laughing out loud.

With a sudden comical wipe of expression, her face regained composure and she lifted her eyes to his. 'Let's go.'

'Hang on a minute.' He held up his hand. 'Where's *your* Granny Mim hat?'

She grinned at him and produced a blue beanie shaped like a homestead, complete with a sad little gum tree. The verandahs drooped over her ears. '*Spirit of The Land* — my home among the gum trees. Tada!'

'To think I would have missed this if I'd slept in.'

She grinned at him. 'I was hoping you wouldn't.'

They slipped out of Zac's door, straight onto the verandah and around the side of the house to the paddock. Zac was pleased she reached for his hand at the same time as he reached for hers. Then Reggie appeared beside them wagging his tail and Ava scratched his neck with her free fingers. 'You can come too.'

Zac's hand tightened on hers as they moved towards a slight rise, with another hill he hadn't noticed behind it. They hurried up the incline, crunching dirt and scattering rocks as the sky lightened.

She said, 'I try to watch the sunrise in the first couple of days when I come home. It reminds

251

me how it must have looked to Mim when Pop brought her here and it connects me again to the land.'

They crested the slight rise before them to the left of the higher mountains and the view opened, multifaceted, shrouded in the last of the night. Shadowy features of rocks and small trees appeared slowly out of the gloom with the approaching dawn like waiting soldiers in the camouflage of night.

They climbed on top of the red outcrop of boulders, one of half a dozen different-sized rocks, bumping each other like a group of giant marbles waiting for a new game.

He eased down to sit on the scratchy rock, next to the most restful woman in the world, and took her hand again, watching the sun inch fingers of orange paint across the dark vista in front of them. They peered over the roof of an old stone shed below them, which Ava told him had been the original settlers' dwelling.

As it rose in the sky, the sun reflected unevenly off glistening rocks and washed down ravines, until it deepened the colour of the red dirt to the far horizons. The endless vista held a magic he hadn't expected. He also hadn't expected the seeping peace that seemed to fill him at the sight.

As he sat there holding Ava's hand, soaking in the silence, taking in the tranquillity, something seemed to be osmosing into him, like the sun's early rays healing the darkness in his soul. He'd never experienced anything like it and wondered if that was where Ava drew her strength of spirit from. It wasn't hard to imagine that was so. They stayed there, quietly, for almost half an hour.

On the way back down, he listened to Ava talking about her grandparents' adventures and those of their friends, both Indigenous and settler, and the stories of hardship made him appreciate the distance they were from the comforts of the city. Not for the first time he considered that Ava should never leave here, and, more pointedly, that he didn't fit.

This intrepid outback woman had her beliefs nurtured by a never-ending sky, with a vision untethered by human construction, the endless plains tempting her with adventures he'd never thought of. Realistically, he wasn't actually worthy of finding a future with Ava, so it was lucky he didn't expect one.

Back at the homestead, the saliva-inducing aroma of bacon and basil swirled in the air, and Zac couldn't remember ever being so hungry. This truly was turning out to be a place of firsts.

When they walked in, Granny Mim stopped, snorted and cackled with laughter, then demanded she be allowed to take a photo of them for her beanie album.

★   ★   ★

Jock arrived after breakfast. They were taking the Polaris, an all-terrain buggy Jock had picked up second-hand from one of the clearance sales, and it fit three adults comfortably across the front.

'Hana not coming up to the house to wait here?' Ava asked.

'She's got an order that came in last night that

she'd like to start on.' Jock took a cold bag with food and drinks from Stella. 'Thanks, Mum. Did you put any of Mim's Anzacs in there?'

Stella gave him a sardonic look. 'Yes, dear. Your grandmother would like Zac to get some too.'

'What about me?' Ava teased, and Zac watched them all, soaking it in. A family that worked and talked and squabbled and let emotion sit front and centre, not pretending that 'feelings' was a dirty word. Each determined to get their view out there but happy to listen to those of others.

It was incredibly different from the way he'd grown up, which was: *Listen to your parents until you leave home.* Even with Roslyn and their marriage, which had been a little more relaxed than his parents' house, it had never had this sort of playfulness. It was strange, the ease with which he could slip into this rapport. Something he'd lacked in the busy world of medicine. Ava would always be a part of this, and maybe that was why he found her so different and so incredibly appealing. But his time here was short-term and had a purpose. To find his memory. He needed to remember he was trying to remember, he thought with a wry smile.

'Let's go.' Jock's voice broke into his thoughts and he and Ava headed for the door with Jock carrying the cool bag.

Stella pressed a broad-brimmed hat into his hand with a little squeeze. 'Don't do too much. It's supposed to be a fun excursion to show you around. They can forget,' she warned.

He nodded and jammed the old Akubra happily on his head, where it sat worn and soft, with a hole in the brim that gave extra character, something he hadn't expected to feel comfortable in.

Ava smiled at her mother, and he had no doubt there was something significant in the loan. He'd donned a pair of lace-up walking boots for the climbing, though Ava had said they'd do little today. Hopefully he'd be able to keep up.

Ava had her own hat, which looked better than the homestead beanie, and their buttoned, long-sleeved shirts seemed too warm for the day's heat.

They climbed into the all-terrain vehicle and settled back. The vehicle, which was open to the air, had bench seats and swing doors. Jock jogged back to the house for something he'd forgotten and Ava said quietly, 'Jock expects to find dead livestock. That's why I insisted we come with him. Hope that's okay.'

'I remember you said he's taking it hard. I'm happy to help in any way I can.' When Jock returned, he said, 'This vehicle looks like it can climb mountains.'

Jock jumped back in and heard the last part. He patted the bare, dusty dashboard. 'It's a good quad. I like the roll bars — not that we're going to try them out, but sometimes we can be at an angle on a ridge and it can get dicey. It's got a good twelve inches of ground clearance, so it can climb up and over rocks and over stumps if we need to, and it's a mission to get it bogged even in the river sand. I don't try that hard,'

Ava was watching her brother and he could feel the undercurrents of concern she was trying to hide. 'So where are we going?'

Jock glanced at Zac. 'Out the back. There's no feed at all out there. Ava tell you?'

He nodded.

'Good. I want to look at all the trap yards. I've been making them with a plan in mind for the future — the future when the cattle aren't dying.'

Zac looked from one sibling to the other. 'What's a trap yard?'

'A set of cattle yards in the bush with a one-way entry and a one-way exit for cattle,' Ava answered. 'You can put the yards around a water source and they come in, drink and leave again. But if you want to catch or work with particular cattle, you lock the exit and they come in for the water and can't get out until you let them out. Technically,' she added, then glanced at her brother and they both smiled.

It was all fascinating stuff. 'Technically, eh?'

Jock nodded and steered around an ant's nest that was bigger than a grown man. 'If you get a mean enough scrub bull in there, he'll just carry on and demolish the place until you let him out. It's better to give in to him than take him on.'

'So you can muster cattle like that?'

'You can. Though you end up with pockets of cattle near water sources as opposed to a mob at the house yards if the muster crew bring them in and get them loaded onto trucks from the same place. But an overall control system with remote taps could nudge the cattle towards the yards by turning off consecutive troughs and making them search out the next one. It's no good for now as the cattle are too weak, but when the season is good I reckon it would work well.'

He glanced at his sister. 'I've wanted to move to that way of mustering for a couple of years now, but Mum is old-school. And Mim even older. If we went that way, we could look to the future of just using the yards and lose the expense of the stock contractor.'

Ava didn't seem sure because she frowned.

'Muster's a lot of work for us,' Jock added. 'And we're too few. But the contractors wouldn't like that and might not back us if we needed them later. If we still have a station when I'm finished with it.'

'Your ideas will work,' Ava said, but Jock's labile mood had plummeted again. She frowned.

'What are you thinking?' Zac slipped his hand across and took her fingers. He decided she needed comfort. She flashed him a grateful glance which made it all worthwhile.

Jock looked away. 'Maybe we should just sell. Like they did over at Dreamtime.'

Ava and her brother exchanged an unhappy look.

Zac stretched his brain to try to catch the nuances, but his thoughts were less flexible than he wanted. He was also trying to understand the intricacies of running a cattle station. 'So you hire extra people to help with the muster?'

'In the past, yes. And probably this year as well. We hire the already assembled regional gang. The head musterer runs it. He has his own crew, and usually a contact who has an R22 helicopter or two if the mob have really taken to the far boundaries. We don't have the workforce for scattered stock, and he does the rounds of the stations that need manpower. That's his livelihood. But the old man has retired and his son's come home to take over.' Jock glanced at Ava. 'I don't like Jai. Never have.'

Ava screwed up her face and Zac's brain tickled him again. Then it clicked. *Jai. The father of Ava's daughter. The one who wanted to marry a fortune.* No wonder Jock didn't like him. Zac had never met him and he definitely didn't like him.

The flies buzzed annoyingly when they slowed down to a crawl to move over or around obstacles, and the heat in the day was building despite the breeze they were making with the forward motion.

Ava was saying, ' . . . Not so many stations this year either, so if we pull out then the business will be down for them. With the Wilsons gone. Have the new people taken over Dreamtime yet?'

'Just. Mum said it was bought by an Italian guy for his son. Apparently, the son and his wife have been working on stations for a couple of years and Dad has enough money to buy them one. He came over last week with a cut hand.'

'Over here? Mum's met him?' Zac felt Ava stiffen. 'Our new neighbour came over here and she didn't say?'

Jock's eyes were roving across the landscape, unlike his sister's, who watched the road when she drove. But then they weren't on a road, they were driving through a paddock, Zac guessed and winced as Jock ran over a submerged boulder. 'Mum stitched him up and gave him a tetanus shot. Said he seemed pleasant enough.'

'You didn't meet him?' Zac felt Ava's curiosity beside him. 'Did he meet Mim? Funny. Mum didn't mention it when I spoke to her.'

Jock peered at her, then back at something that caught his eye out to the left. 'Why would she?'

'She doesn't get that many visitors, and it's not exactly commonplace for a new neighbour to drop in. Especially for an injury. She's usually full of that sort of news.'

'Not lately.' Jock shrugged. 'She's not that forthcoming.' Then he pursed his mouth. 'I do remember Mim mumbling something about how she missed out on meeting him and Mum being all flustered. Then our mother shut her up. Maybe she's not game to mention him in case Mim starts again?'

Zac could tell Jock thought it wasn't an interesting topic, yet Ava leaned towards her brother, particularly intrigued. The dynamics amused Zac and he wondered what it would have been like for his own childhood to have had siblings to squabble with. Roslyn had been an only child as well, and hadn't taken teasing well, and that was possibly why she'd been in no hurry to have babies. Another regret . . . He pulled his mind away from the past.

They rounded a large outcrop of rock and tufts of some flowering grass, and he saw the first of the cattle under a tree not too far to the left of where they were driving. 'Are they Brahman?'

'Mostly, though we have Charolais, Senepol and Brahman crosses as well.' Ava pointed out the different breeds.

The beasts were bigger than he expected, predominantly white or brown, most with the Brahman floppy ears and long noses. 'Is there a water source around here?' He couldn't see how. They were out in the middle of what looked like a desert.

'There's a bore that feeds a trough, so we'll check that while we're here. The cattle come between one and three times a day to drink. This is another area I want to put the yards on, but for the moment the musterers would just drive them back towards the main yards from here. Some of the other properties are remote-controlling the far bores and bringing the cattle in closer to the yards by shutting off the water sources the way I'm looking to do.'

'Ava said I could join the muster.'

Jock nodded. 'Sure. The more the merrier. Mustering's a big workload when it happens. Up before sunrise, doesn't finish till after dark, sleeping out in a swag, so it's cold and no showers. Can't waste time getting to and from the mob by driving back and forth, so we need to cook and maintain a camp as well.'

Ava cut in, 'If you've got a dozen people that's a bit of work.'

Zac was seeing that. 'I can imagine.'

Ava's gaze flicked to her brother and she smiled. 'That's where Mum comes into her own. She's the best camp cook in the Territory and

Granny Mim is good at sorting problems. Jock is good at managing the stock problems.'

Ava was bouncing on the seat beside Zac, and he realised he'd lost her hand when she'd pointed something out earlier. He might have to get that back. 'And what are you good at?' he asked.

'I'm the peacemaker, and the dogsbody.' She smiled at her brother. 'And I look pretty.'

Jock laughed. 'You do at that.'

She was more than that. 'You look beautiful,' Zac corrected her, his sudden need to say that surprising him.

Jock peered over his sunglasses and Ava caught the look and said primly, 'Thank you, Zac.'

They travelled around the closest paddocks, pointing out the direction of the local Aboriginal community, and then the trails that led towards the rising MacDonnell Ranges. They drove to the top of Lone Tree Hill, a local landmark with the graves from their family dating back to their grandfather Max's father, the first settler of Setabilly.

While Jock drove off to check another set of troughs, Zac and Ava set the thermos and the contents of the esky out for morning tea. When she lifted a section out of the bag she laughed.

'Mum's put in some fresh sausage rolls and a bottle of tomato sauce. Jock'll be in seventh heaven — he'll want to travel with you more often. We're getting spoiled.'

Zac leaned over and peered into the bag. 'Happy to be of service.' He couldn't remember if anyone had ever packed a picnic basket for him. Or put something special away like Granny Mim's Anzacs or Stella's sausage rolls. Another poor little rich boy moment that he needed to get over.

Soon they'd eaten far too much and packed away the remains, the sun was past the middle of the sky and Jock looked at the blue sky above them. 'We'll head down to skirt the bottom of the ranges, steering into indents in the rock, looking for canyons or a place where cattle could be caught by weakness,'

They found half a dozen cattle, enough to make them all pale. Jock went silent as he dealt with those he couldn't save and mapped the ones he'd come back for. With each successive tragedy, Jock withdrew further into himself.

Zac watched Ava grow more concerned as she assessed her brother's mood. 'We should go back,' she said. 'I want to check on Jessamine over at the community today or tomorrow. Mim will be wondering where we are and it's Zac's first day back doing normal activities.'

Jock grimaced and turned for home. 'I guess.'

Ava had explained that the whole family depended on the number of breeding cattle to get them through the lean years, so Zac could understand his devastation.

'We'll just check the trap yard in the next gully. Then we'll go back. I haven't been out here for a few days,' Jock muttered.

This time Jock noted the marks of a small herd that had stood for a while, whether too tired to move they couldn't tell. 'Okay. We'll go home.'

But Jock set his face and said, 'I'll be coming back.'

'If you do come back,' Zac said quietly, 'I'd like to come with you.'

Jock raised his brows and nodded his head in acknowledgement. 'Sure. Be glad of your company.'

Ava didn't say anything, but Zac could tell by her face that she was relieved he'd offered.

33

Ava

The next morning, Ava drove with Zac over to the local Indigenous community to talk to Jessamine. The community lay spread across the expanse of desert, a busy, dusty place, with the occasional motorbike or old car, and a group of shirtless young men playing footy on a patch of bare earth out to the side of the settlement.

A drop-in with Zac seemed a good opportunity to have a doctor cast his eye over the twins now that they were more than a week old. Zac carried the big first-aid kit Ava never left home without. Normally, Ava would check the babies herself, but she wanted to share her world with Zac and this was one of the best parts of it — reconnecting with mothers and babies in their own environments. The prospect of seeing Jessamine and her twins again made her wish she'd phoned Denise.

'I should have asked Denise to come out and meet us there, but it's too late now. We should have come yesterday, but the light was fading by the time we made it home after touring the boundary fences.'

'And Stella had been adamant that I rest before tea,' Zac said dryly.

Ava laughed. Last night, she'd seen Zac's

eyebrows rise at her mother's bossy orders, which amused her, probably unkindly, but still. Zac wasn't used to it. She couldn't help if it tickled her sense of humour to see him take himself to his room with a frown. But this morning, even her mother couldn't complain about how well he looked. It was a shame Ava's heart didn't feel so healthy.

She dragged her thoughts back to their task. Hopefully Jessamine, who'd been home for a few days now, would be able to see them unless she'd gone north to see relatives.

'The birth was amazing,' Ava was saying as she steered into the sprawling settlement.

Zac said, 'It'd be nice to remember that I've seen a spontaneous twin birth. And breech!'

That's not all you can't remember, Ava thought wistfully. She wished there were a brain exercise she could offer him, but there was only the healing of time. All she said was, 'We don't have breeches every day. And no more babies until I get back to work, please. Did you want to tell Jessamine about your memory loss, or do you want to just wing it?'

He looked weary as he thought about explaining. 'I'll wing it.'

When they arrived, they found Jessamine sitting on a blanket under a tree, Mother Earth with her two little babies feeding twin fashion at the breast. Ava's heart swelled at the sight and she beamed at the young mum.

'Look at you, sitting up there as relaxed as a grandmother. Go you, Jessamine.'

Jessamine smiled shyly at both of them, and

glanced at Vivian, a woman Ava had shared midwifery care with in Alice Springs two years ago. Vivian, a cousin of Big Jim's, knew Ava well as her baby had been born premature, and she'd had to spend weeks in Alice waiting for him to grow enough to come home.

Ava had tried to be available for Viv in the beginning, during her visits to the neonatal nursery. Their rapport was obvious by the warm smile Viv sent Ava, and Ava sighed with relief to see her. She hadn't been sure Jessamine had friends yet, and Viv would be a support person with good sense.

'Viv — ' she gestured to Zac — 'this is Dr Zac. Zac, this is Vivian. Dr Zac was there when Jessamine had her babies, so I brought him with me today. I thought Jessamine might like him to check the babies over?'

'Good to meet you, Vivian,' Zac smiled at Viv.

Ava explained, 'I was lucky enough to be at Vivian's son's birth — a terror of a two-year-old now.' As if on cue, a dark-skinned, dark-eyed cherub appeared from behind his mother, clutching a battered green truck. 'Ahh, there you are, Willy. When he was born he was as big as your hand, Zac'

Zac smiled. 'Hello there, Willy.' They all pretended they didn't see Jessamine taking the babies off the breast and tucking herself discreetly away. When she had covered herself, Zac turned to her.

'What do you think, Jessamine? Would you like me to look at your boys?'

'Be good,' Jessamine agreed. 'He makes a

noise when he breathes and this one's got a funny belly button.'

Zac smiled at that. 'That sounds like healthy variations of normal, but let's start with our noisy one. What's this man's name?'

'Jarrah.'

'A good, strong name.' Ava watched Zac with his calm, friendly manner and the way he put Jessamine at ease while examining her babies. It made her heart ache for what might have been — a desert medical duo reaching out to those in need — and she turned away, blinking away the sting in her eyes as she gathered the little set of portable baby scales.

After Zac examined each baby, she weighed the little one then handed the naked baby back to his mother to dress. She wrote the weights down to pass on to the child-and-family nurses for their records.

Vivian had left; she'd taken Willy's hand and they were small figures in the distance walking along the dusty road on some errand. Another mum hustled her toddler towards Zac, and Ava wondered if all the mothers would bring their children to see the doctor. Zac would enjoy that and the mums would be pleased to have any concerns clarified by him.

They'd seen most of the small children and had begun preparing to leave when the roar of a motorbike made them look up. The motorbike skidded to a halt beside them and the boy riding it gasped, 'Viv, on the road! She needs the doctor now!' He waved his hand behind him. 'I didn't see him.'

'What happened?' Zac voice was calm but firm.

The boy gulped, his eyes wild. 'Willy. His arm. I hit him with the bike.' His big dark eyes pleaded with Ava to understand. 'I didn't see him. He ran out.'

Ava scooped up the first-aid kit they'd just packed. 'We'll go. I know it was an accident,' said Ava quietly. 'Go find Willy's dad and ask him to come and help Viv.'

The young man looked terrified at the thought; Ava didn't blame him. 'Can you find an elder and they might go with you?' The boy nodded, relief clear in his eyes, and he took off at a run, leaving his motorbike on its side in the dirt.

Ava took off at a brisk pace towards the vehicle with Zac close behind her. A couple of kilometres down the road they found Viv kneeling in the dirt clutching 'Willy to her chest and they pulled over next to her.

Willy lay in his mother's arms, a red welt crossing his thigh where the bike tyres had caught him, his mouth wide as he hollered his distress and thrashed. One thin arm lay obviously damaged across his chest, and every time Willy moved it he screamed louder. Zac's eyes met Ava's as he nodded at it.

Zac eased Willy from his mother as they knelt beside her, careful not to move the arm, and lay the screaming child down on the ground in front of them to quickly assess him. Zac's big hands ran gently across the child's stomach and thighs, the latter causing a shudder from the little boy as he pulled away, but the main damage seemed to be from Willy putting out his arm to protect himself.

'His arm needs looking at, but the rest should be fine in a few days, Vivian,' Zac soothed her. 'Though he needs to be taken into Alice. You can see it's out of shape.'

Viv sobbed a croaking agreement.

'Zac and I will bind his arm to his chest, get the RFDS to come pick him up, and they'll set his arm when he gets there.'

Ava put her arm around Viv's shoulder. Willy continued to holler every time Zac adjusted the sling. 'He's very loud,' Zac said with a smile. 'He'll grow up to have a very impressive voice when he's big.'

'And that's a good sign. He's well enough to let us know he's not happy,' Ava said, giving Viv's shoulder a squeeze.

Tears streamed down Vivian's face, but she was calming and Ava soothed her. 'Poor little Willy. Poor Viv. Your boy is determined to cause you worry. One day, he'll have babies of his own and then he'll see what worry does.'

Viv hiccuped a small laugh and sniffed, and she nodded. 'He's so fast. Here one minute, gone the next.' She glared at the spot on the road where it had happened. 'That boy shouldn't be riding so fast on the bike.'

'No, he shouldn't.' Ava shook her head in agreement. 'You reckon that will be Willy one day? Riding bikes too fast on the road?'

Viv gave Ava a rueful nod. 'Maybe.' Then she said, 'You got that phone you always carry?'

Everyone knew Ava was the one with the sat phone. 'Yep. We'll phone for the plane. They can land on Setabilly and Mum will give you a nice cup of tea while we wait.'

They strapped young Willy up with his arm to his chest and sedated him, and by the time they got Viv and her son back to the homestead, the RFDS were on their way. They were lucky. Sometimes it took longer for response depending on the emergency calls, but today they'd be there soon.

34

Hana

An hour later, the RFDS aircraft arrived on the
station airstrip with the flight nurse. Hana drove
out to pick up the nurse in Ava's car and brought
her to the homestead. Another car pulled up at
the same time and a tall, dark-haired, older gentleman climbed out as Hana directed the nurse
through to the house. She walked over to see
what he wanted.

He bowed his head with an Old World gesture.
'I am Lorenzo DeFortelli.'

Hana smiled. This was different. 'I'm Hana
May. What can I do for you, Mr DeFortelli?'

'It is I come to see if. I can help you. I heard
the emergency flight and I've come to see if
Stella, Mrs May — ' he sent a hopeful look
towards the house — 'requires assistance?'

'Ah, thank you. You know my mother-in-law?'

'Yes, she was kind enough to repair my injured
hand last week. Though we have met before. I
came across from Dreamtime Station.'

Oh my goodness, Hana thought with a
suppressed smile. 'Our neighbour. Yes. I heard.
Thank you for the kind thought. Stella is well. A
small child from the community has had an
accident and they are flying him back to Alice.
Would you like to come in?'

Stella hadn't said he was gorgeous. 'The doctor says the child will recover well.' She gestured to the house. 'Stella's daughter is a midwife and her doctor friend is with her. We're fine, but you're welcome to come in.'

How fascinating that this lovely man had rushed over to see if Stella was okay. Hana had been intrigued by the way Stella had brushed off Mim's and Hana's questions about him last week, and they both wanted to meet him. Mim had been dying to, actually. She could see now why Stella had been flustered. He was a middle-aged hunk. 'Come in. Stella will be pleased to see you.'

Lorenzo shook his head. 'No. No. There are enough people if another family is involved. As long as all is well.'

As long as Stella is well, you mean? This good-looking man had been worried about Stella. And he had such a commanding stance. That thick head of hair, greying at the temples in just the right amount, made him extremely distinguished.

Hana wasn't letting him get away that easily. Mim would kill her if she did. 'Then come tomorrow for morning tea. Ten o'clock. Stella can tell you all about it. It's good for us to have visitors.'

Lorenzo nodded and smiled, and Hana wanted to grab Ava and whisper the news to her, but Ava and Stella would be busy with the child and his mother until they were transferred. She smiled as she watched him stride with that particular European elegance back to his expensive car.

She couldn't wait to tell Ava. She might leave Jock to find out a little later. He could be a little over-protective.

35

Ava

The next morning, Zac and Jock went off to 'check the bores and fences' just before ten, and Ava watched them go with a small frown because she hadn't been invited.

Hana waggled her brows. 'I've been wanting to catch you alone. They'll be fine, Jock likes him and Zac understands about life and death with humans so he can listen to Jock's heartbreak with the animals. He took me aside and said he'd talk to Jock about the mood changes and suggest that he make an appointment with a psychologist next time we're in Alice. I almost threw my arms around him. It's a big ask for a man who's really a guest.'

Ava touched Hana's shoulder in sympathy. 'I'm glad. He'll be good.'

Hana lifted her chin, and if her smile was a little forced then Ava was still happy to see it. 'In lighter news, I want you here and Jock out of the way for our visitor this morning.' She rolled her eyes. 'My darling husband can be a bit off-putting until he gets to know people.'

Ava remembered Jock's response to Zac holding her hand yesterday. 'Which people?' Her brother needed to get out more and stop carrying the worries of the world on his shoulders. 'Who's our

274

visitor?' They both sat down next to Mim, who held a pot of tea for refills.

Hana glanced towards the hallway and lowered her voice. 'Lorenzo DeFortelli's coming over for morning tea to see your mother.'

'Is that the Italian who bought Dreamtime?' Ava didn't understand. 'The one Mum sutured the other day?' Hana raised her brows suggestively and Mim nodded gleefully. 'Why is he coming?'

'Hana asked him.' Mim looked archly satisfied, while Ava wondered how her sister-in-law and grandmother had managed to arrange this 'surprise' for her mother.

'Does Mum know?'

Hana's eyes sparkled. 'He arrived last night at the same time as the RFDS to check we were okay, but wouldn't come in. He's a lovely man who seemed relieved it wasn't Stella they'd come for. We told Stella he asked to visit today and that we'd offered morning tea.'

'Did he really ask to come?' Ava's scepticism didn't come out as subtle as she meant it to. As if Mim or Hana cared.

'Sort of.'

'Shhhhh. She's coming.' Mim jumped up, hurried over to the sink and picked up a tea towel. Hana stood and reached for the broom. Ava raised her brows and sipped her tea. They were mad. There were no dishes to dry and she was pretty sure her mum would have already swept. She watched Mim grab a clean cup out of the cupboard and polish it furiously.

When Stella walked in, Ava realised her

mother had actually put on mascara and perhaps a bit of blusher. Curiouser and curiouser. Maybe Mim and Hana had it right?

Stella said, 'Where's Zac?'

Trying to keep a straight face, Ava gestured vaguely towards the hills. 'He went with Jock to check the bores.'

Her mother frowned. 'Mim and Jock did that two days ago.'

Ava could see Granny Mim gesturing behind her mother's back for her to carry on, and her control stretched. She racked her brain as she tried to remain composed. 'Zac seems interested in the running of the station.'

'Oh. Okay.' Stella tilted her head at her, staring her down. 'I like him, Ava. Despite the fact that you've known him less than a week and already slept with him.'

That wiped the smile off her face. Hana's broom stilled. Ava threw her hands up in the air. 'Is nothing sacred around here?'

Stella's 'No' made Ava wave her away. *Grrr.*

'Tea,' said Mim. 'The first cup of tea of the day is sacred. Nobody says a cross word until after that.'

Ava and Stella both looked at her. Ava growled, 'Right. We had that at six this morning.'

'I know,' said Mim. 'You asked if anything was sacred. That's all I was saying.'

Mim was saved by the sound of a vehicle pulling up on the gravel. Her eyes sparkled. 'You get it, Stella — I just want to dash to the bathroom.' Hana slipped out to the laundry with the broom.

Stella peeked hopefully at Ava, who said innocently, 'Who is it?'

Her mother spun on her heel and headed for the front door. Ava saw her quickly checking herself in the mirror on the way and she had to smile. Mim and Hana reappeared magically, all discomfort gone. Mum was on the back foot now. Ava had to hand it to them. 'Go, you guys. I'm impressed.'

36

Ava

Hana, Mim and Ava craned their necks as they peered avidly through the kitchen window. Her mother was making lots of hand movements and the man was watching her with a small smile on his face. As they turned to come back inside, Mim and Ava collided in their haste to get away from the window and Hana laughed. They'd only just managed to stop giggling by the time her mother returned.

The colour was high in Stella's cheeks when she brought the big man through to the kitchen. 'Lorenzo, you've met Hana, apparently, but this is my daughter, Ava, and my mother, Mirium Mason.'

Lorenzo DeFortelli stood almost six feet tall, had muscular arms and a barrel chest. A bear of a man who moved with surprising lightness of foot as he entered. Ava decided he was probably a few years older than her mother, judging by the brush of expensively cut hair that held distinguished grey around his temples, and the creases from laughter etching lines at the corner of his kind eyes. Ava had met few Italians and wondered if many older Italian men looked this George Clooney-esque in their expensive shirts and trousers. He was also extremely polite and gazed warmly at Stella. She could see why her mother was flustered if she was the reason he'd called.

Lorenzo made an infinitesimal but elegant bow. 'Enchanted, Miss Ava. Mrs Mason.'

'Call me Mim, please, Lorenzo,' her grand-mother said.

Ava resisted the urge to say, *Just Ava.* 'Nice to meet you, Lorenzo.' He held out his hand and she shook, and slowly, while still holding his hand, turned his wrist. 'Nice stitches.'

'She is clever, no?' Lorenzo laughed and it was a deep, delighted chuckle that had Ava smiling too. They dropped hands. There was something vaguely familiar about him, but she couldn't catch it. 'Your mother repaired my foolishness very neatly.'

'She's a good cook, too,' Mim said and deftly avoided the daggers Stella shot her way. 'The jug's boiled,' she went on blithely. 'Would you like tea or coffee?'

'Black coffee,' Stella said for him and Ava hid her smile. She was so glad not to have missed this, or worse, to have had Jock in tow.

They all sat at the table and Mim brought out her Anzac biscuits, and Stella had made one of her special carrot cakes with lemon icing and a magnificent bacon-and-onion quiche. Hana sat quietly amused. *Quite the party*, Ava thought, and tried not to catch her sister-in-law's eye in case she laughed.

Lorenzo complimented her mother on every-thing, and Mim on her biscuits. He turned to her. 'Do you cook, Ava?'

'Ava makes very nice scones,' her grandmother said loyally. That was about all Ava made. Cooking held no interest for her and her grandmother knew it.

'Thank you, Mim.' She gestured to the food on the laden table. 'Do you cook, Lorenzo?'

'*Si*, though I have no one to cook for. My wife passed five years ago. My son and his wife met while backpacking in Australia two years ago. She is from Australia. These young ones are fearless.' He shook his head.

'I thought you buying Dreamtime was a little fearless,' Stella said with a shake of her head.

'No. You thought it foolish when you discovered it, but you will see. Again, you underestimate me, Stella.'

What was Stella underestimating? Ava raised her brows at her mother, who looked away.

Lorenzo caught the silent question between them and went on smoothly. 'I digress. My son, Leo, and his wife, Aimee, have worked on cattle stations in your Northern Territory for several years now and have held their wish to return here to Central Australia.' He shrugged. 'So I came to see last year, and I too — ' here he glanced at Stella — 'was drawn by everything.' He shrugged. 'My wealth is only to see my family happy. Happiness is all that I need.'

He certainly appeared happy while he was watching her mother. 'I look forward to meeting them.' Ava thought an outback station a particularly radical gift for his son, but she wished them well. If the son was used to working on stations, then with a good manager they'd work things out. It would be good for Jock to have young people near, too. Interesting changes were afoot.

'*Si*. And they you. They are in Sydney at present with plans for the station. I am home alone — ' he spread his hands and pretended a mournful face — 'except for my Mrs Digby, the keeper of house.' He looked at Stella. 'And the cows. In Italy we have the Chianina, they are the oldest breed in the world. I will cook the *bistecca alla fiorentina* for you all one day with this meat and see how it turns.'

'Turns out,' Stella corrected gently.

'*Si*. Turns out.' Another warm glance was directed at her mother.

'Thank you for coming over last night. It was very thoughtful of you.' Stella gushed a little and Ava stared. Her mother caught the look. 'Lorenzo and I met at last year's races. Do you remember, Ava?'

Ahhh. Now she remembered seeing him in the crowd. 'I did think you were familiar.' Her mother had been flustered and unlike herself at the time. Behaving pretty similarly to this, actually. She'd thought then that it was just not her mum's scene in her unaccustomed heels, though there'd been a small crowd she'd stood with. A merry crowd. 'How lovely.' This delightful man obviously remembered Stella very well.

'Have you decided to settle in Australia, Lorenzo, or are you having an extended holiday?' And her mother worried about her future with Zac. Italy was a long way away, so did this even have a future?

'My son is settled, so I will not be far. I retain my villa in Italy, but my plans are fluid for the moment. It is not the place that is important but the people.' This was said with a long look at her mother.

Her mother actually blushed and Ava caught Mim's look. Her grandmother's satisfaction dusted the situation with another layer. If Mim was happy, and Hana avidly interested, then this situation had a history she'd been unaware of. But then that was fair. She hadn't talked to her mother about the true situation with Zac.

By the time Lorenzo had left, Ava was pretty darn sure her usually sober mother was slightly drunk with infatuation. Of all the left-field occurrences, this was the biggest she'd seen for a while, Zac notwithstanding.

37

Stella

It was after morning tea, on the fifth day since Ava had arrived home, when Stella May climbed the rocky hill to calm the agitation in her chest. The others were out in the back paddocks somewhere, and she'd cleared the benches and tidied. But the tablecloth of her family stability felt as if it were fraying at the edges on all sides and her own inner turmoil wasn't helping anyone.

For the last few days, Stella had watched her daughter battle to keep the heartbreak out of her eyes and her hands to herself. Stella knew just how that felt. She never saw Ava touch Zac, except for that day of hand-holding that never returned.

She saw that Zac listened to Ava with intent concentration and appeared to soak up everything about the world that was Setabilly Station with avid interest, but the distance between them was growing and Stella suspected it was a kindness of Zac's doing that he had taken a step back.

In Ava, Stella saw the aching loss, and the gradual acceptance that while Zac had no memories, he would return to Sydney and the relationship would progress no further than the making of a 'lovely' friendship.

The proposal Ava had quietly shared with Mim and Stella after Lorenzo's visit, but it was never mentioned to Zac. Everyone skirted the edges of their strained relationship as if it were a minefield.

Stella wished Lorenzo was there. It was extremely uncharacteristic of her to look for support from others. She stood alone, had done for twenty-four years, so why now did she need support?

But the empty kitchen didn't make her want to cook and the silent house didn't ask her to clean. Even the dog had wandered off, because Jock and Hana had gone for a drive. Mim was resting. Everyone was doing something except her, the cattle were weak and the ground dry, and her brain gyrated and galloped with the worries of the week, with no one to spill it out to. She really wanted to walk and stomp and shout, but an unusual loneliness stopped her.

The arrival of a car out the front jerked her head up. She knew the sound of that engine, so she turned and walked, with the occasional slip in the gravel in her haste, back to the house. *Slow down, goose,* she admonished herself but couldn't help the sigh of relief and anticipation that he'd come.

'How did you do that?' she said as she made it to the driveway and marched across to meet him.

Lorenzo climbed gracefully from his seat, smiled at her and stepped close. 'Do what, *bella*?'

284

She gestured a little wildly with her hand in a half-circle. 'Arrive when I'd just admitted to myself that I wished you were here.'

He steepled his hands in a very Italian gesture. 'It is our connection, *cara*. We transcend mere telephones.'

She snorted. 'I don't believe you.'

He slid his arm around her and drew her close. 'I missed you. It is good you missed me.' Then he shrugged. 'Also, your mother rang. She believed you could benefit from my company this afternoon. She is an excellent woman.'

Stella couldn't believe her mother had done that. Her cheeks heated in dismay. 'I'll kill her.'

'And I will kiss her.' He bent his head, 'And you,' Which he did with a quirk of his brows and with masculine thoroughness. By the time he had finished, she wanted to kiss her mother too.

He let her go but held onto her hand. 'Is it so bad that I am here?'

'No,' she mumbled into his solid chest. Had she said that grudgingly? Her mouth felt soft and swollen and her head half dazed. She needed to be careful of that — the man could sweep her away with his kisses.

It was only the second time he'd kissed her and it was even better than the first. He was moving the pace along. She wasn't sure she was ready, but it felt so damn good to be held again.

His voice vibrated in his chest under her cheek. 'You could say 'grazie for coming, Lorenzo'.'

She made an exasperated noise in her throat. 'Don't push your luck.'

He laughed, stepped back and let her go. 'Come, *cara*. Let us walk along this dusty Australian track. Share your thoughts from the last few days while you show me these little houses your mother has so cleverly designed.'

She glanced once back at the homestead, considered taking the sat phone, and decided against it. If anyone was worried, they could ask her mother. As for herself, she was already feeling better. She took his strong hand in hers and it felt so good, she didn't give a damn if anyone saw them. Everyone else seemed to think her attraction to Lorenzo was a great idea, so why was she fighting it? And how could she not be attracted to him when he made her feel like the desirable woman she'd thought she'd lost?

38

Ava

By the end of the fifth day, Ava's strain of having Zac here, but not here, felt like the weight of a big Brahman bull tied across her shoulders.

Zac was still polite, unintentionally endearing, and interested in all the things he'd been interested in when they'd first begun to discuss each other's lives in Alice. But the loss of her lover had broken Ava's heart, and sitting next to him on the verandah now, watching the lowering sun cast shadows along the ridge, made her eyes sting.

'So, Dreamtime stories tonight over at the community?' Zac asked into the silence between them.

She couldn't do it. Couldn't sit in the dark with Zac and imagine what it should have been like if he had remembered what lay between them. Her reserve of strength for today was gone. 'Poddy's offered to take you. Something's cropped up that I need to do tonight.' *I need to get rid of this depressing headache*, she thought.

Zac had turned to cast a searching look in her direction and she was relieved to see Hana's brother walking towards them, 'Here he comes now.'

They both turned towards the approaching stockman. Poddy epitomised the glory of the

Maori with his big, dark eyes in his big-boned face and swirling tattooed sleeves on his muscular arms and legs. Like a haka-roaring footballer, Poddy seemed larger than life, but his soul was gentle, and after the death of their parents, his protective love for his sister had carried him across the Tasman Sea to share her life in Australia, where he'd slipped with remarkable ease into the role of foreman for Jock.

Poddy had taken Ava aside today and shared his concern about Jock. They'd agreed he'd take Zac to the stories tonight and discuss Hana's worries. Ava would ask Zac if he thought they should speed up the referral for help.

'Hey, bro.' Poddy slapped Zac on the shoulder and Ava winced at the solid blow. Lucky it was his good side, though the idea of knocking some memory into Zac was beginning to appeal. She sighed inwardly — she really did need a timeout.

'We gonna tie a bit on and sink a few beers?' Poddy's jovial greeting made Ava smile and almost wish she was going with them now. She probably needed that sort of recreation more than Zac.

'Sounds good.' Zac stood. 'I'll keep in mind the recent head injury.' He said this with a smile at Ava and one last glance towards her. 'Sure you don't want to come?'

'Can't.' She kept it short.

Poddy cast her a searching look. Ava knew Hana had told him her problem with Zac. 'I'll teach him what I've learned with the didgeridoo. Should be a laugh.' Poddy was notoriously bad at the didgeridoo.

'Sorry I'll miss it.' Ava could smile at that.

'Liar.' Poddy grinned at her and she thought again how lucky they all were to have him in their lives. 'Come on then, Doc'

When she'd waved them off, she went back inside where her mother and Lorenzo stood quite close to each other as they looked out the window towards the river. Cups and saucers were set out on the low table. Formal supper in the sitting room?

Stella directed Lorenzo to the large chair, and she sat and patted the couch beside her for Ava.

'You look less pale but more worn out,' her mother said with a hint of worry in her voice, and Ava straightened her shoulders. She was fine. Her mother looked so much better now than she had when Ava had first come home. At least someone's love life was being sorted out.

There was no doubt Lorenzo appeared happy too. He said, 'I am sorry your Zac still has no memory.'

And now everyone was feeling sorry for her. Better and better. *Not.* 'Thank you.'

When his gaze moved to her mother, Lorenzo's admiration for Stella shone for a moment and then was hidden. Ava wondered when he'd first realised her mum was for him. She couldn't help a trickle of self-pity when she thought of what it would mean to have Zac look at her in such a way again.

Granny Mim returned with a pot of tea and Lorenzo jumped up to take it and set it down for her. Mim took a seat and Stella leaned forward to pour the tea when the four of them were settled. Small sections of a slice were arranged on a plate, so ordinary and pleasant, yet her world had been shaken and stirred like a bloody mary cocktail.

To add to the surreal environment of normality, her mother said, 'Lorenzo and I went for a walk. He's very impressed with your cottages, Mother.'

'Jock and Poddy built them.' Mim still seemed out of sorts, though she smiled. 'But thank you. I must show you my workshop one day.'

'I would like that.' Lorenzo's sincerity was obvious.

Mim nodded and smiled for a brief moment before the smile fell from her face. Her eyes were full of worry when they landed on Ava. 'How.are you, sweetie? No breakthroughs today?'

Ava truly didn't intend to say anything in front of their guest, but you know what? It was okay that Lorenzo was there, especially if the vibes she was getting meant what she thought they did. And she needed to unload. 'I think the hardest thing is we'd only just found each other and now he's forgotten.' Ava leaned into her mother and rested her head and closed her eyes against the sting. Her mother's hand stroked her hair.

'I know. It's so hard being strong.'

Her mother would know. She studied her concerned face. They did need to share more. She said softly, 'I never believed in love at first sight, Mum. I do now.' She qualified the statement. 'It grew from the first moment we saw each other. He said that too, and now his memory of it all is lost.'

'Love is the hardest thing to trust and you've had your challenges. But it will come back to him. I'm sure of it.'

Ava gave a bitter little laugh. 'That's what I thought. Five days he's been here and now I'm not so sure. I thought coming here would help. It's tough with him treating me like a stranger.'

'I have a prescription for you,' her mum said, patting Ava's hand. 'You need a timeout for Ava and her worries. Less than a week ago you were in an accident too. You were shocked, and you saved a life. Probably at the end of a very torrid time at work before your holidays?'

The question hung in the air and Ava closed her eyes. Yes, the past week and all its dramas were all there behind her eyelids. 'Hmm,' she agreed.

'It's surprising, really, that you're still standing after the week you've had. I prescribe a virtual holiday. Just for twelve hours. You shelve everything for tonight. Take time out. I'll hold all of your problems here.' She tapped her chest. 'Safe. You'll go to bed early, sleep and rest for twelve hours. Then we'll see what happens when you have your reserves back.'

It was a nice fantasy. 'How can I do that?' Ava sat up and squared her shoulders as if to take up her burdens again, and Stella stroked her hair.

'Try.' Stella tilted her chin and looked into her daughter's eyes. 'I'll relieve you. Pretend I'm your midwife. You know you do the same for those mums who have problems with their babies and they've tried everything. The ones who struggle into the maternity ward totally exhausted, not

291

knowing which way to turn, totally bushed.' She lifted her hands. 'I'm your midwife. It's your turn. Forget your troubles briefly.'

Ava rolled her eyes. 'I don't have breastfeeding problems, Mum!'

'You're sleep-deprived and stressed, with a recent head injury.' Stella hugged her. 'Is it surprising then that the most resilient girl in the world thinks everything is too much?' She patted her hand. 'Your problems will all still be there when you get back from your timeout. We'll all be here for you. But your head will be clearer.'

Ava sagged into the lounge. Could she just pass it all over for the night? Pretend her mother held it all between her capable hands in a fanciful ball, like one of Mim's skeins of wool for her beanies? Ava met her mother's gaze with her own and admitted the idea held sense. 'It does sound wonderful.'

'It's done. I have all your troubles here.' She patted her chest. 'Now, I'll make you a special pot of chamomile-and-vanilla tea and tell Zac when he comes back that you've gone to bed. Tomorrow is a new day and will come soon enough.'

★　★　★

When Ava woke the next morning, she did feel surprisingly more in control. Mim arrived with the first cup of tea for her and then perched on the side of the bed.

'How do you feel, Ava?'

She couldn't believe it. 'Better. I don't know

how Mum did it, but I did seem to be able to turn off my whirling brain for the night. Maybe the tea helped.' She sat up straighter and took the cup and saucer. 'Thank you, Mim.' She could breathe without a heavy weight on her chest, which was a good thing. 'If his memory doesn't return and we don't end up together, then perhaps the magic I thought we had was grounded in an illusion.'

'Oh, darling.' Mim struggled with not offering advice and lost. 'Are you sure you shouldn't just tell him he proposed?'

'Positive.' She kept her voice level. 'I refuse to make him feel trapped.'

With a supreme effort of will, Mim said, 'You know what's best for you.' She squeezed Ava's hand. 'Be yourself. He has to fall in love with you. I have no idea how he's held out for so long. How could he not?'

Ava thought about the last night before they'd left for their ill-fated proposal. Zac staring down at her as he bared his soul. Why hadn't she said yes then and there, and gone to Uluru the next day? *No*, she told herself. She would not languish in the what-ifs and maybes. That way lay the tension she'd vowed this morning she'd release. Instead, she would be grateful that they were alive and still had the chance to rediscover each other.

She would hold on to hope until the very last moment before he left Setabilly. She just prayed he'd give them time.

★ ★ ★

293

The new beginning started at breakfast.

'Hello, Zac,' she said brightly. He looked up and she smiled because he was alive. He could have been brain-damaged. Maimed. Dead. She was thankful!

In truth, the man seemed determined to scare the dickens out of her. Yes. It was wonderful to see him whole. He appeared a little startled by the warmth of her greeting, and the last thing she wanted to do was scare him away, so she explained.

'I've been thinking about the accident, so it's good to see you looking so well.' She shook her head and sat down, trying not to stare. He was so broad and sexy, and she just wanted to feel him wrap her in his arms and tell her it had ail been a bad dream, but for him there were no 'magic times' between them, no memories, certainly no proposal. She drew a breath. *Things can turn out well if you allow yourself to trust,* she told herself. *Trust.*

He put his spoon down in the middle of eating to look at her and she gestured to the teapot. 'Would you like a refill?'

He nodded and she filled his cup so carefully it could have been liquid gold. She needed something normal to say. 'Did you enjoy your evening with Poddy?'

His face lit up. 'The stories! And the didgeridoo. Did you know didgeridoos are made from logs hollowed out by white ants?'

He was so animated. A lovely man eager for new experiences, just not *her* lovely man. 'Yes,' she said, shutting down that line of thought.

'There's a gorgeous Dreamtime story of the first didgeridoo. Denise's husband, Ernie, tells it really well. If you see him when you're here we'll ask him.'

Then she did something she'd avoided the whole time he'd been here. 'I know we decided to let things work themselves out, but does it upset you to talk about your memory loss?'

Zac shook his head and his shoulders lowered a fraction with an obvious release of tension. He sat back in his chair. 'It's not interesting for anybody but me.' He shrugged. 'And thankfully, you. But I haven't wanted to upset you by asking about the accident.'

There was a new eagerness to him, as if he had a million questions, and he sat forward a little. 'You sure?'

She nodded.

'The feeling of doom worries me most, though I get that both you and George say no one died. George said I could be subconsciously repressing memories because I fear them. Maybe something to do with when I lost my wife.' He glanced at her from under his brows, as if he was worried he would offend her. 'Do you know of anything that I could be trying to forget?'

Ava didn't know what to say. She couldn't think of an instance that would be so horrific to Zac that he would fear its memory. Then a horrible thought occurred. What if his subconscious had rebelled at the fact that he'd betrothed himself so soon after his wife had died and the guilt had caught up with him?

Her stomach sank and she tried to keep her

voice level. 'Not that I can think of, but then I can't compare this experience to the one where Roslyn was injured. In our accident, I woke up and you were unconscious.'

He shook his head with frustration and looked around the room awkwardly. 'If I remembered my time with you this would all be different. As it is, I feel like I shouldn't be here.'

This is exactly where you should be, she wanted to shout. Instead, she stared into her teacup as if the future were there. She drank the bitterness of lost hope, put her cup down and said brightly, 'Then we need to beef up the hospitality aspect if we can't keep guests feeling welcome.'

He threw out a hand. 'Oh, I feel welcome, just a fraud. And I think I'm hurting you by being here.' He reached across and took her hand for the first time in days and her breath caught. 'If I am, I'm sorry. In that case, I shouldn't have come.'

He squeezed her palm, wrapping his strong, warm fingers around hers. She didn't think he realised he was doing it, but she reeled as the memories rushed in of other times he'd held her hand, times she'd taken strength from the feeling of his hand on hers. The tears welled up and she closed her eyes tightly to hold them back. She would not beg him to remember that he'd said he loved her. But, oh, how she wanted to.

Ava pulled her hand free and stood up. She walked a few steps to face out the window overlooking the river, surreptitiously wiping her eyes. 'Do you think you'll ever get your memory back?'

The creak of the kitchen chair told her he'd followed and then his hand was warm on her shoulder, pressing softly, and he turned her to face him.

'Apparently,' his voice was low, gentle, sharing the bad news, 'the longer it takes, the less likely it is that it will return.' His voice dropped lower still, as if he was afraid of the answer. 'Is there anything else I should know?'

She lifted her head. This was all a big, painful waste of time and emotion. 'Nothing important.' *Maybe you should just . . . leave,* she told him silently.

She felt like a bird that had just hit a window, drawn to the reflection but smacked off a hard surface. Hiding her pain, she forced a smile and stepped back from him. 'Okay. You stay here, finish your tea, and I'll talk to Mum and Mim about an expedition. Find you another fantastic experience of the outback before you go back to Alice.'

She pushed open the screen door and went down the steps to Granny Mim's work shed. She'd glimpsed her mother through the window and she needed some comfort away from Zac.

When she ducked in through the side door, her mother and Mim were standing very close together at the workbench. They stopped talking when she came in.

'What?' She glared at them suspiciously.

'Nothing,' Mim said.

'How are you?' her mother answered at the same time.

'I'm fine. I'd be better if you didn't whisper about me.'

They shared a guilty look, then her mother said quietly, 'We don't know what we can do to help. We think it's getting too much for you.'

Ava pushed the hair carefully off her forehead around the raised bruise and scar. Her mother had removed the sutures yesterday. She didn't think she could carry on. 'I think . . . ' She made a decision. 'He can ask if he wants something, but I think he'll leave soon. Maybe even tomorrow.'

Her mother sighed. 'That's what I think. Though your grandmother wants to tell him he loves you and see if he wakes up.'

Ava's eyes pricked and she blinked rapidly. Fighting the sudden well of emotion that squeezed her lungs, she struggled to take the deep breath she needed to force away the tightness in her throat. Yes, they'd had something beautiful and now it was lost. Something precious that slipped further and further away every second.

She imagined discussing the proposal as if it were an interesting lab result. *Oh, by the way . . . Then there was the proposal looking at Uluru from our hotel room.* She wasn't explaining that to Zac. She'd had enough trampling on her tender heart. 'Please don't do that, Mim.'

Mim crossed to her, leaned up to give her a kiss on the cheek, and patted her arm as she stepped back. 'If that's what you want, sweetie, then that's my plan too.' She turned to Stella, then handed her a paintbrush. 'I'm not in the mood to work. Can you finish this, please? I might have a wee lie-down.'

Ava and Stella watched Mim walk away and

Stella dipped the silver paintbrush in the tin. 'She's feeling everything is out of her control and she's not used to that.' She grimaced. 'I'm not used to it, either.'

Ava crossed to her mum and leaned in, avoiding the wet paint on the tiny homestead. 'Thanks for last night. I did sleep well.' She rested her head on Stella's shoulder as they both gazed over the paddocks. 'The women in this family like to be on top of everything.'

'Or at least look like we are,' her mother said cryptically. 'We'll all hope your Zac gets his memory back, darling. But if he goes back to Alice, we'll still be thankful you're both alive.' She straightened into Sergeant Stella. 'That's the most important thing.'

39

Zac

Zac waited for the moment when Ava left the shed. When she reappeared she didn't look his way, but turned and headed towards the river. Watching from the verandah, he strode quickly to catch up.

She walked fast but he was faster. 'I'm sorry, Ava.' He spoke to her spine, which was ramrod straight, pushing the distance between them as she walked a little ahead. He caught up and touched her shoulder until she stopped, and as if impatient, she spun around.

Her eyes were glinting with unshed tears and a well of protectiveness swelled in him as she looked up to face him. Her features were so beautiful, her eyes so tragic, he couldn't help pulling her closer to curve his fingers around her chin and draw her in. 'What have I lost, Ava, and how much has it cost you? What was I thinking doing this to you?'

'We've both lost, Zac, lost a lot. It's not just me.' She stretched up on tiptoes to reach his mouth with hers and the light touch of her made him pull her closer.

For Zac, something did shift in his mind at that second touch. Her blue eyes were dark pools, like a mermaid's lure drawing him in, her pupils dilated and bottomless. He stared into them, and she stared back, and the moment lengthened as each of them tried to see into the other's soul.

When, finally, inevitably, he bent down and put his lips on hers again, he felt her tense under his mouth and paused. This time when he kissed her, it was as if he was transported back to another moment, kissing this woman, holding her in his arms. He closed his eyes, the past skipping and slipping through his mind, and no matter how hard he tried to hang on to the memories, they slid and evaded his attempt at tethering them like will-o'-the-wisps in the breeze. Fiercely, he wrapped his arms around her and lifted her closer until her toes left the track and she was crushed against him. She felt right, perfect, incredible in his arms.

Even that wasn't close enough. Her tongue invited him in and the kiss deepened and he forgot where, or why, he was here as he breathed in the scent and the taste of the woman in his arms. And she answered him with a longing that touched the core of him with a feeling of homecoming, so tantalising, so welcoming, but still just out of his grasp.

He couldn't remember.

Finally, their lips parted and he lowered her slowly, running her body down the length of his in slow torture until she could step back. Letting her go was the hardest thing he'd ever had to do.

When he looked into her eyes he saw the heartbreak he'd caused, and deepened, with his intense embrace, and his finger rose to brush her tears away as they fell on her cheek.

Obviously, she was struggling with him being here and he cursed himself for putting her through this. He was a jerk. A thoughtless, arrogant jerk. It had been too big an ask and he knew without a doubt that he had taken advantage when he shouldn't have.

'We've kissed many times before.' His words were a statement and she didn't deny it, but she stepped away further and the back of her hand rested across her mouth where he'd left his imprint. He could tell she was having trouble with her emotions.

She wasn't the only one. His heart thumped like a piston in his chest and he wanted to snatch her back instantly, back into his arms, and do that all over again. And more.

There was only one way his thoughts could go and he didn't understand how he could have allowed himself to risk this woman by making love to her when he must have known it couldn't last. *Damn*.

'Were we lovers?' His voice was harsher than he'd intended, angry with himself, not her. She flinched at the baldness of the question.

She raised her chin and he remembered that from the first time she'd visited him in the hospital — he'd known she was no shrinking flower. She held his gaze, lifting her chin higher. 'Yes!'

He glanced down at her body as if to remember, and his gaze lingered on her generous breasts. Before he could say anything, she spun away towards the path again.

God, this must be hard for her. What the heck had he been thinking of to involve someone as obviously decent as Ava when he was never marrying again? Especially someone who was as honest and smart and generous as this woman. Someone who could never leave here and be happy. What had he done just now? He'd almost lost control. *Bloody hell.*

He spoke to her back. 'I think I should leave for Alice Springs tomorrow, I can arrange for a car to pick me up.'

She sighed and turned back to look at him. Her eyes were shadowed now. 'I don't know. Yes. I suppose. Maybe you *should* just go.'

Strangely, now he didn't want to. 'If I think of something, can I call you?'

This whole mess was nowhere near finished, but suddenly it was important to give her space because she needed it. He needed it too, to think. Whatever had been between them was gone, and he should be as well. Especially if he'd led her on unfairly when there could be no future.

'Sure.' Except the one word sounded anything but sure.

When he had his own transport he could return. Or maybe, for Ava, he would not.

He stopped following her then and watched her increase the distance between them, down towards the waterhole. Soon she'd rounded a bend and disappeared out of sight.

★ ★ ★

Poddy arrived at his door an hour later with an 'experience' for Zac. To get him away from Ava for the day, he had no doubt. He didn't blame her family for arranging it, so he followed Poddy to the vehicle and climbed in to go hiking for the day.

That night, he tossed in his wrought-iron bed and remembered the confusion and pain in Ava's eyes. He hated that he'd caused her such distress. It would be better when he'd just left her in peace and returned to Alice Springs. He was almost completely certain that was the right thing to do, but he wasn't ready to go back to Sydney. Something held him back from doing that.

He'd sat outside before going to bed. He could hear the dull murmur of voices from inside the homestead, and not wanting to eavesdrop he'd stood up and walked down the steps to gaze up at the enormous sky above him. The full moon hadn't risen yet and the dark sky lay with such a dense carpet of stars, swirls and stick figures of constellations. To the left of his unobstructed view, the glorious Milky Way cut a swathe across the sky like a silver cloud. Even the occasional taunting flicker of a shooting star zipping past and extinguishing out of the corner of his eye seemed fitting in this moment.

Like Ava. A bright star who'd appeared in his world and then was gone.

In the night hours, the brief snatches of sleep Zac managed were filled with the worst of dreams. He was cold, freezing cold, and he could hear a woman's screams. Somewhere. In smoke.

304

He couldn't find her. He ran this way and that as he searched for her, but the cries didn't seem any closer. He had to find her before something terrible happened, something he'd never survive, but then it was too late. Her screams were cut off and he sat bolt upright in bed.

The light from the moon shone into the room at a low angle — it must be setting. It was nearly morning, reminding him where he was and that he'd be leaving today. Leaving Ava to heal the heart, which he could now see he'd broken.

His hand shook as he reached across and took a sip of water to clear the ache in his throat. When he sat on the edge of the bed, his heart pounded in his chest.

Ava was the key. He still believed she could help him remember, but at what cost to her? He'd never felt closer to seeing past the block than he had yesterday, but he'd also seen the toll it had taken on the woman trying to help him.

Because she'd confirmed they'd been lovers, he had more questions. How had he begun a relationship so soon after Roslyn? Why hadn't he stopped it? How long had it been going on for? He'd only been in Alice Springs a week. How could he not remember that? How had he come to the point where they'd slept together?

He massaged his scalp with tense fingers. If they had been lovers, surely they'd taken precautions? What if they'd made plans he didn't remember? That would explain her persistence in bringing him here. These were all very serious questions that he should have asked, but it all came back to what had possessed him. Possessed him to become involved when he was transient, when he'd already royally screwed up one marriage with far more chance of success than this balls-up.

He lay back down, feeling restless and staring out at the moonlight shining on the barren landscape.

Maybe a miracle would bring answers before he left.

Maybe when he saw her this morning, it would all come back in a deluge.

Maybe pigs might fly.

40

Hana

Hana was thinking of Jock and the loving way he'd left her this morning. She knew Zac was leaving soon and she felt for Ava's loss. She glanced at the clock again. Jock should be back. He'd left early, said he wanted to check the cattle he'd moved closer to the east troughs, but it was after morning tea and he usually would have checked on her by now. Plus, they'd be going together to say goodbye to Zac.

The uneasy feeling she'd woken with this morning gnawed at her gut and even her baby wriggled more than usual, as if feeling her tension.

Damn this drought.

Damn this fear that was creeping over her skin, making her cold.

Damn her husband's state of mind, which had skewed his normal rational thinking so that he'd turned all the blame on himself.

It had been financially devastating when Setabilly had lost the international beef market, like so many others, right after Jock had ordered the expensive improvements. They'd been critically overstocked at the wrong time, through no fault of Jock's, in a glut as everyone had tried to downsize their herds in the local market.

They'd seen more than one family fall straight into bankruptcy, and now the viciousness of this drought on top of a few lean years had affected them all. Nobody could have done more to care for the infrastructure, the innovation and the monitoring of the feed and water levels than Jock.

She rang the house and Mim answered. 'No, Jock isn't here. You coming Over to see Zac off soon? Want me to ask Stella if she knows?'

Hana murmured 'No' quite quickly, because her mother-in-law had been almost overwrought, something Hana hadn't seen in the time she'd been here, when Ava had suggested Jock might be depressed. Stella would instantly worry. 'I'll be over soon.'

Hana took down the spare satellite phone and clipped it to her jeans as she walked to the shed. The Polaris was gone, which wasn't surprising, but the quad bike was there. She glanced in the direction of the house and contemplated calling Ava, but then shrugged. Her sister-in-law had enough on her mind.

Hana clambered onto the tall quad bike, swinging her legs and belly awkwardly, and settled herself. She knocked it into neutral, started the engine and pushed into low gear. She'd go slowly. Poke along until she saw Jock, who would rant and rave about her riding the bike, but perhaps next time he wouldn't leave her to worry.

Such sudden inexplicable worry, along with an icy-cold fear that chewed inside her. As if she could feel the angst inside her husband through some telepathic bond.

Jock had been saying nonsensical things about letting the family down, the responsibility of being the fourth generation, of losing Setabilly. Making it all his fault. She suspected that despite Jock's euphoria over their coming baby, the responsibilities of being a new father could very well tip him deeper into the spiral of depression, and she wasn't having that.

For some reason she remembered him saying she would be excited to find out the sex. As if he wouldn't be there. Hana pushed the throttle on the bike a little harder to increase her speed.

She saw the Polaris as she rounded a bend, rolling erratically down the hill, and then it came to a stop. Her breath eased out. Unconsciously, she slowed until she saw the vehicle was empty, oddly parked at the bottom of the hill, as if it had driven itself there. She glanced to the top of Lone Tree Hill.

When Hana first saw the thing hanging from the tree, she thought a branch had come down. It looked odd, misshapen, and it swung, jiggled, and suddenly, the full horror dawned on her.

Hana began to swear as she gunned the engine, bounced wildly across the rock-strewn paddock from rock to rock, roared up the hill and aimed for the lump. Angry, incredulous, heartbroken words poured from her lips as she swung the bike under the swinging body of her husband as he hung suspended above the ground, and she tried to let the bike take his weight.

She threw open the small tool chest on the

back of the bike and reached in for the knife that was always there. When her fingers closed about the hilt, she dragged herself up until she stood, swaying unsteadily on the seat of the bike, and sawed at the tight rope at his neck, the tiny gap opening as she kept his weight off the rope. Seconds mattered. She kept her eyes on the rope, strand by strand as it separated, eyes away from Jock's hideously purple face, and sawed, and sawed. Her grunts gasping from her mouth, her whimpers getting louder. Finally, the rope separated from the branch and Jock's body toppled with an appalling thump onto the ground. He took her down with him, and with a gasp she fell forward and landed on top of him with a painful, solid slap and lay there stunned.

Until she heard it, under her cheek. She could hear his heart beating.

41

Zac

For Zac, no miracle had arrived with the morning he'd spent with Ava. No memories. Despite all of Ava's efforts, Zac remembered nothing since Sydney prior to waking in the hospital in Alice Springs.

It was time to leave.

Poddy had offered to give him a lift into Alice and would be here soon. Poddy had said he'd been going anyway, and that he'd pick him up at eleven. Standing outside his bedroom door, the one that led to the verandah, Zac felt the immenseness of this place in the middle of Australia envelop him as if trying to ease into his soul. The sweep away to the MacDonnell Ranges seemed even more mesmerising and he wished they'd gone to the foothills again; the top of the path down to the river made him think of when Ava had taken his hand. He looked away to the distant red dirt and sparsely covered paddocks, where he knew that so many turns and fence lines led to places he'd never see. The sadness for something lost that he didn't remember sat on his shoulder like one of the crows he'd woken to the sound of this morning. *No.*

It was time to leave.

His backpack sat on the verandah and the

front door stood open as he looked to the entrance of Ava's home.

She came through and headed his way, moving gracefully, like a dancer. She'd told him that story of when she was little and the memory made him smile . . . A thought intruded as a fragment of recollection, tantalising, beckoning, so close . . . Something sizzled for a moment, then it was gone. He grimaced with the frustration.

What did you say to a woman you've found out you'd slept with and didn't remember? *Bloody hell*. He had no idea except, 'I'm sorry. So sorry for any distress I've caused you and your family, Ava.'

'It was never your fault.' She held out her hand, composed and pleasant. She was all class and he wished he had more to offer her, but the feeling of impending doom that he seemed to be carrying around made him anxious to leave before he hurt this family any more than he already had.

'I'm sorry I couldn't help your memory,' Ava said as she touched his outstretched hand very briefly. She stepped back to stand beside her diminutive grandmother, who had also appeared, and he couldn't read the expression on either of their faces. The thought crossed his mind that they'd never looked so similar as they did in that moment.

'Goodbye, Zac' He heard finality in that farewell and it jarred with him. Jarred like a cymbal on his head, but the ringing didn't produce memories. Just a headache. *Come on, Poddy. Arrive.*

She'd be better off without his dramas.

Then the odd ringing tone of the satellite phone went off in the house and Ava turned away to answer it. He and Mim just looked at each other.

When she reappeared, the shock on her face made him step towards her. 'Ava?'

Her eyes held his and he saw tears were running unheeded down her face. 'Jock. Still alive. Hana's with him. Hanged himself.' She hurried towards Mim, who'd gasped and reeled with her hand to her mouth.

'Mim. Find Mum and tell her to set up the sick bay. Phone RFDS for retrieval. Send Poddy as soon as he comes so we can bring him back fast. Lone Tree Hill. I'll get the utility.'

Zac strode towards the house. 'I'll grab first aid and Stella's intubation equipment. Throats swell and occlude.' Jock would need ventilation if he was going to survive.

42

Ava

Ava jerked to a halt at the front door in the farm utility and wiped the tears off her cheek with a trembling hand. Zac jumped off the verandah and slid into the passenger seat. 'Go.'

Her brain was whirling and all she could think was, *It's my fault.* She'd missed it. Zac had agreed that Jock's depression was concerning and they'd made the appointment, but none of them had thought him this urgently in need of assessment. 'Hana went looking for him. Found him hanging and cut him down.'

Zac made a noise through his teeth. 'How long?'

'The ute was still running down the hill when she saw it. He'd used it to swing off.'

Zac sighed. 'Poor bloody Hana.'

Ava didn't want to think about poor Hana. 'She had the sat phone. Imagine if she hadn't.'

He touched her arm. 'Don't imagine anything until we sort this.'

Thank God you're still here, she thought. And that was something else she didn't want to imagine. All she said was, 'Yes.'

Then she glanced at him as they tore up the hill they'd walked so enjoyably down almost a week ago. 'Have you seen hangings?'

314

'Intubate. Ventilate. Resuscitate,' he recited. 'We'll go from there. He's alive now, so his odds are good.'

She blew out her breath. *Okay*. 'Thank you.'

As soon as she spotted them she jerked the car to a halt. She saw Hana sitting on the ground beside the quad bike, her back against the wheel, her body stiff. Jock's head lay in her lap. His neck purple and face swollen, his lips bloody where he'd bitten them. He was unconscious, and rattling gasps slowed as his wind pipe closed with the swelling and air entry began to shut down. Hana had blood on her mouth, and Ava guessed it was because she'd kissed him.

Ava said, 'Can you slide out, Hana?'

Zac moved her aside. 'Take his shoulders as I lift her out. He's occluding.' Zac had Hana out and Jock flat on his back in seconds, and Ava reached for the kit to hand him the airway. 'Straight to endotracheal or we won't get it in?' She lubricated it.

'Yep.' Zac slid the tube past the obstruction and blew up the balloon, then attached the bag to hand ventilate. They both shuddered with relief as Jock's chest rose and fell with Zac's squeeze of the bag. The simplified version of emergency airway.

Ava reached for his wrist. 'Pulse one eighty.' Her voice broke and she sucked back the sob that wanted to explode.

'Same as mine,' Zac said quietly and Ava blinked and then nodded.

'Mine too. Thanks.' *Focus on reality*, she told herself. Jock was breathing. He had a pulse. It could have been worse. She glanced at Hana, but her sister-in-law's eyes were glued to the rise and fall of Jock's chest, her lips moving in prayer. *Bloody, bloody hell.*

They put in a cannula for access in case they needed adrenaline and Zac gave some sedation in case Jock woke with a tube in his throat. Though he was still unconscious, they should be able to keep him stable until he could be airlifted out. What happened after that they could pray about. Ava fumbled until she found the blood-pressure machine.

When she'd completed the measurement she said, 'His blood pressure is okay, Hana, which is a good sign.'

'Mine isn't.'

There was something in Hana's voice that made Ava plead silently to God. 'Hana?'

'I fell. After I cut the rope. I hit my stomach and the contractions have started.'

Ava crawled away from her brother across the rocks until she knelt beside Hana and rested her hand on her sister-in-law's stomach. The uterus below her fingers was rock hard. 'Oh, sweetheart. You are so brave and wonderful. Hold on.'

43

Stella

The Royal Flying Doctor aircraft landed at Setabilly Station for the second time in a week, but this time they came from a distance and didn't arrive until almost three in the afternoon.

Stella waited for the engines to wind down, and unlike her daughter-in-law's calm last week, she wanted to run across to the plane and beat on the doors for them to open.

'Zac says they'll be fine. Zac says they'll be fine.' She chanted the litany over and over, mouthing the words, mashing her hands together, moaning a little between the sentences. She wished Lorenzo were here, but he'd gone out into the paddocks and couldn't be contacted.

Stella relived the horror she had felt when Hana had phoned Ava. Jock hadn't woken during the transfer from the hill. She and Mim had remained at the house to phone for retrieval, and they'd clutched each other's hands until Jock had been carried in by Zac and Poddy, and Hana had limped in, held up by Ava.

Her darling boy, her baby Jock, sedated with a tube in his throat to keep his airway open, carried in like the dead. Like her dad had been that horrific day ten years ago. Stella's lip quivered and she brushed away the trickle of tears on her cheeks. She glanced at Mim, who looked just as shocked. She'd thought nothing could have been worse than her dad being carried in. Now it was her son. And her dear daughter-in-law and her grandchild.

Ava and Zac, both professional to the core though their faces had been blanched ashen, confirmed that Jock's vital signs were stable, but Hana's uterus had been contracting, they hoped only from the stress. Though they didn't say it, everyone was thinking, *Please, God, not from the fall.* She had no blood loss or other pain, so Ava said that was a good sign.

Usually the calm one in emergency situations, Stella had felt small and frightened, and finally asked Mim to phone Lorenzo again to come and just be there in case they needed help, but really, she just needed his presence. His housekeeper had said she would make sure he drove over as soon as he returned. He should arrive by the time she got back to the house with the doctor and the flight nurse.

Come on, people. Get out of the aircraft.

Finally, the propellers stopped turning and the door swung down to form the steps. The flight nurse and the doctor seemed unhurried, but they appeared beside her very quickly.

'Thank goodness,' Stella said, and her hands seemed to shake more visibly the longer it took for them to put their equipment into the car.

The flight nurse nodded in greeting. 'We get that a lot.' Then, when she looked at Stella, she said, 'Would you like me to drive, Mrs May?'

Stella touched her cheeks and realised she was

crying. 'Yes, please.'

When they arrived back at the house, Stella's heart squeezed at the sight of Hana's face, pale and wooden, with two tear trails from lid to chin as she held Jock's hand in hers. Her beautiful dark eyes were huge and hauntingly tragic as she stared down at Jock,

Mim sat with Ava, squeezing her granddaughter's fingers as the medical team concentrated on Jock. Stella could see how the fragile, veined hand shook, and she crossed to them both to rest her hands on their shoulders.

Ava turned her way. 'Mum. He'll be all right. He's tough.' Then her voice cracked. 'We'll never let him do that again . . . Poor Hana.'

Stella's heart was breaking. 'I know, sweetheart. I know.'

★ ★ ★

The next half-hour saw them stabilise Jock and load him, still on the spine board they kept for medical emergencies, still sedated, back into the station utility, with Poddy driving. This time, Zac and the doctor rode in the back tray with Jock for the slow and careful drive out to the aircraft, and Hana, in Stella's car with the nurse, was driven out by Ava and accompanied by Mim.

Stella stood watching them leave the house, Lorenzo's arm around her, her face a mask. When he came back, Poddy would drive into Alice to be there for Hana until the others arrived.

Stella watched the tail-lights fade and shivered. She was so, so cold.

'They will be well, *cara amica*.' Lorenzo's deep voice seemed to come from a long way off and she blinked several times to break the stare she had fixed on the receding red glow. The ice seemed to be spreading through her body and she shivered again. His arm tightened around her, and she slowly turned her head to look at him.

She was being weak, leaning into this man, who she barely knew yet felt she did. If he hadn't been here the house would be empty while she waited for Ava and Mim to return, and she'd be left with the detritus of a field hospital and the crushing worry all by herself. She thought perhaps she might have lost herself in the emptiness if he hadn't been with her.

'I'm sure they will.' All of them. The words sounded hollow and unconvincing even to her, but Jock was alive, and Zac had said he'd get the best care. Stella wanted to shriek to the sky. She would defer it until later. For now, she tried to calm herself.

Please, God, let Hana and the baby be fine. She couldn't cope with another lost baby like Ava's Amelia. But Ava had said there'd been no bleeding. And if the contractions didn't stop, Hana would be in the right place to get the necessary care. But thirty-one weeks?

Hana should stay in Alice now until the baby was born. She'd tell them both.

Zac and Ava had been incredible. Especially Zac. He'd intubated Jock, sedated him, kept him stable until he could hand him over. Zac. A few days ago, she'd wished he'd go home so Ava could recover. Because Stella herself had decided that her daughter would be unhappy and lose her way like her mother had. How foolish she'd been. Life was too short not to grab happiness when you could.

Life could end. But not like this. Never like this. There'd been too many funerals in her life already.

She felt herself pulled into strong arms more securely. 'Come. We will drink your tea and all your *bambini* will be well.'

Lorenzo's arm steered her back into the house through the hall and into the kitchen, where he settled her down on a chair. She was barely aware of the move.

Big, beautiful Jock. Her son. So close to death, so lost and alone. How would they come back from this? Though Zac had been reassuring, and help was being given now. Importantly, he had breathed before the swelling because Hana had cut him down quickly.

Stella thought of her daughter-in-law. 'Hana will be beside herself until he wakes,' she said. She should have listened to Ava when she'd said he was depressed. Made something happen right away. But she'd been too busy thinking of Noah and the way he'd dealt with her leaving. That too had been suicide of a sort, and she'd panicked into denial. More evidence of her being useless again.

Lorenzo patted her shoulder. 'I see you are creating the *disastro* in your head. We will be

321

positive. Say 'yes, Jock will recover'. Say 'yes, Hana's baby will be safe'. I will say this with you every hour until this happens.' Lorenzo crouched down in front of her. 'Let me drive you to Alice tomorrow.'

Stella shook her head. 'No.' She needed to go with her family. Though when she looked at him, she wished they could leave now, but they'd wait for daylight. It was the sensible thing to do. They couldn't afford any more accidents, and travelling so far at night wasn't safe.

Lorenzo frowned slightly, but all he said was, 'I will be here for you. You need to remember this. But I will explain another day.' Then he stood and began to rifle through the cupboards behind her.

She heard the chink of glass on glass and a thimble-sized shot of amber liquid appeared beside her face. 'Sip while I make the tea.'

She took it absently, sipped and grimaced. He'd poured from the bottle of cooking brandy she kept in the cupboard.

'Medicine,' he said.

'Are you trying to get me drunk?' *Yuck*, but the sip she'd taken had warmed a trail in her chilled centre. She took another.

'One day I would like this. Not today.' She heard the smile in his voice and that hidden thread of someone sane in this suddenly cracked world sounded reassuring, so she clung to it.

She turned her face. 'Why do you like me, Lorenzo?'

His dark eyes stared down at her and his face

softened. 'You stay in my mind. And burn my heart like this liquid burns you. But that too is for another day.'

44

Hana

Hana lay in her bed in the antenatal ward of Alice Springs Hospital with her hand resting on the mound of her tummy. The machine they'd strapped to her stomach beat out the clopping heart sounds of her baby in a steady, reassuring rhythm and showed no contractions. Inside her belly, below her fingers, a tiny jiggle of movement dragged a small smile onto her pinched face. 'Thank you, baby, for being a warrior, and staying in there. Now we just have to sort out your father.'

A noise at the door turned her head and she saw Ava, holding a pot of tea and two cups, and Hana waved her in. Thank God for Ava and the whole of Jock's family. Though Poddy had been a star to drive through the night and be here for her first.

Her sister-in-law put the pot and mugs down on the bedside table and leaned over to give Hana a kiss on the cheek.

'You okay?' The words were quiet because it was too early for visiting hours. The perks of working here, she guessed.

Hana thought about the question. Was she okay? She settled for 'As good as could be expected.'

Ava nodded. 'Baby?'

'Jiggling.' Hana patted her belly and Ava smiled.

'Contractions?'

'Stopped.' Thank goodness. Part two of the world's most frightening night flight. A flight to save her husband and as an added bonus the worry that she'd have a premature birth or lose her baby.

'Good.' Ava nodded again and sat down. 'Zac's spoken to the psychiatrist on duty, and they'll keep Jock sedated for another twelve hours. His neurological signs are good, no fits, no obvious signs of brain damage. The intubation meant he could breathe until the swelling subsided. The rest is recovery. They've had consistently good outcomes from that scenario. You got him down quickly.'

Hana flinched. 'I dropped him.'

'Good.' The two women looked at each other and both sets of eyes filled with tears. Ava's hand snaked out and held Hana's. 'Thank you for saving my brother.'

'It was too close.'

Ava's eyes narrowed. 'Maybe it needed to be close to wake him up.'

'You don't mean that,' Hana whispered in horror.

'No.' Ava sighed. 'No, I don't. Nobody will be sorrier that this happened than Jock. I should have seen how unwell he was.' Her eyes met Hana's and there was a fierce intensity Hana hadn't heard before in her sister-in-law's voice. 'That wasn't Jock who tried to die. That was an illness, an illness that got away from all of us, that we should have seen and treated. We won't miss it again.'

'He hid it.'

Ava shook her head again, no doubt in the movement. 'The illness is devious. Jock is not.'

Hana's lips trembled no matter how hard she tried to keep them still. She was struggling to comprehend the horror. 'He must have convinced himself that the insurance policy would save the family farm.'

'The disease did that,' Ava said again.

Hana nodded. 'I know. It twisted the truth until it seemed real. Created the scenario in his mind that everyone would be better off with him dead.'

Ava sighed again. 'I know. All decisions at Setabilly are joint ones. But we have him safe now, thanks to you.' Ava squeezed Hana's hand. 'And he will get well.'

Hana glanced down at her stomach. 'He's only got ten weeks.'

'He'll be more himself with the meds in four. Zac says the psychiatrist is brilliant. He checked him out with friends in Sydney. We're lucky to have the best care.'

Hana jumped on the change of subject. Diversion was good. 'How is Zac? He was amazing.'

'Yes, he was. And he's fine.' Ava's voice was noncommittal.

'Will you see him while you're here?'

Ava shook her head. 'He's going down to Uluru for a week. Mum and I will go home as soon as Jock is awake and stable. We still have a muster to organise. Is it okay if we take Poddy back with us?'

'He'll want to go back to help now that he knows I'm okay and Jock's okay.'

'Poddy did well to get here so quickly. I wanted to come with him, but I thought Mum would lose it if I went.'

'He's a wonderful brother.'

'Brothers are wonderful. And you saved mine.' Ava blinked away fresh tears and changed the subject. 'If Poddy will come back, that would be a bonus.'

Hana put her head back and closed her eyes. 'And I'll be no help?'

'Having you here in town will be an enormous help.' Ava gestured to the phone with her hand. 'You're our contact with Jock. Mim's staying with you at the flat until Jock's out of the mental-health unit. Lorenzo's son is back from Sydney and has organised a muster gang — goodness knows how, but I don't care. We'll go back in a few days and get it over with, though the numbers will probably be small. I don't think Mum even cares.'

Hana thought about Stella. The way she'd seemed to shrink when she'd looked at Jock. 'Your poor mother.'

Ava lifted her chin. 'Mum will be fine. We all will be. You worry about yourself and Jock. He's got the help he needs now and he will get better.' Hana could hear the certainty in Ava's voice and it comforted her. Ava would be onto the mental-health team like a . . . What did she say

327

Granny Mim was like? An eagle onto roadkill.

The gruesome image sat well in Hana's determined mind. She'd be like one too, until her husband had healed.

45

Zac

Zac looked around his impersonal apartment at the hotel in Alice Springs and decided it was decent but too big for one person. The view from the window faced the MacDonnell Ranges — he guessed a different side to that he remembered from Setabilly — but looking at the rugged mountains made him feel closer to a station he had no cause to return to and held a barb of regret.

Apart from his own things in the room, he didn't recognise anything here or anyone he ran into. He'd cancel the booking and pack his stuff. Just move into a normal hotel room next week when he came back from Uluru.

It was best he left town while he waited to go back to work. He knew he needed to give Ava space. Her family had been flung into the worst kind of turmoil. He felt as if he'd let them down by not seeing the perilous depth of Jock's depression, though he had broached the subject of a consult for Jock and made the referral for the next time he and Hana would be in Alice. But it had been too little too late.

The horror of yesterday would stay with him for a very long time. He could feel his heart rate pick up and blew out a breath to reassure himself. At least he'd got the tube in. Jock would recover physically and Zac staying around here wasn't helping anyone. George had suggested another week off, but he'd be back to work after that.

He glanced at his phone and checked the time in Greece — 8.15 am. He placed the call to his parents and checked in, as well as letting them know the latest from George. Then he began to pack his things.

★ ★ ★

The next morning, Zac drove down to stay at the Ayers Rock Resort in Yulara, because he'd be going back to Sydney soon and Ava had been quietly persistent that he should see the Uluru-Kata Tjuta National Park before he left.

His first sight of Uluru made him stop the car and stare. Even from a distance the monolith rose as an immense protrusion into the sky, and as he drove closer it reared up from the surrounding desert, drawing his eye back like a magnet from the road to the rock.

Yulara township was a surprise. It appeared suddenly after miles of desert, a collection of buildings, a turn, and a row of verandahs from the hotel on his left looking out to the road and across to the monolith. The township was bigger and more modern than he'd expected. An isolated outpost with desert gardens and smiling staff and tourist buses, and he could see why it drew visitors from around the world.

There was an adventurous feel to the place, an excitement and a buzzing of expectation, and despite his tiredness from the five-hour drive, he could feel the effect lifting his mood. And the smiling Indigenous woman at check-in with her brown eyes crinkled in good humour and the expansive wave of her arm towards his room left him with a definite feeling of welcome.

He climbed the stairs to the Rock View Room he'd requested, a recommendation he'd taken from Ava. On opening his door, he could see why she'd pushed him to be specific. The room itself was fine, an upscale hotel room in desert reds and greens, but it was the view that drew him through the screen door onto the small balcony.

Across the road, and across the far red desert, past the rocks and low, scrubby desert foliage, Uluru sat grandly in the distance as it had sat for millennia. Drawing the eye with a subtle power and insistence that kept his eyes roving over the shadows and lines of the face. He'd go there soon.

First, he dropped in to the medical centre where George had said he'd almost died, and one of the nurses there made a fuss of him. Actually, she became quite animated about how agitated and critical he'd been and remembered the smoking ceremony the traditional healer had performed. Ava had mentioned that briefly and now he wished he'd asked more at the time. The nurse kept touching his arm as if reassuring herself he was real, and he had to laugh, which he was severely reprimanded for as 'it's no laughing matter'. Ava's name came up a lot and he found himself growing wistful the more he heard it.

He left there and drove the twenty-five kilometres out to Uluru, stared in awe, walked a little way along the winding base walk path, and when he could, at different sections, he ran his fingers along the rough surface of the rock, but the magic wasn't working for him. All he felt was loss and being lost.

He drove back to the resort and sat in his room, out on the verandah, and contemplated the rock in the distance as he remembered his time at Setabilly and how much more interesting this would be if Ava were with him.

The next day, he drove to the cultural centre in the shadow of the monolith. He examined the history wall and marvelled over the artefacts and artwork, which seemed to draw him in. A tall woman with glowing ebony skin rose from her seat where she'd been creating a dot painting and came across to him.

'Zac. Welcome back to Uluru.' She held out her hand. 'You don't remember me. I'm Denise. Ava's friend. I was there when the twins were born and the night they brought you in from the accident.'

He took her hand and shook it. 'I'm afraid I don't remember anything from before the accident.' Then he recalled what Ava had told him about her friend. 'Was it you who helped me with your traditional medicine?'

'Yes.' Her eyes were kind and very calm. 'Both you and Ava needed me. She asked me to look out for you while you're here.' She pressed a small card into his hand. 'My mobile number. Either I or my husband will have the phone on us most of the time. Leave a message if you need assistance.'

'Thank you.' He wouldn't, but the kindness he'd

met here was unlike anything he'd ever experienced. 'I love your paintings.' His eye was continually drawn to a blue-and-white dot painting.

'Ah, you like the medicine art. That's not surprising. There are curtains made of this design inside the medical centre at Yulara and perhaps you're remembering that, too.'

He had a vague picture of that from earlier today. There seemed something so familiar and calming about the blue-and-white waving lines that he bought a painting as well as a small postcard of it to tuck into his wallet. It was getting tight in his wallet and he needed to clean it out. Denise wrapped the painting carefully and he carried it while she gave him a tour and explained the artefacts and artwork to him.

When another tourist came over to ask questions, he wandered away and spent another hour listening to the explanations on the free running video and reading the interpretive texts along the warren of nooks and flowing walls.

He'd booked for dinner so he left to give himself enough time to drive out to The Olgas. Kata Tjuta. He needed to be back at Yulara for the bus that took those who'd booked to the sandhills for the Sounds of Silence dinner.

★ ★ ★

Despite his feeling of displacement, Zac stayed for a week: did the sunrise, the lunch and the sunset tours, went again out to Kata Tjuta, up to Kings Canyon, and took short hikes that connected him more to the feeling of timeless space around him. He attended several Indigenous events which he enjoyed, but the Sounds of Silence dinner out in the desert under the stars that first night remained the highlight. Though he wished he could have gone to it with company. The Dreamtime stories told that night reminded him of the night he'd spent with Poddy and the desert community, but his mind kept returning to Ava and how it seemed they'd been doomed from the start.

On the last day, he drove back to Alice Springs for his pre-work check-up. He'd moved no closer to the past, but was more easy with it, and had come to the conclusion that he probably never would remember.

George looked up as Zac entered. 'Zac. Welcome back. How was the rock?'

'As amazing as they say. And the resort is excellent. I'm glad I went.'

George studied him and Zac raised his brows. 'Well? Do I look human?'

'Well rested. How are the headaches?'

'Almost gone.' Most of the time, but George didn't need to know they still came, though each one was milder than the last. He didn't mention that the dreams were getting worse, either.

'Let's have a look at you, then.' George came around the desk with his ophthalmoscope and proceeded to attend to the neurological examination Zac had expected. His hand ran over the rough area at the back of Zac's neck. 'Stitches out, I see?'

'The clinic at Yulara obliged. The nurse there is very friendly.'

George laughed. 'You were very exciting for them.'

Five minutes later it seemed George was satisfied. 'I'm happy to tick you off. Are you ready to come back to work?'

Was he? 'I believe so.'

'On night shift because I have no one else?'

'Sure. Nights are fine.' He wasn't sleeping well anyway, and maybe the nightmares would stay away in the day.

'Great. Then come back tomorrow night.' He cleared his throat a little sheepishly. 'Ah, in view of a shortage of doctors — ' he coughed — 'is there any chance you could do an extra fortnight's locum if you feel up to it?'

'Of course.' And funny how quickly that had come out. Why wouldn't he just want to go as soon as he could? Zac frowned at himself. He'd answered so quickly in the affirmative that anyone would think he wanted to stay here. He wasn't thinking that, of course not, he reassured himself — he just wasn't ready to return home yet.

George had gone on, rubbing his hands. 'Do two shifts and then two days off. And then we'll add another four after that and see how you go.'

George wasn't giving him a chance to change his mind. Which was fine by him. Sitting around was driving him mad. 'Do you want to go back to the same hotel?' The hospital provided the accommodation.

'Sure. I don't need the apartment, though. Just a room will do. I need to sort my things and get ready for the week.' In fact, it would be good

335

to have a purpose, and his gear was a mess from moving so many times in the last couple of weeks.

An hour later, sitting on the bed of his new hotel room, Zac cleaned out his wallet. As he tipped out the change from the zippered section at the back, something else fell out with the coins he'd accumulated over the last few days. A ring. He stared at it, nonplussed. Judging by the single pink diamond, it was an engagement ring.

He kept watching it as if it were a lizard about to dash off the bed.

Why would he have an engagement ring?

His mind darted to thoughts of Ava and reared back. There were only two answers. One: he was holding it for a friend, and that was unlikely. Or two: he was going to ask someone to marry him.

Ava? After only a week? Not yet three months after Roslyn had died?

If things had progressed so far, no wonder Ava had been devastated when he hadn't remembered her.

An engagement ring!

Gingerly, he picked it up in his fingers. The faceted diamond instantly captured the light and flashed brilliant. It was a beautiful ring, and on the very expensive end of the price range, he'd guess. What had he been thinking? Had they even talked about it, or was it all in his plans for later — assuming he didn't get hit by a car and suffer amnesia!

Bloody hell.

But did it change anything, apart from giving him some understanding of how intense their relationship must have been or was becoming?

What the hell had he been thinking?

He kept coming back to that. Had he planned to move to Alice Springs, which seemed radical considering his life was in Sydney? Or was Ava going to leave the place she loved — surely, he hadn't been stupid enough to ask that or even think that? His head began to pound and he put the ring back and zipped it away.

He had no idea.

He needed to think.

There was no rush. The ring had sat there at least since the accident — and diamonds didn't age. What was a little more time ?

* * *

Zac returned to the emergency department the next evening, and apart from having to learn everyone's names again, to his relief he had no problem with the work.

Hana and Jock had both been discharged — he'd asked the night-shift clerk to check, though they were staying in Alice Springs because Jock was coming up to the hospital twice a week to see his case worker. Before he'd left for Uluru, Zac had left his number with Hana, but he still thought it for the best that he didn't see them unless they asked. Neither needed to be reminded of the last time if it caused them pain.

After the first night his headaches stopped and he slept better, though once it was dark, his nightmares developed into epic disasters that left him sweating and cold. The agitation and feeling of loss each time he woke up grew, but the stress eased once he was in the rush and drama of work. When his two-day break came he drove off-road, went back along the Red Centre Way, and took to any walking tracks he could find with a vengeance.

46

Ava

Finally, the day that had crept towards Ava so slowly through all the noise and exhaustion of muster was upon her in a rush. She returned to the family flat in Alice Springs, and when she pushed open the door Hana practically threw herself at Ava.

'Ava!' Hana hugged her and she squeezed her sister-in-law gently in return. Jock stood back and waited, and her eyes stung to see how diffident her brother had become, and thinner. Gaunt-looking. But his eyes were clear.

'Hey, you,' she said and stepped up to hug him, and after an initial hesitation he hugged her back fiercely. They'd spoken on the phone, but this was the first time she'd seen him since that fateful day.

'Love you,' she said.

'Love you, too.' Jock heaved a sigh, gesturing vaguely. 'I was nervous.'

She touched his shoulder. 'Don't be. We miss you, but we can wait till this baby of yours arrives and then we'll have you home.'

She tapped her ear. 'I hear your psychiatrist is pretty cool. Hana said you really like him?'

Jock smiled. 'He's amazing. And I'm feeling better. Almost good.' He looked from her to

Hana. 'I'm feeling stronger.'

'And it's only been ten days. That's excellent,' Ava said to the both of them. 'By a month you'll be yourself again.'

He sighed. 'I hope so.'

'Don't rush. We'll do this properly.'

Jock nodded.

'How was muster?' Hana asked the question they both knew Jock wanted to ask and she dragged Ava into the lounge room so they could sit down. Jock and Hana sat opposite her and Hana held Jock's hand in hers. It was so good to see them together that Ava felt the tightness in her throat easing.

'Well, we all fell asleep in camp at night physically exhausted. Lorenzo's family are awesome. Though everyone's sad you and Hana missed the camaraderie.' it would have been great to have had Zac there, too, but she wasn't saying that out loud.

She went on. 'Your wonderful trap yards, with the entry and exits, were a huge success. The cattle self-mustered into the yards to get the water. Even Mim noticed how calm the cattle were and how few people were needed.'

'That's great.' Jock practically beamed and Ava saw Hana's eyes mist at the obvious cheer he drew from that.

'Mum went so far as to say she should have listened to you earlier.'

Jock clicked his fingers in disgust. 'And I missed it.'

'Yeah, but I'm telling tales so it's okay.' They smiled at each other. Hana beamed at them both and Ava imagined how hard it must have been to carry the spirits of both of them by herself this last week since Jock had been discharged.

'I have more good news,' she told her brother. 'The cattle numbers might not be as dire as your estimates. We'll wait for the sales, but they look more generous than we hoped for.'

'That is good news.'

'And in breaking news, Big Jim came across to help at muster with his own vehicle. He didn't want wages, he said, because of the support I'd given Jessamine and the twins.'

'What did Mum say?' They both knew Stella didn't accept help easily.

'She surprised everyone. She said thank you.'

Jock's eyebrows went up, but Hana didn't look too startled.

Ava went on. 'He came to the barbecue with Jessamine and the twins, which we combined with Dreamtime Station's. Poddy and Lorenzo's son, Leo, took to each other like a house on fire, but it might have been the beer.'

Hana laughed. 'Sounds like my brother.'

Ava smiled. 'You'll like Leo's wife, Aimee. I think you and Jock and Leo and Aimee will be the next social set. They're fun people.'

'And Lorenzo?' Hana glanced at her husband with a little smile.

Ava held back her own. 'I think Mum's found some happiness. He certainly admires her.'

Jock frowned.

'I told you,' Hana said. 'It's perfect. I think they'll be very happy.'

And in the devastation of the last month,

someone needs to be, Ava added silently. She just had the last of her own devastation to complete.

Ava knew Zac had only two night shifts left before he flew back to Sydney, and there was a chance that even back at work she might not see him. Tonight she would see if she could arrange one last meeting because she couldn't quite let go.

★ ★ ★

Four hours later, on presenting herself to the night supervisor's office for her ward allocation, Ava didn't know whether to be excited or horrified to be sent down to help in the emergency department straight off. However, with maternity being unusually quiet, she had no choice, which meant she couldn't be a chicken.

She tried to settle her pounding heart as it thumped with a foolish hope that things had changed and Zac simply hadn't had a chance to tell her, no matter how sensibly she admonished herself to stop.

Her ID card wavered a bit as she held it over the scanner and she blew out a breath as she slipped through the staff entrance to emergency. Skimming the large open area quickly, she zoomed in on him. There he stood, side-on, talking to a patient. Her heart sped up and she growled at herself, *Easy*.

She hung back a little just to savour the tilt of his head, the breadth of his shoulders, the flash of his smile as he joked with the man on the gurney.

She remembered Zac so vividly beneath her hands that she couldn't help the slow curl of anticipation that grew in her stomach. She tried to keep it in check, but damn it. Just once more, if she got the chance, yes, she would fight for him one more time. She stepped towards him and waited for a break in the conversation.

'Anything you'd like me to do, Doctor?' Ava's voice came out quietly, but still it made him freeze without turning. He tilted his head as if the cadence seemed familiar, and for a heart-stopping moment she thought he remembered, but when he slowly turned to look at her she knew he hadn't.

'Hello, Ava,' he said.

She extended her hand, forcing him to touch her. He hesitated, but she stood in front of him with fingers outstretched and she gave him no choice. When he did his hand felt warm and wonderful beneath hers, and she felt his shock at the moment of contact. They dropped hands.

'You look well,' he said. Yes, her scar was healing well and the bruising was gone, but she didn't feel as well as he suggested. Her heart played up.

He'd gained a little weight and his shoulders seemed broader, and the colour in his cheeks meant his skin shone with health even under the emergency department's fluorescent lights. She dragged her eyes away from him to the patient waiting behind him, to ground herself. She smiled vaguely at the fellow.

The man lifted a finger but kept texting on his phone, so the silence between them remained.

'Your holiday is over?' Zac's voice broke the unexpected trance completely.

She cleared her throat. *Right*. 'Yes. I've been seconded down here from maternity. I hear you're busy. Is there something I can do for you?'

He indicated the man beside him. 'I've suturing to do, I thought in SR 1, if you'd like to set up for that? Thank you.'

She walked towards the little suture room and pushed open the door. She'd done this many times, but until Zac walked in pushing the gurney she'd forgotten how small the room was. The best thing she could do would be to concentrate on setting out the instruments. Work. There was always enough of that.

Ava felt strangely content to hover quietly and pass Zac the instruments he needed, although the job felt successfully completed in too short a time. Assisting him soothed her and the sight of him, so tall and vital, eased the part of her that still woke sweating with memories of when she'd thought he'd died. He, on the other hand, seemed a little distracted and she wondered if her arrival had unsettled him. She mentally crossed her fingers. She damned well hoped so because that was only fair.

After he'd finished an impressive repair job, she dressed the man's wound and the orderly came with a wheelchair to take the patient to his relatives. Yep. It was all over too soon.

Zac turned from the sink, where he'd removed his gloves and washed his hands. 'We work well together. Did we do that much?'

Normal conversation. She could do that. 'Enough. Mostly maternal emergencies when we called in extra help.' She steeled herself to say it. 'Before I see if anyone else needs me, would you like to meet up tomorrow, one last time? I thought, since you've come back here and some time has passed, you might have questions you'd like to ask me.' She'd rehearsed that in case she needed it.

His head shot up and her heart skipped to see he was relieved she'd offered. 'Yes, thank you, I would.' There was no hesitation there and she eased the breath she'd been holding out of her frozen lungs. 'Are you working any day shifts?' he asked.

'No. I mostly work nights.'

'Me too. I'm off tomorrow until eight in the evening. What time do you wake up? How about supper before you come to work?'

'How about we meet in the morning, instead? Then I'll sleep after.' She knew she wouldn't sleep waiting to see him.

'Even better. Breakfast, then. Eight o'clock. My shout. Do you have a place you prefer?'

She named the hotel he'd stayed at the first week all those weeks ago and he nodded. 'That's where I'm staying.'

She didn't say, *I know. We slept there together.* Instead she said, 'Fine, see you in the dining room there at eight. If I'm late it'll be because of work.'

He smiled at her and it was that sweet, caring smile she remembered. It almost broke her heart. 'No problem. I'll be patient.'

She nodded and glanced at the swinging suture-room door. She should go and do something useful and so should he.

'Ava.' His low voice held such a gentle quality she could have wept.

'Yes?'

The blue-green of his eyes shadowed. 'I can see this isn't easy for you. Thank you for offering.'

She felt her eyes sting. *Do not give me sympathy. Do not!* 'I'd better get back out there.' And with that she left. It felt incredibly difficult to walk away, but at least she'd seen him. She had a plan. Now he just needed to find his memories in that big, beautiful head of his and fall in love with her again. Or she would have to say goodbye forever.

47

Zac

The next morning, Zac waited and the minutes ticked past. He wouldn't blame her if she didn't show at all, but what he did know of her said that wouldn't happen. He wished he'd met Ava ten years ago. When he'd still believed in fairytales.

Now he knew about this ring, he needed the story behind it, but it was the one thing he wasn't going to ask. The risk of upsetting her was too great.

When Ava arrived, he watched her with an intensity he couldn't prevent, and his heart kicked with unexpected recognition his brain didn't get. It didn't help the decision he'd come to.

There was something about the way she moved, though, that was distracting him. She had dressed casually in long shorts and an open-necked shirt that tugged at him, but he couldn't pin it to a memory. Her blonde hair hung loosely around her face in damp tendrils and she brushed it away from her face as she walked. She'd stopped to shower but looked unhurried and graceful as she sailed past the doorman with a smile, then raised a hand as she crossed the foyer towards him.

He could feel his mood lift, and automatically

he stood as she approached. 'You look too good to have just finished night shift.' The words came from somewhere deep. Though now that she stood closer, he could see her eyes seemed weary but not defeated.

'I'll get my rest. How are you?'

'Looking forward to breakfast with you.'

She sat and he did too. As she studied him, she said, 'Why do you think you feel that way?'

It was a challenging question, especially since both of them had been up all night. He smiled quizzically at her. 'Isn't it usual to feel uplifted by having breakfast with a beautiful woman?'

'I have no idea. You tell me.' She shrugged and didn't seem particularly thrilled by his compliment. He had the feeling she was focused on a course of action or conversation and wouldn't be swayed.

He grimaced. 'So, maybe finding some answers to things I want to know is a relief as well.' He handed her a menu. 'I thought we'd order off the menu. To save bouncing up and down for courses from the buffet.'

'Sounds fine.' She looked over the top of the menu sheet. 'Have you remembered anything?'

He shook his head in frustration. 'I'm beginning to think I won't. There's plenty of medical literature that says it can go either way'

She sat back in her seat and regarded him sombrely. 'I think I'm coming to a sort of peace about that.'

Lucky you. 'I wish I was.' The nightmares wouldn't let him.

'Maybe you should. Though I guess it's easy

for me to say — ' she grimaced as she went on — 'but it's two weeks of your life, not mine.'

'I took a week of yours trying to remember.'

'Yes, you did, but I don't regret it.' She sat straighter in the chair. 'So? Would you like to know the details of our first meeting? You know how we met, but we never did get down to the nitty-gritty of how we spent our time together.'

Too right. He needed the details of why he'd created such an impact with a woman who at most should have been a fling. And why he'd bought a ring. 'Yes, I would. If you're happy to put it out there.'

The waiter arrived and they ordered. As soon he'd left she said, 'As I said before, we met on a flight from Sydney. During the flight we had a few wines, talked a lot, and after it — we ended up in your bed instead of at dinner.'

He blinked. *First night?* Then he watched her cheeks flush, but her eyes didn't waver. He had the feeling she'd rehearsed that line to get it out in one go and that was brave. She really was incredible.

He wanted to hug her and say he respected her fearlessness, except he was still replaying what she'd said. 'That doesn't sound like something the Ava I met at your family station or the one at work would normally do.' He spread his hands. 'I'd have to say it doesn't sound like me, either.' He lifted his chin and met her gaze. 'We must have connected?'

'Oh, we connected, all right.' She looked away and he wished she hadn't. But he guessed he owed her the privacy of her own thoughts when she was being so open. When she turned back to him, her face showed only a slight smile. 'It was a crazy rush the first time, but — ' their eyes met — 'even in the rush, we were responsible adults.' Her meaning was delicate but clear. He had been concerned about contraception and felt himself relax.

She didn't miss his relief and her smile disappeared. She went on in the same quiet voice, as if giving clinical handover on the ward for a patient. Her control impressive. 'You gave me the idea that one night was a one-off, ships-in-the-night thing, and we made no plans to meet again.'

That he could believe. It was most likely his decision, not hers, judging by her care of him since.

She went on quietly. 'Then, unexpectedly, the next night we met again at work. On the flight you'd asked not to discuss work or family, and yes, it was a small shock when we ended up on the same ward. I followed your lead and pretended we were strangers, but you approached me the next morning and asked me back to your place again.'

That sounded so ballsy and not like him. 'I was that crass?'

'Can't have been too crass.' She shrugged and spread her hands. 'I said yes.'

Indeed. 'I must have been persuasive.' He wouldn't have thought he'd have had it in him after Roslyn.

She didn't comment on that. 'We had four days, every hour until the next shift started, until my move on to Yulara before holidays. You said you'd come down to the rock for the weekend,'

The waiter arrived with her black tea and his coffee. Another arrived with her cereal and toast and his eggs. When they left he asked what he'd been dying to ask. 'Did I talk about when I'd go back to Sydney? Did we think we had a future?'

She took her time pouring her tea. 'I was off to Yulara on Sunday and then holidays and wouldn't be back in Alice for a month. You were meant to be back in Sydney after that.' She raised her gaze to his. 'I tried not to have expectations before Yulara.'

'I'm sorry.' He must have thought it was going nowhere, then. But when did the ring come into it? 'That seems a pretty big ask. And you're still talking to me?'

'Funny that.' She laughed, but it sounded too hollow to be amused. 'You never promised anything, so my expectations were low.'

So he hadn't asked her to marry him. Was the ring planning or in case? It was pretty impulsive after four days and so hard to believe of himself. But then Ava was a very special woman — he'd certainly learned that at Setabilly.

She was going on. 'I half expected we would end when I left after our last night shift together.' She shrugged. 'Except you came to Yulara.'

He couldn't help leaning forward in anticipation of discovering what happened next.

She smiled at him and the memory must have been pleasant. 'You arrived as Jessamine had her twins.'

'The forgotten twin birth.'

'Yes. The birth went smoothly, thank goodness.

351

It was good to have you there.' She looked away before she went on. 'Then we drove out to Uluru and the accident happened.' She'd left something out. He didn't know how he could be sure of that, but he was. She obviously had her reasons.

'And then the accident happened,' he repeated.

He remembered the description from the nurse in Yulara. His agitation, his loss of blood, which Ava had stopped before he'd bled out, and his critical condition in a place where advanced care wasn't available. And Ava, who had refused to let him die.

He'd put her through a lot. 'I'm sorry I got amnesia.'

She cast a critical eye over him. 'You are high-maintenance.'

He laughed.

48

Ava

I shouldn't have said that, Ava thought, but when he laughed, the tension that had been building between them began to disappear like the tea in her cup, which she was hiding behind. And she hadn't told him the most important thing.

He held up his hands in surrender. 'I admit, I have been very high-maintenance.'

They both smiled. 'To be fair,' she said, 'only when you're being knocked unconscious and refuse to remember you know me. And in your defence, I was driving.'

She would have taken that workload any day. She loved him and she was terrified of this not going anywhere if he didn't remember. But she wasn't telling him that. She needed to see if he'd thought about a future with her even if he didn't remember what had gone before.

'Do you still have any expectations, Ava?' He ruined her set-up. *Damn. He got in first.*

She hadn't mentioned the proposal. Technically he hadn't asked, and she'd decided she wasn't going to risk him feeling trapped if she told him.

'I'm learning not to have expectations, Zac.' She gave him a level stare. 'But that's not my question to answer. It's yours. I've put myself out there, told you how it was. Now you tell me what you think.' Did he feel enough for her to stay and try again?

'Fair enough.' They stared at each other across the table and the tension rose again.

The waiter arrived, unasked, with fresh tea for Ava, which impressed her because she'd been trying to squeeze more out of the empty pot and the idea of having a whole new array of things to use to avoid his eyes was a great relief.

'Would you like more coffee, sir?'

'No, thank you.' He didn't take his eyes off Ava and she could feel the tempo of her heart increasing like she was running down a hill and couldn't stop. She did hope there wasn't a brick wall at the bottom of this hill. But she would live if she hit it.

The waiter left and the silence stretched.

Finally, he spoke. 'Thank you. You've been very open and honest. And all I can say is if I gave you the impression that we had a long-term possibility then I'm sorry. Maybe I had a madness that made me ignore the reality of any sort of relationship between you and me, but you belong here.' He spread his hands helplessly. 'Long distance, different worlds . . . ' He looked as unhappy as she felt. 'Maybe I was ignoring the truth.'

She needed him to say it out loud so she could stop this false hope that was killing her. 'And what is that truth, Zac?'

'I think you'd be much better off without me.'

Bang. She wished now she hadn't asked as

agony sliced through her and she concentrated fiercely on hiding it. Running downhill into a brick wall could not have been more painful. *Get yourself out of here, Ava.*

She rose from her seat. 'Thank you for being honest. I wish you well,' she said: no inflection, no subliminal message, just a pleasantry. 'Goodbye, Zac'

49

Zac

Zac fingered the ring in his pocket as she walked away. His eyes stayed on her until she passed through the door into the car park. He watched her disappear, feeling like he'd just missed a brilliant opportunity or a very important event.

One that he might have waited his whole life for — except that he couldn't remember what it was.

He hated the feeling. He also felt bad for Ava, though he had told himself he was doing this for her benefit — in the long run. At least he'd learned that he hadn't made a commitment he didn't follow through on. No breach-of-promise suit — not that she was that kind of woman.

But there was no doubt that now was the time to leave the midwife alone. No more meetings or rehashing or creating opportunities to hurt her. *Enough!* He could see it was too dangerous for her and they needed to let go.

★   ★   ★

When Zac arrived at work that night, he tried very hard not to think of Ava. But it was quiet when he needed crazy busy. Now, three hours later, he glanced at the clock. Eleven pm. She would be on shift in the maternity ward.

The circle of thought started again. *She'd been so fearless in the telling . . . She'd looked amazing . . . She was so incredibly brave . . . Her mouth . . .*

He wished someone would come in with chest pain or something equally critical that he'd need to concentrate on. But the night dragged unusually slowly.

Of course he and Ava wouldn't have worked. He was no cowboy sitting on a fence in the centre of Australia chewing . . . what had Poddy said the cows chewed out here? Mulga. He wouldn't be chewing mulga grass as he ran a station. And she'd never be happy in Sydney, away from the people she cared about, both her family and the women who needed her advocacy up and down the road from here to Katherine. He'd seen firsthand her passion for the women of the communities and remote midwifery. Stella had that right.

They lived in different worlds, had different agendas, so he had no faith at all that it could have possibly worked, despite the undeniable sexual attraction he didn't have to remember to acknowledge.

When it all boiled down to it, Roslyn and he had been from the same world and they had definitely struggled.

The sound of a car screeching into the emergency-department driveway pushed his butt out of the chair. *Yes. Thank you. A welcome distraction.*

Zac grabbed hygienic gloves and beat the rest

of the staff to the front, where he was halted by a distraught man at the ambulance entrance.

The tall, blond bloke threw open his door and hurried to the rear of the car. 'Thank God! Zac'

Zac shot a quick look at his face and recognised a much thinner and more haggard Jock. 'Hana's in labour. She's thirty-three weeks — too early.'

'Got it.' Zac turned to the nurse behind him. 'Leave the wheelchair for me. Get maternity down here.'

Zac shelved Jock's appearance for another time as he concentrated on the young woman in the rear seat of the car. He opened the door and leaned his hand on the seat next to her. 'Hello there, Hana. You scored me. Okay if I help until the midwives arrive?'

The young woman turned huge, frightened eyes towards him and then drew a shaky breath to calm herself. 'Zac.' She blinked. Then she said firmly, 'I think the baby is coming, Zac.'

Zac glanced behind him. 'The nurse has gone to ring maternity. Let's get you out and into this wheelchair.' He offered Hana his arm. 'You're doing fine. Tell me what you're feeling now.'

Hana drew another shuddering breath and swallowed. 'I think there's something hanging out down there and I don't know whether to push or what.'

Zac had the strangest feeling that he was being divinely tested, and the urge to foster calmness felt stronger than anything. 'Well, we'll find out very soon, but could I have a quick look in case I have to catch a little someone?' He met Hana's eyes and smiled, and Hana lifted her bottom and pulled her trousers down to her knees in a no-nonsense movement. 'Of . . . course.' She panted and gestured her permission with a wave. 'Go . . . ahead.'

It was awkward but not impossible for Zac to see what was happening, a task made no easier by the dim light. There was a baby, but if he wasn't mistaken it was coming bottom first. Were breech babies a Central Australian speciality? Not really statistically surprising, as thirty-three-week babies were often breech. At least this one wouldn't fall anywhere dangerous except inside the baggy trouser legs, Zac thought wryly.

'Not coming head first. Let's meet the rest of your baby in a more comfortable place. What do you think?'

Hana gave a strangled laugh of relief as she agreed.

'Good girl. Can you climb out backwards, maybe slither along on your bottom and I'll lift you into the chair? We'll get you inside so we can see what's going on.'

'I'm scared to move. Here comes another pain.'

Jock's head poked around Zac's. 'Is she having it?'

'Yes,' Zac answered calmly. Then in an even softer tone, 'That's okay. Breathe through it. You're doing fine. But we need to get you inside and the maternity staff are coming. I bet your baby would much prefer to be born on clean sheets.' A fervent agreement came from behind his head and Hana grinned.

Something or someone kept chanting in his head, reminding him that if this was happening smoothly they'd be fine, and not to touch anything yet.

Zac turned his head and waved to someone behind him to push the wheelchair closer to the car. He gave Hana his arm and together they inched her along the seat. As soon as she was at the door and the contraction finished, he put his arms around Hana on one side and Jock took the other, and they lifted her into the wheelchair. She was inside and onto the waiting gurney before she'd barely taken a breath.

The nurses whipped a curtain around and Hana's pants were swiftly pulled off. 'Lying on my back's no good,' she gasped, and tried to shift on the narrow trolley.

'Stay there. The doctor needs to see,' the nurse said briskly, at the same time as Zac said, 'That's fine. Move where you need to.' He shook his head apologetically at the nurse and gave his arm to Hana again to help her roll onto her knees. As soon as she knelt the baby began to descend in a smooth downward arc, and with a sudden flick that startled everyone except Zac, first one and then the other leg plopped out.

'Good grief,' said the nurse.

'Perfect,' Zac said, and hovered nearby without touching, and marvelled at the jiggling of the baby's legs as it wriggled its way out. Umbilicus, nipples, one arm, second arm and the baby sat, head still inside, and all the time Zac felt as though a calm voice were describing what would happen next. Zac took the warmed towel the nurse offered, still not touching the baby.

Behind him, he ignored the sounds of others arriving, as the baby descended further. He waited, his hands still, ready for the tiny chin to drop and the face to fall into sight, allowing gravity to do the tricky traction of a breech birth all by itself.

Across from him three nurses watched open-mouthed. Hana gasped, Jock swayed, and the baby's head freed and dropped. Zac caught the little face as it fell into his hands. He closed his eyes for a second, holding the weight of the baby as a medley of images of another breech birth passed through his mind.

Just like this. The world swirled, and he rested the baby on the bed until the kaleidoscope stopped. One still photograph in his mind gelled. Ava, in another time, in another place, and two baby boys.

On automatic pilot, he handed the baby to the paediatrician, who checked Hana's baby as the midwife, one so suddenly, so dearly familiar, hurried into the room.

Concentrate on what you're doing! his mind yelled. He turned towards Hana to find Ava had helped her flip onto her back, with her baby on the way to her arms. Suddenly she gasped again, and looked up to catch Zac's gaze, her eyes widening in question.

He saw the gush of blood. 'Placenta,' he said simply.

She sighed and relaxed. 'I didn't think it was twins.'

361

Zac delivered the placenta into an awaiting dish and stepped away. 'Done.'

The paed, who'd paused for the third stage to be completed, passed the baby to Hana. Her little girl. Zac watched the tiny bundle be drawn safely into her mother's arms and blew out a long breath.

Finally Zac's eyes met Ava's.

'Congratulations,' she said, but she looked straight through him as she turned towards Hana and Jock. Was that to them or to him? Did it matter? All he knew was that he felt bereft and he'd thrown away the best thing he'd ever found.

Zac saw that Ava had turned her shoulder to assist Hana to position the baby safely. The bed rails were pulled up. Sweet memories were crowding in his brain. He could just hear Ava's murmuring voice as the pictures in his mind twisted again in the vivid kaleidoscope. 'She's so beautiful,' Ava said as she bent to catch the tiny baby's waving hand, and he wished he'd taken an extra glance at the newborn, but his mind had been whirling.

Jock stood stock-still in awe, watching, and Zac didn't miss the glint of tears bumping down the man's unshaven cheek. Emotion stung his own throat as he looked at him. Poor bloke. He'd had the wildest few weeks of his life, but hopefully this would be the start of a new chapter for them.

Ava was hugging her brother now. 'I'm so excited for you all. We'll push the bed straight to the special-care nursery and she'll stay toasty warm on Hana's skin until the paeds can check her out again up there.'

Hana said something he missed and Ava responded. 'India, that's beautiful. After Mim's middle name? How fabulous.'

Then Jock said something and Ava shook her head. 'No. India's breathing fine. She's a fighter like her mum. You were amazing, Hana. Congratulations.' He could hear the quiet joy in Ava's voice as he stood back from them, rightly, on the outside of a family he was nothing to.

It seemed Ava had wrangled it so Hana could keep hold of her baby for the transfer upstairs. *Skin to skin.* One of Ava's pet crusades. He remembered that too, now.

Of course she was far too busy to look at him as they moved. Zac glanced back at the paed, a friendly face in all the drama, who smiled at him and said, 'Nice delivery.'

With a half-smile that he couldn't contain, he indicated Ava with a nod of his head. 'I had a good teacher.'

'You're a good student,' the paed said as she hurried away to follow the bed.

Zac moved sideways from the bed to elbow on the taps at the sink and stripped off his gloves. Silently, he rinsed and soaped his hands. The rhythmic washing of his wrists gave him the privacy to allow the memories to wash over him. The crash, the tumbling, the stop, and the sight of Ava injured. He'd thought she'd died. Or worse, had been rendered brain dead. He breathed deeply to clear the swirl of images in his head. The horror to end all horrors.

Now it was all there. Right from the start.

Being in the aircraft with Ava's laughing face next to his, the crazy ride in the taxi and the wild, uninhibited, explosive night when they'd made love until all hours of the morning.

And the next four days.

He remembered the ring.

He remembered Yulara.

The ring made so much sense now. He could remember his euphoria when he'd bought it. How could the memory of how much he loved Ava have been buried so deep? It was unbelievable, really.

Lord, he remembered Yulara and the emotion and joy and anticipation as they'd headed out to the perfect spot for him to properly propose.

All of his memory had returned. As he dried his hands, still feeling dazed, he caught sight of Ava's disappearing back as she helped push the gurney upstairs. Her brother, Jock, was beside her.

No wonder she had looked through him when he'd told her all hope was gone. She'd had to deal with that final loss of faith.

Others had taken over. He saw a nurse sitting on the chair, pale and stunned. She glanced up and he smiled and shrugged. 'Things can turn out well if you allow the presence of trust,' he told her. Like Ava had told him after they'd helped deliver the twins. And hopefully, that would work.

Trust in Ava — that would be what he'd have to do now.

50

Hana

Hana lay in the dark, listening to babies cry in the maternity ward — not hers, though — with Jock sleeping next to her on the trundle bed in her room. She could hear his breathing, a sound she would never, ever take for granted, and she counted her blessings in a fervent prayer of gratitude.

Her fingers stroked the polaroid photo of India that Ava had taken before they left the special-care nursery, even though it was too dark to see her daughter's features. She didn't need to see. Her daughter had blonde hair, and deep-blue eyes like all babies — she laughed at herself. But she bet India would have eyes like her dad's. She had his beautiful mouth and that funny tip on one ear.

Hana had held her for the start of her life against her skin, warm and so incredibly soft, stickily secured to her until she'd needed to be lifted into the crib in the special-care nursery. And she was so thankful for that brief time of connection that could never be taken away. But India had been impatient to arrive and they would have to be patient before she could stay with them without observation.

Thanks to her darling Jock, who had managed

to get here in time through some inventive short cuts and magnificent driving. All that off-road racing had honed his skills — there hadn't been much time to spare once she'd been woken by her waters breaking.

And thanks to Zac's gentle handling of her birth.

And Ava. Dear Ava; Smoothing and explaining and making sure she and Jock were involved in all decisions for their daughter's wellbeing. Gliding in to check on her in the dark, whispering little snippets of what was going on with India as she found out, checking that Hana was well and comfortable and happy. Laughingly telling her that of course it wasn't strange she was awake after such excitement.

Hana sighed and blew a kiss to her darling Jock. Blew a kiss in the direction of her new daughter. Then she closed her eyes. Her daughter was safe. The doctors said she was perfect, just early, and India would grow and grow until she came home, where she would evolve into another strong May woman.

Like her mother.

And her aunty.

And her grandmother and great-grandmother.

Things would work out just as they should. Hana was blessed.

51

Ava

In the few brief occasions she'd had time to think during the long, busy night on the maternity ward, Ava had smiled with a mixture of fierce soaring pride and plunging bittersweet regret at the memory of Zac's management of Hana's birth. He may not have remembered Jessamine's breech births, but he'd done everything right tonight and she wished she could tell him so.

It could have turned out much differently for Hana and her baby if the precipitate delivery had been managed by someone who hadn't been able to trust and leave well alone until needed. Baby and mum were both great thanks to Zac.

Ava was also thankful to have been lucky enough to be there for the end, to see the birth and to be with her brother and his wife this morning. It was a shame it had been so busy and she hadn't had much time to visit the special-care nursery to soak in her new niece and the starry-eyed wonder of Jock's joy. Hana, of course, had been amazing.

Yes, Zac had been great, but Ava wouldn't tell him. She couldn't tell him.

Because she was done.

Finished.

Over.

The pain of loss was too great and she'd be going home to her family as soon as Hana left the hospital. She wouldn't be back in Alice until he'd gone. She might even go to Weipa.

Zac Logan had been a comet in her past and their love had disappeared without a telltale trail.

A little break in Arnhem Land sounds perfect, she thought, jollying herself along. It was nice to think of somewhere different. During her uni studies for nursing, she'd shone in tropical medicine, and the lure of steamy — as opposed to searing, oven-like — heat had always seemed particularly exotic to her.

Her mother and grandmother were strong single women. She could be one too.

She would not see Zac Logan again.

⋆　⋆　⋆

Except when the clock reached seven-thirty, and she pushed open the ward's door, a tall, dark-haired, serious man was waiting for her in the hallway.

And as had happened once before, he asked simply, 'Can we meet for breakfast?'

Another fragile part of her heart broke. 'No.'

There, she'd said it.

Except this time he added, 'At our hotel?'

She frowned at the 'our', and notwithstanding her brain shrieking *no*, and all the arguments she'd assembled in a neat stack that now threatened to topple onto her, she sighed. He'd said 'our hotel'. Her mouth opened to refuse again, but instead she heard herself say, 'I'll be there in a while.'

★ ★ ★

And here she was. *Why am I doing this to myself?* she asked herself for the millionth time.

He stood when he saw her enter and remained by the table — the same table — with her tea waiting, and the same waiter hovering nearby.

Zac came around to meet her, and instead of pulling out her chair he took her hand and lifted her fingers to his lips, then kissed her palm. 'I'm sorry,' he murmured. Then he pulled her towards him, gently, slowly, watching her face, asking her with his eyes to trust him, staring into her soul as if she was the woman he loved more than life itself.

Oh, too, too cruel. I can't do this. Her chest struggled to get enough air. 'I can't do rejection again, Zac. What are you doing?' She stared at him for a second more and then, incredulously, felt the realisation crash in on her.

'I remember,' he said simply.

'You're back?

He nodded.

'You remember?' she asked again, afraid to believe.

Again he nodded. Her eyes stung and she blinked away the distortion of tears because she wanted to stare at him. To see in his face that it was true. He looked like he wanted to crush her to him, just as somebody cleared their throat, and they both glanced around at the interested breakfast diners.

Zac lifted his head, daring anyone to complain, and stepped closer to her. 'My poor, darling Ava.' He pulled her against his chest, wrapped his big, beautiful, loving arms around her, and for the first time in weeks she felt herself come alive. His smile made her want to melt. 'I really did hope I would remember,' he said, and his other hand came up and trapped her face to hold her still, as if he intended to infinitely savour the next moment. She held still, barely able to wait.

Their lips touched, ever so gently, and with the first warmth of his mouth, the first inhalation of his breath, her breath caught and held as she too remembered. When his mouth brushed hers again, and his hands slid down to pull her closer against him, all the memories rushed back because she knew this was what she'd hoped for.

'I remember,' he repeated, his voice low and vibrant. 'I remember it all. Everything came back after Hana gave birth.'

'Everything?' She didn't think she could believe this after he had sat here yesterday and said the opposite.

'All of it. All of you. All of us.' Then he pulled back and gazed deeply into her eyes. 'You're so pale,' he said and hurriedly pulled out her chair. 'What have I done to you? Sit.'

She sank into the chair, suddenly glad to be off her jelly legs. He kept hold of her hand as he went around the table to his own chair, watching her the whole time, then caught her other hand so he had all of her fingers — like he was waltzing around her. Her hands looked so small in his. Clasped in his.

Words drifted over her head like feathers falling in a dream. 'I remember I love you. I remember I want to spend the rest of my life with you.'

It was true. She couldn't believe this was happening. A tiny voice whispered, *Why can't you believe it?* Suddenly, the dream popped like a soap bubble on its way to the sky. She slid her hands from his and sat back. She mentally stepped back as well and stared at him, blowing out a long stream of held breath.

Yes, she wanted to believe him, but . . . 'So what dark and dreadful memory stopped you from remembering that before? Why were you so frightened of remembering me?'

His intense gaze captured hers and held it. 'It wasn't because I was afraid of us.' He ran his hand through his hair, tousling it, and she tried not to be diverted by the urge to lean forward and touch him.

'I remember the crash, the tumbling, the stop, and then I saw you. I thought you'd died. I was conscious the whole time we rolled.' He leaned forward and very gently touched the pink scar on her forehead, a pale reminder of a close call. 'The blood,' he said, shaking his head. 'The position of the blow in the centre of your forehead. It was so similar to Roslyn. I thought you'd died too. Or worse. That you were comatose, like she was. My brain couldn't bear it because it was my fault again.'

Okay. She could see it had a form of deja vu horror attached. But . . . 'How was it your fault?'

That she didn't get. She'd been the one driving. The campervan had instigated their involvement.

He threw his hands out, probably aware he had no explanation that would satisfy her. 'You looked dead. I wasn't thinking straight. I promised myself I would keep you safe. I failed.'

She shrugged. 'It's my job to keep myself safe.'

He squeezed his hair again, took a deep breath and settled. 'It was my fault that you ended up like Roslyn and I blocked it out. Who knows? Maybe my subconscious decided that if I forgot you then you'd be safe. Safe from dying. Safe from me.'

She could even get that. A little.

'I don't care why.' He cupped her cheek in his hand. 'But now that I've remembered, I can't do that. Please don't be safe from me. I want to live my life with you.'

She narrowed her eyes at him, but inside her heart had begun to bounce around, chirping and singing like a desert cricket. 'I love you, Zac. But I've got to be a bit cautious after everything.'

He stopped. Looked at her.

'The fact that we come from different worlds has been a major factor. What's the plan?. Where will we live? Part-time together, part-time long distance? Do we both travel to work in places like Weipa and have adventures?'

'I had that prepared in Uluru. We'll have a long engagement and we'll try it all. I know you belong here.'

She could see the truth in his words: he had thought about it. Maybe more than she had until this moment. Then it was true. They could and would do this and this would work, because he was her destiny. But he'd put her through hell and she couldn't help giving a little back.

'I'll think about it.'

'Good. Think about it.' He raised his brows and pulled her closer until she leaned across the table towards him. 'You have ten seconds.' Then he swooped in and kissed her. He pulled back and touched her cheek with one gentle finger. 'You have such strength and love and — ' he waggled his brows — 'and humour, because that's a joke, right?' He didn't look too worried.

She smiled at him and nodded.

'Thank you.' His smile back nearly blinded her. 'You help me appreciate things I forgot to appreciate years ago. But most of all, I need you because I love you.'

Did she love him? This big, beautiful, high-maintenance man of hers? *Hell yeah.* But she was soaking in this outpouring of declarations. She had almost given up — she actually had given up yesterday — and she did need the reassurance.

The repetition.

The comfort.

'Marry me,' he said, and pulled his wallet from his pocket. 'See what I found and didn't know why I had it.'

Now we're talking. 'You almost asked me once before.' She smiled and he reached over and took her hand, lifted it to his mouth and kissed her fingers. Then he slid the gorgeous pink diamond ring onto her finger.

'I'm not waiting to do this. Be my wife.'

She stared with blurred eyes at the beautiful engagement ring. Then she leaned over and met him above the middle of the table and kissed his waiting mouth. 'Yes.'

'Let me show you how much I love you.' He looked around at the other diners and smiled. 'But not here.'

'Yeah. Get a room,' one of the older men said teasingly, and the people around them laughed. Some applauded.

Zac smiled and stood, then went around to pull out her chair. 'Let's start again.'

In a room, a different room, Ava wrapped her arms around the man she'd thought would never hold her like this again, and savoured the strength and vitality that she'd thought was out of her reach forever. She held him as if she would never, ever let him go.

She kissed him, putting into that kiss all the love she'd been holding back, all the fear, all the frustration she'd felt at his loss of memory, and to her absolute delight he returned it tenfold. Her hands slid up and over the taut muscles bunched beneath his shirt, and she curved her fingers into his shoulders and neck with a sigh of delicious deja vu as the kiss deepened. Tongues touched, tasted, entwined, and she jammed herself closer.

He slid his hands down her back and cupped her bottom so that he could lift her slightly towards him. He groaned, a deep, growling noise that made her mouth tilt under his. *Oh yeah.* Her big, strong man was the perfect size. Ava wasn't sure if it was the loss of the ground beneath her feet or the sudden depth of his kiss that made her feel as though she were flying. Either way, she didn't want Zac to stop.

She felt like she'd been starved of this. As though she'd waited a lifetime to be back in his arms,

'You sure you remember? You're not just tricking me into seduction?'

'Absolutely.' He leaned over her and brushed the hair away from her eyes, and the expression she saw on his face and in his eyes stopped the world and the laughter, and brought the sting of tears as well as a swell in her heart. Her hand lifted unconsciously to her chest and pressed. *Speaking of hearts. What if the love of your life finally remembered who you were?*

He took her face between his fingers and gazed into her eyes. 'Ava, I'm serious. I want us to be like this always. Talking. Hugging. Loving. Forgiving. Me holding your hand. Wherever we are, till death do us part. I need to marry you. Forever. I can see us being one of those old couples walking along hand in hand. Into a desert sunset.' He dipped his head and kissed her once more. 'I promise I'll renew the vow at Uluru soon. But for now, will this do? Please?'

There was no doubting the searing need and also the slight trepidation she could see in his eyes. Was he that blind not to see how deeply she cared for him? She blinked away the tears that threatened to make this magical moment too misty to see.

She drew a deep breath. 'I love you, Zac. I loved you from the first morning after our unexpected night together.'

He stared at her, momentarily speechless, then shook his head. 'You did not.' He brushed his lips against hers with so much tenderness she shivered.

'Okay. Maybe not the first day. But the next day when you asked me back for breakfast. Seriously. Breakfast. So many promises of food that I didn't get.' She lifted her face and kissed him again.

They didn't speak for a while. They were too busy. Too enthralled.

Finally, he lifted his head. 'I couldn't take my eyes off you on the flight.'

'I watched your hands.' She reached down and pulled one up to kiss his fingers, then laughed. 'I was berating myself for just following you when you waggled your fingers. I do love these fingers.'

'And they love you.' He undid the last button on her shirt and he pushed it aside. 'My wife-to-be.'

52

Stella
Two months later

Stella looked across to where Zac stood in the centre of a red sandy knoll. He'd been positioned directly in line with Uluru's blessing under a white metal archway that fluttered with ribbons. He'd been instructed where to stand by Ava, with Poddy as best man, as they waited for her to arrive.

The archway, intricately welded together by Mim, would later be returned to stand in the rose garden at Setabilly Station. Stella and Lorenzo had already made good use of it at their own wedding a month ago.

In a few minutes, Ava and Zac would celebrate their nuptials on one of the many ochre-red sandhills between Uluru and Kata Tjuta.

The whole event would be framed by the benevolent ancient mountain range in the distance and the endless plains filled with promise. This was all the Anangu people's country, stretching away forever. An orange-brown dusted land, with the sage of desert foliage, between two magnificent icons glowing as the afternoon prepared for sunset. A land that Stella, and many other people here today, loved with a passion.

Round tables had been set below the sandy

hillock, white chairs and linen tablecloths in the desert, waiting to seat the guests who stood with rounded eyes, awestruck by the venue, turning this way and that at the desert beauty around them.

They'd arrived from Sydney like vivid birds in their colourful shirts, hats and dresses, streaming from the resort bus along the maroon carpet walkways. Others had arrived from the stations around Alice Springs, from the hospitals, big and tiny, and remote health centres. All were waiting for the bride, and Stella enjoyed the excitement of Ava's friends, the respect she'd earned from her workmates, the warmth of the smiling faces. Most of all, she enjoyed the expectation of the groom.

A whisper of noise heralded the long black car as it slowed and stopped beside the carpet at the base of the hill. Stella clutched Lorenzo's hand.

Jock stepped out in a dark suit, tall and sturdy, a quirk of a smile on his handsome face as he moved to the rear door. *My baby is well again. Whole.* He opened the door and Denise, Ava's best friend, stepped out dressed in a magnificent maroon strapless dress, Australian wildflowers in her hand and her thick dark hair coiled like a crown.

Then Jock reached in to give the bride his arm and Ava stepped out.

Ava's white dress fell simply from the top of her breasts to the tips of her silver shoes and she drew a gasp from the onlookers as she came to stand behind Denise. Her face radiated a serene, glowing joy that softened the faces of everyone she touched with her emotion.

Stella felt the tears sting her eyes and she heard Mim sniff beside her. '*Bella* Ava,' Lorenzo's whisper carried to his wife, as his daughter-in-law stepped onto the carpet and stopped, waiting. '*Così bella*,' he whispered.

'*Così?*' his wife looked at him. 'So beautiful?'

'*Sì*. Like her mama.'

The crowd hushed and silence fell over the sands until the low, growling sounds of the didgeridoo filled the air with rumbling cadences, drawing emotion with a command that carried to the rear of the assembly. The wedding party began their entrance. Denise's husband had offered to play the didgeridoo when Ava had asked Denise to be her bridesmaid, and the pulses of sound lifted the hairs on Stella's arms as her daughter walked up the red carpet to the top of the sandhill.

It's perfect, Stella thought.

Denise trod the carpet in a stately walk, and on the knoll ahead of her Zac's gaze fixed on his bride.

Ava seemed to float behind her bridesmaid in a shimmer of white light until, finally, she stopped beside him. The delicate grevilleas in her bouquet didn't shake as her gaze held his with a wealth of love.

Just before sunset, with the burnished copper of Kata Tjuta glowing like the heart of a fire, they pledged in front of family and friends until husband and wife turned to face the desert and those who loved them.

Zac raised Ava's hand and the magnificent

pink diamond flashed in the light, along with the wedding ring beside it. 'I introduce you to my wife, Ava May-Logan.' His voice resonated deep and clear and full of pride, and those who watched applauded and cheered. The sound of the didgeridoo rose strongly, swelling with the joy of the moment above the cacophony, and promised in vibrating throbs the fullness of their life to come.

As they descended into the throng, Zac held firmly onto his wife's hand. Stella saw Ava pause and dip her head as she pointed to the ground, and Mim and Stella laughed as they both saw the subtle movement in the dirt as a thorny devil lizard wandered away. *Ngiyari*. Ava's desert friend had come to watch the ceremony.

Acknowledgements

As you come to the close of my new book, *The Desert Midwife*, I hope you have enjoyed the time spent in the Red Centre of Australia. I have grown to treasure these people and places in my heart. This story gave me some labour pains — funny how some book babies are more intense than others in creation! — but here we are. The End. And I'm proud of her.

As always, there are so many people and places I drew inspiration from, who supported me, whom I want to thank with sincere gratitude for their role in the birth and nurturing of this book. As for places, of course, there is Australia's glorious Uluru and the evocative desert lands that surround this most magnificent natural wonder. As I rested my awed hand on the rough walls, walked the base and sat at the waterhole, I could almost feel its heartbeat. I hope this book encourages everyone to seek the chance some-time in their life to spend a while at this mystical power centre on earth and perhaps learn from the wisdom of the Anangu people.

In this book, I offer my view as a non-Indigenous midwife, and so I want to thank those who helped me write about Indigenous women and communities. My thanks to Suzie Dean, a real desert midwife, who read the early version and shared insight into situations and people she came across while working in remote communities in central Australia. You are a champion, Suze. To Rachel Scoltock, a friend and mentor, who referred me to Jennifer Cowley, author of the book *I Am Uluru*. Jen kindly referred me to the incredible Linda Rive, who coordinates a digital archive of all things Anangu called 'Ara Irititja'. Linda's insight and generous offer to share my relevant chapters with women elders was such a bonus, and together with Penguin Random House I send a.huge thank you to Linda and to elder, Yanyi Bandicha, for their guidance and kindness in relation to my story.

Thanks to the wonderful staff at the Desert Gardens Hotel, who really are as fabulous as Zac said, and the 'rock view room', which really is special. When you go to stay, please don't miss the Sounds of Silence dinner. Soak in that night sky.

To Kym Cramps, way back in Broken Hill, for the second use in my writing of her mailbox, a tiny metal homestead complete with miniature working windmill, which Granny Mim creates in this book. It really does stand outside Mount Gipps Station for mail, and if you want to see it there's a small video of it turning in the wind on the Facebook page for my book *The Homestead Girls*. Kym, I hope I have captured some of the angst of station owners waiting for rain while the land dries out and your animals suffer. You are all such heroes, those who live on the far-flung stations of the outback and greet each day with hope for the land and livestock you love.

At Penguin Random House, I'd like to thank

my publisher, Ali Watts, and my editor, Amanda Martin, for their faith in my writing and for their fab input all through this book journey. Thank you also to the insightful Alex Nahlous for her lovely compliments and work on the manuscript, and Penelope Goodes. And not forgetting the wonderful cover designer and the huge team of wonderful people who launch a book from my computer into the world!

Thank you to my agent, Clare Forster, and Ben Stevenson from Curtis Brown for your support and advice as always.

Thank you to my writing friends — there's nothing like having your own tribe to feel nurtured — especially my dear writing pal Trish Morey, way over in South Australia but just here beside me via email. You pushed me towards the finish line as we leapfrogged our word counts, a new game we both draw strength and story progression from as life gets busy at inconvenient moments like deadlines. To Annie Seaton and the Wicked Writers of Words in my local writers group, you guys rock. *The Desert Midwife* is in fact the longest book I've ever written, and the first I've ever had to cut scenes from. I can hear my writing friends laughing — especially Rachael Johns, who very kindly provided the lovely quote on my cover. You really are a wonderful woman, Rachael. Thank you.

To you, dear readers, who buy and borrow my books, and send me fab messages on my Facebook, and share photos of my book babies when you see them on the shelves, I am so blessed to have you in my life and will always be grateful for your support and kindness. Thank you.

And lastly, and always, to my own dear hero Ian, who has suffered along the sometimes torturous, zigzag trail this book has taken, the book he called the never-ending story, with each new version not quite the last. It's done. I'm yours. Until the next one, dear Ian. xx

We do hope that you have enjoyed reading this large print book.

Did you know that all of our titles are available for purchase?

We publish a wide range of high quality large print books including:
Romances, Mysteries, Classics
General Fiction
Non Fiction and Westerns

Special interest titles available in large print are:
The Little Oxford Dictionary
Music Book
Song Book
Hymn Book
Service Book

Also available from us courtesy of Oxford University Press:
Young Readers' Dictionary
(large print edition)
Young Readers' Thesaurus
(large print edition)

For further information or a free brochure, please contact us at:
Ulverscroft Large Print Books Ltd.,
The Green, Bradgate Road, Anstey,
Leicester, LE7 7FU, England.
Tel: (00 44) 0116 236 4325
Fax: (00 44) 0116 234 0205